Praise for *Re*
An Amazon Best E
(Mystery, Thriller, and Suspense)

"A dark, visceral novel of shame, trauma and secrets, told in two distinct timelines . . . Enigmatic and intricate, this first novel will chill even the most hardened of Scandinavian noir fans with its considerations of human nature, self-determination and animal instinct." —*Shelf Awareness*

"*Reptile Memoirs* is the perfect novel for those who like their mysteries and thrillers delivered in a manner that is a bit left of center but still contains all the crucial elements you would expect from a classic noir investigation story. Silje Ulstein is a talented author, and I am excited to see what she has in store for readers next." —*Book Reporter*

"Everyone seems guilty in this well-written, pitch-black psychological thriller, whose tense, lost-child theme conjures twisted fairytale tropes." —*Booklist*

"*Reptile Memoirs* is a magnetic ocean tide: a bold, heart-stopping and genre-defying debut which compels us to sink toward the darkest depths of our past. A masterfully shocking and at times wonderfully uncomfortable exploration of obsession, desire and rejection, sexuality and taboo, Ulstein leaves us breathless in her quest to examine which version of the self is capable of love and violence."
—Sarah Schmidt, author of *See What I Have Done*

"This book is a shapeshifting marvel. I found it compulsively readable, and not just for the unexpected paths by which it unpacks its secrets. Silje Ulstein writes about snakes in ways that made me feel I've never really seen them before: In language that is as seductive as it is prickly, she pries open the boundaries between reptiles and humans, adults and the children they once were, and criminals and victims. An uncanny, unsettling, and totally immersive read."

—Emily Fridlund, Booker Prize-shortlisted author of *History of Wolves*

"Extraordinary and terrifying, *Reptile Memoirs* sinks teeth into you from page one. Through relentless and, at times, almost unbearable tension, Ulstein delivers a menacingly layered thriller unlike any you've read before."

—P. J. Vernon, author of *Bath Haus*

"A beautifully dark and twisty story with jaw-dropping twists and pin-point plotting."

—Joanna Cannon, author of *The Trouble with Goats and Sheep*

"Ulstein has written the best and creepiest Norwegian crime debut in years . . . A novel that stands out due to both its dark, clever and intricate plot as well as the author's solid insight into the human mind."   —*Adresseavisen* (Norway)

"A nerve-wrecking and highly original psychological thriller . . . The book is very hard to put down and if you do the plot will keep playing out in your mind."   —*Dagbladet* (Norway)

REPTILE MEMOIRS

a novel

SILJE
ULSTEIN

Translated from the Norwegian
by Alison McCullough

Grove Press
New York

Originally published in Norway in 2020 as *Krypdyrmemoarer* by Aschehoug Forlag.

Published simultaneously in Canada
Printed in Canada

This book was set in 12 point Adobe Garamond Pro by Alpha Design & Composition of Pittsfield, NH.

First Grove Atlantic hardcover edition: March 2022
First Grove Atlantic paperback edition: March 2023

This translation has been published with the financial support of NORLA.

Library of Congress Cataloging-in-Publication data is available for this title.

ISBN 978-0-8021-6235-9
eISBN 978-0-8021-5887-1

Grove Press
an imprint of Grove Atlantic
154 West 14th Street
New York, NY 10011

Distributed by Publishers Group West

groveatlantic.com

23 24 25 26 27   10 9 8 7 6 5 4 3 2 1

I is another.

—Arthur Rimbaud

PART ONE

Liv

That first time, his body was a paradox. Like living granite, or silken sandpaper. He was hard and soft at the same time. Coarse and smooth. Heavy and light. The first thing that struck me was how warm he was. As if I had believed his body would be cold both inside and out. As if I hadn't wanted to believe that he was alive. Only later would I learn that he didn't give off any heat of his own, only absorbed what was around him.

He lay in my arms, barely a metre long and still just a little baby. He lifted his head, supporting himself against my arm and turning his shining eyes in my direction. Perhaps he was trying to understand what I was. Whether I was prey or a potential enemy. His split tongue vibrated lightly in the air, and he moved slowly up along my chest, towards my throat. Once there, he stopped, half of him suspended in the air, his stony dead eyes on mine. I looked straight into his narrow pupils, into a gaze that was completely steady, free of any impulse to blink. He seemed to be seeking some kind of connection, despite the impossibility of communication between us.

There was something ethereal about him. This ability to hold such a large portion of his body in the air without the slightest effort, or so it seemed. As if he had no need for contact with anything earthly and could have simply remained in constant weightlessness had he so wished. Just the thought of having such bodily control seemed impossible—it made me feel weightless, light-headed. I lifted my arm, and he hung down from it as if from a branch, moving searchingly towards my face.

"He likes you," said the woman with the American *r*'s and *l*'s, bringing me back to the cold attic room that housed all kinds of species in cages that lined the walls. There seemed to be a propensity for laughter in the woman's voice. "Do you like him? It seems so."

Like. The word was insufficient. Something I might have said about a cool jacket. This was something else entirely.

"Can I hold him?"

"When can *I* hold him?"

Ingvar and Egil looked on from either side of me. I had almost forgotten that they were standing there. Despite the fact that Ingvar was a couple of years older than Egil—and although Ingvar had a beard and long dark hair like mine, while Egil was wearing a white shirt, his hair slicked back and blond—right now they seemed like twins in their early teens. For them, the word *like* made sense. The two of them "liked" the snake in the way that they liked bands and beers and anything else that might briefly preoccupy them. What was it that I felt? Maternal affection? Love? A connection that crossed the differences between species. When I looked down at that tiny face, so far removed from my own, I thought it looked back at me with trust, even understanding.

It wasn't long since the idea had come to us. The living room had been heavy with smoke at five o'clock in the morning in Ålesund's coolest basement apartment, where the red lava lamp stood spewing up its globs 24/7. We were the small group that remained of what had previously been a living room full of people. Close to calling it a night, but not quite ready to do so. The mood was subdued, the air sweet with smoke, and Ingvar sat in the armchair playing classic rock tunes on his guitar. Even Egil, who had spent the entire evening pumping the living room full of 50 Cent and OutKast, had rolled down his shirtsleeves and settled on the rug with his arm around a girl who was probably in some of his classes at the Norwegian Business School. I was high on the atmosphere and one of Ingvar's strong joints, had withdrawn into myself. I lay on the sofa, concentrating on the ceiling, which was undulating, up and down, up and down, as if it were breathing. Having found the rhythm in it, I had intended to lie there until I fell asleep, but then out of nowhere a guy appeared. He had been outside and came wandering back into the apartment. He must have been an acquaintance of Ingvar's or Egil's, I didn't care which. Later I couldn't remember his face, only that he sat on the floor beside my head and wanted to talk to me, but I was too busy watching the ceiling breathe. After repeated attempts at getting my attention, he went and sat with the others instead.

I slept, or became one with the ceiling and ceased to exist, but soon enough I was back. It was Ingvar's exclamation that woke me. The girl Egil had been hitting on was half hidden behind his back, her hands over her eyes. Egil himself sat with his eyes glued to the TV. On the screen a man was standing in the jungle, half submerged in a muddy puddle and pulling something from the water. It was a snake with gleaming brown and black scales, as thick as an alligator but much longer. The snake got bigger and bigger as the man drew it out of the water. Its skin was brown, black and yellow. A huge python. The man called out as he pulled forth an ever fatter, ever rounder coil. "This is a big snake!" he cried. "The head, there's the head!" An Australian accent and quick movements. At that moment the snake opened its jaws and lunged at its captor, furious. The man backed away, giving a stifled cry, the snake following after him.

I swallowed. Heard Egil's nervous laughter and curses as if from somewhere far away. My heartbeat seemed to drown out everything, filling the room with the sound of my blood. My cheeks turned hot, my hands clammy. I didn't usually feel such an intimate connection to my body—not like this. There was something about the coiled snake's soft movements, the muscle power that must be hidden beneath the sleek scales. I felt drawn to the screen, where the man had taken a camera from his pocket and positioned himself to take a photograph of the enormous animal. Right then, the snake and I yawned, almost in unison. We stretched our necks, displaying a long and flexible oral cavity with tiny teeth that almost merged into one. A wet soft palate, a tongue that waved in the air. Then we struck. The room erupted in unanimous fear and fervour as we sank our teeth into a thick, hairy arm.

"I thought I was going to die," the Australian man said. "I thought it had me." He sat in a deck chair, a tent in the background. "It would have killed me, had it not got its lower jaw stuck on my trousers. I never would have had a chance against it otherwise." The clip of the snake biting the man was shown over and over, in rapid succession. The soft pink mouth darted forward, darted forward, several times at speed and then again in slow motion. I saw how the snake bit, how a pale-pink tooth snagged on the fabric of the man's trousers before finally breaking free. The thought of that tooth, how it would feel against my fingertips. I closed my mouth. Swallowed.

"I know where you can get one of those." It was the new guy who spoke—the one who had come in from somewhere outside. "Not as big as that one, obviously, but I know where you can buy smaller ones like it—babies."

When I think back, try to remember what the guy looked like, I recall only a head without features, free of eyes, nose or mouth. But I remember that the room fell silent for a moment. Egil turned his head and flashed me a huge smile. I tried to mimic it, but struggled to overcome the intensity of emotion I was feeling. I was afraid they would notice how fast I was breathing, how I was swallowing saliva, how my cheeks burned. I nodded, slowly. Egil turned to Ingvar, who had a similar smile on his face. He nodded, too. And so, wordlessly, we decided. We would get ourselves a snake.

The evening came to life again, the room filling with laughter and voices. The new guy held up a glinting silver digital camera and snapped some group photos of us. Me, Ingvar, Egil, the girl, the guy, and in the background the TV screen featuring the frozen image of a six-metre-long python.

The new member of our family was a metre-long tiger python. Still just a baby. But I was already lost in this tiny creature. Had the feeling of being suspended in midair above an abyss—an astonishingly pleasant sensation. Before I passed him on, I lifted him to my face and whispered, "You're coming home with me."

It must have been a figment of my imagination, but I thought I saw him nod.

Mariam

Kristiansund
Friday, 18 August 2017

"Mamma, can I get a magazine?"

Iben holds up a pastel-coloured comic book covered in glitter. The character on the cover is supposed to be a sexy zombie with shimmering lipstick, pouting with overly large lips. As a rule, only Tor takes Iben along to the store—I like to get the shopping done on my own. But today is mine and Iben's "just us" day. It was my suggestion. School starts on Monday, and I wanted to be the one to take our sixth grader out to buy new clothes and school supplies. Wanted to set aside time for the two of us, in the hope that we'd become closer again. Our relationship has become more difficult as she's got older. Distant, somehow.

We've been at the Storkaia shopping centre for almost three hours. I let Iben choose herself an outfit, and she picked out a pair of skinny jeans, a lace top with a button at the neck, which suits her, and pink shoes and a matching hoodie that she put on straightaway. We stood before the mirrors of the clothing stores, taking pictures and messing around. We even found a yellow sweater in her size that looks like the cashmere jumper I have on today, and we sent Tor a photo of us. Iben is so like me when I was her age. It sometimes hurts to see it, how alike we are, but today it's been sort of nice. After we finished our shopping, we sat in a café and ate ice cream. I asked her safe questions, and she answered them. We talked about horses for a while. She has a friend who's taking riding lessons and is eager to join her. I promised to speak to Tor about it, but she smiled as if I'd already given her my permission.

Iben is a beautiful eleven-year-old, with locks of fair hair that fall down into her eyes, a narrow nose and thin lips. The absurd figure on the zombie comic book she's holding up to me provides a garish contrast. Iben puts on a face intended to charm. It probably works on Tor—who lets his softhearted nature guide him far too much—but this is a poor tactic to try on me. It makes me feel duped. For eleven years I've looked after her, made sure she wouldn't come to any harm—wouldn't fall off the sofa, get food stuck in her throat or swallow any Lego bricks. I've comforted her when she has cried, when she's been ill. She doesn't appreciate any of that. Gifts, and permission to do things—that's all she cares about.

I take the magazine from her hands. For a few seconds she looks at me, a light still shining in her dark eyes, and seconds pass in which she still has hope of getting, getting, getting. I flick through the magazine. More conceited zombie girls gazing from the pages with big, made-up eyes. They do everyday activities, go to school and put on makeup. The people behind the magazine know how to take advantage of the way young girls' eyes twinkle at the sight of all that glitters.

"What can you learn from this?"

Iben looks down. Scrapes the floor with her new shoes.

"Iben. What can you learn from this?"

"I don't know," she whispers.

"It looks to me as if there's nothing at all to be learned from this. Why do you want it?"

She continues to look down at the floor, half shrugs the one shoulder in response.

"Their hips are narrower than their necks," I say.

I set the magazine back in her hands. Stand behind her and open it to the first page.

"Look at this. No story. Almost no text, and the text that is there is nothing but jabbering prattle. The only thing this magazine offers is ugly pictures of half-dead girls in makeup. Why do you want this, Iben?"

She shakes her head. Tries to move, but I restrain her. Turn to the next page.

"Look at this." I turn the page again. "Do you see? Ten pages, and still no story. It isn't about anything—it's about nothing at all."

I can hear the strictness in my voice, but I can't let my daughter continue to fall for something so tasteless. Next time, she'll know better. She tries to twist away, but I hold her in place with my elbows. She looks down at her new shoes, lets go of the magazine so that only I'm holding it—along with her now-limp hand. She whimpers, tries to pull her hand away. I've gone too far.

"I'm sorry. I didn't mean it like that. I just think you shouldn't read things that are going to make you dumber. Find something better, and I'll buy it for you."

Iben snatches the magazine from me. Ducks her head and walks with quick steps, disappearing off behind the shelves.

Then my mobile rings. I rummage around in my handbag and find Iben's phone first—she's asked me to look after it because her pockets aren't big enough. I dig around some more and find my own. It's one of the accountants—he's probably looking to arrange a meeting about employing more personal assistants. OptiHealth, my health-care company, won a major contract in June—there was a photo of us in the *Tidens Krav* newspaper. We were pictured with marzipan cake and sparkling wine, and after spending the summer planning, we're now ready to start delivering. But today my daughter is more important than my role as the company's CEO—I've promised myself that. I put the phone on silent and let it ring on.

Iben isn't at the magazine racks when I reach them. I pick up another comic book that seems better, along with a book of crossword puzzles. Stand there for a moment, looking at the magazine with the heavily made-up zombie girls. We can talk about it this evening.

Iben isn't at the checkout, either. Not by the shelves of sweets, and not outside the store. I take the items from my shopping trolley and load them onto the checkout's conveyor belt. Take out my mobile to call her, but then realise that I have her phone. I think she's too young for a shoulder bag, but I'm clearly going to have to buy one for her soon. At the till, I pay and try to ask the boy sitting there whether he's seen an eleven-year-old girl, but I may as well have asked the till itself. I pack my items into carrier bags, roll my shopping trolley through the exit and stop between two stores, glancing left and right. When I still can't see any sign of her I start to shove the trolley hard in front of me, taking long strides out along the pavement, aware that my patience is wearing thin.

I grit my teeth as I force the shopping trolley up the hill to the multistorey car park.

She isn't at the parking meter; nor is she waiting beside the car. I turn, looking about me in all directions, but there are only a few cars to be seen, and no little girls. This is probably the point at which I'm supposed to start running around hysterically—call on the security guards and have a message read over the shopping centre's PA system, in fear that someone has taken her. That's what she wants. But she will not punish me—I refuse to be part of her game. I begin to load the groceries into the car, throwing in the carrier bags ever more aggressively. The eggs have probably been crushed in their carton, and I hope they're on top of the magazine I chose for Iben. I thrust the empty shopping trolley against the wall with a crash; it topples over and lies there, wheels spinning, as I get into the car. The hem of my four-thousand-kroner coat gets caught in the door, its fabric ripping as I pull it towards me. I start the car. Iben is such a fast runner that she'll likely be home in ten minutes. I refuse to follow her. I'll soon be out on the road. If I want, I can simply keep driving. Put family life behind me and never come back.

Liv

Ålesund
Saturday, 23 August 2003

He had his hood pulled up over his head and was walking hunched over, with his characteristic gait. I recognised his sweater from a distance, its grey and green stripes, worn thin after years of washing. We came close enough that I could see the sweater was spotted with flecks from the light rain. Then he lifted his head, and I met his ice-blue gaze, the smile that was almost expressionless in his pimpled face. As ever, he had a pouch of snus tucked under his upper lip. It was almost possible to believe that he had always looked like this. He must be twenty-eight by now.

Patrick waved, and nausea surged through my body. I spun around, looking down and making a sharp turn into the doorway of the first and best store—the jewellers—but I regretted it as soon as I was through the doors. This was no escape route—it was a dead end. I walked over to a wall of cabinets containing gold jewellery and heard the jingle of the bell as he came in after me.

The bright memories came first. Our laughter as he swung me around and around in the living room until we both crash-landed on the floor. The way he would put slices of ham and cheese on his face to make me laugh. Memories from the time before I started school, before the woman who called herself my mother began to disappear for months at a time. It was as if those memories were wrapped in cotton wool, as if my head turned to cotton just thinking of them.

After the bright memories came the glimpses of everyday life. Patrick, who never woke up on time. The clock radio that buzzed and served up a dry newsreader voice into the darkness of the windowless room. It buzzed until Patrick pulled its plug from the socket. I would stand there tugging at him until he got up, or until he told me to go to hell. Then I would spread butter on a slice of bread, drink a glass of chocolate milk and walk to school. When I came home in the afternoon he might be lying on the sofa, or he might be out, or he might be standing in the kitchen making toasted cheese sandwiches for us. The days drifted into each other, an entire life made up of things we did or didn't do together. The breath from his nose when he tickled me, the TV that was almost always on, glasses of congealed milk and bowls of leftover porridge on the counter. The blobs of toothpaste he would leave in the sink, which I would smear across the porcelain with my finger. Everyday life gradually became less the three of us and more just us two.

The darkest memories came last.

By this point Patrick had moved so close to me where I was standing before the cabinets of gold jewellery that I could smell him. These memories, I couldn't bear. I wanted him to leave so I would be spared having to think of them. I stared at the gold

jewellery—things I could never afford. The only piece I wore
was a gold-plated key on a chain around my neck. I saw its
reflection there in the glass case, and I saw Patrick, who at that
moment reached out a hand and touched it with his fingertip.

"Have you become a latchkey kid, Sara?"

A shock flashed through my body. I shrugged him off.

"Oh, Sara," he said.

I held my breath for several seconds, trying to keep the
nausea at bay.

"My name is Liv," I said. "And I don't know you."

Roe

Kristiansund
Friday, 18 August 2017

The clock on the computer screen is approaching twelve. I check it around every four minutes, occasionally glancing out of the window where the Sundbåten ferry is returning to the harbour. The wind blows tiny raindrops against the pane. When I first came here, I thought the window facing the sea would be something that gave me pleasure. Now all it does is remind me that Kristiansund is just as depressing as Ålesund, only with a better view from the office.

I've long since finished the interview with the girl who claims she was raped while asleep—I'm just giving her testimony a final look-over. Of course I could have eaten lunch with the others, could have joined them for a piece of the Dane's latest "apology cake." When I was new on the force, I used to like these gatherings over cakes. I even pretended to love them when I went for the job interview in Kristiansund—anything to get out of Ålesund. But apology cakes aren't the same when you have a desk job and are no longer in the field. You just

become the person who eats and never bakes—who hears the
stories and analyses them but never experiences them personally. Some of the old guys who are no longer in the field bake
cakes to share regardless, but that's just idiotic.

It isn't just that I'm no longer out in the field. After all that's
happened, I can hardly stand to be around people anymore.
And when police officers eat cake together, they ask questions.
They want to dig around in you, know everything that's going
on inside your head. I don't intend to share a bloody thing,
I have no intention of revealing a single detail they have no
need to know. They think picking up a junkie off the street is
tough, that it's a tragedy if nothing comes of their attempts at
flirting. I can't talk to these people about what it's like to have
lost everything meaningful, without ever having realised just
how important it all was. Or what it's like to be sixty years old,
with every year that passes just another year wedged between
Kiddo and me. It's too late for me. In the past lies an ever
more distant memory of the people I didn't value while I still
had them; in the future, only death awaits. But I can't say this
to my colleagues. So I remain the grumpy old man who sits
there in silence, eating their cake. I won't let them force me
into being that guy.

My stomach rumbles, but I intend to wait until there are
as few people as possible in the cafeteria before I go for lunch.
To kill time, I play the video from the interview with the girl
again. She sits with her head bowed as she speaks, her hands
in her lap. Her hair hides her face from the camera. "I knew
him, from before," she says. "From school and stuff. He had
never, like, made a pass at me—there wasn't anything between
us. That night, at the party at his place, he tried it on, but he
wasn't pushy or anything." My own voice chimes in after a

clearing of my throat: "Now, you say 'he tried it on'—what did he do?" Silence. Then: "He wanted to talk about things. Private things. Then he wanted to kiss me, but I pulled away. I said I wasn't interested, and then he gave up. Afterwards everything seemed fine. He's the kind of guy you feel safe around. I wasn't afraid to lie down next to him and go to sleep." The girl begins to cry. I watch myself hold out the box of tissues. "Tell me what happened next," I say. "I slept," she says. "I didn't wake up until he'd started. He . . . did stuff to me, while I was asleep—" My own voice interrupts again. "I know this is difficult," I say, "but you have to try to be as specific and detailed as possible. When you say he 'did stuff,' can you tell me what you mean by those words?"

I remember how I felt on those first occasions when a young girl cried like this in front of me. How incensed I became at the perpetrator, or perpetrators. At times, I had more to give those girls than I had to give my own daughter. They needed me more, too, with all they'd been through. Now the empathy stops at the halfway mark. I can no longer bear to feel that emotion—I'm afraid I'll see red and then lose it.

I stop the video in the middle of the statement. Look for a moment at the young girl's bowed head. Remember Kiddo running up the street towards the house where we lived as a family. She was always so happy to see me. All at once my heart starts to pound in my chest. I shake off the memories and close the video.

I walk towards the stream of police officers who are on their way back to their desks in the operations centre. Soon many of them will be gone—the operations centre is being moved to Ålesund in a few weeks. Everything disappears from Kristiansund. There's only me swimming against the current.

On my way up the stairs I stop to tie my shoelaces. Listen to the police station's hum of voices, like a swarm of bees. I know that I can't stand much more of this, but I can't fucking stand any of the alternatives, either. I straighten my spine and decide to jog up the rest of the stairs, even though nobody can see me, running past the wax dummies dressed in old police uniforms. The worst thing is that I used to wear one of these myself back in the early eighties, when I was new to the force and wore a neat police cap atop my thick mane of hair. Engaged to be married and full of anticipation for all that lay ahead. All of that would go up in smoke.

Birte walks out of the cafeteria, a bottle of sparkling water in her hand. Her face is so densely covered in freckles that she looks like a map; her customary red plait hangs down over the epaulette of her uniform. She raises her hand in greeting as I pass. People greet each other far too much here—it's exhausting. Once I'm through the door, I hear a shriek, followed by piercing laughter behind me. I turn and see that the Dane has dressed up as a mannequin, in a wig and an old uniform. The tall man is doubled over with laughter. Birte has to sit down on the steps and dry her eyes, she's laughing so much. I know it's stupid of me, but I can't help but think that the Dane was standing there as I passed by just a few seconds ago. That he waited, stock-still, as I walked past so he could jump out and scare someone other than me.

There are still a few small groups of people sitting in the cafeteria, the ones who take long lunch breaks. None of the food looks especially appetising, but I decide to go for a chicken salad. Pick up a newspaper and make a beeline for one of the tables by the window. The football coach Magne Hoseth is on the front page of *Tidens Krav* today—he wants to help

Kristiansund retain their position in Norway's premier league. I flick through the paper's pages to find the interview. Don't really give a toss about how Kristiansund FC are doing in the football league, but at least the article will be about something other than the business sector or hospitals. Wrong. Even Hoseth has an opinion on the planned regional hospital that has already cost taxpayers 450 million kroner to try to figure out. It's a week since Kristiansund lost the appeal in the hospital court case. The hospital will instead be built in Molde.

Plucking up my courage, I stab a piece of chicken with my fork. I've just managed to open my mouth over it when from the corner of my eye I see someone coming towards me.

"Well hello there, stranger!"

Åsmund is wearing a greyish-brown sweater that matches his white hair in a way that is far too clichéd. He doesn't get that I'd prefer not to be seen with him. That his presence calls attention to the silver strands on my own head. There's nothing to do but brace myself for Åsmund's inevitable stories of school visits and concerned conversations with the town's youth.

"How's it going, Åsmund?"

He sighs and sets down his tray on the table.

"You know, the longer I work here, the more convinced I become that there's simply no hope for the next generation."

"At least you don't have to deal with the sexual assault cases. Give me a drunken brawl or a break-in any day—the sexual assault cases are the ones that really get you."

One of the most difficult things to accept about Åsmund is that we actually get along pretty well. It's depressing.

"I've heard that you're pretty skilled at handling those cases, Roe. I was talking to a couple of guys over a slice of cake earlier. They say you're a capable interviewer."

I'm surprised that they've been talking about me, but I suspect Åsmund isn't telling the whole story—that there was a *but* in there somewhere.

Åsmund starts relating a story about some young boy of thirteen he's been trying to help. I quickly zone out. Look down at my salad and consider whether I should bother taking another bite. Fill up my fork and look at the pale meat, the dressing the colour of mustard.

"Roe!"

Birte is calling me from the door. Her freckled face is serious this time.

"Meeting. Team room."

I can see it in Birte's bearing, how she suddenly seems ten years older—I can smell a big case from miles away. That's what I need right now, for something to happen. I wasn't hungry anyway. I get up, taking my lunch and newspaper with me, and walk over to the rubbish bin. Throw both items into it with both hands, the plastic lid giving out a loud crack.

We hurry down the stairs to the third floor. But in front of the door to the team room, Birte stops. She holds out an arm, wanting me to go in first. I turn my head and see that Åsmund has followed us—he's standing on the stairs and looking in our direction. As I reach for the door handle, I suddenly feel unwell.

The room is half dark and full of people sitting in silence, all looking at me. Then there's a bang, and the air is filled with raining confetti. On the wall a sign that says ROE—60 TODAY! lights up, and in chorus the room erupts into a rendition of the birthday song. They sing, bow, curtsy and turn around, just as the song's lyrics dictate. I should have known. Of course the bastards intend to rub it in.

Liv

Ålesund
Thursday, 28 August 2003

"Oh no, no-no-no, no, no, no!"

The car on the TV screen spun off the road, straight into a concrete wall, and was flipped over onto its back. Egil swore, flinging the controller at the pedestal with an angel figurine on it that stood in the centre of Ingvar's room.

"What the hell are you doing?" Ingvar smirked, giving his long dark hair a flick as he swerved his car neatly across the finish line. "You have way too much of a temper."

"But Egil's dad will happily buy us a new Xbox if this one gets broken," I said. "You let it out, Egil."

"Oh shut your mouth," Egil answered.

The mocking, the bickering—under all this was only good feeling. This was one of the things I liked best about these guys—that we could yell at each other without it being taken the wrong way. You don't talk like that to someone you don't like, not in that tone. We each knew that the others could take it, and that they wouldn't go too far. Nobody

misunderstood, nobody fell out, and it gave us all a chance
to let off some steam.

Egil flopped down on the bed beside me and straightened the beige Lacoste shirt he was wearing. It was slim fit,
of course—he hadn't spent all those hours at the gym for
nothing. Egil was irritatingly well proportioned in everything from the breadth of his shoulders to his jawline and
cheekbones to his nose, forehead and eyebrows, which met
in the middle. He was the kind of guy many girls convinced
themselves they wanted, because they thought that was what
everybody else wanted, too. Girls who looked like images
from a glossy magazine thought they were looking for an
image from a glossy magazine—and Egil used this for all it
was worth. Only I knew that in Egil's case, there was actually
a good guy underneath it all.

I lifted my arm—Nero hung down from it, his scaly body
seeking to return to the heater below the window—and Egil
took the snake from me. I sat down on the floor next to Ingvar
and grabbed the controller. Ingvar started the game again, and
the vehicles lined up for the race, my white Jaguar and Ingvar's
black Lamborghini next to two other fancy cars. The intoxi-
cating sound of four motors filled the room. Some women in
short grey skirts came up and prepared us for the start signal.
Then we were off. Full throttle through dark streets. I was so
overeager that I cornered with my entire body. I turned the car
too hard, so its back end bumped into the crash barrier—no
high score for me. Ingvar was soon in pole position, sailing
elegantly across the asphalt, taking a long jump from the crest
of a hill and making a controlled landing into the next turn.
I was too concerned with what he was doing, and so crashed

into a Vauxhall with red stripes along its sides—we lost control, both of us. Egil laughed loudly in his usual taunting way, seeming to have forgotten that he was in my position just a few minutes earlier. I regained control of the car and swerved around the Vauxhall into a perfect turn, only to find that I was now going the wrong way. I was soon at the back of the race again. I sighed, pulled carefully over to the roadside verge, and parked the car.

"I think it's obvious what you're doing all day, Ingvar, when you're supposed to be writing music," I said.

Ingvar raised an index finger as the words NEW HIGH SCORE appeared on the screen.

"You're just jealous," Ingvar said. "Because I'm so good."

"Good at not having a life," retorted Egil.

Ingvar drove on without saying a word. I went and sat on the bed beside Egil while Ingvar carried on, driving alone in the lead, scoring points.

"You'll be here for the party on Saturday, right?" Egil said.

He tried to get Nero to lie like a cat in the crook of his arm, but the snake didn't seem to understand. Instead he sank, pulled by gravity down onto the bed, resting his head on his coiled body. Nero was calm by nature. It was rare that he moved at all—he could lie in almost the same position for hours at a time, saving his energy until the next opportunity to hunt presented itself.

"I don't have any money," I said. "Or any leftover booze."

Egil let out an exasperated breath.

"You always scrounge your drinks off me."

"And anyway, I'm not really up for it."

Egil looked at me.

"I actually just want to spend the weekend doing my course reading," I said. "Seriously. Go to bed early and stuff, spend all Sunday reading instead of lying in bed hungover and hating myself."

Egil raised an eyebrow.

"I'm sure one party isn't going to stop you from becoming a nurse. Come on, it won't be like last time, it'll be cool."

Egil probably remembered more than I did about the things I'd rattled off at some point in the early hours between last Saturday and Sunday. I'd vowed never to tell them about Patrick, but bumping into him in town that day had had such a strong effect on me.

"You'll be up for it as soon as you start drinking," Egil said.

That's what I'd thought, too, when I'd come back here that day and started to get ready to go out partying. Mostly I just wanted to bury myself under the duvet and ride out the anxiety that was flowing through me. But instead I'd decided to make it the best night ever—told myself that it would be fun just as soon as I started drinking. It wasn't. I couldn't even remember what I'd said, only that I had said far too much. I didn't even know that Ingvar already knew Patrick.

Egil stared at me, giving me a dejected look. He was waiting for an answer and seemed to have no intention of accepting a no. I sighed.

"Just kidding. Of course I'm coming."

I extended my index finger and touched one of the narrow stripes of pale scales on Nero's head, right at the top of his neck. If you looked at his head from above, the pattern looked like an arrow, a stroke of white at the very back and a dark arrow tip that pointed towards the snout and jaws. I had spent so much time staring at this head, this wondrous signpost, in recent months.

"He's so beautiful," I said. "I just can't get over it."

"Jeez," said Egil. "Way to make a guy feel good."

"I mean it—just look at that body."

He had shed his skin a week earlier. I'd been able to watch the entire process, from when his body had taken on a greyish cast—his black eyes included—until he scratched himself against the bedposts to pull off the brittle grey-white membrane. The new scales that were revealed shone in vivid colours, polished and gleaming. People once thought that snakes were immortal. They saw them being reborn from their own skin, again and again. His skin was now hanging from the ceiling light in my room. I wanted to keep every rebirth, remember all the snakes he had been.

"Can't we bring the snake out at the party?" Egil asked, fluttering his eyelashes.

I looked at him.

"Just at the after party, then?"

I shook my head.

"It's not as if there are policemen on the guest list or anything—just cool people. If he gets scared, we'll put him away again. It'll be fine."

"Until he bites somebody and she calls her mummy."

"I'll keep an eye on him. Warn everybody not to startle him."

"Egil. We're done talking about this."

"It's not just your snake. Ingvar—what do you think?"

Ingvar had turned off the Xbox and was now putting on a CD. Electric Wizard's *Dopethrone*—his favourite album. Slow guitar riffs filled the room as Ingvar slumped down onto the bed on the other side of me. He was wearing a band T-shirt that was so faded it was no longer possible to see what the image on it depicted. He had a book in his hand.

"Shall I tell you what I was thinking about earlier today?" Ingvar said, holding up the book.

"*Alice in Wonderland?*" I said. "Children's books, Ingvar? I thought you only read Russian novels the size of bricks."

"It's a classic. Who do you think we'd all be if we were characters from *Alice in Wonderland?*"

Egil laughed. "I certainly know who you'd be, Ingvar. You'd be the caterpillar that sits on a mushroom, smoking all the time."

Ingvar threw his arms wide.

"All the time? It happens once a week at most!"

"For some of us that's pretty often," Egil answered. "And who knows what you get up to when the rest of us are out at lectures."

"That's a lie—and anyway, it's medicinal," Ingvar said.

Ingvar had epilepsy. He rarely had seizures, but he was always on guard against them, and he rarely drank alcohol. We had agreed that if he was ever home alone and called one of us but couldn't say anything, then we should assume he'd had a seizure and go to him straightaway. Luckily so far, he'd only ever had seizures while someone was with him.

Egil grinned. "It hasn't been proved that cannabis helps epilepsy sufferers, Ingvar, so don't try to make excuses for your drug use."

"Egil's easy, too," I said. "He's the Mad Hatter. One never-ending, meaningless party—that's your life, isn't it, Egil?"

"Well, you're fucking rude," Egil said. "And anyway, you're way crazier than me when you drink. Who's Liv then, Ingvar? Is she the cat?"

"She could be the Cheshire Cat." Ingvar raised an index finger. "Or I could have gone for Alice, too. But there's an even better option. Liv is the Queen of Hearts."

"Because I'm the boss of you two?"

"Well, that—and you're the party queen. But the Queen of Hearts is the most important character in the whole book. She makes the story dangerous—there's no story without her."

"I don't get it. You think I'm dangerous?"

"I don't get it either, Ingvar," Egil said.

"But think about it. Who was it that dragged us out for a midnight swim in February? Who climbed up Sukkertoppen in the pitch-dark with a gang of drunken fools? Who crawled through a bush and into a fancy garden to steal *that* thing?"

Ingvar pointed to the angel figurine standing atop the pedestal—one of those fat, babylike cherubs that you saw everywhere, but discoloured by green stains and seagull shit, it looked far from cute. I had named it Beelzebub.

"I remember when the light came on in the first-floor windows," said Egil. "You ran like fuck with that angel."

"Exactly," said Ingvar. "How many nights would we remember if Liv hadn't been there to liven them up? Without her, there wouldn't be much that was memorable. Just an eternal absurd tea party."

I shook my head. "For a guy who smokes all the time, Ingvar, you're actually really fucking smart."

"I *don't* smoke all the time!"

"Liv is the one who's going to end up in prison," said Egil. "I'd put money on it."

"Just wait and see how wrong you are," I said, laughing.

"So then it's decided," Egil said. "Ingvar's persuaded you. Nero can come to the party?"

"Actually, I agree with Liv," said Ingvar. "The snake will end up biting someone, or maybe even trying to choke them. I want no part of it."

Then my phone rang. The number on the screen wasn't one I had stored in my contacts.

"Hello?" Her smoker's voice was rasping.

"Yes, you called me?" I said, getting up. I walked out into the hallway, past the walls covered in embroidered decorations from our landlady's youth, towards the bathroom. Thought I caught a whiff of a scent, a strong spray of perfume.

"Sara? Is that you?" She sounded emotional. I flipped down the toilet seat, imagining the face of a middle-aged woman floating at the bottom of the bowl. Pulled down my jeans and underwear and sat down.

"It's Liv," I said, and peed.

She fell silent as I pressed the telephone hard against my neck, studying the sea of various dust-covered soaps, after-shaves, razors and other male beauty products, along with the washing powder, hair bands, some nail clippings, a tennis sock. I generally kept my own things in my room unless I was taking a shower.

"It's Mamma."

I heard the sound of her breath as she drew smoke down into her lungs, a darkness. I wiped, flushed. The toilet half filled and sucked the paper down into the drain. I washed my hands under piping-hot water. The woman on the phone said, "Hello? I heard Patrick ran into you in town last weekend." Her voice cracked. I dried my hands. Imagined how they would feel if they were covered in scales. My skin was such a thin layer, so delicate.

"I'm so sorry about that, Sara."

Her lies forced their way through—it felt as if they were working to loosen something within me. I looked at myself in the mirror, my face pale in the harsh light. I tugged on the gold chain I was wearing around my neck, bringing the gold-plated key out from under my sweater and fiddling with it, stroking the small teeth at its end with my fingertips. I cleared my throat, which put a stop to her torrent of words—a relief.

"You've got the wrong number," I said. "This is Liv. Not Sara."

"Are you doing well, honey?"

"You don't understand," I said, louder. "I don't know you." I closed my fist around the key and tried to shut out the smell, the voice.

"Surely we can find our way back to each other again?"

I hung up. Her voice remained in the room as a vibration. I left the phone on the sink and went back to the bedroom. Egil and Ingvar looked at me.

"So many wrong numbers these days," I said. I took hold of Nero and held him up in front of me. Studied the deep hollows in his snout, which he used to observe the infrared rays in the room. He could "see" our body heat. I wondered what that looked like.

Nero parted his tiny jaws and hissed. Egil and Ingvar shuddered, but I wasn't afraid. I didn't think he would do anything to me. Instead, I tried to listen. Wanted to open my mind and understand his language. Could I make out a word, deep inside there? If I simply looked past everything that sounded like an *s* or an *h*, ignored my human alphabet, I might be able to discern what he wanted to say. He had no lips, so if he tried to make an *m*, how would it sound? If he tried to make a *t* with his forked tongue, a *g* without vocal cords? His words could never be like human words, so he would have to use his own. Subtle nuances of *h* and *s*. If I listened closely enough, I would understand.

Did I dream about it that night? That I saw myself as a burning flame, ablaze in the bed, and heard my own voice whispering? Or was it his? I don't remember what he said.

"We should try feeding him live mice," I said to Ingvar and Egil. "Don't you think that must be better for them—more natural?"

Mariam

Kristiansund
Friday, 18 August 2017

The windshield is full of tiny dead flies. I turn the wipers on, squashing them into reddish-brown streaks that arc across the glass. I drive. The road lies behind me as more of it appears up ahead, an eternal ribboning movement. On the dashboard is a pile of bills, because I'm an eternal self-contradiction—I run a regime of tidiness in my home that I'm unable to follow myself. I spray the windshield with wiper fluid. Continue to drive. I could keep going until I reach Trondheim and stay there tonight, drive on in the morning. Make it a fair distance before Tor becomes so unsettled that he reports me missing. A phone starts to vibrate again, mine or Iben's. He's calling constantly. Probably thinks that his young wife has gone off to visit some lover or other, and now he's afraid our happy facade is about to collapse. That politician Tor Lind and his trophy wife—of whom everyone has such a good impression—are about to part ways.

The ringing stops. I follow the turns that twist their way through the still summer-green landscape. The fjord occasionally disappears behind houses or trees, but it's still there, pursuing me. The cool water is on the hunt, lying in wait for the right moment to pounce. I'm so tired of mountains and fjords. Would probably be just as tired of jungles and savannas, if that was what surrounded me. I don't know much about the world out there, other than that it feels as if my heart is trapped here. It isn't enough to cast a glance at the horizon and see the water disappearing into the distance, I want to disappear myself.

On the ferry I stay in the car and close my eyes. One of the phones starts to ring again, then the other. The sound of the vibration is more muffled, as if it's tightly wrapped in something. I don't know why he continues to call when no one answers. I take a few bites of the baguette I bought at a petrol station. It tastes vacuum-packed, and reminds me that everything is perishable. I put the sandwich down on the seat next to me; sit there staring straight ahead in the closed mouth of the ferry as I wait for its jaws to open and show me another world.

The landscape changes as I drive deeper into Sør-Trøndelag. Less fjord, more forest. A rock face appears on my left-hand side, a perpendicular wall that bears obvious signs of blasting, to clear the way for people. In my bag one of the phones buzzes again. I increase my speed, feeling the power in the turns, how I'm ripped along by the car's muscle.

I think about what it would mean to simply take off, to leave for good. Feel the impossibility of it. It wouldn't just involve leaving the company I've spent years building up, or my house, my husband, my life. Am I to demand that Iben come and live

with me—become a single mother? In many ways she's more
his child than mine—I could never take her from him. It's more
that I want to remove myself from *them*. I weigh heavily on
them, dragging them down. They'd be better off without me.

Another fjord peeks forth through the landscape. I slam on
the brakes, pull over onto the shoulder. Turn off the ignition
and sit there with my hands in my lap. There are women who
leave their children. Nobody understands them, how they
could do something like that. But even if the longing to vanish
like dust in the wind remains, that too now seems impossible.
When I think about disappearing completely and never being
able to see my child again, it hurts. In my mind's eye I see how
Iben pushes her hair behind an ear as she sits and reads, and
this awakens a warmth in me, tiny bubbles in my blood. She
is, in spite of everything, my child.

I get out of the car. Lock it, even though there's not a soul
in sight, and cross the road to continue down the sloped bank
to the fjord. It's quiet here, nothing but the occasional crow
nearby. I bend down and stick my hand into the water. It's cold
against my fingers. I look around. A car drives past, is gone in
a flash. I pull off my expensive work shoes. Lift my skirt and
grab hold of my tights, pull them down. Leave them lying on
the ground like a dead skin. I step out into the water. It stings
my toes, my ankles. I haven't been swimming this far north in
years—it's Tor who takes Iben swimming, on the rare occasions
when the sun is just about out and the wind warm enough that
he can be bothered to put on his swim shorts. I had forgotten
that there's something good about the stabbing sensation of
feeling your feet go numb in cold water. I lift my skirt, walk
out until the water almost wets my underwear. Stand that way
for a moment, looking out across the calm water.

I so wish to be timeless, placeless, free from the meaningless laws of physics. It isn't the house, the town or my family that traps me—it's my body. I wonder how long it would take for somebody to find me, were I to disappear completely into this dark water. But I'm not brave enough, don't mean it enough. There's something that stops me, some insistent force.

I turn and start to walk back up the slope, my underwear and skirt wet because I move too quickly; the cold stings, and now I'm probably going to get a urinary tract infection. I return to the shore, sit down on the grass and look out across the water. My freshly laundered skirt is flecked with wet earth, but it doesn't matter.

It's as if an old memory floats up and lies there, bobbing on the water's surface. A bubble that refuses to burst. I can't run away like this. It won't do any good. The thing will stay with me, regardless.

I get up and walk back to the car, shoes and tights in my hand. The asphalt is unfamiliar underfoot, and small stones gnaw their way into the soles of my feet. I brush them away, get into the driver's seat. Take my phone from my bag and wait until it's finished vibrating yet again. I'm being unfair to him. Know that I'm much more than a trophy wife to him. I don't want to listen to any of the countless voicemails. I turn off the phone, then do the same with Iben's. Then I start the drive home.

I sit in the car for a while with the engine switched off, looking up at my house. It stands there in all its banality. The curtains in the windows I selected precisely so that they would stand out as little as possible. The coniferous hedge has been cut exactly as coniferous hedges should be cut; the gates are freshly painted, the garden furniture new and clean. Nobody who walks past this house will see the slightest trace of decline. It's on the inside that we're collecting dust and rotting away.

I have a mental fantasy that tends to calm me whenever my emotions get the upper hand, and which has often helped me fall asleep. I start by emptying the entire house of furniture, clothes, toys and all the myriad things we've filled it with over the years. See a van driving it all away. Then I take a bucket of water, a scrubbing brush, a cloth and some strong cleaning products. I start at the innermost end of Iben's room, working my way out the door and continuing with mine and Tor's. I spend a long time scrubbing and cleaning the bathroom upstairs, where we most often shower. When I'm done up there, I wash my way down the stairs and continue with the living room, kitchen, bathroom and toilet on the ground floor, as well as the large room we only use to store old clutter. Finally, I scour the hall until it's gleaming and white, the way it was when we moved in. A freshly polished chandelier, clean white carpet treads on each step. I wash my way all the way out onto the front step, where I stand, alone, before a closed door that no longer bears any trace of us. Not the tiniest bacterium, not a single strand of hair. It's a laborious ritual, which I can drag out infinitely. It always brings me a sense of calm.

I slowly open the car door and then sit there, staring straight ahead as if I'm waiting for something. Perhaps for something to fall from the sky and make my life different. Rain falls into the car, but I'm already wet.

When I finally get out of the car, I crane my neck to look into the living room window. It doesn't look as if the TV is on. Regardless, it's so late that she's probably gone to bed, and

Tor is probably relieved not to have to listen to the sound of the TV for a while. He'd prefer it if we only ever watched the news. *Anything for you, dear daughter*, he often says to Iben, touching her fair-haired head as she sits in front of the screen. He's always been a good father to her. Reasonable, and patient, too. That patience is like a warm embrace that protects his little flock.

It's actually strange that he's called me so many times today. He's never called me like that on the occasions I've taken a little trip by myself before. Not even the time I spent the night at a campsite before driving home again in the morning. All his prior experience dictated that I'd be back again. He knew that all he needed to do was be his usual, patient self—and wait. What's different this time?

On the front door hangs a sign that Iben made at school. Three smiling faces, two adults and a child, and our names printed in childish letters. Beside the faces is a large tree, which the teacher must have helped Iben draw. The Lind Family. I pass a hand across the sign. I so want to understand the mothers who say they would do absolutely anything for their child. Those words have come out of my own mouth, too, but I haven't meant them—not deep down. The tiny bubbles are there—the pride I feel when she does well, the comfort I offer her when she is ill. But when I try to find that deeper bond, it slips away. Would I jump in front of a train for her? Fight off a bear? I'm not sure.

Iben must have actually tidied away her shoes for once. Perhaps she's taken something I've said on board after all, big girl that she is. I smile to myself and open the closet, but her shoes aren't there, either. Nor is her jacket hanging on its hook. It's not on the chair, nor balled up on the shoe rack, where she would often leave it when she was younger. Was she really so angry that she rushed upstairs with all her outdoor clothes still on?

Tor is sitting in the kitchen. He glances up from his laptop, meets my gaze. His phone is beside him on the bench; on the table an empty coffee cup. His face glows with worry. His skin seems greyish, and his forehead is creased with deep lines. I look at his blue eyes, the deep curves of his receding hairline he dislikes so much—even though it actually suits him. The slightly too large glasses he wears when he can't find the pair he likes. I suddenly feel a tenderness for my husband. How could I have thought of leaving him?

"Where have you two been?" He gets up.

My gaze lands on the kitchen counter, freshly wiped clean. I realise that the food I've bought is still in the car. I look at the chair where Iben usually sits, at the window ledge where she tends to set her mobile to charge at night, but of course I have her phone in my bag.

"You two?"

The words come out in a squeak—I'm unable to say any more. See how his face takes on a confused expression. I turn on my heel and walk in the opposite direction, towards the hall. Take the stairs two at a time and flatly ignore Iben's KNOCK BEFORE YOU ENTER! sign that's been hanging on her door since she was six. I storm into her room and take a deep breath, ready to shout at her, give her a huge telling-off. But the bed is neatly made, and empty, as is the chair at the desk. I jog back down the stairs. Stop in front of the living room door, feel the adrenaline surging through my body—that's what she wants, for me to be afraid; she's probably sitting in there laughing at me. I tighten my grip on the door handle, throw open the door.

The living room is bathed in dim evening light. I look towards the sofa, the dining table and the empty chair in the corner. Turn and walk towards the bathroom, but there's nobody in there, either. I remember that I haven't checked the bathroom upstairs, so I run back up again and wrench open the door.

"What's going on?" I hear Tor say from downstairs.

The walls tremble from my own hard steps across the floor. I check the bedroom that Tor and I share, almost collapse as I walk back down the stairs to the ground floor. Open the door to the room of clutter and stand there staring stupidly into the chaos. I go back to the kitchen.

"Has Iben gone out?" I try to sound normal, unworried, but my voice is faint.

Tor stares at me. The muscles in his neck tighten. His eyes seem to bulge. It dawns on me that he's angry. And if Tor is angry, then this is serious.

"You're telling me that you don't know where Iben is?"

The realisation reaches me at the same moment as his words. The clock on the microwave says 22:23. The shopping centre has been closed for several hours. And I don't know where my daughter is.

Liv

Ålesund
Friday, 29 August 2003

We gathered around my bed as if around an altar, Egil and Ingvar on either side at the foot and me at the head, standing next to the headboard. We had spread out a large white sheet, which Ingvar and Egil were holding up at the corners. Inside the sheet a little white and brown mouse was running around, scrabbling and slipping against the white fabric. Egil leaned forward and peered over the edge, making little puckered kissing noises at the mouse.

Nero lay resting in my arms. He lifted his head and stuck out his tongue in quick thrusts. I sat on my pillow in the lotus position and set him down on my legs. Pulled the white sheet down for him. He scented the air with his tongue, aware of the prey now. His scaly body began to move, sliding towards my naked feet and making rough-smooth contact before he slipped over the sheet's edge.

In the night I had been woken by a sound in the room, like a wind coming from far away. Something barely audible but present, like an itch. The bright summer night made it impossible to tell whether it was two o'clock or six. I picked up my phone, saw that it was five past four. The sound was faint, but there was no doubt that I had heard something real. It was a sound full of smells, full of dreams. I bent over the edge of the bed and peered under it. Nero's stone eyes stared at me. He lay curled up on the rug. For a moment I thought the sound had stopped, but then it started again. So low that I thought it might have been with me my whole life, or never existed. It was coming from him. I lay down on the floor, closed my eyes and listened, thought I could make out the traces of this energy that danced in the room between us. Pure contact.

Then I heard the first word. His voice sounded ancient, full of dust. When I first heard it, I thought that this must be what he had wanted to say to me all along. His meaning was so clear, despite the fact that it was expressed with just a single word. *Dear.* A warmth spread through my body. I crept close to him and whispered, "You're dear to me too, Nero." Then a new susurration rustled out into the room, and I heard another word. *Liv.*

I had never thought any living creature would be able to make me happy. Had believed that I would carry loneliness with me wherever I went. But last night, when I lay under the bed with Nero after he had whispered his first words to me, I felt a happiness spread through my veins, out into each finger and down through my feet, back to my heart and out again, as if I had found the way into my own body. The next word I heard from the depths of him was a wish. *Hunt.* It was a long time since he had last been fed, and he was dissatisfied with the frozen mice we dangled in front of him to create the illusion of living prey. He missed hunting. It was in his nature.

When I woke again early this morning, I was lying alone on the rug. I hit my head on the slats of the bed when I tried to get up. For a moment I had the idea that he'd abandoned me, had found a way out and fled. But then I found him hanging around the plant on the window ledge. The rays of the morning sun hit his glossy skin. Yet again I was fascinated to see his body balancing in this way, resting, yet simultaneously tense, in order to hold himself aloft. I lay down on the bed. Tried to coil myself up, as far as my stiff spine permitted, and then stretched out, bending from side to side with my arms alongside my body. Had any person seen me, they would have wondered whether I was having a seizure. But Nero looked at me and understood what I was trying to do. That I was attempting to get closer to him.

Now the mouse was running around and around in the white space we had created for it, its little paws clawing and scrambling. Continuously turning in new directions and failing to find a way out. I wondered whether it forgot where it had already been, or whether it tried a route again because it could see no other option. There would soon be no more directions in which to turn. The white space was being slowly filled by snake. Nero approached, a shadow in the mouse's world, seemingly new but something that had always been there, a clouding of the mouse sky.

In the next moment the white and brown animal was trapped. The mouse thrashed about for a moment, stopped, then thrashed again. From its tiny mouth came a succession of desperate squeaks. Nero held the mouse firmly, squeezing until the animal stopped its thrashing. Blood spattered the white sheet. I felt a tickling sensation inside me. In my chest, my belly, and deeper. Egil gave out a long, half-whistling exhalation. Then the body of the snake carefully tightened itself around that of the mouse.

"This is totally sick," Egil whispered.

None of us said anything further. Nero continued to squeeze, ever tighter. It didn't seem to cost him much effort. His body was tense, but calm. Then something happened to his face. It seemed to open into a smile. His huge jaws slid apart, the skin at the corners of his mouth stretching like soft cloth. He enveloped the prey with his mouth, its white fur sticking out. The snake's brown and beige head was broad and flat, and took on an even wider and more absurd leer as he swallowed. Soon, all that could be seen of the mouse was a pair of pink feet and a tail, before that too sank into Nero and was gone. Egil and Ingvar dropped the sheet onto the bed. They both stepped back without a word.

A small lump moved down the snake's long stomach, a barely visible protrusion in the radiant skin. I stretched out my hand and carefully stroked it with my fingertips. Wondered what it would feel like to be in there. It must be warm, probably wet and cramped, too, like being in the womb.

Reptile memoirs

One day, I just knew. My tiny world was inside a thin, white shell from which I now realised I could break free. I pushed my head against the white membrane, carefully at first, testing the elasticity of the tough material, then harder, until the shell cracked. Through the opening, I found something cool—this new substance that I would learn to recognise as air. I had of course drunk all my amniotic fluid, and when I first felt the cool air descend into my lungs it brought the sweet relief of finally having something I'd had no idea how much I needed.

I looked around at the new layer of the world that had opened itself to me. A layer in which the universe's boundaries were an enormous, shining snake's belly, curled around its countless white eggs. Mother. Siblings not yet hatched. I slipped slowly out into the day, gliding across my unhatched brothers and sisters. There was so much to take in. The heat that glowed from above. A distant taste of life in the air. All

manner of loud and piercing noises from some place unknown
to me. Sounds that rose and fell, vibrations from Mother as
she kept her eggs warm.

By the time the light and the darkness had switched places
several times, I had a dozen brothers and sisters who slipped
in and out of their eggs, depending on whether they wished
to sleep or to play. We coiled ourselves around one another,
keeping our bodies close, each pulling in our own direction.
Found new hollows between coils, slipped under, up and out.
We learned the strength of our muscles, how easily we could
duck away and hide, only to emerge again. Where one body
ended and the next began was immaterial. We were both ourselves and all the others at once.

Mother was hiding something from us. She shielded us from
what awaited behind the great coil. At first it didn't interest
us. We thought the coil must be the limits of the universe. For
us, the days were a single intense wave of movement, heat and
taste. Still, we knew that there was something we must learn.
That there was a reason we tested our muscles on one another.
We knew in our bodies that there must be some purpose for
our strength.

I clearly remember the first time I glanced up and found
Mother's back was gone. It hadn't been an end after all—rather
a beginning. Around us the ground was bare, the path open.
I was hungry, and the air smelled faintly of food. Small creatures that were hiding somewhere close by. Now it was up to
us. Now we must spread ourselves like a river across the soil,
on our way to replace the bitter taste of amniotic fluid with
that of flesh.

I sought my way down from the empty eggshells, towards
the dry earth. Tasted my way ahead between small stones,

completely silent. The animals must be here somewhere, but the tastes in the air were distant and unclear. The only living heat I could see around me was from my brothers and sisters who came up on either side of me.

I readied myself to dart forward, to streak across the ground with the hunter instinct that existed in my body and commanded me, requiring no conscious effort. I discovered that the air, too, had a boundary. No matter where I slithered, I met invisible resistance. I licked at the air with my tongue, but the barrier had no taste. The barrier simply was—a new truth. Confused, I lay beside the barrier and tried to understand. I knew there must be something on the other side. I could clearly see it, hear it and smell it. Now I could even feel its motion. It was a creature so enormous that Mother's back was small by comparison. It was its height that was most impressive, how the being towered over me. It came closer, lifted one of its long limbs and tapped on the barrier, tap, tap, tap, shooting vibrations through my body.

Liv

Ålesund
Saturday, 30 August 2003

Everything was spinning. The room was moving in a circle, so I could no longer distinguish the walls from the ceiling, my arms from the hands that held on to them, swinging me around. People, in an erratic stream of skin and colours rushing past in red, yellow and white. I saw hair and clothes and somebody laughing. I laughed back, unsure to which face. I'd had too much to drink. Tried to focus on a fixed point. The black leather sofa and matching armchair. The dusty paintings on the walls that the landlady had probably bought secondhand for cheap. The chest of drawers in the corner, bright red—Ingvar's chest of drawers that was never used for anything. Egil's CD player with its speakers spewing out rhythmic words—it was always Egil who was first to choose the music in the living room. I liked Ingvar's better—it was more depressing and psychedelic, more in line with how I felt. Egil's dance music, all his racket, his burning need for life to be one endless party and nothing but fun, fun, fun, made me uneasy. Had it not

been for the fact that I knew him to be an entirely different
person when his noisy coursemates weren't hanging around, I
wouldn't have bothered to maintain our friendship. That's just
how our relationship was. We gave and we took.

The person swinging me around had a shifting face, like
sand. I wanted to stop, tried to pull my arms away, get them
loose, but instead he pulled me closer. Moved more slowly.
Stroked a hand over my hair. I was dizzy; I grabbed his arm
so as not to fall. He embraced my shoulders, pressed me to
him and rocked me from side to side, in time and then out
of step with the rapping from the stereo system. It was as if
the movements in the room didn't correspond to the sounds,
everything seeming to lag behind. Nor did I know whether I
could trust gravity. Up wasn't always up—sometimes it was
to the left, and I had no idea where my head, stomach and
legs were, which way was up and which way was down on my
body, whether any of it belonged together. Pieces that didn't
really fit, but which could still be hitched to each other, an
unsuccessful attempt to solve the puzzle. That's what I was.

I lay my face against his sweatshirt. It had a design on
the chest that I touched with my hands. The music pounded
through my fingers. A while ago Egil had tried to give me
water and asked me to sit down. I had simply laughed at him
and emptied the half-full glass over his head. The thought of
how furious he'd been made me giggle.

"What are you laughing at?" the guy asked.

I looked up at the silver chain around his neck and then at
his chin, a round chin.

"I was just thinking about how bad this band is," I said,
pressing my finger hard against the print, although I had no
idea what it depicted. I giggled again, louder this time. Right

then he grabbed my chin, hooking hard fingers under it and lifting my face. He pressed his lips against mine, shoved a reckless tongue that tasted of something bitter between them. A burning rose in my stomach, a bubbling at the very back of my throat.

I twisted out of his grasp, in need of air. Shoved my way between dancing bodies as I headed for the door. Suddenly remembered the glass of banana liqueur someone had put in my hand, how vile it had tasted. I leaned on a chair and tried to force down the vomit, but it was no use. I managed to open the door and throw myself outside, leaning over the low wall that surrounded the terrace. Brownish yellow puke spattered down the wall and across the flower bed, drops of it flecking the green leaves and pink petals. We were supposed to look after the garden—it was our responsibility—but the landlady had given up caring long ago; it was she who cut the grass and weeded the flower bed. At least I had now fertilised it.

I walked across the grass, still with the taste of puke in my mouth. Grabbed a large leaf from the plum tree and licked it, trying to rid my tongue of the taste. I leaned against the tree trunk, felt the cool dampness of the leaves against my face. Closed my eyes and tried to find my way back to a world that didn't feel as if it were bobbing on the high seas. At least it felt good to get away from the music, all the people and the noise.

"Cigarette?"

The guy I'd been dancing with was leaning against the house wall, holding out a packet. The lighter flared up beneath his face. A childish face on a tall body. His head was shaved almost completely free of hair; the tiny remaining strands were so pale they seemed to merge with his skull. His body was skinny, and he was wearing a hoodie that made him look small, a copy of Eminem. In his ear was a shining diamond.

"Fuck yes," I said.

He came over to me with the pack of cigarettes, leaned against the tree, his arm propped above my head. The smell of his aftershave made me feel unwell. His face was so close to mine; he wanted me to light my cigarette using his—to "screw it," as we said in high school. But then the nausea returned. I held the cigarette to one side and bent over; he grabbed my hair as the vomit sprayed out once more. I retched and felt my muscles tighten. My stomach was empty, but my body wasn't ready to give up just yet. The guy's hard groin pressed against my behind. His hand on my stomach was farther down than I would have liked.

I wiped my mouth on my arm, leaving behind a viscous yellow trail. Sucked on the tiny glow that was left on the end of the cigarette until it blazed as I walked towards the steps. The guy stayed standing on the lawn, watching me as I smoked. His eyes were so dark they were almost black. He had a narrow face, almost free of facial hair. Still, I thought he must be several years older than me. Sometimes you can just tell, without knowing how. He waited as I stubbed out the cigarette against a step. If I went inside now, he would only follow me. *Why can't I see your room, why not, why not?* I'd have to dodge him, slip away as unnoticed as possible.

"I usually win," I said, feeling that the cigarette had helped a little, although I was still very drunk.

"You usually win what?"

I pointed at him. "Staring contests. I'm the most stubborn person I know, actually, but you're a real challenger."

He came all the way up to me, put a hand on my hip.

"I like to stare," he said, letting his hand slide back to grab one of my butt cheeks and squeezing it.

A new nausea surged up in me—I remembered Patrick's breath. I ignored the impulse to flee and instead leaned in closer.

"You're really fucking pretty," he whispered, pinching my lower lip between his fingers and tugging it.

I smiled and dragged him closer to the house, to a place not far from the terrace door, but where nobody could see us without coming outside. I sat down on the grass and pulled him down beside me. I giggled and put a finger to my lips.

"Lie down. Close your eyes."

He did as I asked. Lay flat on his back with his face turned up and his eyes closed. He smiled absently as I began to open his fly. I pulled down his jeans, simultaneously taking off his shoes and socks, which I set neatly beside the flower bed filled with large salmon-pink flowers. Under his jeans he was wearing boxer shorts with a logo around the top—boxers to show over sagging jeans. I got up and grabbed the garden hose that lay alongside the house wall, flipped up the red handle that started the water. The guy shrieked as the stream of cold water hit him. I dropped the hose and ran laughing towards the house. Heard loud cursing behind me.

I slammed the terrace door shut and twisted the lock with a click. Squeezed my way through the mass of people, saw that Egil was dancing with a girl with long red nails that she was using to scratch his face. I was pretty sure she had breast implants. I was constantly fascinated by the women he conjured up. They must come from a place where the bimbo photocopier was in operation twenty-four hours a day.

I forced my way between clusters of bodies who talked, jostled and laughed at each other, fake smiles and artificially high voices, fingers playing with glasses. I pushed past a couple who were making out. I walked towards Ingvar's room, opened the door and was met by a wall of music. The vocalist from Bongzilla was roaring and grunting from the speakers. Ingvar lifted his hand in greeting as he passed a joint to the person next to him. The room was dense with smoke and with people; the bed and the rug on the floor abounded with jabbering bodies. I sat down on the floor, shoving myself halfway into a group of kids who looked like they were in high school.

When it was my turn, I took my time with the joint, taking several long drags and letting it fill my chest, closing my eyes. I soon felt less drunk and more content. The voices around me lowered, and the room became more remote. I could no longer hear the words, as if something had crept into my ear canals, something that was expanding. It was nice. I took a last drag and opened my eyes to pass the joint on. In the doorway a man stood looking at me. It was the Eminem guy. He had a large wet patch on the front of his hoodie. Behind him were two dudes with big arms, bulging muscles. The way they were standing was like a parody of a Tarantino film. The Eminem guy looked at me. I'd expected him to look away, but far from it. His gaze held as if it were black stone. It didn't suit him, standing there with the two gorillas—they made him look skinny, like a weakling. It was so comical that I started to snicker, and once I'd started, I couldn't stop. I bubbled over, tears of laughter gathering, and soon I fell backwards and lay there, laughing loud and heartily.

When I looked back towards the doorway, the guy was gone. At the same time, I noticed that the room was quieter.

As I leaned against the bed, giggling to myself, I felt someone prod me in the shoulder. I lifted a hand and gently pulled on Ingvar's beard.

"Good shit, Ingvar," I said, wiping away the tears.

Ingvar's expression was stern.

"What the hell was that?" He pointed towards the door where the Eminem guy had stood.

"Just some guy who wouldn't stop pestering me."

Ingvar sighed.

"Well, that guy who wouldn't stop pestering you is my dealer."

I sat up. "*That's* David Lorentzen? You always make him out to be so scary!"

"He looked pretty pissed off."

I shrugged. "I'm not going to sleep with somebody just so you can get your hash."

Ingvar sighed and sat up again on the bed. Coming from the speakers was Weedeater, a band I liked listening to when Ingvar, Egil and me spent afternoons alone together. But right now the music was far too loud, too heavy. Mixed with the voices in the room, it was transformed into a seething mass of chaos. I thought that must be what it sounds like in hell.

"Hey, Liv!"

Egil was suddenly standing over me. I made space for him to sit down next to me on the rug, but he only leaned halfway down and cast a glance at two girls who seemed to be waiting for him.

"I was just wondering. Those two ladies over there are curious about Nero—don't you think we could bring him out here, just for a bit?"

"Stop it, Egil."

"Just for a bit? Or they could go into your room and say hello to him?"

I pulled him closer so that he lost his balance and had to sit down.

"I don't even get why you told them about him. Can't you get yourself some action without Nero's help?"

"He's not just yours, you know. He was supposed to be the whole flatshare's snake."

"Forget it."

Egil bent down to my ear. "Give me the key," he whispered, but I squirmed away.

Beside my door, I pulled on the gold-plated chain I was wearing around my neck, and the key emerged from beneath the neckline of my top. I carefully stroked my thumb across it. I'd had it plated in gold when I moved here. My first key to my very own room, a place nobody would be able to enter unless I let them. Of course I'd had a key to my so-called childhood home, but my room was always open, and for many years I shared it with Patrick. There was something holy about having a thing like this, my very own lucky charm.

I turned and checked to make sure that Egil wasn't standing behind me before I stuck the key into the lock. Not long after, I was inside, locking the door behind me. I breathed out. Walked over to the specially constructed terrarium by the window, where Nero lay resting on the heat mat inside. When we bought him, the American woman had advised us to keep him in a locked room. Even though the terrarium had a sliding lid, he still might be able to get out. And if he got out of the house, it would become a story on the national news. I'd let him out onto the grass a few times anyway—but only under strict supervision. Ingvar and Egil left the doors to their rooms open all day, so the snake had to stay with me. I opened the terrarium lid, carefully took hold of Nero's pliant body and lifted him up. His forked tongue sought the air. He stretched, seeming to be on the lookout from this new height.

"Hi," I whispered. "Have you missed me?"

I crept under the duvet, taking him with me; his small scales tickled my stomach when I put him under my T-shirt. I stroked my fingers over his dry surface. When we got him, Egil said that he'd thought snakes were either slick, like snails, or sticky and soft, like worms. Perhaps I, too, had had such an expectation in my fingertips—but it was wrong. It was more as if his body were strewn with a blanket of tiny, smooth fingernails. I couldn't get enough of it, the feeling of touching the roughness of his back.

When I had just moved in here, I might have ended up getting it on with that guy. I might even have brought him here, just so that I wouldn't have to sleep alone. I'd tried it a few times. It didn't help in the slightest; it only ever ended in a sense of unease, stinging genitals and too little space to turn over while asleep. This, on the other hand—sharing a bed with Nero—provided a kind of relief. I lay there, listening for his voice in the room, trying to find my way back to the words he had whispered the previous night, but he was silent. Had it all just been a figment of my imagination?

"Talk to me," I whispered, and felt a tear run down my cheek. It surprised me. I wasn't usually one to cry.

Roe

Kristiansund
Friday, 18 August 2017

"Come dance with me?"

Ronja smiles and holds out a tiny hand. She's intoxicated, and her cheeks have a rosy flush. Her brown curls, usually pulled tight into a hairband, now hang loose. Ronja Solskinn is her name. It's a surname that promises sunshine, and nobody honours that promise better than Ronja. She's the very embodiment of "open and welcoming," still marked by the naiveté that adult life hasn't yet managed to quash. Needless to say, she still has a fair bit to experience in life.

"Thanks, that's very nice of you, but I don't dance."

The bar they've chosen is crowded, full of drunk people staggering and speaking in excessively loud voices, suddenly leaning over a chair to talk to you. The most popular place in town, they say, because of the karaoke. The screeching of drunkards who have lost all inhibition, clinging onto a microphone. Great fun, they think. Not knowing the lyrics makes it even more amusing.

Ronja leans across the table. Casts a glance at the others, who seem to be occupied with other conversations. She types something into her mobile, her thumbs moving quick as a flash, and shows it to me.

I just want to say that I think you were right to be angry. They have no right to ask you about those things.

I arrived at the restaurant late—the others had gone there straight from work while I'd been given permission to run a few errands, change into a fresh shirt. Consequently, I ended up at the worst place at the table, the innermost end, where I sat right in the firing line for personal questions from police officers I haven't had a damn thing to do with since I started working here. They wanted to know whether it was true, what they had heard—that I had lost my daughter. Creased their faces into emotional expressions. The worst thing is that they think they're being kind. They think it helps me, their dragging Kiddo to the forefront of my memory to wave her about in front of me. They don't get that she's not a conversation starter—she's my daughter, my flesh and blood. I ended up asking them to shut up—bluntly. I nod to Ronja, give her a smile in thanks.

Kiddo used to call me a grouch. Back then, I wasn't angry the way I am now. Irritable, perhaps. Principled—absolutely. At times I was distant because my job was such a huge part of my life. Now, however, I'm a grouch. The grouch in me has become a friend, a protector. I hate the guy, but I need him. That's just how things are. I look down at the message from Ronja. Delete the message she's written and type back with clumsy fingers: *It's always okay to be angry. Not at the bad guys, not when making arrests or during questioning, but otherwise always.*

She takes the phone and reads what I've written. Then she nods and straightens up, and heads off towards the dance floor. She seems so unworried, so free. I'm at least happy that the music is too loud for any tentative attempts at intimate conversation. Most of the others are up on the dance floor with Ronja. She soon has her arms draped over the Dane's shoulders, while he finds a place for his on her back. I wonder whether he's the right type for her—he seems decent enough, I suppose. But she'll get bored. These young girls, they need time before they settle down. Constantly on the lookout, and so bloody open. She'll be hurt over and over again before she learns to close herself up.

"Do you want anything?" Shahid asks. "I'm buying."

His eyes are swimming, and he's leaning in to me, unnaturally close. Shahid has often struck me as being one of the most practical people I've ever met. His glasses are functional, his shoes comfortable, and he cycles to work wearing a grey and orange rucksack with a water bottle tucked in its side pocket. Training and transport in one. Now my usually sensible boss is waving his Visa card in the direction of the bar. Drunk people can smell sobriety from a mile off. They do everything they can to obliterate any sign of clear diction or self-restraint. I point to my half-full glass and say that I'm fine.

"Are you doing okay, Roe? Are you enjoying it, working with us at the station?"

So he's going to try to have an intimate conversation despite the fact that he has to shout to be heard over some tottering woman in her forties who thinks she's hitting all the high notes. Even if I'm not doing okay—which, in a sense, isn't untrue—I'm not exactly going to sit here and shout it out to my boss. I consider not answering at all, or asking whether this is an employee appraisal interview.

"Everything's fine, but I think I need to start heading home soon."

He places a hand on my shoulder, a gesture of drunken intimacy.

"Stay a little longer, Roe. You're the guest of honour, after all."

The guest of honour never wanted any sixtieth birthday party, but none of them seem to have realised this. Shahid is in his fifties himself—I'm sure he loved being the centre of attention when celebrating his last major birthday.

"Stay awhile," he says again. "It's nice to have you here. It isn't so often we're all out together. You need the social side of things. I'm sure you know that, too, with all your experience— it helps to know your colleagues if you're going to get on well at work. We have to be able to talk, air things out. Given all the stuff we go through. But tonight's just about having fun. Cheers."

I chink my glass against his. He turns to face the people sitting on the other side of him, and I look down into my beer, trying to breathe and count to ten. Want to say that I don't need to be taught that it's good to have a debrief. Of course it's good to have a debrief. About work-related stuff, the kinds of things you experience when you're on the job. And it's good for people who have little stress in their lives, who simply need to let off a bit of steam every now and then. For me, on the other hand, it's impossible.

A slow song begins. Ronja and the Dane are slow dancing, her head resting against his chest. She's so small and slight, while he's tall and huge, seeming to fold himself around her.

Hands that drown her hands, shoulders that overshadow hers. They almost suit each other, but not quite, as if he's too large a version of what she should have had. He's polite, someone with a good head on his shoulders—that's good for her, at least. I'm not sure why I care so much about which guy she's seeing. I just think she's nice to talk to—I want her to be okay.

There's a vibration on the bench—it's coming from Shahid's jacket, but he doesn't realise that his phone is ringing and continues to talk to the guy on his other side. I have to nudge him to get him to react. Instead of passing me on his way out he elects to go the other way, making three other police officers move. I end up with Åsmund next to me. He's managed to change into a fresh shirt and a knitted pullover.

"So how are things going with the new guy?"

If I had ten kroner for every time I've been asked how things are going this evening . . . Things are not going well. I've run away to a new town, only to discover that nothing changes. It's so stupid, just like that old nursery rhyme about the man who wanted to move from the gnome. Everybody knows that the cursed gnome is going with him. I lift my glass to say cheers and, just to have something to talk about, ask whether he's ready for the autumn term school visits.

There's a reason Åsmund is easy to talk to. To him, everything stays at surface level. Work, the weather and feeling worn out. He's eagerly awaiting his retirement—has just eighteen months to go, and is looking forward to finally being able to sit in the chair on his terrace and watch the birds in his garden. An old bachelor with dreams of lonely domestic bliss. I share his interest in birds, but for me it's something darker. I watch the birds because they remind me of what I miss—a sense of purpose. I watch them build their nests and collect food for their young, and think of the day somebody will come along with a chain saw and cut down the entire tree. Åsmund wouldn't understand if I told him this. So we generally talk about which species have visited our bird tables. Me in my former life and he in his current one.

The music stops. Someone clears their throat, and then a female voice comes over the speaker system and says that we have a birthday boy here tonight. I look towards the stage, where Birte is standing with four other police officers around her.

"Roe Olsvik is sixty today, so let's sing 'Happy Birthday'!"

Åsmund grabs my arm, tries to pull me up; I insist on staying seated. But most people have quickly narrowed in on the birthday boy. The entire bar looks in my direction and sings along. A woman wearing a shirt with the bar's logo comes towards me with a huge cake full of burning candles that blaze in the dark room. I clench my fists beneath the table, know that I have to smile and say thank you and blow out the candles and make a wish, but I don't know how I'm going to manage it. I should have been the one who died, if anything in this damn world made sense. I shouldn't have been left behind to get older like this. I get up. Can feel my smile as a stiff, fake line in my face. I wave, bow and nod as people film me and take pictures on their phones. I blow out the candles. Have to take another breath to extinguish the last of the flames.

Soon half the bar has gathered round my table and is trying to congratulate me. A woman who must be in her sixties herself wants to buy me a drink. She's so drunk that she hasn't noticed that half her bra is sticking out of the neckline of her top. I politely decline. The next person to talk to me, though, will be told to go to hell. My stomach hurts, my chest is tightening with pain and my cheeks are on fire. I try to jostle my way through the crowd. Just have to get down the stairs and out the door, out into the fresh air. God help me if I have to spend another fucking second here.

"Roe!"

Shahid sticks his head in from where he's standing out on the balcony in the middle of a group of smokers. He's holding his phone against his chest, has seen that I've stood up to leave. He signals for me to go join him. For a moment I actually consider going out to him, but I'm all out of patience. I'm going home. I pass a couple who are clinging to each other in the corridor and make my way down the stairs. On the pavement outside, I stop and take a deep breath. It burns my lungs.

"Roe!"

Shahid has come running after me. He tells whoever is on the other end of the phone that he'll call back.

"Something's happened."

He looks pale. Is holding his mobile between two fingers as if he's holding something that's too hot to touch. He looks around him, at the bouncer and a few girls who are standing a short distance away.

"A girl's disappeared. Eleven years old. Been missing for nine hours."

I clear my throat.

"And they just reported it now?"

He nods. "Seeing as it's a child and she's never run off before, I'm opening an investigation immediately. Hopefully they'll find her tonight, but just in case. You know how it is. Time can be costly, should it turn out to be a major incident. We can't have all our investigators out partying right now if it turns out she's still missing tomorrow. We have to go home and get some sleep, all of us."

I nod. Feel the knot in my chest loosen, a relief. I clear my throat again.

"I'm good to work now."

Shahid looks at me, astonished.

"You have to sober up first."

I look down at my hands. Haven't wanted to admit what I'm about to say.

"I've been drinking alcohol-free beer all night," I say.

Liv

In a dark room sat a dark girl. Her long black hair was brushed forward over her face. She sat on a straight-backed chair, at the centre of a ring of water. There was the whispering of a missing TV signal and a faint tone. The film's female protagonist approached the dark girl, stretching out a hand to touch her. Then, in an instant, the girl grabbed the woman's hand, the room spun in a circle, and a scream rang out. The woman woke in her own bed. She had a bloody mark in the shape of a hand on her arm.

I greedily helped myself to the contents of the popcorn bowl and rested my head on Egil's shoulder. Nero lay on the back of the sofa behind us, his tail touching the back of my head. Outside, wet snow was blown against the windowpanes. The lights we had hung above the terrace door before Christmas were only just hanging on after the season's festivities. Egil had spent Christmas Eve with his family and had returned with a strong need to reassert himself. It felt as if the entire town had marched through here between Christmas and New Year's.

"We could have made a film like *The Ring*," Egil said. "You would have slipped straight into the role of Samara, Liv."

"Shhh!" Ingvar said. He was sitting in the armchair, his feet up on an old bottle crate. His dark hair hung down into his eyes.

"It could just as easily be Ingvar who played Samara." I laughed. "We could have swapped roles."

Ingvar threw a kernel of popcorn across the room so that it hit me in the face. I sent it back, but it flew lopsidedly through the air and landed on the rug. Egil came to my aid by taking a fistful of popcorn from the bowl and sending a shower of it towards Ingvar. I let out a silly shriek and clapped my hands.

"Knock it off, children," Ingvar said. "One of us is actually trying to watch the film!"

"You've seen the Japanese version," I said. "You know what happens."

"I don't watch films to find out what happens," Ingvar said.

The doorbell rang, and the front door opened. Several voices could be heard chatting out in the hall.

"We're just setting up," one of the members of Ingvar's band shouted from out in the corridor. Ingvar answered with a wordless cry.

On the TV screen, the lead character had found the dark girl's childhood home, and had begun to discover the neglect to which she had been subjected. Egil stretched out his muscular arm, onto which Nero had seen fit to climb.

"I'm just saying," said Egil. "When he's grown so long that he stretches all the way across the back of this sofa, we're going to fucking bring him out when we have people over. I'm going to do it no matter what you say. One day before too long you'll both move out of here, and then I'll get to do whatever I want."

"Forget it, Egil," I said. "I'm taking Nero with me when I move."

"It isn't just *your* snake, so that's not your decision," Egil said. "I've paid for pretty much everything—including the snake and the terrarium."

"Your dad has, you mean."

"Shut up."

"Could you two quit it?" Ingvar grunted from his chair.

"And what's with you, anyway, Ingvar?" I said. "Time of the month?"

Ingvar got up and brushed the popcorn remnants from his clothes.

"I can't be bothered with this shit. It's impossible to watch a film with you two."

Ingvar disappeared into the hallway. I turned my eyes back to the TV screen, but I'd lost track of the plot.

"I don't like it when you do that," Egil said. "Drag my dad into stuff like that. It actually kind of bothers me."

"I know," I said. "I'm sorry."

"At Christmas I had a dream about shooting him. Like, in the head." He formed the shape of a pistol with his hand. "He's a total psychopath—I mean it. He has no emotions, other than greed and discontent. I don't think people like him deserve to have any power over others."

"People like him *obtain* power over others," I said.

He nodded.

"I should rebel. Make sure he gets what he deserves, some-how. One day, I'm going to do it. Something that hits him where it hurts—in the wallet. Burn down the house, empty his safe."

On the bench beside the TV the lava lamp sent up a large yellow-green bubble.

"Is there something wrong with Ingvar?" I said. "He isn't usually so touchy."

Egil took his time chewing the popcorn he had just put in his mouth.

"There is something, isn't there?" I asked.

He sighed. "I've been at him a bit over some stuff. It's nothing to worry about."

I paused the film and turned towards Egil. Nero licked the air in my direction.

"Why don't you want to tell me?"

Egil looked down.

"Because I really don't think you'll want to hear it."

"Just spit it out, Egil."

Egil held the snake in front of him, focusing his gaze on the scaly creature.

"He's seen Patrick a few times," Egil said. "In town. I saw them talking."

I immediately closed my eyes, trying to squeeze away the memories with my eyelids. How Patrick smelled of beer and stale sweat. He was clumsy, with dirty skin and greasy hair. The girls would talk about him, making sure he overheard. In the evenings he would stand before the mirror, picking his spots.

"Ingvar says it's hard," Egil said. "When the guy just comes up to him like that—I mean, they're old friends—but he's promised that they don't hang out anymore."

Old friends. That was just the way it was. People knew each other. It wasn't enough to simply move across the fjord if you wanted to get away.

"I think Ingvar should have punched him in the face," Egil said. "In fact, I think we should get somebody to go teach him a lesson. Like that guy David, Ingvar's dealer—he could help us."

"Not going to happen," I said. "He is my brother after all."

Egil shook his head.

"You care about him. He doesn't deserve it."

"Has he been here?"

The apartment was suddenly filled with the loud, piercing sounds of instruments from Ingvar's room. It sounded as if they were trying to mimic a circular saw. Nero seemed stressed by all the noise. I took him down from Egil's shoulders.

"Fuck this," I said. "I'm going to read."

Ronja

Kristiansund
Friday, 18 August 2017

August smells of fresh aftershave and whisky. His arms are folded around me so that I'm almost drowning in his embrace. He bends his head towards me, all the way down to my face, so close that I can see the pores of his skin. Blond stubble is just starting to appear on his otherwise super-smooth chin. In the bar, everyone is singing "Happy Birthday." We're standing on the steps, slightly hidden away among strangers, but someone from the station might pop up at any moment. I glance towards the bar, but can't see anyone I know. August is very drunk. I've never seen him like this before. His eyes are swimming, his smile a long line. I giggle. I'm not used to seeing his face this way. There's something peculiar about having my arms around his neck, feeling the warmth of his breath; it feels so strange. It's not a good idea, this—not a good idea in the slightest: we're colleagues—but it's almost as if it isn't happening for real. He smells good, and surely a little kiss won't do any harm. I have to stand on my tiptoes to reach him.

His lips are thin, a bit softer than I'd imagined. His tongue moves carefully, a small, pointed slug. A little smacking sound escapes my lips as I pull away. I giggle again and rest my head against his chest. Shake my head at myself, hit my forehead against his rib cage. He breathes warm air into my hair.

"Maybe we shouldn't go any further, right now," he says in Danish.

"No." I giggle, mimicking his speech. "Maybe we shouldn't."

Somebody bumps into us on their way past. I lift my head and see Roe's broad back as he makes his way down the stairs. The boss follows him—they hurry down the staircase and then disappear. August backs away from me. I hide my face in my hands, heat smouldering in my cheeks.

"Do you think they saw us?"

I take a few steps, straighten my hair—I have no idea what it looks like after he's been running his fingers through it. "I think we should go inside and join the others, before they come back." I start to leave, trying not to fiddle with my hair. I realise that I have no idea how my makeup looks, either— maybe my mascara is all over the place, but it's unlikely anyone will see. I lift my head, meet Birte's gaze across the room. She looks from me to August, then raises an eyebrow and smiles. I should have known we wouldn't fool anyone.

I stand in the queue at the bar. Don't want to talk to anyone, just to drink a glass of water and then go home. But Birte comes over and grabs my arm.

"I love this song, come dance with me!"

I shake my head, but she doesn't want to hear it; drags me out onto the dance floor. She puts a finger under my chin, tilts it up.

"Chin up, Princess."

So we dance. It feels better already, freer than standing at the bar feeling ashamed of myself. Perhaps that was what Birte was aiming for, why she came over to me like that. I throw my hair back, look up at the ceiling and lose myself in the movement. The disco ball colours our faces with its shimmering silver light, and we sing along to "Wannabe" by the Spice Girls and laugh.

Then someone takes hold of my elbow, turns me around. For a moment I expect to see August, but it's Shahid. He seems stressed.

"Party's over," he says. "We have to go home and sober up, all of us."

Liv

Ålesund
Tuesday, 3 February 2004

Her kitchen cabinets seemed like a portal to the world of cakes. She pulled out aniskringle, wienerbrød, vørterkake and thick butter in a glass dome. The serinakake biscuits must have been there since Christmas. She poured coffee into porcelain cups decorated with flowers. Brown cheese stuck to the roof of my mouth; I swallowed down the bread and cake with big gulps of milk.

"They're making such a terrible mess down there," she said. "It's too much work for an old lady. My son . . ." She picked up a photograph of a middle-aged man and showed it to me. "He wishes he could help, but he has enough on his plate as it is. Last time he was here, he took half of them away to the vet. It's awful to have to take such steps, but when you can't take care of them . . . Well, it's nice that there are at least some young people like you who love animals." She patted me on the arm with a soft, slightly damp hand.

When the old woman walked, she bent her elbows, hunched her back and thrust out her chest. She seemed like some kind of rare bird. I never had a grandmother, at least not one I'd ever met. Didn't know whether I had one who was still living, or what she would have thought of me if we ever did meet. I didn't know if her arms were like this woman's—the skin hanging in heavy folds from her underarms, wrinkled and strewn with moles, like stars.

She led me down into the cellar, where she lifted the blanket that hung like a curtain from a countertop. They were there in a box beneath the counter, a mother cat and two tiny balls of fluff. The kittens squeaked when the light hit them, and they began to toddle around. The woman lifted a small white and yellow-brown kitten, which squealed in terror at being picked up. Its coat was thin and damp. The kitten lay there on its stomach in my palm, as if in a ladle, helplessly waving its little legs. It meowed weakly, clawing at my hand. I gently lay the kitten against my chest.

"Hey you," I said. "You're coming home with me."

I had to walk home. Didn't dare take the bus for fear that someone on it might recognise me. I glanced at the people I encountered along the street, trying to figure out whether they were anyone I knew so I could avoid them before they saw me. I kept my back straight and chest lifted despite the impulses I felt to hunch over, to run, to hide. At the same time, I did my best to avoid the slush, but it was no use. Water soaked into my shoes, making the legs of my jeans wet.

It was a boring walk home, but never before had it elicited so much anxiety in me. In my hand rocked the cage. Every time

I held it a little lopsidedly, the kitten slid over to the opposite end, letting out a fragile mewling. It was only twelve o'clock. The streets were relatively empty—this wasn't an area that was busy at all hours of the day, and I'd be fine as long as I avoided the high school students' breaks. Nor would Egil and Ingvar be home for a few hours yet.

Nero was no longer satisfied with a live mouse or a rat every now and then. He took them and swallowed them, but they didn't satiate him. He kept me awake at night. Drilling into my ears with his ancient voice. He went for me whenever he got the opportunity—wanted to show me how furious he was at not being fed enough. Now I never heard the words *Liv* or *dear*, only *hunt, hunt, hunt*. He hadn't bitten me yet, but he had come close.

I crossed the road. Walked as close as I could to the remains of the old mounds of roadside snow, black with soot. Tried not to increase my stride—the risk of being seen was low, but my nerves didn't believe me. The mewling continued. What would I say if I bumped into anyone? There would have to be a partial truth if the lie was to be believable—that was always the case—but what would the partial truth be? I was looking after it for an old lady while she was in the hospital. A good friend of the family at one time. No, it would be too complicated. The cage smouldered between my fingers; the mewling made my temples pound. Just a few metres left of the main road. I avoided glancing into the car that braked to drive past me. It was a totally normal day, a totally normal day. I'd just been to the vet with it, I'm looking after it for a friend. She was taking an exam. Who was she?

I was finally almost there, the mewling returning as I took a sudden turn. I had to stay calm. Just a single obstacle left now, and the riskiest one. To walk past the windows on the ground floor, come up with a lie in case the landlady should happen to see me—as if *this* would be the thing that was most unacceptable to her. She never peered out of the window, not during the day, nor in the evening, either. She stayed hidden behind the curtains—but who knew? Maybe today she would peek outside just as I happened to walk past. With the cage heavy as a coffin in my hand, I walked calmly over the square in front of the house and glanced across. There she was, in the kitchen window, her grey-white hair like a cloud around her emaciated head. She was standing there, busy with something, and just as I looked into the window, she looked out at me. I automatically lifted my free hand to wave, but she just turned back to what she was doing.

I did all I could to curb the shaking as I walked down the stairs. I had to stay calm. I had only borrowed it for a few days; *of course* I was going to ask for permission if I decided it was something for me. Tried to unlock the front door with a shaking hand as a squeaking came from the cage. If I had only borrowed it for a few days, why hadn't I said anything to Egil and Ingvar? On the other hand, why would anybody care enough to ask me these questions?

My eyes slid across the shoe rack and the floor, then over towards the living room, even though I knew that Egil would be at lectures and Ingvar was at a friend's house—he'd be prac- tising with his band all day. I stood in the hall and looked out of the window at the patch of garden and the picket fence. A few cars slid past. I could still go back to the old lady who gave me the kitten and say that I was allergic, that I had changed my mind. Perhaps I would have felt better if I'd been able to involve Egil and Ingvar. With others I could have written it off as something that got out of hand. We would have egged each other on. But I hadn't dared to ask them—nor had I wanted to. I'd wanted to experience it alone, guided only by the desire, the drive, to feed my snake.

I let myself into my room with the gold key. Set the cage on the floor and went to lift Nero out of his terrarium. I would often leave him free to rummage around the room as he pleased, but it was warmer in the terrarium. Even though I could tell he hated lying in there, even though I could hear him spitting out furious words when I put him in it, I knew that he needed the warmth of the heat mat. He wanted freedom, but I was fairly sure he didn't understand what that involved.

Nero allowed himself to be lifted and set down on the dirty beige rug. He had grown so large in such a short time and had become more difficult to handle, but he was always energetic when he smelled food. He had already caught the scent of the new tiny creature in the room. He crept closer to the cage, his split tongue seeking the air.

I opened the cage and stuck my hand into it, grabbed hold of the small body. The kitten whined and waved its little legs around; its surreally thin fur created electrical wisps in the air. It whined at being picked up, at being stroked along its back, at being set down on the floor, at being in a room with air and movement—at existing. Perhaps there was nothing that didn't scare such a creature, apart from the heat of its mother, from which it had now been taken. An alarm went off in my body, my ears ringing and adrenaline pumping through me, but I reminded myself that this animal's fate had been sealed long ago. Nobody else had shown an interest in the litter; the others had already been taken to the vet to be put down. It would have been better to let them loose in the forest as food

for the foxes. There were already far too many cats in Norwegian homes—their owners wallpapered the walls of local stores
with posters of kittens that were to be given away, to no avail.
Better to give it to a hungry animal as food, I thought, than
to fill the back room of a veterinary surgery with the remains
of people's inability to take care of their pets. This way, at least
it would be of use.

Nero moved quickly in the direction of the prey, which swayed
unsteadily on its tiny legs. Perhaps the kitten saw the movement
first, a gliding wave of body gathering around it. Then it noticed
the snake's head. It screamed. Not a kitten's mewl, but a terrified
scream like that of a person, which was immediately silenced by
Nero's teeth as they sunk into the kitten's delicate neck. Then
there was only movement that remained, the snake's body as it
pulled ever tighter around its prey.

At least snakes were honest. They didn't try to conceal their
actions with talk of morals. One minute we humans were
speaking about good and evil; the next we were sinning against
all we'd just said. The human being was a species that built
walls of wood and stone around itself and its own so-called
evils. Called its prey beef and pretended it had never been alive.
Why play such games? When a woman killed her husband,
she was condemned, her actions deemed unnatural. Why not
instead look to the female spider, who devours her partner as
soon as they have mated? Realise that *this*, too, is part of us?
That *this* is also nature?

Nero's stone gaze fell on me for a moment, as if thanking
me, before he began to swallow. I felt nauseated, overwhelmed.
There was a hard pounding in my chest, belly and crotch. I
pulled down my jeans and underwear, and with somewhere
between ten and twenty hard rubs reached climax.

Mariam

Kristiansund
Friday, 18 August 2017

I sit at the dining table in the living room, paralysed. The walls are coloured by the flashing reflections from the blue lights outside, the warning signal to the entire neighbourhood that something terrible must have happened. Nothing has happened. I refuse to believe it. She must have just gone to visit somebody. In the worst case, she got some idea into her head and got on a bus. I refuse to believe that anything serious has happened. They'll find her in an hour or two. She'll ask for help from an adult or come home on her own. These things happen all the time—children go missing and then they turn up again.

They asked me to stay by the phone, just in case. My mobile and Iben's are lying on the table in front of me, neatly arranged beside each other on the place mat. I watch the blue lights flashing against the wall, take a deep breath and let it out. I should have gone to bed, really. Tomorrow is Saturday—Iben has a handball game, and I've promised to bake a cake. The bags of groceries are still on the kitchen countertop—the eggs are probably broken, all of them, and the milk sour. I'll have to go to the store again early tomorrow before I can start baking. She can help me when she comes back. I hope she hasn't ventured so far that she doesn't come home tonight—I don't like the thought of her being cold and afraid. Or that she might talk to the wrong kind of grown-up.

"Mariam Steinersen Lind?"

There's a man standing in the doorway. He's taken off his shoes and is standing there in his socks, wearing jeans and a white shirt. He's tall, broad-shouldered. His dark hair is shot through with a few grey strands here and there; he has thick eyebrows and a crooked nose. In his hand is a worn leather bag with a press stud fastener. He looks like a cross between a plumber and a geography teacher.

"Chief Inspector Roe Olsvik." He has an ID card in his hand, greets me. Gives me a firm handshake.

"Roger?"

"Roe. *R-O-E*. It's a Norse name—it means 'honour.'"

He's from Ålesund. His dialect dances in my ears. His large chest lifts when he says his name. He lets go of my hand, opens the leather bag and pulls out a Dictaphone. "I have to ask you some questions, Mariam. I hope that's okay?"

My eyes automatically start to flit about the room. More questions is the last thing I need. I just want to close my eyes and pretend this day never happened. Tomorrow everything will be back to normal again.

"I've already spoken to . . . I've forgotten his name?"

He nods. "I know. That's good, but I'd like to talk to you, too. As long as that's all right."

I don't like his tone. Think his pleasantness seems feigned, as if he's trying to charm me. I don't find him pleasant at all, actually.

"Could I ask a favour, Mariam? I came here in a rush and seem to have forgotten to bring along something to write with. I don't suppose you happen to have a pen and some paper I could borrow?"

I wonder whether he's the kind of person who thinks it's nice to be called by your first name all the time—as if I don't know my own name.

"Isn't the Dictaphone enough?"

He gives me a smile that's difficult to read.

"Of course, but you know how it is. Old habits. I like to note things down on paper—it reassures me that important information won't somehow disappear. If it's not too much trouble?"

I get up and go out to the kitchen. Think I have some paper lying around here somewhere, but I use it so rarely. I rummage around between the cookbooks, open a drawer that contains wooden ladles, serving spoons and a whisk; finally I find a notepad containing a recipe for sweet rolls and a shopping list. I can find nothing to write with other than a turquoise glitter pen that must belong to Iben. I look at it, at all its glimmering colours. She loves pastels, little girl that she is. Why didn't I just let her have the magazine?

When I return to the dining table, the policeman is standing there holding one of our family photographs from the dresser shelves. He nods at it, puts it down.

"You have a lovely family, Mariam."

My daughter is gone. Why is he standing there singing the praises of an amputated family, as if it were whole? I look at the picture, in which Iben is sitting between Tor and me, smiling, sunlight in her face. She must be hiding from me. When she comes back, I'll be sure to show her just how much trouble she's caused. I'll drag her down to the police station and get them to tell her how many people were out looking for her. Tor will be able to tell her how he walked the streets shouting her name, how scared he was. The previous policeman asked whether I had the phone numbers of any of Iben's friends. I was taken aback, but I gave them the entire list for her class. Tor's the one who keeps an overview of these things.

We take a seat opposite each other at the dining table, where I've been sitting with the two phones in front of me for the past hour, staring alternately down at them and at one of Iben's old magazines that she's read over and over again while eating supper. It's become such a major part of our routine that I no longer tidy the magazines away—she removes them herself each time she gets a new one.

"Let's see," says Roe, noting something on the paper. "I've been provided with a reasonable summary of the statement you've already given, but I have some additional questions. You said that Iben ran away from you after an argument in the grocery store?"

I feel my throat turn dry, nod.

"Tell me what happened when she ran off."

"Iben wanted a comic book, but I didn't want to buy it for her. We argued, and she ran off. I thought she would be waiting for me outside the store or by the car, but she was gone."

He nods. "Did you talk to the shopping centre's security guards, or anyone in the store?"

I was too wrapped up in my own emotions to notice other people.

"I had a full shopping trolley. It wasn't very easy to move around. And anyway, I really thought she had to be waiting by the car."

He makes a note on the notepad.

"When she wasn't at the car, why didn't you go back to the shopping centre to ask the security guards whether they had seen her?"

"I thought she must have just run back home. It isn't far."

He looks up. "Would there have been anyone here if she came straight home?"

"Tor was at work."

"She has a key to the house?"

I shake my head. She used to have a key, but she lost it and didn't dare tell us until several weeks later. We'd had to change all the locks.

The policeman taps the little glitter pen against the notepad. "I don't quite understand. If she didn't have a key, why would you have thought she would run home?"

I look down at the table. Know that I should have been the good mother with her heart in her throat, running around looking for her child. Crying and calling the police, even if only half an hour had passed since she last saw her little girl, because she's so afraid, so afraid. Instead, another Mariam took over—the one who is furious instead of afraid, who storms off instead of staying to search. I'm unable to explain this to the police, but nor do I need to, after all. She's just run off and is hiding somewhere.

He clears his throat. "So you thought that Iben had gone home. Then you got in the car to leave, but you didn't go home, did you?"

"I went for a drive. Towards Trondheim. I've already said that."

He nods.

"You were angry, felt unfairly treated by an eleven-year-old, and so took yourself off for a drive?"

He makes it sound so childish. That facial expression again, which I can't quite decipher—there's something in it, a darkness. He notes something or other on the paper, perhaps that I didn't answer the question.

"How long were you gone?"

"Like I said to your colleague . . . I was back here around ten, ten thirty."

"Which means that you were gone for between seven and eight hours. Do you have a habit of driving off, disappearing for hours at a time?"

I clear my throat. "It isn't a usual occurrence."

His eyes bore into me. Why is he so angry?

"Why did you just drive off, Mariam? Why didn't you look for your daughter?"

I've raised my shoulders without noticing. Forcefully lower them and take a breath.

"I don't know."

"You see, I'm getting the impression that you're lying to me, Mariam."

My shoulders automatically hunch again.

"Why would I lie?"

He clears his throat, strikes the pen against the notebook with rhythmic clicks.

"Only you can answer that. Perhaps what you're saying isn't true—that you didn't try to look. How can I know you were alone in the car, that she wasn't there with you? How can I know that, Mariam?"

He's started to say my name continuously now. It feels as if he's stabbing me with it, thrusting it at me.

"She wasn't," I say. My voice is shaking. "She wasn't in the car."

"Another thing that's occurred to me," Roe says, "is that she might have been in the boot. Was she in the boot, Mariam?"

"No!" I strike my palm against the table in front of me, so my tea sloshes around. "I haven't done anything to her!"

A flush spreads across the policeman's face. He coughs. Then he opens the leather bag with the press stud fastening. Pulls out something packed in plastic, a brochure or a magazine. A comic book. He sets it on the table before me. It's in a Ziploc bag. Sexy zombies wearing glitter lipstick.

"Was this the magazine Iben wanted you to buy for her, Mariam?"

If he doesn't stop saying my name soon . . . I can't take it anymore.

"Where did you find that?"

"It was found around here, down by the kindergarten. There's a shortcut up here, right?"

I nod. The policeman flicks through the notepad, holds it and the pen out to me.

"I need an overview of where you went. If you stopped anywhere, to buy food or whatever, I'll need the names of those places. If you were gone for seven or eight hours, I guess you must have eaten something? I'll also need the time at which you took the ferry to Halsa. Since you said you were driving towards Trondheim, you must have taken it at some point. Unless you've been driving round and round a roundabout for seven hours."

I look down at the notepad he's holding out to me. Back at the comic book with the glittering lipstick mouths. So she stole it, and ran here, but she never made it home.

"I apologise for the brusque tone," he says. "We are of course working on the basis that she's just gone off somewhere, stopped in to visit someone. Still, you know—the police must leave no stone unturned."

He's still blushing. He gesticulates towards the notepad.

"Snack bars, petrol stations, if you went to a restaurant or wherever. A list of everywhere you've been today."

I grip the pen. Think about what I've done. How I've tried to pretend there's something normal about all this, about how I've behaved, about the fact that Iben is gone.

"Do you think somebody might have picked her up in a car?" My voice trembles.

"I don't think anything," he says.

"It hasn't sunk in for Tor just yet," I say. "He hasn't had time to think it through. That I wanted to . . . you know, just drive away."

The policeman nods. He holds my gaze for a moment before releasing it again. Looks at the notebook between my hands, waiting for me to start writing.

Liv

I was five or maybe six years old, and lying in my bed. Patrick was in the living room watching TV. I could hear strange sounds coming from out there; it sounded as if he was watching a film. He had told me I wasn't allowed to leave my room after bedtime, but I desperately needed to pee. The glass of milk I'd drunk just before going to bed—he'd said I would regret it, and now it wanted to come out again. I imagined how the pee would be white in the toilet bowl. If I opened the door in total silence, he wouldn't notice, and I'd be able to creep past him. I closed my hand around the door handle, began to push it down slowly so as not to make a sound. If I bit my tongue, I could concentrate better. I didn't want to disturb him, would just hurry to the toilet and then go straight back to bed. The sounds became louder as I pulled the door to me, just a little—the sound of women giggling. I cautiously stuck out my head. Patrick was sitting on the sofa, his back to me. His hair was long at his neck. I looked up at the screen and tried to understand what I saw there. The faces of two women at the edges of the image, the ones who had been giggling. Heads cocked to one side, long tongues, dancing hair. One of them had her hand around a man's thing, which filled the middle of the screen: a lizard, a slug. The women laughed and looked at us, sticking out their long tongues. What were they doing? "Sara." Patrick laughed. "What are you doing up?"

I shook my head. Wanted to duck and look away, but right then something happened. The thing on the screen grew, stretching itself out to become long, like a big worm. It came out into the room. Undulating towards me through the air, an enormous earthworm. Patrick's laughter thundered in my ears.

I jumped up into a sitting position. The curtains fluttered inwards, into the room, dancing like a huge cape. I got up and went to close the window. Returned to the bed, where Nero lay stretched out right next to where I had been lying. When I lay down again, he extended his long body, showing me his yellow, brown and black scales. He had grown so much in such a short time—he was now twice as big as when we got him. I stroked a hand over his glossy surface. Snakes don't usually enjoy being petted in the way that warm-blooded animals do. I often thought that our relationship was something special, but for all I knew, this stroking might be bothering him. Sometimes it seemed that way, like now, when he reacted by winding himself up, coil upon coil, to become an accumulation of snake at my feet before sliding down onto the floor. He slipped across to the heater below the window and lay against the wall under it.

I got up, walked the few steps across the room and kneeled down before him. Stretched out a hand in order to reestablish the connection between us. I pulled on the coil, wanting to drag him out, but he resisted. Lifted his head for battle and hissed at me. As usual I heard enraged commands within that hissing. He went for me, and I had to back away.

It was now a month since he had been given the kitten. Snakes could go much longer than that without food, but I had noticed that he seemed hungry again. I tried to give him a chicken breast, but he no longer touched dead food. He darted after my arm instead, hissing out his orders. The only thing that governed our relationship was my inability to give him food. He couldn't possibly conceive of how hard it had been last time; the risk it had involved, or how it had felt. For him, it was incomprehensible that prey did not simply arrive when he needed it.

My body quivered as I put on a dressing gown and went out into the kitchen. I found the local newspaper lying on the floor with the paper recycling, opened it to the "Free" section of the classifieds, and sat down at the kitchen table. The column was full of advertisements from pet owners.

"There you are!" Ingvar was standing in the doorway. He was wearing a T-shirt that said SLEEP on it in large green letters, along with an image of a dark caravan moving through a desert. I recognised the image from the artwork for the album *Dopesmoker*. I folded the newspaper, put it down on the table.

"You're up late," I said.

He shrugged. "I'm a musician."

He opened a cupboard and took out a cup, which he filled with water from the tap.

"We don't see you very often these days. You're just in there all the time." He jerked his head in the direction of my room.

"I have a lot of studying to do."

"In the middle of the night, too?"

I looked down at my feet, bare against the linoleum floor. A dust bunny had got stuck under my big toe. I brushed it away with the other foot.

"Sleeping badly, then?" Ingvar asked.

"I had a nightmare," I said.

He took a seat at the table opposite me, ran a hand through his beard. "Have you spoken to Egil lately?"

I shook my head. "I'm just in there all the time, aren't I?"

"He failed his exam. His dad won't give him any more money."

"I didn't know things were that bad," I said.

"It gets worse. His dad doesn't like him living here with us. Thinks we're a bad influence."

I laughed. "You have to admit, he's kind of right."

"He's threatened to write Egil out of his will. Egil is raging. You're coming to his birthday party, right?"

I picked at my thumbnail.

"Yes."

Ingvar fixed his eyes on the tabletop.

"You know that it's okay to . . . like, talk to me. If you need to."

I tittered. "Yeah—you're the best girlfriend I have, Ingvar."

"Stop kidding around." He looked at me. "I mean it."

I tried to squeeze away the memories with my eyelids. The rhythmic slapping sounds in the room when Patrick thought I was asleep. The later visits in the half dark.

"You've stopped meeting him in town?"

Ingvar nodded.

"And he'll never come here?"

He calmly shook his head. "I promise."

I looked at Ingvar, shook my head. "It's too dark."

"For you, maybe. Not for me."

The stains Patrick left behind were sticky, and smelled sweet. It was no use trying to wipe them away, and there was no guarantee we would have any clean bedding the next day. When I thought back to that girl, the one called Sara, I remembered that smell. I looked at Ingvar, then back at my feet. Kicked at the floor in front of me. I didn't want to call up those memories.

"What did I tell you?" I asked Ingvar. "That night, when I got really drunk and started talking about Patrick. I don't remember what I said."

"I don't want to repeat it," he said. "He should have had his dick cut off for what he did."

"That's not the worst of it," I whispered.

There was part of it that I didn't have the strength to put into words. How, over time, the little girl I once was had changed. She became more clingy. Held her brother close, demanded his attention. Danced around him in the kitchen. Sometimes it was even she who crept up into his bed.

"The worst of it is that I loved him," I said to Ingvar. "That's why I had to leave."

I accepted his hug. Ingvar's warm, bearded cheek, his arms around mine. I let out a sob against his shoulder.

"That wasn't love," he said. "Love isn't like that."

"Love is like that, for me."

Ronja

Kristiansund
Saturday, 19 August 2017

I pop into the store on my way to the police station to buy painkillers, salted biscuits and an energy drink. The Storkaia shopping centre stands there as it always has, showing no sign of whatever it was that happened here yesterday. I pay at the checkout and open the packet of biscuits as I make my way out the door. Put the first one in my mouth and throw myself onto my bicycle, pedalling the last stretch into work. It occurs to me that no matter what happened, it happened almost right under the noses of the police—perhaps even while most of us were out partying. I'm not even sure whether I've managed to fully sober up, but I don't intend to wait a minute longer. This is too important.

I hope August hasn't made it in to work yet. It would be nice to pretend just a little longer, act as if yesterday never happened, but as soon as I walk through the door of the department, I hear his voice. Not only that, but I'm sure that I hear a muffled "for fuck's sake" in his thick Danish. I've never heard him angry before. I follow the sound of the subdued cursing. It's coming from Shahid's office. The door is closed, so he must be speaking really loudly in there. I don't catch the rest of the words, but his voice rises and the boss answers in a tone that is probably intended to calm him down. Then the door opens, and August comes out. I have to take several steps back so he doesn't crash into me, and I drop my energy drink on the floor in the process. He looks down at me in surprise before he turns and continues on down the hall to his office.

"Hi, Ronja," I hear the boss's voice say.

I feel the blush spread across my face and bend down to pick up the drink.

"I was just on my way down to my office," I mumble.

"It's great you're here early," says Shahid. "You're one of the first to get here. Listen—Tor Lind, the father of the missing girl, is coming in in half an hour. We have to conduct another interview with him, and one with his wife later today. We need somebody to observe the interviews and take notes. Can you do it, do you think?"

"Of course."

"If the case drags out, you'll be assigned to other duties, but for now this is what we need most. I'm going to watch the recording myself, I just have to see to a few things first. Talk to August about how you want to play it."

This isn't what I'd imagined—I normally work with Birte. Usually I'd have no problem being flexible—and nor will I this time, either. Nothing unusual to see here, no problems at all. I grit my teeth until I'm back in my office. I have half an hour to sober up, to get myself really awake and extinguish this headache, half an hour to get my heart rate down and rid myself of this blush. It'll be fine.

As I walk through the door to August's office, I notice that he's wearing a facial expression that is difficult to interpret. Expectant and sceptical at the same time. I can still feel a little glow on my lips from yesterday's kiss, even though it feels strange. I feel awkward. I would prefer not to look him in the eye, but it will only be even more uncomfortable if I don't.

"Shahid asked me to observe the interviews," I say. "Take notes."

He seems relieved. As if he thought I wanted to talk about last night. I involuntarily rub my shoe against the floor, making a sound that causes him to look down. He's an interrogator, used to looking for signs of nervousness. It apparently takes so little for me to make a fool of myself.

"That's good," he says, pretending not to see the heat rising in my face. "I'll conduct the interview alone, but it would be good if you could watch from the observation room. Take as many notes as you can."

He passes his hands over his thighs twice as he gets up— so I'm not the only one displaying signs of nervousness. He holds out an arm, and I walk in front of him down the hall to the observation room while he goes to the interview room to check that everything is ready. We can collaborate. No need to feel uneasy, not about the fact that I'm going to sit and stare at him on a screen for an hour or so, not about what my colleagues think—who cares about things like that? I'm a professional. I can keep my private life out of it and just do my job.

On my way into the observation room I realise that I ought to go to the loo before the interview starts—it would be stupid of me to miss anything. I hurry into the bathroom, feeling like a hungover teenage girl. Just manage to get back by the time

August enters the interview room with Tor Lind and starts reading him his rights.

August slides easily into the role of reassuring interviewer. He asks whether Lind has problems understanding his Danish, whether he would like a glass of water, and apologises for the state of the premises. Tor Lind sits straight-backed in his chair in the cramped interview room. He keeps his hands in his lap; there's a little potbelly under his blue shirt and buttoned-up grey cardigan. He has silver-plated blond hair and a hairline that's receding at the temples; a pair of silver framed glasses surround his blue eyes. He's in his fifties, and therefore some years older than his wife, but he bears his age well. Lind is a handsome man, in fact. He has a certain radiance about him. I note that he seems calm and composed, gives clear answers to the first questions about the case. As he told the officer who interviewed him yesterday, he got home at around five o'clock. He had expected Mariam and Iben to be home already. When they weren't there, he called his wife and daughter repeatedly on their mobiles, but got no answer. Mariam didn't arrive home until around ten thirty. She came home alone.

"Is there anyone who can confirm that you were at home?" Lind gives a ready answer.

"My neighbour across the street was out cutting the grass. Haven't you talked to him yet?"

August nods. "We have. He says that you came home at five o'clock, but is there anyone who can confirm that you didn't go out again, that you were home the whole time?"

"If so, they would have had to have seen me through the window. I was home alone."

I become engrossed in August's fingers. They're thin, and surreally long where they curl themselves around each other on the table before him. All of him is too tall and too thin, like a cartoon character. I touch my lips. Stupid. So, so stupid.

"Did you use your computer?" August asks.

"Yes! Yes, I did. I sat and read quite a few articles online. When I wasn't trying to call Mariam, that is."

"What did you read about?"

"I was looking for news. Traffic accidents and that kind of thing, something that might explain why they hadn't come home. I called the hospital, too, to check whether they had been admitted."

"When did you call the hospital?"

"Around seven or eight, I think it was."

I write down the times. Now we have to check Lind's browser history and call the hospital. I note that he sits leaning forward across the table, that he looks into August's eyes and doesn't seem nervous. That he asks several questions about the investigation, and whether we believe we will find Iben alive. It takes a lot of self-discipline to present yourself this way if you're not innocent, but we have to remember that he's a politician. He has the gift of the gab; he's used to making sure that he appears trustworthy.

"Tell me how you met your wife," August says. "Was it here in Kristiansund?"

"It was. She was a waitress at my favourite haunt. She came on to me, actually."

"'Actually?' Why do you say it like that?"

"Well, as you might have noticed, she's younger and better looking than me."

He's perhaps twenty years older than his wife. Not an unusual age difference, but it's obviously something that bothers him. I wonder whether he's insecure about something in their relationship. Perhaps he's afraid that she's not as taken with him as he once thought.

"How is your relationship with your wife now, after so many years of marriage?"

"We have our bad days, of course. All married couples do, but I love her—I feel that every day."

"Does she love you?"

He hesitates, thinks.

"Yes, I believe she does. Although you can never know for sure. Mariam has it tough sometimes. There can be days where she isn't able to show us her love, but I trust that it's there. I tell her that, too."

I write that the interviewee seems to answer questions about his relationship with his wife openly and honestly, and I add in parentheses that he seems like a good man. Think a little more and note that it seems as if he might be embellishing his family life. As if he wants to cast even the darker aspects of it in a good light.

"Does your wife have a diagnosis?"

Lind shakes his pale head.

"No, nothing like that, but she's had a rough time. And, just so you're aware, Iben isn't my biological daughter. I'm not able to have children myself. Iben is the result of a rape."

The interview room falls silent. Tor Lind clasps his hands on the table in front of him, gives August a serious look. I write *rape*; underline the word several times. Mariam hasn't said anything about that. Everyone has been working on the assumption that Iben is Tor's child.

"Mariam is strong," Lind says. "She manages. It's just that some days I really see how that incident has left its mark on her. She can be hard on Iben, too—and I know that it bothers her when she lets her problems affect her daughter. Mariam also had a difficult upbringing, and that probably makes being a parent even more challenging. Of course nobody wants to repeat their parents' mistakes."

"Did Mariam report the rape?"

Lind gravely shakes his head. "She doesn't know who he is. It was an attack, it was dark, and she never cared to report it. When I met her, it was already several months in the past, otherwise I would have tried harder to convince her to make a report."

"So Iben isn't your biological child. But tell me in your own words about your relationship with Iben."

"She's my child. I couldn't love her any more if she were biologically mine. And now, once I'm done with this interview, I'm going to go straight back out there and keep looking for my daughter."

Liv

Ålesund
Saturday, 20 March 2004

I lay under the warm duvet, his body against mine as the bass vibrations from the party outside spread through the bedposts and mattress. My earrings chafed against my throat, my tights against my waist. We lay there, Nero partly under my dress, his dry, rough body against my belly. He moved up towards my neckline a few times, tickling my skin with his coarse-smooth scales.

A sudden hammering on the door, hard fists.

"Liv, for God's sake," Egil called, tugging on the door handle. I put my head all the way under the covers. Drew the snake closer and studied those largely lifeless eyes with their vertical slashes for pupils.

"I'm not going out there," I whispered to Nero. "I'd rather stay here, with you."

Just a couple of hours ago I had been ready. All dolled up in a new dress, I had leaned against the edge of the sofa, putting on my makeup in front of the mirror on the wall. Egil had come in wearing a shirt that looked as if it cost half the price of a car. I refrained from asking him whether he'd used his credit card. EGIL—20 TODAY! hung on the wall in large letters. He'd paced back and forth, rattling off all the names of everyone who was coming, said it was going to be such a great party! It had been nice, almost like when I'd just moved in. I had felt a tiny spark of expectation as we stood there preparing trays of red, yellow and green vodka jelly shots.

I *had* been ready—even to risk meeting David, or some other idiot who wanted to pressure me into things. I had *wanted* to be ready, so that Egil would have the celebration he deserved, because he was a friend, through and through. The only thing I hadn't been ready for was that he would start to bug me about Nero again, even before a single guest had arrived.

"That's the only birthday present you need to give me, Liv. Nobody understands why they never get to see him. They think I've made him up."

"I don't understand why you've even told them about him," I said.

"Because *I* don't have weird rules," Egil snarled.

"Do you have to brag to get attention or something?" I said. "Are you worried that they won't have the same respect for you now that daddy has cut the cord?"

Egil's mouth fell open. He gave me a look that indicated he couldn't believe what I'd just said. Then he lunged at me. His fingers clawed for the key that hung around my neck; he tore at the chain. I thrust an elbow into his stomach. Worked myself free of his grasp and turned and walked with long strides straight into my room. I pulled the duvet up over both of us and lay still. The party moved the house around us. Voices hit the walls and ceiling, feet tramped against worn wood and linoleum, and Egil's fists hammered at the door. They couldn't break in, couldn't reach us where we were. We lay with our heads beneath the duvet, breathing each other's air in the dark.

"Have you ever thought," I whispered, "that life is a brick wall you just hammer away at, to see what's on the other side?"

He answered by licking the air with the two tips of his tongue. Many Native American peoples believed that snakes were messengers between humans and the underworld—they used to pray to these animals, asking them to carry their messages to the rain gods. Then, when it finally began to rain and the snakes crept forth from their holes in the ground, they took this as a sign that their prayers had been heard.

"You're the one who's closest to knowing what's on the other side," I whispered.

Egil finally gave up his insistent hammering; we were surrounded only by the bass vibrations once more. I'd really messed up this time—he would never forgive me, but I couldn't stand even the thought of going out there now. The past week had been long and heavy. Sitting in lectures was fine, but having to do group work with girls who seemed to have a natural ability to know what was right all the time was harder. When they weren't talking about how to make up beds with hospital corners and how to dose medications, they talked constantly about boys. I didn't see myself in their problems—men didn't approach me in the same way. With the other girls, they flirted and invited them out to do things together. They approached me as if getting ready to defeat an enemy.

I had found girls difficult ever since I was small. They sat on the edge of the sandbox wearing pink bubble jackets, brushing the tails of their beautifully pastel-coloured My Little Ponies.

They had perfect features, hair that fell softly around their cheeks. They looked at my grey jacket, a hand-me-down from Patrick, saw my worn-out trainers, my ash-blond hair that was uncut—and probably unwashed, too. They saw all this, and then they turned to each other and snickered.

With the boys it was simpler. It was enough just to be a girl who didn't act like a girl. I'd climb trees, fight—that sort of thing. This was, on the whole, a successful strategy—until one of them tried to push me down a steep hillside. I just managed to keep my balance, then grabbed hold of the first stone I saw and threw it at him. I didn't mean to hit him, but the rock sailed through the air, grazing his head as it passed him. It was all fine in the end—he wasn't badly scratched up—but his mother was furious. After that, none of the kids were allowed to play with me anymore. Only Patrick.

I had read that snakes feel no sense of belonging. That they are not pack animals. When you see them hunting together, they're not collaborating—they're competing. Snakes do not bond to individuals; they do not make themselves dependent on others. As soon as all her eggs are hatched, the mother snake leaves her children. I believed I could have lived like this, completely free of friendships and familial bonds. To have contact with other members of my species only when they could be used for something. In a way, I thought that this was what bound him and me together—the fact that we were so independent.

"I only wish I could get properly close to you, Nero," I whispered.

At that moment there was a knocking on the windowpane, quick and insistent: tap, tap, tap. I glanced over and saw a face peering in at me. I always kept the curtains open during

the day so Nero would get as much sunlight as possible. I
had almost stopped putting him in the terrarium, wanting
to allow him to move freely. Now I'd forgotten to draw the
curtains again. I reluctantly slipped Nero out from under my
dress and walked over to the window. It was David, the stub
of a cigarette between his lips. The same closely shaved hair
and eyes like black holes. He was wearing a hoodie that was
even baggier than the sweatshirt he'd had on the last time I
saw him, if that was possible. I opened the window a crack.

"What do you want?"

"Are you sick?"

"Just not in a partying mood."

"Cigarette?"

It was the only word that would have made me open the
window right then. I hitched myself up onto the windowsill
and reached out a hand for the pack, but he snatched it away
with a smile.

"Let me come in first."

I made space for him next to me; he jumped and pulled
himself up onto the ledge. His shoulder touched mine. He lit
my cigarette, and I greedily sucked the smoke into me, taking
deep drags down into my lungs. It was Patrick who taught me
to smoke. He showed me how to inhale properly and laughed
at me when I started to cough.

David said nothing. He just sat there beside me, blowing
blue-grey clouds out into the night's darkness. He finished
his cigarette, stubbed it out against the wall of the house, and
threw the butt into the blackness that blanketed the garden.
He turned his head and looked into the room. His body jerked;
then he laughed, a booming chuckle.

"So that's Nero," he said.

With great difficulty, he managed to get a foot over the windowsill and come into the room. Nero had climbed up into the plant just beside the window. David gently took him down, holding him out in front of him.

"Well, hello there, Nero," David said.

For a moment I wondered how he could know the snake's name, but of course he would have heard it from Egil. I quickly took the last drags on my cigarette and climbed back into the room.

"It's crazy hot in here," David said. "Must be over thirty degrees."

"Snakes need heat," I said. I'd got used to how warm it was in the room. Just as I had got used to the floor being covered in newspaper so that Nero could slither around as he wished, even after feeding.

Nero licked the air with the tips of his tongue. Held his head aloft, seeming to study this new person in the room. His radiant eyes moved a little now, as if he were trying to register what was going on. Then he opened his mouth and gave out a low hiss. He felt threatened. David, on the other hand, seemed to take the situation in his stride. He carefully set the snake across his shoulders. Did a couple of dumb dance moves and stopped in front of me.

"Sexy, huh?" He laughed.

His mouth tasted of beer and stale smoke. In some ways, it was a relief to kiss him. Our tongues twisted around each other. Nero continued to slide up over David's neck, draping himself over his shoulder on the other side. I tugged on David's white T-shirt, trying to pull it up—he wanted to move Nero, but I stopped him. I lifted the snake long enough for him to pull off his T-shirt, then put Nero back across his naked shoulders.

I didn't really like having sex. If I did it, it was because the other person wanted to, and to pass the time. It didn't matter who I did it with, or whether they were men or women—it was only ever something to do. It did sometimes give me a little bolt of joy at feeling superior, because they liked me more than I liked them. David let me hold him down as I sat on top of him; the snake crept across his chest. He laughed nervously as I pushed him down into the mattress, harder, just to feel him sink into it.

I closed my eyes and tried to concentrate on the tiny throb of pleasure that fluttered in my diaphragm but didn't want to reach its full potential. I placed a hand against David's throat and held him down. Squeezed my hand around his larynx. Thought back to the first night, when I had been woken by Nero's communication, that pure contact. The words I believed I could discern among the flow. *Dear, Liv.* I knew that he was longing for something greater, something bigger. He wanted to thank me for the live prey. He hoped to get more, and that I would be his hunting mate. Had I dreamed all this? Had I not lain here all these nights and heard it all?

David coughed. He grabbed my wrist and pulled my hand away. Pushed himself away from me. With his red face and messy hair, he looked as if he had wandered straight out of a psychiatric facility. I couldn't help but laugh.

He coughed.

"Jesus, Liv," he said. "You're fucking insane."

Roe

Kristiansund
Sunday, 20 August 2017

"Hey, Roe."

Somebody nudges me in the shoulder, shaking me awake. The light between the blinds dazzles me. I turn my head and see Ronja standing over me with a friendly smile, her brown hair tightly pulled back from her heart-shaped face. *Just like the wandering heart she is*, I think, and feel immediately embarrassed at the idiotic thought. Wandering heart. Jesus.

"It's time for the morning meeting," she says.

I must have spent the night asleep in the staff room. The last thing I remember is pouring myself a cup of coffee and sitting down for a five-minute rest. The next moment an incredible drowsiness came over me, and I must have decided to lie down, thinking I'd just close my eyes for a few seconds to rest. And the next thing I know, it's Sunday morning. I sit up. My neck is stiff and painful from sleeping with my head against the sofa's armrest.

"Thanks for waking me, Ronja. I haven't even prepared for the meeting."

I empty the dregs of yesterday's coffee into the sink, refill the water to make a new pot. Ronja leans against the kitchen counter as I start to make the fresh coffee.

"Have you been here since Friday?" she asks. A typical young woman taking the responsible role towards an older, male colleague. She probably does the same for her father. Such roles go in cycles. You provide the care during those early years and then move gradually—almost imperceptibly—into being the one who is cared for. If you're permitted to keep your child, that is.

"You know what—I have. I've become completely engrossed in this case."

She nods. "I feel the same way. It's like things can't happen fast enough. I dreamed about Iben last night, woke up several times." She smiles to herself as she says this. She's open about her feelings and tries to cover them with a smile, a tried and tested defence mechanism. This girl is the only person in this place who doesn't annoy the shit out of me. She doesn't try too hard—she's simply herself. I know all too well why I've had a soft spot for her all this time, why I've kept an eye on her and wanted her to be okay. It's because she reminds me of Kiddo—of course it is—but she isn't my daughter, and I can't protect her from the world.

"It's hard not to take your work home with you with a case like this," I admit. "Let's hope there's a breakthrough soon."

I turn away so she can't meet my gaze. Take the coffeepot from the machine and set my cup under it so that it catches the first few drops. Ronja takes a colourful mug from the cabinet.

"I'm going to do everything I can to make sure we solve this case quickly," she says.

She's ready for battle. It was once like that for me, too—I would be chomping at the bit to get started. But it's no longer enthusiasm for the job that drives me—that train left long ago. These days I run on pure rage. But I can't say that to Ronja. Instead, I clink my cup against hers.

She checks her phone.

"It's five past," she says, surprised, then turns and begins to walk ahead of me, down the stairs. I follow after her, close at her heels, hoping that everything is ready for the presentation. I spent almost all of Saturday going through the security footage from the Storkaia shopping centre, every second from every camera during those central hours, picking out the clips in which we see the mother and daughter disappear, each going in different directions at different times. A simple job, perhaps—but an important one.

Ronja carefully opens the door to the team meeting room. Shahid is standing in front of the projector screen, gesticulating. He nods to us as we enter and take our seats beside the window. Behind him on the screen are the points we set up at yesterday's morning meeting, more and less probable hypotheses as to what might have happened to Iben Lind: running away, accident, sudden illness, suicide, kidnapping, murder. Shahid wants to remind us of these possibilities so that we don't lose sight of them in the task that lies ahead. Under "suicide" is a list of potential reasons a child might take their own life. It happens rarely, but is not an impossibility. Under "kidnapping" and "murder," possible motives are listed: financial gain, paedophilia, revenge, familial conflicts, conflict among friends. The murder of a child by a friend is also rare—but not an impossibility.

"Although we hope the search efforts will give us positive results," Shahid says, "and we all want to find Iben alive, it's also important that throughout the investigation we keep in mind that the worst may have happened. This will make us more open to finding answers and ensure that we're better equipped to handle the situation if the answers don't turn out to be the ones we're hoping for."

He likes being up there, in front of everybody. I can see it in the way he lifts his chest towards the ceiling, how he uses an authoritative but pedagogical tone of voice. Even though he's neither particularly tall nor broad-shouldered, he has a natural authority about him.

"Before we talk about today, I'd like the head of each group to summarise the work that's been done since yesterday," he says. "We can start with the group who interviewed members of the immediate family."

The Dane gets up and moves to the front of the room. The tall man towers over his far shorter boss, who takes a seat in one of the chairs at the front.

"My team has interviewed Iben Lind's immediate family," the Dane says. "That is, her mother, father, grandparents and aunt on her father's side. The family has informed us that the grandparents on the mother's side are deceased, and that there has been no contact between Mariam Lind and her other family for many years. Mariam has been interviewed several times, first on Friday evening and then on Saturday morning." He casts a glance in my direction, apparently still angry about how I got all riled up in the interview I held with Mariam Lind on Friday.

While August relates Mariam Lind's statement regarding what happened at the shopping centre on Friday, I take a quick glance around the room at all the other police officers.

So many of them have been out trawling the local area, ringing doorbells and searching the streets, parks and car parks. What have I done? I've been sitting staring at a screen, trying to hide what a bad job I'm doing. They all know that I'm too old to be working on electronic tracing—I have none of the competence that the others in the group have. I've just been stowed away somewhere. In front of me a colleague has the *Tidens Krav* newspaper up on her phone. On the front page is an image of Mariam and Iben Lind, smiling and wearing almost identical yellow sweaters—the last photograph to be taken of Iben before she disappeared. Pale locks of hair frame the face of both mother and daughter. "Investigation is stepped up." Who chooses a picture like that when trying to find their missing daughter? It seems calculated, as if Mariam Lind is taking full advantage of the opportunity to showcase herself. Perhaps she thinks it will help bring in more money for her firm. People are weird like that. *Wasn't that the company, the one with the CEO whose daughter disappeared? What a tragedy.* I have no problem imagining she might be that cynical.

"In the interviews, we've focused on whether Iben had exhibited any unusual behaviour recently," August continues. "Signs that something or someone had been bothering her, signs that might lead us in the direction of what might have happened. None of the adults say they noticed anything out of the ordinary. One of the girls in Iben's class says that at some point earlier in the summer, Iben had said that you can't trust adults. Not even those you know, she supposedly said. When the girl asked what she meant, Iben didn't respond, but the girl says that Iben had a strange look on her face. We've noted that the friend remembered this as something unusual, but that doesn't necessarily mean it's of any significance."

Shahid nods patiently at the Dane's lengthy report. "Thank you, August. Can you tell us your plan going forward?"

"When interviewed, both Tor and Mariam Lind have related that Iben was the result of a rape that occurred here in Kristiansund in 2005," says the Dane. "We're going to interview individuals previously sentenced for rape and check out their alibis. It will be especially important to check whether any convicted rapists had been released and were in Kristiansund around the date on which Mariam Lind claims she was assaulted."

After the Dane, it's Birte's turn to present findings from the inquiries thus far. She stands straight-backed as she speaks, like an actor onstage.

"We've made inquiries at the Storkaia shopping centre and in the area around Iben's home, and we've also collaborated with the tip line." She gives a toss of her head, so her long red plait dances on her shoulder. "There are many witnesses from the shopping centre. We've also spoken to witnesses who claim to have seen Iben in the period after she disappeared. The most dependable are two people who say they saw her on Hagbart Brinchmanns vei—one of whom says he saw her stop at Myra's Flowers."

Shahid puts a map of Kristiansund up on the projector, on which details pertaining to the case have been marked. It shows a probable route between the Storkaia shopping centre and Iben's home.

"There are also uncertain sightings," says Birte. "People who didn't know her, who may have thought they remembered something after seeing Iben on TV. We've also had a number of sightings reported in Kirklandet and Gomalandet, but we regard the sightings in Hagbart Brinchmanns vei as more probable. They're closer in time and place to the disappearance, and supported by other evidence. These observations strengthen the hypothesis that something happened to Iben on her way home to her residence in Siktepunktet. As does the fact that none of the neighbours in Siktepunktet saw Iben around the time she disappeared. It's likely that somebody would have seen her had she made it home. Two neighbours were outside in their gardens around the time in question, and they confirm that they saw Tor come home, but neither of them saw Iben. Since the comic book was found not too far from the house, we regard it as probable that there was somebody there who stopped her from making it all the way back."

Shahid thanks Birte for her presentation. "I think that leads us nicely into hearing from the electronic tracing team?" he says.

When I get up, my legs feel like jelly and my heart is hammering in my chest. But this is no longer visible from the outside; I manage to keep it to myself. Should anyone happen to hear it in my voice, they'll just think I'm nervous about speaking in front of an audience. But inside me, Kiddo's house is ablaze. I often think of those flames burning deep within me. I take over Shahid's computer and bring up the video clip of Iben running out of the supermarket in the Storkaia shopping centre.

"Video surveillance from Storkaia shows that Iben Lind leaves the supermarket at 15:47 on Friday," I say. "As you can see, she's wearing blue jeans, a light pink hoodie and a pair of pink trainers. From the supermarket she runs out through the first door and turns to the left. This would be the natural route for her to take if she were walking home. At 16:02 we see Mariam Lind come out of the same store with a shopping trolley full of groceries. She looks around for her daughter and then moves quickly out of the same door that Iben just ran through. Mariam, however, turns right, towards the car park. She's captured on video again at her car. The footage clearly shows that she's angry, throwing bags of shopping into the vehicle before shoving the trolley against the wall in rage. Then she gets into the car and drives off. The car leaves the shopping centre at 16:16."

Shahid shifts back to the map again, and I show where Iben walked after leaving the shopping centre, pointing out where she was captured on a webcam at the Sparebank 1 savings bank in Langveien. I ask Shahid to switch back to the larger map, which shows Mariam Lind's movements and the places we can assume with reasonable certainty she visited after leaving the shopping centre, all confirmed by credit card payments: a snack bar and two petrol stations, as well as the ferry to Halsa, where she was also captured by a surveillance camera.

"In interviews, Mariam has said that she was on her way to Trondheim. She set off in anger, wanting to leave her family. On the way, she changed her mind and turned back. I believe we should search here"—I make a circular movement above the map in the area Mariam visited. "As I've said before, we cannot rule out the fact that Iben may have been in Mariam's car. Even though they left the shopping centre at different times, we cannot be sure that Mariam didn't pick up her daughter later, and that something may have happened. The fact that there was conflict between mother and daughter before Iben disappeared is a factor we mustn't overlook in this case."

I look over at Shahid, who puts on his stern boss's face.

"Where are you suggesting that we look along this route, Roe? It's a huge area to search."

"I believe we have to do the same as we're doing here in Kristiansund. Map out likely places we should search—places where Mariam may have stopped along the way, and places we know that she stopped. Search any areas of forest and bodies of water."

I'm starting to stutter. Realise that it's becoming difficult to argue for this project.

Shahid holds my gaze, gives me an encouraging smile.

"The mother's movements may warrant following up, Roe; they might be important. There are many possible leads—as you know. But we have no eyewitness sightings of Iben outside the town centre. We've spoken to the employees at the snack bar and petrol stations where Mariam Lind made purchases. None of them remembers having seen a child. Furthermore, Mariam Lind has no criminal record, and none of the witnesses described her in a way that should give us cause for concern. Even if Mariam did kill her daughter, it's just as likely that the body would have been dumped here in Kristiansund. It's a big enough operation searching with divers and helicopters here in the local area—never mind if we're to do the same from here to Halsa. I'm not saying we'll never expand the search, but we're not going to do it right now. Thorough checks using cadaver dogs have also been completed on Mariam's car."

This last fact I interpret as a direct reference to my interview with Mariam.

Shahid clears his throat. "For now, we have to prioritise mapping and following up on eyewitness accounts before we start going out and searching at random. However, it's important that we know where we should focus our search efforts should the investigation move over into the next phase—something none of us hopes will happen, of course."

Next phase. He means if this becomes a murder investigation.

"It would be great if you could take the lead on that, Roe, if you have the capacity for it," Shahid says. "Now—any findings from Tor Lind's computer?"

I feel my face flame red. Of course I should have provided proper justification. I was working on the assumption that the mother would be a natural suspect. I clear my throat.

"The data traffic supports his statement. He spent a lot of time browsing online newspapers and using search engines between 17:00 and 22:30 on Friday. We've also confirmed that he called the hospital at 19:25 and inquired about Mariam and Iben."

"Anything from Iben's mobile phone?"

"There were no findings of interest on the mobile. She seems to have only ever called her parents on it. She was logged into Facebook, so we've looked at her messages from recent weeks on there, but none of the conversations stand out. A thorough search of her iPad didn't turn up anything of interest, either."

"Good," Shahid says. "Then we don't need to spend any more time on that. Thank you, Roe."

I look down at the floor as I thank my audience for their attention. Blood rises to my head. I hear the boss asking the crime scene technician to come up to present the total lack of fingerprints on the soaking-wet comic book, how it's been sent to the National Criminal Investigation Service for further testing. The whole investigation is made up of hints and missing leads. I can't take any more. I have to get out of here.

I close the door to the team room behind me. Wonder how long it will take before somebody figures out that I'm on the surveillance footage from Storkaia. Wonder whether there's any way out. Whether I can jump on a plane, flee to a far-off foreign country and put this whole fucking mess behind me. But it's no use. They'd find me, no matter where I went. It's only a matter of time.

Reptile memoirs

I rested my head on my belly. It was warmer here on this side of my living space than on the other. Should I feel the need to cool down, I would move over to the other side, but for the most part I lay here. I kept close to the invisible barrier, trying to understand and break through it, but it was no use. This was how the days passed. Outside the window, the sun rose and set. I could slither to the other end, and I could slither back again. I could close my pupils so that everything turned dark, sleep a little, and open them again. Observe what was going on out there. My brothers and sisters, inside their own glass barriers, lay just as still. I heard the scratching, flapping and scrabbling of animals kept behind bars and doors. I knew how those animals smelled, because I had detected the scent of them on the few occasions I had been permitted to spend time on the other side of this glass. In here, it smelled only of my own excrement.

Hunger tore at my body, making me irritable. I kept an especially close eye on the animals out there, as it was a long time since I had last been given food. Animals with feathers, fur and scales—animals that flew or ran or jumped, with tails dancing after them. I could have eaten them all. I could almost taste the fresh blood in my mouth, even though I had yet to experience it.

I yawned. Slowly moved my body into a new position, instead resting my head farther down my body. Closed my pupils and slept. The same dream as always. A world I had never properly seen—a memory from previous generations that must have been stored in my cells. I lay resting under a bush, where the sun wasn't so strong. Insects scuttled around me, and the air tasted of bushes, trees and living creatures. There was also water close by—I could see the sun's rays glistening on its shining surface.

Right then, a movement entered my field of view. A tiny lizard on skinny little legs, toddling across the pebbles, clambering over small stones. I knew at once what I had to do. That was the best thing about instinct—it always knew what to do. I darted forward, following the prey along the ground, over tufted mounds and under roots, and managed to stop it just before it disappeared up along a tree trunk. Just as I was sinking my teeth into the tiny reptile—just as I was about to use all I had learned, all my strength—I woke up. This was how my days passed. Always this dream, and then waking to this frightful, dead room.

One day, the cold woman was standing outside the barrier once again. A being that towered high above and controlled the world. I called her the cold woman because she was cooler than the other live animals I had seen, and because she served cold food. The cold woman was hard. It was she who had put me here. It was she who held me captive, who only ever let me out of this odour-free confinement when buyers came to visit. She who tormented me with all these noisy creatures I couldn't have, who tapped on the glass with their gruesome limbs. Before I met her, I'd thought life was good. I thought the world had something to offer a hunter like me. Now I knew that I myself was prey. Not for a hungry hunter, but for the human need to imprison and gawk at other creatures.

The cold woman opened the hatch above my back. I licked at the air, and detected that she had a carcass with her. It smelled of death and cold, as usual. A long time had passed since I was last given a meal. My body ached for food, but still I didn't want to eat. This cold carcass was an insult. I wanted to show her that this was no food for a creature like me—that I knew better—but it was no use. All she needed to do was gently shake the carcass and the movement triggered something in me, an internal reflex. Despite my lack of appetite, the intense feeling of never being able to have what I truly wanted, I never fought my reflexes. I darted up and snatched the piece of meat.

Flesh of this kind filled my stomach, but it gave me no satisfaction. I ate only because my body needed food. It was the same with the lamp. It glowed, providing the warmth on which I depended in order to stay alive, but it gave me no spark, no energy for life. It seemed there was nothing to do but accept this. Acceptance was the only truth my mother had instilled in me, the utmost virtue for creatures like us. The limitations we faced—they simply existed. Trying to fight them, or doubting them—it was all wasted energy. Acceptance, on the other hand, cost nothing.

The days passed. The sun continued to rise and set outside the window. I had looked out through it a few times. Had seen that there were lush plants, that there was a heat outside too. All this made me downcast, here where I was forced to lie beneath the artificial light. The days passed, and soon it was a long time since she had last brought food. Even more time passed, and the hunger ached in me.

My lamp hadn't worked in days—it flickered on and off at appalling speed. Without the heat I felt listless and empty; I lay still in my corner and waited for death to come. I decided to end it all. To stop drinking from the dirty water bowl entirely. If more carcasses appeared, I would not eat them. I would simply lie there and let my life ebb away. The cold woman wouldn't notice a thing until it was too late. I was tired—it took energy to rebel. And so I slept.

When I woke again, there was an entire flock of people outside the barrier. They were buyers. That meant that they had come to lift me up, make noise. I licked the air, but sensed nothing here inside the glass. I reminded myself that acceptance was a virtue; it would shorten the suffering. This was my life—successive pain and suffering—and I awaited its end. So when the cold woman grabbed my coil, hard, and pulled me out into the room beyond, I remained calm. Licked the air, getting to know the group of individuals that stood around me. Humans smelled of so much other than themselves—of flowers, dead plants and foreign animals. It seemed as if they took on the scents of other animals in order to camouflage their own. But they couldn't hide their true odour from me. I licked the air and tasted all the sourness, all the salty bitterness that oozed from their bodies. Tiny drops of sweat on their skin. The distant taste of the digestive juices on their breath. Other juices from their genitals.

Then I was set in the arms of a human female. It was easy to see that this was a female—their sex was something that humans clearly exhibited. She had long, dark hair, which danced and smelled of acidulous plants. A more powerful glow emanated from her than from the others. I licked the air and noticed too that the bittersweet taste of her sex was stronger. She felt desire.

She took me between her hands and lifted me across to the window, permitting me to feel the bright rays of the outside world for the first time in months. My body was renewed at once—enlivened. As I enjoyed this revival, she touched my spine with her ape-like fingers and whispered in her curious language. I didn't understand the meaning of the sounds, but I understood that they were expressed with affection. I didn't like such caresses, but I had seen parrots stroking their heads against each other and cleaning each other's feathers, cats that licked each other's coats. They moved their bodies in a way that testified to contentment. Personally, I felt satisfaction only at good food and warmth. Caresses were for pack animals—those unable to cope alone as individuals. They gave and received caresses as a form of subordination, in order to be able to use each other at will. I understood this, as the rays of sunlight from the window brought my body back to life. It was her submission that had given this gift to me—and it could give me more.

Liv

Ålesund
Saturday, 10 April 2004

I was all out of my usual shampoo. I sniffed my way through Egil's many bottles of powerfully scented soaps and hair products, looking in vain for something neutral. I'd just have to smell like a man tonight. Maybe it might even keep the worst of the hunters at bay. The shampoo created a plume of foam that rose and fell around the drain. I wondered what the other girls on my course were doing now—whether they were meeting up beforehand and getting ready, enjoying a glass of wine together before the dinner. Such organised gatherings were only really good for the students who had already found each other, but it was better than staying here.

There was a knock at the door.

"Hello? Is there anybody in there?" It was a girl's voice.

"I'm in the shower!"

I let the water run over my face, into my ears and on down my neck.

"Hello? Can I come in and pee? There's only me here."

I turned off the shower. Sighed and wrapped a towel around me, stepping out onto the tiny patch of floor that remained between the wet towels and dirty clothes. Unlocked the door. In came a girl with long, bleached-blond hair and a nose ring. A few years older than the girls Egil usually went for, but other than that, she seemed to be his type.

"Be quick," I said.

"Oh, thanks! Really—thanks!"

The girl took several long steps into the room, moving across to the toilet.

"I'm really sorry, honestly—I wouldn't have disturbed you if I wasn't desperate. But then I thought, well, since it's just us girls here . . ."

I dried myself as she peed. I'd never liked the feeling that anyone might see me naked. Didn't even like being naked alone. There was something tragic about it, something colourless, like a duvet without a cover. I waited for her to say something. To give me advice about hair removal, or comment on my body in some way. Instead, she flushed and moved across to the sink.

"Is it okay if I do my makeup, too? Since I'm here?"

I shrugged. Hung my head and dried my hair with a towel. She took my makeup bag from on top of the washing machine, pulled out an eyeliner and began to line her eyes.

"You weren't here yesterday," she said.

I shook my head, making my tousled, uncombed hair dance.

"I was busy. Do you have a hairbrush? Mine's in my room."

She handed me a white brush and continued the laborious process of applying her eyeliner. Slowly but surely, she began to resemble a cat.

"Egil says you've stopped hanging out with them."

"I know." I tried to brush out the worst of the tangles with hard strokes.

"Is it true that you have a snake in your room?"

"Lots of things about me are true," I said, dragging the brush through my hair with extra force. A few black strands remained on the white brush. They didn't belong with the blond ones that were already there.

"Does snot get stuck on your nose ring?" I said.

She laughed. One of her front teeth slightly crossed the other. "All the time."

"It's more original than a tramp stamp, I'll give you that."

"Oh, I have one of those, too." She pulled up her sweater at her back. "Look—right here. I love clichés, they're so fun. Don't you have anything like that?"

I looked at her—at the tattoo on her lower back, at her nose ring and her crooked front teeth. She wasn't like the other girls who constantly turned up at the apartment door. She seemed cool, different.

"I did consider getting a tattoo of a snake on my ass," I said. "Seeing as Egil insists on going around telling people that I have a python in my room."

She clapped a hand over her mouth.

"You're kidding? So it's just something he's made up?" She began to laugh loudly, clutching her chest. "Oh, you've just made my day! Liv—that's your name, isn't it?" She took my hand. "I'm Anita. What are you doing tonight?"

"I'm going to dinner with the people from my nursing studies course."

She laughed. "Sounds like great fun."

I shook my head. She put her face right up against the mirror and wiped away some mascara that had ended up on her cheek.

"I'm going out with some friends from my course, too—
from the art school. I reckon we'll go to Lille."

She rouged her cheeks with quick brushstrokes. I occasionally went down to Lille Løvenvold on Fridays to drink cheap
wine. It wasn't like the Smutthullet pub where I usually went
with Ingvar and Egil. Lille Løvenvold was a more decent kind
of place, cleaner. True, an atmosphere of drunkenness pervaded
there, too, once it started to get late—after midnight all the
bars in Ålesund were exactly the same. But there was something
different about Lille Løvenvold. The crowd was different.

"Are you an artist? Like, a painter?"

She nodded. "I paint, mostly, yeah. And not just my face,
either." She laughed and met my gaze in the mirror. "Of course
my body is a work of art, too, but I mainly paint on canvas."

I realised she was making fun of herself. There was something that cut through her laughter, a sort of stutter. Her eyes
met mine in the mirror.

"By the way—I hope you don't mind me saying this, but
you have such interesting eyes. You'd make a good model for
a painting."

I looked down at the chaos of towels and other clutter on
the floor. Felt my cheeks turn hot.

"I hope that wasn't a rude thing to say," she said.

Interesting eyes. What did she mean by that? For some reason
it felt more forward than if she'd commented on my body.

"No," I managed to say. "Just a bit weird."

"Well, I'll leave you in peace," she said. Then she packed
up her makeup bag, leaped over the dirty laundry basket and
opened the door. "If you get tired of the nurses, just drop by
Lille." Then she disappeared into the hall.

I dressed quickly, surprised to feel that I was warm all over, as if slightly feverish.

I heard Egil's agitated voice coming from the kitchen. I followed the sound and saw him pacing back and forth across the tiny kitchen floor, his phone pressed to his ear. The voice on the other end sounded flat, emotionless.

"Do you know what you are?" Egil said. "You're a sea cucumber! You have no feelings for others, you're nothing but a blob!"

The voice on the other end of the line continued, unchanged, like that of a strict headmaster.

"Nobody likes you. No wonder Mamma left you."

Suddenly he turned, saw that I was standing there. The look he gave me was so hard that I immediately backed out into the hall again. My heart was pounding. I peeked through the open doorway to Ingvar's room.

"So there you are," Ingvar said. There was a tension in his voice.

I entered the room, where the blind was pulled down so that no more than a few strips of sunlight made their way in around it. Ingvar lay on the bed with a book. I sat down beside his feet.

"I was just reading about you." Ingvar smirked.

On the book's cover was a portrait of a man with a long chin and nose, wearing a headdress of green leaves. Dante Alighieri, *The Divine Comedy*.

"You're such a nerd, Ingvar."

"Listen."

Ingvar began to read from the book. It was a verse that described two creatures, a man and a snake, that were turned into each other. The poem described the entire process—how the man's legs became entwined and his tongue split, while the opposite happened to the snake. How the snake grew hair and ears, while the man's skin turned hard. In the end, the man who had become a snake disappeared, hissing along the ground, while the snake who was now a man stayed standing.

"That's exactly what's happening to you." Ingvar laughed. "You're turning into that snake. For all I know, it's already you lying back there in your room, and Nero who walks here among us."

I shook my head, moved towards the door.

"You're leaving?"

"See you in the next life, Ingvar," I said.

Then I left.

Mariam

Kristiansund
Monday, 21 August 2017

The light seeps in through the cracks around the curtains. A treacherously faint blaze that exposes everything I can't bear to think about—that day has arrived, that the world exists, and that I myself exist within it. Pulling the covers over your head is always futile—the head knows that the day exists. The head knows that it's still late summer outside, that today is the first day of school. The head doesn't forget her breath coming in little puffs when she was a tiny baby, her voice when it said *Mamma* for the first time. Or the feeling of standing before the mirror with her and pointing. The head insists on remembering how it was to kiss those little feet, to point to each toe and tickle them. The little lips that puckered as she slept, her forehead wrinkled by unknown dreams. The head knows it is guilty of destruction.

There's a knock at the door. Tor comes in with a tense expression on his face. He's wearing one of his finest blue shirts with the silver stitching, the top button undone. It complements his eyes and his grey-blond hair so well. In his hands he carries a plate and a glass of milk.

"Have you eaten?" He puts the glass and plate on the night-stand, frowning when I shake my head. "More than two hundred people have signed up to take part in the search today. The entire school is going to join in. School isn't going to start without Iben."

He doesn't look at me as he speaks. Has a distant look in his eyes as he gazes up at the wall somewhere, at the family photographs that hang there. He isn't going to ask me to join them, and nor am I going to say anything. It must cost him a lot to be here in the same room as me and to keep speaking to me, after what I've done. And yet he's still his usual patient, caring self. I always feel that his care for me should tell me something about how I should be towards him. That he's trying to teach me something, but failing. I sit up, take the glass and drink small sips of milk out of sheer gratitude. Pass my hand across the bedding, with its pattern of spring flowers. Then he goes.

I squeeze my eyes shut and try to pretend that I don't exist. Small flashes of memory, of a little girl's laughter, burning my ears. I see her over and over in the minutes before she disappeared, with her head bowed and that ridiculous comic book in her hand, moving away from me. The magazine they found. Her, they're still looking for. As if an eleven-year-old girl could simply get lost on the streets of the town centre, or in the hundred-metre-wide forest opposite the house. She's sensible. She knows exactly where she lives. If she'd had any problems, she would have asked an adult for help or gone straight home. Almost two days have passed. Someone has taken her. No other explanation makes sense. If they find her out there today, no matter where they might look, she'll be dead.

A memory from spring returns to me. I was sitting in the armchair in the living room, having just got home from work. I was waiting for Tor and Iben to get home. No—that's wrong. I wasn't waiting. I was pulling myself together. Preparing myself for my family's return. I could tell from the sound of the door opening that it was Iben who had made it home first. Her cautious nature sent vibrations through the house, as if from a frightened sparrow. She was on her way into the living room, probably to watch TV, but when she saw me she stopped in the doorway.

I saw how guilt-ridden she looked. How she didn't want to meet my gaze. A kind of irritation came over me, completely irrational. I felt mean. My body wanted to be unreasonable.

"How did the English test go, Iben?" I stared straight at her, waiting.

"It went okay," she mumbled.

I knew she was lying, so I pressed her.

"You'd done enough practice, hadn't you? You remember what you said to me yesterday, that you'd done enough practice so you could play instead?"

"Yes. I practised enough."

Her entire body showed that she was lying, and I—I took a mocking tone with her. I said, "Wonderful! Then I'm looking forward to seeing your results."

I didn't stop there. Later, when the three of us were eating dinner, I said to Tor, "Iben says she did so well on her English test today." Tor never picks up on my mean jokes—he'd smiled proudly at Iben and said, "That's great, Iben! You see, it pays off when you do the work, right?" Right there is where I know I hit Iben's conscience the hardest—Tor's pride in her. But I didn't stop there, either. Later that evening, when Iben had got into bed, I went into her room and said, "I'm so proud of you, Iben, working so hard at school. Pappa is so proud of you, too—he's just bursting with pride." Then I kissed her on the head and said good night.

When I think about this, my stomach aches, but still I wasn't done with my game. In the morning, when I saw her at breakfast, I spoke English to her. Asked her whether she would like bread, butter, cheese. Then I asked her about other things, using words I knew she didn't understand. She hung her head and answered yes to every question I put to her.

How often have I treated her like this? It isn't really Iben I want to torment in this way—it's the *idea* of a child. All the things I'm afraid that she'll become. I get lost in the dark place she came from, about which she's entirely innocent. Maybe she really has run away after all.

I open my eyes. Force the thought out of my head and get up. The cold floor against my feet feels deserved. My legs are heavy, my entire body stiff. The house will be empty now. Tor is out searching for Iben. Who by now might be just a cold body, lying out in the woods somewhere. Images I do not wish to see constantly appear in my head—her skin is grey, cold and damaged, her hair dark with blood. I don't want to think about it.

The wardrobe is open, so I can see all my beautiful suits hanging neatly next to each other. It gives me a certain sense of calm to buy nice clothes, something I can put on and show the world that I'm a woman who has style. The garments and shoes automatically make me stand taller, lift my head. They give me confidence when I'm about to enter an important negotiation at work. Clothes are far more than just clothes— they're control. At least that's what these clothes are. I pull the wardrobe door closed and see myself in the mirror on the front of it, standing barefoot in worn-out pyjamas, blond hair dishevelled because I've been tossing and turning all night. I turn away and leave the room.

I stop for a moment before the capital letters on Iben's door: KNOCK BEFORE YOU ENTER! It's years since she wrote this message—it hangs there as both a souvenir and a warning. The rule has long since been violated by forensic technicians in white suits, with tiny brushes and swabs in their hands. I set the flat of my hand against the sign, push open the door and peer into the tiny yellow room. A chest of drawers with flowers painted on it. Walls covered with posters of horses. Pink bedding. In just a few years it will look completely different. All stripped down and teenage, with pictures of boys on the walls. I've been looking forward to watching her grow up.

The desk is overflowing with sheets of paper, stationery and toys. Whenever I ask her to tidy up, she only ever tidies things off the floor. I start to lift the pieces of paper, going through them. Am suddenly afraid to find one of those drawings you hear about, of something grown-up that's frightened her. Remind myself that the police would have taken anything like that. The drawings on the desk all feature safe motifs—princesses, horses, dogs.

On the wall hangs another drawing, sketched by an artist at a fairground. I remember that day so well. We took Iben on a roller coaster for the first time. Tor hit a bull's-eye and won one of the biggest teddy bears for her. That might be the happiest day we've ever spent together as a family. To top it off, we visited the booth where you could have your portrait done. Were drawn together as a family, sitting on thrones in a castle. The king and queen, with the little princess on her father's lap. Extravagant costumes with padded shoulders and narrow waists, beautiful and pure faces. Smile upon smile upon smile. A happy family.

I creep into her bed, pull the duvet over me and inhale her smell. Again I'm struck by memories of a little girl, newborn, two months, a year, her first milk tooth, riding around on a tricycle in the rear courtyard of the building in which we lived, petting the neighbour's cat, trips to the beach with sunscreen and inflatable armbands. Ice-skating, jumping on a trampoline, eating lemon for the first time, sitting on Pappa's shoulders as she moves through a crowd towering high above everyone else. Her first day at school, running with friends in the playground, learning to ride a bicycle and to swim. My little girl.

I pick up my phone. Flick through old photos—Iben unsteadily riding her bike with stabilisers. A video from a school play in which she's dancing, looking shyly down at the floor. I watch it several times. Find a photograph in which she's two years old and eating porridge for all she's worth. She was so happy back then. Used to shout *Hello! Hello! Hello!* with rippling laughter. The police have Iben's mobile phone and iPad. Perhaps they'll find conversations she's had on Facebook with a grown man she doesn't know.

They're out there looking for her—something crawls through my veins at the thought. When I close my eyes, I try to see everything in black, only the black, to disappear into it. But the head wants to remember. A little girl sticking her small, chubby hands into the sand. A six-year-old with a new rucksack and new shoes.

I open my eyes. See the empty chair where Iben has sat so many times with her head bent over her homework. Her blond hair in a braid at her neck. Her hair, so thin between my fingers that it's almost weightless. I can lie under the duvet and try to forget all this, but my head knows that they're out there, searching. My head knows that her hair is out there somewhere.

I get up, go across to the bookshelf full of books for young girls, trail my fingers across the pastel-coloured spines. A dedicated shelf full of boxes: a jewellery box, an old cigar box, a bowl full of beads. I start to open the boxes, one by one. Look at the tiny pieces of gold jewellery she was given as christening gifts, the clip-on earrings she wore when they had a carnival at school. The largest box has MY SECRETS written on it. It shines, there on the shelf. *Young girls must be allowed to have secrets*, I seem to remember reading in some advice column or other, but now I can't help but open it.

In the box is a hundred-kroner note, a plastic toy horse and a gold chain with something on the end of it. I rummage around to pull it out, hold it up to the light. On the end of the chain is a key. A simple key, of the kind that might belong to any door in any house. The only thing that sets it apart from other keys is that, like the chain, it's plated in a colour reminiscent of gold.

Liv

Ålesund
Saturday, 10 April 2004

Lille Løvenvold was already jam-packed with people, but that doesn't take much. The tiny amount of floor space on the ground floor was hardly enough for a counter and a queue at the bar. I stood on tiptoe, looking between all the heads for a blond girl with a nose ring, then forced my way through the queue to the black spiral staircase up to the first floor.

Disco lights surged across the black-painted walls; at the tables, people were sitting and talking, trying to make their conversations heard above the loud techno music. It was too early for anyone to be dancing—for now, shouted conversations were the favoured activity, the buzz of vocal cords that screeched and rasped beneath glittering necklaces and shirt collars. I had no idea what she was wearing. Didn't even know whether she had actually ended up coming here.

After the student dinner, I'd been left standing alone outside the restaurant as the others went their own way. I'd had too much to drink, and too quickly; my usual clownish antics had emerged. The others had listened—they had laughed and seemed interested—but not in a good way. They had been interested in me in the way that children might be interested in pulling the legs off a spider.

So as I stood there by myself outside the restaurant, the only thing I could think about was something the girl had said—Anita, the girl with the nose ring and the one front tooth that crossed the other. Not that I had interesting eyes—although that, too, was something I'd given a lot of thought over the course of the evening. She had said I should drop by Lille. *Why not?* I'd thought. It was surely better than going home and locking myself in my room. But now that I was here, I was no longer so sure. It was probably the kind of thing you just said, *Drop by Lille*—it didn't necessarily mean that she'd actually be happy to see me here. She was probably with her artsy friends. Maybe she'd turn out to be just like the others. To have a scornful note in her laugh, a false friendliness.

I stood there, looking out across the first floor of the bar in vain. None of the girls looked like Anita. When someone finally shoved past me to come up the stairs, I turned and went back down. A last possibility was the rear courtyard, almost as big as the bar itself and far busier than the first floor. I pushed past smoking bodies, moving out into the cool spring night. Tried to shut out the droning of the voices and look for Anita's blond head. I felt tired. The alcohol was relinquishing its grasp, leaving me shaky. I may as well just give up.

I pushed past the queue at the bar one more time and emerged on the other side. This had been a stupid idea. For a moment I stood out on the street, the art nouveau buildings all around me, frozen there, just as I had been outside the restaurant, until I realised that there was nothing to do but go home. But just as I turned to look down the street to start the long walk back to the apartment, I heard a male voice calling my name. He drew out the *i*—"Liiiv"—like a long howl. I glanced up and down the street, but nobody seemed to be looking in my direction. Then he called out again, a long, howling "Liiiv," and I realised that it was coming from above. There, from a window in the apartment above the florist's, a man's head peered out. David waved. I crossed the street and stood directly below him. I could now hear other sounds from in there, too—rap music and the hollering and jeering of several voices. David stretched out his arm, his hand holding a cigarette; he stuck out his tongue a little and tapped off some ash. It seemed as if he were trying to hit me with it.

I grinned. "What are you doing?"

"Waiting for you to come up. Are you coming?"

I pulled off my boots and set them against the wall along with a dozen other pairs of shoes. Took the beer David held out to me and followed him in the direction of the rap music, loud cries and laughter, down a hallway in which everything seemed to be from the '70s—the carpet was a pattern of red and yellow, the wallpaper striped yellow and brown. There was even an old telephone table in light-brown wood, with a built-in seat. An unease swelled within me when I looked down into the swirling pattern on its cushion.

We turned into the living room, and I saw what people had been shouting and whooping about: on the table in front of the brown striped sofa, a man lay on his stomach. His wrists and ankles were bound behind his back with gaffer tape. He turned his head and took a sip of a drink through a straw;

another fed a cigarette to his lips. Piles of curled gaffer tape also lay on the floor. I looked at David, who was now standing back beside the window.

"He lost at poker," he said.

It was one of those apartments that it was almost impossible to see into. It had a view facing the street but was too high up and too far from the nearest buildings for anyone to see inside. I'm not sure why I noticed this, or why it bothered me. Yes—I did know, in fact. It was something about the people and the atmosphere in there. The exhausted faces, the voices of a couple of them. This was no party—it was a drug den.

David sat down on a pouffe and drew closer to the chair in which I was sitting. He had lit another cigarette and slowly blew the smoke towards the ceiling. He seemed drunk or high, or both. I took a cigarette from the packet he held out to me.

"Welcome to my humble home. What do you think?"

I laughed.

"It looks like an old man's apartment."

He looked around him, at the furniture and curtains. Only the TV and speakers were new—everything else looked as if it were older than me. David chinked his beer against mine.

"Now it's about time you told me something about yourself."

I laughed again. "Like what?"

"Tell me something exciting. Some trauma from your child-hood, something like that."

I cursed my heart. Could Ingvar or Egil have told him something? No—I trusted them more than that.

"You're the last person I want to tell something 'exciting' to, David."

"How come?"

"I don't trust criminals."

David laughed and lifted an index finger.

"My girl. You don't get how it works. It's precisely the criminals like me you can trust. Criminals don't blab—we have too many skeletons in our own closets."

He was sitting closer to me than I would have liked. Probably wanted to find out whether what he'd managed to get last time was on the cards this time, too—and I had to show him that it wasn't. That's what was so difficult about this guy—I always had to be on my guard. But I refused to give in to that feeling of having to be vigilant all the time.

"I have one important thing to tell you about myself," I said, lifting an index finger just as he had lifted his. "I'm not your girl."

He smiled. Leaned forward slightly and passed his hand over his skull, shaved so closely that it almost shone. My body flinched as he came near, reminding me of the last time we'd seen each other. Such memories always felt wrong to me, as if something were cutting into my body from my belly and upwards. Then he closed his eyes and inhaled through his nose, taking a long drag of the air.

"You smell good," he said.

"Men's aftershave," I said. "I'll ask Egil to give you the name of it."

He laughed.

"You really are a mouthy one, aren't you?"

"People tell me it's my best feature."

"Oh. I can think of another feature or two."

"Go suck a clit," I said.

I got up and staggered away from David's laughter, towards the hall. Found the bathroom and went inside. Sat on the toilet and counted to one hundred, slowly. Then I got up, went across to the sink and rinsed my face with cold water. I didn't know why I felt so bad. That was a lie—I did know. For some reason or other, she had noticed me. And now I'd never see her again.

I pulled my sweater up to my face to dry it and immediately noticed that something felt different. Something was missing. I looked in the mirror. Touched the base of my throat, looking for the smooth chain, but my fingers found nothing but bare skin. The key. It was gone. I had taken it off when I'd showered, and forgotten to put it on again. I thought of how eagerly Egil had clawed after the gold chain on my birthday. If he found it tonight, he would undoubtedly use it. I had to get back there.

Mariam

Kristiansund
Monday, 21 August 2017

The rainwater hits the windshield and trickles in small streams
along the glass. The wipers squeak intermittently. They're on
the second setting, a little too fast for the amount of rain, but
the first setting is too slow. It seems as if the rain is like this
far too often—just this exact amount. I put my foot to the
floor through the sharp bends in the road. The forest becomes
a blurred mass of green; the bills on the dashboard sail back
and forth with each turn.

I take a chance and overtake an old wreck, even though we're
close to a bend, accelerating so I'm past it in an instant. The road
is almost free of cars—it's a Monday afternoon. Just the odd lorry
or tractor on its way somewhere. I drive across the roundabout
and over the bridge, winding down the window to feel the fresh
summer rain on my face. I have to drive, have to keep moving. Can no longer stand to lie there following the train of my
thoughts, that muddled collection of memories—becoming a
mother for the first time, the first smile, the first step, the first

tooth. I'd rather follow the road, let it challenge me, throw my body into the next corner, watch the rain change direction and the pile of bills fly across the dashboard yet again. If only I could drive even faster, turn even more sharply; if only the car could be the weapon with which I made an incision in time. On this side of the cut, my daughter is gone. On the other, maybe there's something else.

You don't leave town when your daughter is missing. You don't leave a note asking your husband not to say anything to the police—to wait, that he has to trust you—only to leave it all behind. Of course I get that. And yet, that's exactly what I've done. The phone containing all the photographs of my daughter, the video from the school play—I left it lying there on the kitchen table with the note. Tor won't like that. Maybe he'll call the police right away. If they want to come looking for me, they'll find me—they can do as they please. The only thing I want, the only thing I can cope with, is to keep moving, turning into the bends and out of them, feeling the car's power in my body and the sense that at any moment I might accelerate too hard, underestimate a corner, make another mistake.

This is what I want. To keep making mistakes until there are none left to make. When I don't know how to release these knots in my body, when they pull tighter and tighter with every attempt to loosen them, I'd rather destroy them. I want to break through and tear them to pieces. To turn and then float across another bridge and into a tunnel that is a single long, gentle curve straight to hell and out the other side. The sheep grazing in the fields are small clouds that vanish. I am constantly in motion. Marinas, boathouses, a dilapidated house atop a hill. Black on the inside, just like me.

The weather has begun to lift, but my head is still dense with fog. I brake, and drive the last few kilometres into Molde ferry terminal more calmly. Signal to turn in and stop at the back of the rows of cars with their rumbling engines, standing there waiting for the ferry. In the rear window of the car in front lies a pale-yellow teddy bear, and behind the teddy bear a small child strapped tightly into a car seat. The driver is a woman, her elbow half out of the window. Brown hair fluttering in the wind. There's somebody sitting in the passenger seat, too—I guess it must be the father. I was so angry at Iben when she was small. Didn't feel I had the family idyll that everyone else seemed to have. I thought she had destroyed my life. But I managed to do that all on my own.

I don't think Tor will have called the police just yet. Now that I've asked him to trust me, he'll try to do so. He'll wait for me to contact him. Will perhaps set himself a deadline. He's good like that—always going the extra mile for me. But do I want to be wrong? Do I want him not to trust me this time, to call the police so they can stop me? There's more than just one answer, more than just a single question.

We start to slowly drive aboard. Across the asphalt and the metal ramp, into the ferry's dark mouth. A man points to a vacant space for me. As the ferry moves off, it hits me that I haven't been on the other side of this fjord in almost twelve years. I'm almost about to faint by the time the ticket seller comes to the window and I pay for my ticket, and forget to take the receipt. Sit and stare into the hard metal as the boat carries me across. There's still more than an hour's drive to go, the winding road across the mountains that will take me home again.

* * *

I signal to the right and slow down. Feel a heat in my diaphragm as I turn onto the road, driving up past the other houses with their swing sets and washing lines, not unlike my own neighbourhood, if a little more rural. Larger gardens, and closer to the sea, where there's a better view. As I drive up the hill, the pile of bills on the dashboard finally lands on the floor. It feels like a relief.

I park at the side of the road. Only around this house does the grass grow tall, and the car outside is missing its tyres and windshield. All kinds of junk are scattered about the yard—a spade without a handle, a dirty rag of a thing that looks like an old tent. I leave my leather handbag in the car along with the rest of my proper family life, which has already begun to come apart at the seams; get out of the car and walk across to the front door. Knock. Those who knock have different intentions from those who use the doorbell. Or at least that's how it was twelve years ago, and the same is probably true now.

Some dogs are barking and running around inside. Carol scolds them as she makes her way towards the door—I can hear her voice, loud and clear. She looks through the peephole. Opens three locks and sticks out her head of curly hair—it's longer now, slightly grey at the temples. She tells off the big Weimaraner that is trying to work its way loose from the grip she has on its collar. The dog snarls and shows its teeth. When she sees me, Carol beams.

"I have to see him," I say.

She laughs, loud and shrill. "Not even a hello for an old friend. I see you haven't lost your rudeness." She chuckles, rolling her American *r*'s.

We walk down the narrow corridor between old family photos, the dogs running around us. The baby pictures of her son have been hanging on the walls for years, always the same. Her husband is dead; her son must have reached adulthood long ago. At the innermost door, Carol pulls out a bunch of keys and unlocks it. Shoos the dogs away as I walk ahead of her. The room is full of cages. There is singing, running, striking at the bars. A parrot begins to fly around its cage, squawking various terms of abuse.

"Now, now, Bella," Carol says, going across to the parrot. It calms down as soon as she begins to speak to it. Carol turns to face me.

"I almost sold him once—somebody made me a good offer a few years back. But I couldn't do that to you. I always believed you'd come back."

Carol moves to the door between the cages. Pulls the bunch of keys from the pocket of her large trousers again; it jangles between her thick fingers with their stubby nails. She unlocks the door.

"I'll leave you be," she says, "but you have to come drink a glass of wine with me afterwards."

She nods towards the door and goes. I place a trembling hand on the door handle. Take a breath.

He's lying on the bed, his body in an arc that stretches from the head end to the bottom. The uppermost part of his body rests on the nightstand. He's detected that I'm in the room; he seeks me out. His body glides, its pattern undulating across the brown skin, all the way from the tip of his tail to his head. It's like a prism of dark brown, black and yellow. I sit down on the bed beside him. Wait for him to gather himself around me. To seek out the heat of my body and embrace me, just like in the old days.

Liv

Ålesund
Saturday, 10 April 2004

When the taxi I got from David's pulled up in front of the house, there was loud music coming from our floor. Even the deaf old landlady must be bothered by noise of this volume. A light was on in one of the windows on the ground floor, so she was probably awake as usual. She'd stopped trying to get us to be quiet long ago.

"Wait here," I said. "I have cash inside."

Before the driver could protest I jumped out of the car, hurried down the stairs and opened the door. The hallway was full of shoes and human voices. People standing outside the bathroom door waiting their turn—it wouldn't be free for ages. If the key was no longer in there, I didn't intend to wait in a queue to find out. I could hear howling, and somebody laughing in the living room. Managed to pull off my boots and hurry towards the door to my room. Suddenly felt a jolt when I pushed down the door handle and the door opened. I went in. Was sure that I'd put Nero in his terrarium before I

locked the room earlier that day. Now it was empty. Nor was
he under the duvet, or under the bed or the chest of drawers.
He wasn't hanging from the curtain rail, hadn't climbed up
into the high plant or onto the lamp he used to get up there.
He wasn't in the room. I checked to see whether the key was
in the door, but that wasn't there, either.

Shaking, I pushed my way between the people who were
standing in the corridor outside. Towards the laughter and
the voices in the living room, the high-pitched squealing that
was coming from there. As calmly as I could, I stepped over
a girl who had decided to sit in the middle of the hall to take
a phone call. I forced my way past a gang of people in the
doorway. Then I stopped. The living room was packed. On
the sofa sat a group of girls with big hair, short skirts and rosy
cheeks. They were the ones who were squealing, and they
didn't show any signs of stopping. They whined in rotation,
the squeals of one replaced by those of another.

On the table, towards which all faces were turned, stood
Egil. He had his back to me. From his right hand hung Nero.
The snake was clearly stressed, hissing at the girls on the sofa.
I thought I could feel the anger burning in his veins. Egil
swayed, keeping his arm outstretched, and without warning
jerked forward as if he were about to throw the snake. The
girls squealed yet again. It was incredible that no glasses were
broken. Egil swayed again—he must be really drunk. He jerked
forward yet again, this time towards a girl who was sitting
in the armchair. The girl let out a scream and spilled beer all
over herself. Egil took a step back. Stood still for a moment
and took a deep breath. Then he turned around and threw
the snake. Nero flew through the air and landed on some
guy's face. The guy flung himself backwards, so that Nero fell

down onto the carpet. I lunged through the crowd. Grabbed the snake, which hissed with rage and lashed out at me. I only just managed to grab him around the neck and stop him from biting me in the shoulder.

"What the fuck are you doing, Egil?"

Egil looked towards me, his face still full of laughter.

"You do that again, and I'll kick you in the balls," I said.

Nero hissed and tried to bite me in the face, but I held him. Had to get back to my room with him.

"Give me the key, Egil."

Egil turned serious and sat down on the edge of the table. Only now did I see that there were several ashtrays on the floor, the ash now trodden into the carpet. Egil was red in the face. He swayed, then pulled himself together.

"I don't have your key. The door was open."

"You're lying."

"I haven't taken any key," Egil mumbled, and lost his balance. He groped around in midair, then landed on the floor. I turned and walked back out into the hall. People thronged around me.

Just then I heard a voice. I heard it through the loud music, despite the stress of having to hold Nero and avoid being bitten, despite the raging words I heard in his hiss. I would have known that voice anywhere. It was coming from Ingvar's room. I took long strides towards the sound; everyone who stood in my path stepped aside. It was coming from in there. He was talking to Ingvar. I stopped in the doorway. His icy-blue eyes met mine, and it felt as if crushed glass ran through my veins.

The sweaty fringe, the face full of pimples he always used to pick at with his fingers. His smile was stiff in the way that always made me nauseous, because it awoke so many memories in me.

"Long time no see," Patrick said.

The scent of him didn't need to reach me—I knew how he smelled. I looked at Ingvar, who immediately lowered his gaze to the floor.

"I trusted you," I whispered.

Roe

Kristiansund
Monday, 21 August 2017

It's already late in the evening by the time I leave the police station. I carry my wide bag under my arm, close to my body, taking long strides up the hill. It's a short walk home, and the summer evening is light, but inside me burns a dark flame. I'm wittingly and wilfully putting the brakes on the entire investigation. I know that I'm doing it. Sneaking around in silence like a thief.

Luckily, the stairwell is quiet when I let myself into my apartment building. I don't like bumping into my neighbours—don't like that they see my face and recognise me, that they say hello. On one of the first days after I moved into the building, the doorbell rang. It was a neighbour who had heard that someone had moved in, and she wanted to come and introduce herself. She was in her fifties, wearing a light dress with pockets on the front, which was a little baggy across her chest. When I told her I was a police officer, she began to tell me about how her nephew had fallen victim to a swindler on the Internet and lost huge sums of money, and that the police had dropped the case. That's the sort of thing people do when they meet me for the first time—they see an opportunity to get help from within the system. From the moment they learn of my profession, they shed their skins and become vultures. I mumbled something about a lack of resources, then lied and said I was just in the middle of dinner, that I needed to get back inside. On the times I've encountered her since then I've looked away, walked faster.

I once harboured an idiotic dream of finding a new family in Kristiansund, of starting again. A truly idiotic dream. Any woman with even a hint of emotional intelligence can tell there's something wrong with me from miles away. And if they can't, I manage to scare them off anyway, sooner or later.

It's dark in my apartment. The windows are at ground level and I don't like the fact that strangers can peek in, so I always keep the curtains closed. I shrug off my jacket and hang it up. There's only one jacket on the hook, only one pair of shoes. It becomes ever easier to be me, yet ever harder. I shove my feet into my slippers. Try to think that I now have some time off—that the stress of the day can be released from my body—but I can't remember what it was like not to feel tense all the time.

I go into the living room, simply furnished with a TV, a coffee table and an old secondhand sofa I bought for a hundred kroner, which smells as if someone has died on it. I clear away the dirty cups and plates, find a cloth from the kitchen and wipe the table before I fetch a roll of plastic wrap. Start to wind it around the tabletop in long strips. Soon the entire table is covered. Then I go back to the kitchen and take a light beer from the fridge.

On the table before me are two Ziploc bags. In the first is a turquoise glitter pen and a notebook taken from the Lind house. In the other is a piece of cardboard cut from the cover of a photo album. I've already got all there is to get from the album—images of the fingerprints are in a separate plastic folder, along with some other documents. Nobody at the station knows about this project, and nor am I going to tell anyone there about it. In matters regarding Mariam Lind, I crossed the boundaries of normal work ethics long ago.

I open my briefcase and take out the bag of equipment I've borrowed from the laboratory. The forensic technicians always take so long to leave before the weekend—they stood there in the lab completing various tasks until late in the evening—so I had to wait until today to take what I needed. The field fingerprint kit for use at crime scenes, with a rabbit-hair brush and black and white dusting powder. I've also borrowed a magnifying glass and a decent flashlight. I take a good swig of the beer before pulling on a pair of plastic gloves. Lay out the equipment on the table. She's held the pen between her thumb and index finger, so I start with that.

I take the brush and choose the white powder. Bend over the tabletop and dip the brush in the jar, carefully shaking off the excess. The powder has a slight shimmer, like white sand. I set the magnifying glass over the pen and lightly tap the powder onto it; turn the pen and brush it some more. Repeat the process until I think I can see some ridges starting to take shape. At the pen's tip I think a fingerprint is beginning to appear. It might be my own. I work the brush with care, applying several light coats. Can almost hear Mariam Lind's trembling voice when I asked her where she went after Iben disappeared. Even the voice of the devil can tremble. I know what I'm going to find—I just want to be sure. I apply several more coats of powder to the fingerprint and see it become clearer, more visible. Then I take a plastic strip and carefully cut out a piece I can use. Rub the glue side of the strip against the fingerprint with even strokes before I lift it off and press it down against the ink plate.

I'm left with a little fingerprint. It looks like the middle of a finger. It might be too small for identification on its own, but it might be of help if I find more on the notebook. I set the brush and white powder aside. Take out the notebook, the box of black powder and the other brush. When I open the box, powder flows out over my fingers. Like the white powder, it's finer than ash, and difficult to control. I dip the brush into it, then repeat the painstaking process by brushing the paper. The paper is high quality—far easier to obtain fingerprints from this than cheap notepaper. I find many fingerprints, and several of them will be mine, but I have plenty of time. The black powder is much easier to see with the naked eye.

I find the photographs of the fingerprints from the photo album. Study the new prints under the magnifying glass in the light of the flashlight and compare them. I take a swig of beer. They're only partial prints. My methods are reprehensible. But now even the slightest hint of doubt is gone. The prints are identical. It's her.

As soon as I've gathered my wits, I get up and walk out into the hallway. I think of Iben, the beautiful blond-haired little girl, the way she looked when she came running out of the shopping centre. I open the door to my bedroom and turn on the ceiling light of a dark, unpleasant place. The blinds are always drawn; I hardly know what the view from here looks like. I can no longer sleep in here—the darkness is too heavy for that—and I can't let in the light for fear that someone will see the photographs that fill my wall. Hundreds of photographs, collected over the past few months, cover the wall from floor to ceiling. Old and new images, young people drinking and partying, dancing, smoking. Their eyes red from the flash as they look towards the camera. A young girl with dark hair holding a snake, smiling at the person taking the picture. In the new images she's older. Her hair is blond, and shorter. In the newspaper clipping from *Tidens Krav*, she smiles in her neatly pressed shirt, pearl earrings in her ears. She looks like someone else. In the other photographs she's generally looking away. They're taken from a distance, from behind a bush or a corner. Speaking on the phone, or on her way somewhere at top speed. I've taken the newer photographs on my mobile and printed them out. Times have changed. This room also testifies to that.

I had an opportunity to speak to Iben one morning in July. Had driven around their neighbourhood many times to see if I could find anyone from the family. In the end, she came walking along, alone. I rolled down the window and asked whether she was Mariam Lind's daughter; said I was her mother's friend. After that first meeting I hadn't seen her again. Not until Friday, when I had gone out to buy a shirt at Storkaia before going to that cursed birthday party.

Something quivers within me—it always does when I'm in here. It's like staring straight into a hole in time. I open the door to the wardrobe, where the knife is in place in the tie drawer. I haven't owned a tie since the nineties, so the drawer contains nothing but the knife. I take it out, test the edge of the blade against my nail. It's been recently whetted, so it's at its sharpest.

I put the knife back in the drawer and close the wardrobe door. Stare into the mirror on the front of it, opening my eyes as wide as possible so that I can see myself, how crazy I am. Roe—the raging, the furious. Then I open the other wardrobe.

"Hi, Iben," I say.

Iben doesn't answer. She doesn't move an inch. But her eyes meet mine, in silence.

Reptile memoirs

Those first small twists across the floor of my new home were eager. I quickly perceived that I was somewhere "inside," and began looking for a way out. Slithered alongside walls and under furniture, licking the air for the taste of rain and leaves. But I found only dead wood and dust, materials made by humans. The only living thing in the room apart from me and the warm woman was a plant, and even that was trapped.

I had only just managed to figure out that I had been moved to a slightly larger prison when she threw herself over me. She lifted me up, turned her body from vertical to horizontal, and lay down flat beside me so that all parts of her body were at the same level, like mine. When she lay this way, she immediately looked much smaller. I realised that the size of these animals was only a form of camouflage. They protect themselves by attempting to appear much bigger than they really are.

With her apish hands she clawed at me, everywhere, wanting to squeeze me against her body. For us to lie pressed together, as if we were two members of the same species. I tried to bite her, but her naked ape hands held my head. Even hissing seemed not to scare this human.

Eventually she let me go and concentrated on herself. For the first time, I saw an animal touch its own reproductive organs. I lay there, observing how she moved her long limbs, how gracefully her hands slipped across her body. I tried to imagine how it must feel to have such a body. One that could choose between horizontal and vertical, could bend at an angle and rest head against arms, arms against legs. Which had hands that could perform all kinds of tasks. An animal that could touch its own body. I admit that I was fascinated that first time, but my interest would soon wear off. I would soon come to hate this woman just as intensely as I did the first one.

At night, she lay close to me beneath the blanket, so close that I could taste the sweetish salt of her sweat with my tongue. She touched her own reproductive organs for pleasure. The scents that rose from her became stronger then; her sweat and the taste of her came closer. I lay in the dark and felt a tension tighten in my teeth; I became hungry.

She needed me. She seemed not to be able to function with other humans—that must be why she did things with me and not with them. If anyone could give me all I hungered and longed for, it was this woman. She was my only hope. That's why I continued to lie there, and that's also why I began to whisper faint little prayers to her in the night.

PART TWO

Liv

Ålesund
Tuesday, 8 June 2004

The rabbit sat on the bed. The fat, helpless creature was using all the senses it had to try to find out if the room was safe. Its long ears moved, seeking sounds. Its nose twitched up and down. Shining black eyes stared at me like an accusation. I bent down and patted it on the head. The rabbit flinched at my touch and started breathing more quickly.

Nero came creeping from behind, across my leg. He moved quickly now that he had caught the scent of the prey. The rabbit was too fat and heavy to escape his supple coil. Nero surrounded the animal with ease, his fangs snagging in its neck and forcing the animal down onto the bed. Then he began the slow process of opening his jaws over it.

As I came, the pleasure mixed with a nausea that slithered through my guts, filling my mouth with a sour taste. I pulled the duvet over my head to block out the sight, to ease the queasy feeling that increased with every piece of prey I

watched him devour. I tried in vain to muffle the sound of
Nero's whispering thanks.

Outside the window, the constant sound of passing cars
could be heard, and I could smell cooking from the restaurant
on the ground floor. I set my feet on the tiny patch of floor
in this closet of a room, where there was just space enough
for my bed and a kitchen counter with a hot plate and small
microwave. My clothes lay in a pile on the floor, my textbooks
in a stack by the door. The room was also too expensive for
me—far too expensive—but it was the best I'd been able to rent
at short notice without having to pay three months' deposit.
After what happened, I'd packed up my most necessary belongings and fled here the very next morning. Now I couldn't stand
being here, but I didn't have anywhere else to go, except the
university. It was Tuesday. Since the night Ingvar had betrayed
me, I hadn't wanted to speak to either him or Egil. And other
than them, I had nobody in my life.

Nero was still working to swallow the prey. This had long
since stopped being a game. If he didn't get what he wanted,
his whispering could keep me awake all night. It wore me down
until my body took over, becoming a weak-willed servant who
stood in the queue at the pet shop in order to quench his insa-
tiable needs. He had grown so much since we got him. I'd read
on the Internet that adult tiger pythons needed large prey, such
as lambs or piglets. Where was I going to get hold of a lamb?

I couldn't stay here. I had to get out of this tin can of a
room, regardless of whether I had somewhere to go or not. I
pulled on my jeans and hoodie. Decided simply to get out,
anywhere, just to walk.

Outside, the wind made it difficult to keep my hood up.
I walked down to the wharf and stood there looking into

the dark water that foamed far below, the boats that rocked. Took my phone from my pocket. There were a dozen or so missed calls, most of them from Ingvar and Egil, a few from an unknown number, and the rest from the woman who called herself my mother. She who saw fit to ask me for an apology, while at the same time looking her son in the eyes and accepting his version of events. Who could call me and force all the memories down over my head. They made me sick, all of them. I considered dropping the phone, watching it disappear into the dark water, but changed my mind and put it back in my pocket.

The wind blew my hood from my head yet again, sending my hair out in all directions. I pulled it up once more, turning to stand with my back to the wind. I followed the water to the end of the quay and glanced up at the traffic lights, where I could see the Kremmergaarden shopping centre up ahead. I could warm up a little in the shopping centre or the library, but I didn't want to bump into people. I already walked around too much. Ålesund was not a town in which you wandered restlessly. Here, if you wandered around long enough, you became part of the urban landscape, a curiosity. Still, I had to wander. The only alternative was to sit locked in a room with my own darkness. So I walked to the right and followed the quay farther along. Thought I could walk to the bus station, see whether there was a bus I could get on, get away. Start again, somewhere else entirely. But strangely enough, that didn't feel like an option. It was as if I didn't believe it was possible. This body, eating itself up from the inside out, would be with me no matter where I went.

Instead, I continued over the Hellebroa bridge, walking to the right towards Apotekergata and on past the old buildings, past two hotels and down until I found water again. There, through an underpass, I came to the street that contained the old wooden buildings that remained from before the big city fire. Continued my restless wandering past the old pier and onwards. I just wanted to walk until I was out of breath. Then I saw a poster on the wall of the old factory. GRADUATION EXHIBITION— ÅLESUND ART COLLEGE. The opening was in two days' time.

I came to a stop. Stared at the painting featured on the poster. A dark-haired girl with something in her eyes, a darkness.

She had captured me well.

Ronja

Kristiansund
Tuesday, 22 August 2017

"Stop tarting yourself up, Ronja. You're not going on a date."

Birte laughs at me as she signals right and turns off the main road. Birte often laughs at me, emitting tiny grunting sounds from her nose when she does. I flip up the sun visor. Feel my cheeks grow hot as I fix the last lock of hair in place with a clip.

"I'm not tarting myself up. I just think it's irritating to have loose bits of hair flying around."

Birte lets out yet another grunt.

"But it suits you like that. You know it does."

She lets locks of her red hair fall into her freckled face without thinking anything of it. Birte, who always stands up straight and keeps her elbows slightly away from her body to make herself look bigger, although I don't think she does this consciously. It's a habit, an unconscious defensive posture.

"I want to challenge you, Ronja," she says. "You've been silent, just listening, during our inquiries so far. It's a good and useful tactic that one of us talks while the other listens and takes notes, but you need the practice. So today I think you should have a go."

I've had plenty of practice. We practised on each other at the Police University College, employing all available methods to ensure effective questioning. We made a good team when we practised together, putting our best acting skills to use and laughing a lot. Interviews were a game. It isn't the same with a proper case—one without any set answers or tutors or grades, and where a real person's life is at stake. Not that I didn't conduct interviews during my training—I did. Still, I often choose to withdraw. It happens automatically.

"I know," I say. "It's just that you're so good at it. You always know the right questions to ask straightaway. I only realise what I should have asked when I hear you say it. It would be stupid if we missed something important."

Birte glances in the mirror and turns into the car park of the local outpatient psychiatric clinic.

"You've read all the textbooks, Ronja—you know what to do. Ask open questions where possible and let them talk. Don't interrupt. This guy will be challenging, but he's asked to have a nurse present, so we'll have help in handling the situation. I think you'll do just fine."

Birte finds a parking space and pulls into it with the greatest of ease. Turns the key in the ignition.

"We'll play it this way: you talk, I keep quiet. If I think you're ruining something—which I highly doubt is going to happen—I'll interrupt. Okay?"

Birte is . . . I like Birte. She doesn't use the kinds of expressions some of the men use—*good girl*—as if being good is something negative. And unlike several of the others, she didn't comment out of the blue on the fact that everyone saw me dancing with August on Friday. With Birte, I brought it up myself, and it was really nice to have somebody to talk to, knowing that our conversation wouldn't be repeated in the break room later on. Birte is cool. In her spare time she's a member of an amateur theatre company. She's tried to get me to come along to a rehearsal, but I'm not good at stuff like that, at acting. But Birte is fantastic—the times I've seen her onstage it's been like watching another person. She can make people laugh and cry.

I introduce us at reception and say that we're here to talk with Robert Kirkeby.

"We've arranged to meet him here," I say, feeling Birte's gaze at the back of my neck.

A couple of minutes later a woman with short grey hair comes over to us. She gives each of us a firm handshake, and introduces herself as the psychiatric nurse Kirkeby has asked to be present during our conversation. She shows us into a meeting room containing a long table and chairs. The fluorescent ceiling lamp casts a cool light over the white room. The nurse stays standing as Birte and I sit.

"Robert has asked me to inform you of his diagnosis in advance," she says. "He's been diagnosed with paranoid psychosis. He struggles with delusions relating to conspiracies against him, and he often has problems expressing himself in a way that is comprehensible because he confuses reality and his delusions. Recently, he's read a lot in the newspapers about the decision to build the new regional hospital at Hjelset in Molde, and what that means for the hospital here in Kristiansund. He's created his own fantasy about the hospital, which often comes up when we're trying to talk about something else. It's important to remember that he doesn't lie, nor does he see people who aren't really there, but he can be challenging to communicate with. He can also seem intense, but as far as we're aware, he's never been violent."

My heart pounds as she speaks. I remember one of the tests at the Police University College when I had to handle an aggressive man, someone who called me all kinds of terrible things and who threatened to kill me. I try to remember how it felt, to prepare myself mentally.

"On the day Iben disappeared, it's probable that he was in Nordlandet," the nurse says. "He lives in the area and didn't have an appointment here until later in the day. He's regarded as well enough to live on his own and be a day patient at the clinic. We know that he often walks around the town centre when he isn't here."

Paranoid people don't tolerate being contradicted very well. That was something my tutor told me at some point. The best tutor I've ever had, with so much experience and who took such joy in teaching. It was as if all of Norway's police stations moved into the classroom.

"Is he prepared for the interview to be recorded?"

The nurse nods. "We've explained that that's necessary in order to be able to use his information in the investigation. He's afraid of becoming a suspect himself, but he seems content with the fact that he's only being interviewed as a witness." The nurse flicks aside her grey fringe.

"Thank you," I say.

As the nurse goes to fetch Robert Kirkeby I meet Birte's eyes, which have a twinkle of laughter in them. She can see that I'm nervous.

"You can do this, Ronja. You're doing great."

She lifts her hand in a high five, at which I feel embarrassingly touched, but I return it. Then the door opens, and into the room walks a young man of around my age. He has dark hair that's slightly too long, and he looks exhausted. His shoulders are hunched; instead of meeting anyone's gaze, he looks down at the table. The nurse sits down beside him.

"This is Ronja Solskinn and Birte Lie," she says. "As we discussed, they'd like to ask you a few questions. Is that okay?"

Robert Kirkeby casts a quick glance up at me and Birte before he looks down at the table again and nods. He whispers something, his voice so low that none of us catches it.

"What was that, Robert?" asks the nurse.

He continues to whisper. I catch a few words, think he's maybe saying something about Tom Cruise, but I'm not sure. He seems extremely confused and anxious. It's hard to imagine him seeming threatening, but his mood may of course swing.

I clear my throat.

"Hi, Robert," I say. "My name is Ronja. I'd just like to let you know that this interview is being recorded. You're being interviewed as a witness in connection with Iben Lind's disappearance. Could you tell us what you told us on the telephone?"

He looks up at me, his eyes suddenly sharp.

"What do you get? What do you get? Tor Lind's daughter is big business. How do you know what and what not, the city council has organised the whole thing against Kristiansund hospital and the city, everyone ends up rotting away in their graves before the ambulance comes, it's the council's fault."

His voice is suddenly high-pitched and shrill; it sounds as if he's on the verge of tears. His eyes are full of anger and pain.

I take a deep breath, can feel that I'm struggling to stop my voice from shaking.

"Can you tell us what you know about Tor Lind's daughter? Have you seen her?"

"Little blond girl. In all the newspapers and on TV, they're all showing photos of the missing girl, nobody cares about the man she talked to, no pictures of him, oh no, none." His breath comes in brief panting thrusts; he lifts his narrow shoulders all the way up to his ears. "Little blond girl in the newspapers, but no big man, oh no, nobody writing about him, all the newspapers are looking down at the ground, nobody cares about the city council, that they want to tear down the walls around us. They throw it right in your face and you refuse to see it, turn away, what about all the dead, what about them? Tom Cruise—he's the one they're paying. Tom Cruise is getting the money, hanging off the mountainside, the rest of us have to watch the walls being torn down around us, the hospital we have to get rid of, *Tom Cruise* is the one we want." He hawks and spits a huge glob of phlegm onto the table in front of him. Slams two fists down into the spit, making the tape recorder jump.

"You mentioned a man," I say. "Who Iben Lind talked to. Did you see her talking to this man?"

He turns his head in a sudden movement and sets his eyes on me.

"That's what I'm saying! They don't listen. The man talked to her, and then she was gone. Nobody cares. The newspapers are just sticking up pictures of a sweet little girl and nobody cares. It's the same with—"

"Where did you see this man?" I know I'm not really supposed to interrupt the witness, but with Robert I have to do
something to stop him from constantly going off the rails. It
works—he stops mid-flow.

"Listen to me! Tor Lind was in on it, the city council and
the hospital, he was in on it and now his daughter, sweet girl.
Nobody comes dragging a man with a wide jaw and grey shirt
when it's Tor Lind, Tor Lind and his daughter. The man gets
to go on killing girls, controlling them and killing them, he's
evil, evil. His nose like a big hook, like a witch. In Storgata, at
Storkaia. Grey shirt and a carrier bag in his hand from Cubus.
I should have killed him there and then."

"How close were you?" I ask. "Were you close enough to
hear what they said?"

He shakes his head, hard.

"Spoke quiet, spoke quiet, and planned how they would
exterminate us all. It's like with all the dead, those who can no
longer speak. I know that they hear us, they want to drag us
down to them. She walked away. He was furious, he wanted
something from her, but she walked away."

My heart is pounding. Could this really be something?

"Where did Iben go?"

"Up the road, she kept going up towards Langveien. The
man watched her. Probably planning how he was going to
make sure that the money got to Tom Cruise, it's no use thinking we can change them, they hate us, want to destroy our city,
calling us all towards the earth." His two fists hit the tabletop
again with a bang. "You think it's one of the lunatics, of course
you think so, you never think the powers that be are at fault,
but the powers that be are always guilty. He killed that beautiful
little girl, and you're in on it too, you're in on it." He throws

himself forward and puts his head in his hands. Begins to sob loudly, his face behind his palms.

"I think that's enough for now," the nurse says, taking Robert Kirkeby's hand. "Don't you think so, Robert? That we should stop it there?"

Robert nods and gets up. His cheeks are wet with tears, but he seems to be breathing more calmly and his eyes are clearer.

"I know who it is," he says in a low voice. "You can't make me forget it, no matter how hard you might want to. You'll have to kill me first."

Then he permits himself to be led from the room.

"How do you think it went?" Birte gets into the car on the driver's side.

I'm shaking. Take a box of cough drops from my bag and put two in my mouth. Chew, just to be in motion.

"It wasn't exactly easy."

"You did really well. For someone so new to this, you're great. I mean it."

For someone so new to this. Did she have to put it like that?

"He blamed us."

Birte snorts as she starts the car.

"He also thought Tom Cruise was involved, although I'm pretty sure he was busy elsewhere."

"Do you think we can use any of what he said? The description he gave of the man—can we use it for anything?"

"It'll be difficult. We have to report it, but he's . . ." Birte whistles and makes a hand gesture beside her head, which I find inappropriate. The whole situation is just so sad. That someone has to go around feeling so tormented—has to wander around town afraid of everything and everyone, from politicians to ordinary strangers.

"We have a description," I say. "Perhaps somebody else has seen the same man?"

Birte nods. "We should definitely give the media something to run with, and ask the man to get in touch," she says. "But it's Shahid's decision, of course."

She drives towards Gomalandet for the next witness on our list. A man who believes he saw Iben all the way out there on Saturday morning—something I consider to be highly unlikely.

"He might have a point with his thing about the hospital," I say. "People have been angry at the city's politicians for sacrificing the hospital's location. Could someone have been so angry that they wanted to exact revenge on Tor Lind?"

Birte shrugs again.

"Lind has received threats before, although none of them have ever involved Iben. But who knows? People do plenty of crazy things."

"I feel so sorry for the family," I say. "It's not been possible to speak with Mariam Lind over the past few days, only the husband. She must be so low, to just lock herself away because she can't even bear to participate in the search for her own daughter. I wonder what makes someone kidnap a little girl like that—what makes someone think he has the right to do such a thing."

Birte stops for a red light and frowns.

"It isn't my job to understand the feelings behind people's actions," she says. "I just want to catch the asshole who did it."

That's wrong, I think. Because in order to catch the asshole, you have to understand why he acted as he did. How can you figure out the who and what if you can't link the actions to the feelings behind them?

"I'm still shaking." I laugh. "You would have done so much better than me."

"Oh, stop it," says Birte. "You were great! And by the way, if you think you need more input, you can always watch recordings of previous interviews. I think that can often be useful. Roe Olsvik, for example—he's a good role model. How about watching some of his recordings?"

"Roe seems so . . . I just think he seems to be carrying so much." I don't know why I say this.

"Well. He's extremely competent. And seems to care about what he does. Like the kind of loners you see on crime series on TV. Just you wait—it'll turn out he's undertaking some secret investigation on the side." Birte blinks.

I shudder.

"So which one of us is the female police officer sidekick with the stern expression, who always does everything right?"

Birte laughs. "Doesn't sound like anybody I know."

It occurs to me that I could have asked who she thinks is the young female police officer who sleeps with an older colleague. *That* would be me, of course. He's not an *old* man, though—and certainly not my boss. And anyway, I *haven't* slept with any of my colleagues. Just exchanged some saliva. *Ugh.*

"Roe's little speech at yesterday's morning meeting—it was hard to watch. I just don't get how a policeman with so many years of experience . . ."

"True, Ronja—but even the best of us make mistakes. Do as you like. You can listen to my interviews too, if you think I'm such a good interviewer." Birte takes a left. "Want to come out for a beer tonight? It's the opening night party."

I've been out with Birte and her friends a few times; they're always so full of energy and self-confidence. Playing out their acting dreams in the bar of the Grand Hotel, laughing too loudly at each other's jokes and making a scene by yawning theatrically and patronisingly when I say it's time to go home. I like them—it isn't that. They're too cool for me, or maybe I just don't fit in. One of the best things about being at the Police University College was the sense of belonging we all felt in being part of the police force—it was fine if you didn't care about much other than that. We all spoke the same language. I miss it.

"I need to work out," I say. "And after that, I think I need to prioritise getting as much sleep as possible. I'm planning on working for as long as I can tomorrow."

Birte laughs at me again as she reverses between two parked cars.

"Workaholic," she says.

Liv

Ålesund
Thursday, 10 June 2004

I picked up a glass of sparkling wine from the table of welcome drinks. Cast a glance around the old factory premises with its columns and white-painted walls. There were few places to hide. A couple dozen people were already walking around with price lists in their hands, studying the artworks—a video installation consisting of a torn-up map that was set out on a table, a sculpture constructed of industrial pallets, a collage of sheets of cursive handwriting and notebook pages. At the other end of the premises I could see the outline of my own face. I did my best to sneak around the edge of the room, sticking close to the wall, until I reached the portrait.

She had painted me with my shoulders bare, my hair wet and slightly tousled. Long, gentle strokes, as if done with care. Although I wasn't sure why I thought the person who had painted this picture had wanted to do something good. Now, looking at the painting again, I saw that not everything in it looked like me. She hadn't got the shape of the face quite right; the lips were a little too large, the nose too narrow. The painting seemed like a slightly blurred memory. Still, she'd done a good job after having seen me only once, for a few minutes.

The strongest thing about the painting was the eyes. The woman in the picture had eyes so dark they looked like deep holes, or black stones. They seemed impaled by something sharp. But at the same time there was life in them, something that insisted on its own existence. That gaze frightened me. I couldn't say that it was a realistic gaze—it was too brutal for that. Still, I recognised it so well that it hurt.

At that moment I heard someone say Anita's name. I turned and saw her come in, smiling in a loose pale-blue summer dress with a hemline that came to just below her knees. Her blond hair was put up, and she had huge hoops in her ears. She accepted hugs from this direction and that, and was handed a bouquet of yellow, red and white flowers that were radiant against her blue dress. Beside her stood a man of Ingvar's age, but with a far shorter and more well-groomed dark beard. He seemed to know the same people she did.

I immediately regretted coming. Felt weird, out of place and trapped at the far end of the room, not knowing how I was going to get out without her seeing me. I turned to face the painting again. Suddenly I thought that the girl in the picture looked so naive, almost childish, and that there was something disgusting about her. Something dirty.

"Liv!"

Anita came towards me with long strides and threw her arms around my neck. The locks of her hair closed themselves around me; her bouquet of flowers crackled at my back.

"It's so great to see you!"

"Actually, I have to leave," I mumbled, regretting it as soon as I saw her face change. "Nice painting."

"I'll walk you out," she said. "Mamma, could you hold these?"

She passed the bouquet of flowers to a blond-haired woman who looked strikingly like her, only older. We walked out into the cool evening wind, sat down on some steps.

"I tried to call you," she said. "I got your number from Egil. He says you moved out, that there was some kind of trouble between you. He wouldn't tell me what it was."

"Long story," I said, looking down at my hands.

"I wanted to tell you about the painting before the exhibition, but I couldn't get hold of you. I hope it was okay. You don't think it's rude, do you, seeing as I don't even know you?"

I shook my head. "I like it. It's pretty impressive that you managed that, having hardly even seen me."

"You know, I *was* pretty rude. I was going to ask you if you wanted to model for me, but I couldn't get hold of you. So I borrowed a photograph from Egil."

Anita folded her dress around her thighs. As she did so, I thought her belly had become rounder since the last time we met.

"Yeah, that's really fucking rude." I laughed.

"I can't stay away too long," she said, "but I mean it, it was really nice that you came."

She pushed a stray strand of hair behind her ear. "Listen, Birk goes to sea next week, he works four weeks on and four weeks off."

"Birk?"

She waved the question away with her hand.

"When he goes, I'll have the house to myself. Would you like to model for another painting? So maybe it'll be better this time?"

I thought about the painting back inside the gallery, the dark eyes that seemed somehow impaled. Had she used some red in them, and some white, too? How had she managed to make them look both living *and* dead?

"If I dare," I said.

Mariam

Ålesund
Tuesday, 22 August 2017

I stick the spade in just as the water withdraws, filling it with wet sand that I drop into a yellow bucket. The waves embrace my legs. It's neither hot nor cold. I pat down the top of the sand in the bucket to make it as hard as possible. Turn the bucket upside down so that it sets yet another tower on top of the four that already stand there. Iben is on her knees, eagerly digging out a moat. She's wearing her white sun hat, her face turned down as she focuses on her work, digging even though the water continually returns to tear down everything she's built. She stops. Sticks a chubby hand down into the sand to grab a stone.

"Look, Mamma!"

She gives the stone to me. It's white and smooth beneath my thumb.

"That's nice," I say. "We have to put that on the top."

I hand the stone back to her. She takes it, stretching to set it atop the sand castle. She's four years old. Full of energy. I'm tired—very, very tired—but at the same time so terribly happy to have her, right now.

A piercing, dazzling light breaks through, and around me the world changes colour. Through a haze of sea and blond hair, I'm looking at a wall covered in flowered wallpaper. I sit up in bed, and reality washes over me. She's gone. Someone has taken her from me. Outside, I hear Carol trying to calm the parrot that is flapping and screeching. "Shut up! Goddamn parrot," the parrot shrieks with a dark voice I assume once belonged to Carol's deceased husband.

My head feels heavy after drinking wine with Carol yesterday evening. I turn and see Nero lying there, stretching out his long body. He's now as thick as my thigh, and so long and heavy that if I want to lift and move him, I have to do it in several rounds. His tail hangs down towards the floor, out of sight. When I stroke his back, a quiver runs through my entire body. I didn't think it was possible to feel any more connected to him than I did back then. But now the connection is so strong that it frightens me. I slip beneath his belly, feeling the power of his muscles, and think I'm going to explode from the inside.

Carol lives in a house with many rooms. Doors line the walls, one after the other, as if in a student house. She runs a major operation here, with various animals that are imported into the country, both legally and illegally. Snakes, lizards and fighting dogs. She waves to me as I walk past a room in which she's throwing feed into an aquarium. Her hair is twisted into a large bun on the top of her head, and she's wearing long black gloves. I go into the bathroom. The shower curtain has been drawn aside, and the bathtub is full of water. In it swim a dozen sea turtles that stick their heads up from the water's surface in order to watch me and draw breath.

Yesterday she told me that several people had asked her whether it was she who had the penguins that were thought to have been stolen from Ålesund aquarium a while ago. Carol laughed her usual high-pitched laugh as she told me about it. I find a tube of toothpaste in a cabinet above the sink and look at myself in the mirror. I look ten years older than I did just a few days ago.

The radio fills the kitchen with sugar-sweet pop music. Carol is standing at the closest of the overfilled kitchen's two stoves, swaying in time to the music as she heats milk in a saucepan. Her hands—short fingers, stubby nails—touch her face. She still doesn't wear makeup, doesn't dress up, and lets her breasts hang loose inside a baggy grey sweater. Still, she looks attractive with her grizzled curls. When she was young, she always wore bright colours and heavy makeup. Carol Holloway, a Norwegian American actress who starred in more than a few B movies in the eighties, before she'd had a child with a Norwegian and moved to Norway. She's shown me photographs of how she looked back then, with the baby in her arms and an overly painted face, her head still full of dreams of making it big as an actress. When those dreams were shattered and replaced by new business activities, the need to dress up also disappeared. Now she seems to be facing old age—and the extra kilos she carries—with satisfaction.

"You look good, Carol."

She snorts. "That's the most ridiculous thing I've ever heard."

She pours hot coffee from the pot into two cups, then empties the hot milk into them from the little saucepan. It's always surprised me that there are two stoves in this room. The one at the farthest end is older, and perhaps never used. Carol loves old things. The walls are decorated with old kitchen utensils and rosemålt porcelain. It's like a miniature museum.

I lift the coffee cup she's given me—it has the word *Mamma* on the front, the letters decorated with flowers. The music is interrupted by the familiar melody that indicates the start of the news. Iben is still the main subject; a witness is said to have seen her speaking to a man before she disappeared. The police are asking the man to come forward.

The thought makes me cold. A man. They don't say anything about what he looked like—old or young, tall or short. There was a man, and Iben still hasn't been found. Then the newsreader changes topic. No search for Iben's mother, Mariam Lind. I don't know whether that's because they don't know where to find me or because Tor has chosen not to say anything. And if the latter is the case, how long will it take before they figure it out for themselves?

"I have to have him with me, Carol."

Now the tears come, too. This isn't the first time I've cried in this house, but I'm equally surprised every time I do. It's as if something about Carol's home opens something within me that has previously been closed off.

Carol presses herself against me, putting her arm around my shoulders.

"There, there."

She says no more than this—I'm the one who speaks. The words come in brief bursts, as if something is blocking them.

I try to put all the impressions from the last few days into words, give them names. Carol rubs my back as I speak, big movements with the flat of her hand. My tears stain her grey sweater. She smells of cigarette smoke and something else, something sweet.

"The worst thing, Carol," I say, "is that I actually believed I didn't love her. I thought that it was just a game. That I was pretending."

"Love is not a constant, dear," says Carol. "You don't feel just the one thing. Don't you know that?"

"I'm a pendulum," I say.

I'm a pendulum, swinging between love and destruction. I build up and tear down. I protect and preserve, only to crush everything in the very next moment. When you look at me, you see me as I am—a loving, caring wife and mother who adores my husband and my child. It isn't a game—that woman is no less me than the one who would have liked to see everything go to hell, who finds a perverse joy in the fact that her family is about to be destroyed forever. The person you see when you look at me is also the opposite of who I am. That which is real is also a game. A self-contradiction, but no impossibility.

"Is there anything I can do?" Carol asks. "If there is, just tell me."

She blows another cloud of smoke towards the ceiling.

"I have to have Nero with me. I need him if I'm going to get through this."

"I think I told you I received an offer for him? They wanted to take his skin and make a jacket, or something like that. It was a good price they were offering, too, but I could never have done that to you."

"That means so much to me, Carol. Of course I'll buy him back. Just name your price."

Carol waves the hand in which she's holding her cigarette.

"I'll give you a very good price, dear. Very good—and next time, don't leave it so long before you come back."

Liv

Ålesund
Wednesday, 16 June 2004

I'd almost given up waiting when she finally came to the door. She smiled with her crooked front teeth, her blond locks bold, her face free of makeup. She was wearing a white top flecked with paint. It was stretched tight around her waist and hugged her belly in a way that left no doubt that she was pregnant.

"I'm so glad you came," she said. "I'm just putting the finishing touches to a painting—do you want to come up?"

Her top was a little too short, revealing the tattoo on her back when she turned. I followed her up a spiral staircase to the first floor, into a room that had been fitted out as a studio. An easel stood beside the only window; tubes of paint and brushes lay strewn across a table. On the walls hung canvases featuring all kinds of motifs. Paintings of forests and animals; several self-portraits, or portraits of other people. I bent closer to inspect a painting of a man with a closely cropped black beard, black hair, black eyebrows. He had rolled-up shirtsleeves, his hands on his hips. His arms looked strong; muscular and hairy. It was the man I'd seen her with at the exhibition.

"Birk hates modelling for me," she laughed. "That's one of the few times I've managed to get him to do it."

There was something hard in his gaze, as if he were hiding a side of himself you probably wouldn't want to get to know. I wondered whether the painting exposed something about their relationship.

"You're really good," I said.

She shook her head.

"The painting makes him look older than he really is. He didn't like it. Thought I'd painted him as a mixture of himself and my father." She laughed again, a tenderness in the sound.

I turned to the next painting, a self-portrait in which she was half dressed, with a naked gaze.

"It's beautiful," I said, reaching out a hand to touch the painted version of her collarbone. Then my cheeks flushed hot, and I withdrew my hand. Anita blushed, too, and turned towards the painting she was currently working on. A woman nailed to a cross by one arm, her head turned towards the sea. Behind her the sky was dark; the clouds appeared heavy with rain, and a strong wind blew her hair in front of her face.

"That's intense," I said.

Anita smiled.

"I'm inspired by stories about women who waited for their men, back when they were all out at sea. They didn't know whether they would ever return."

Using her brush, she mixed two colours on her palette and applied fresh paint to the woman's throat. Anita seemed older in these surroundings. Not only because of the bump at her stomach, but because of the house around her. An old house, its floors lacquered with a dark varnish. I wondered which incarnation was most Anita—the young girl I met in the flatshare bathroom, or the grown woman before the easel. I liked both versions.

The daylight from the skylight above cast a mystical sheen over the room. As Anita painted, I walked beside the walls and tables, looking at all the objects there. Piles of paper and sketches, boxes of charcoal, tubes of paint, chests of art supplies.

"What's this?" I asked, lifting up an object made of compact glass, consisting of two balls on top of each other, like a snowman. It was much heavier than it looked, and it glinted in the light.

"It's a glass muller," she said. "It's for grinding pigments to make paint. I hardly ever use it—I buy tubes of oil paint—but it makes a good paperweight."

I put the muller down. Went and sat in an armchair in a corner and studied Anita, how she seemed to become one with the painting on which she was working. It felt good to be in her company. There was something simple about it, which I liked. If we became friends, that's how I wanted it to be—uncomplicated. But at the same time, something gnawed at me, something unclear.

She laughed then, put her hands to her belly.

"The baby's kicking," she said. "I only started to feel her doing it a couple of days ago. It tickles."

"It's a girl?"

"We're going to call her Aurora."

"How pretty," I said. "I love the northern lights."

She looked down at her stomach, stroked it a couple of times.

"How long have you been together?" I asked, pointing at the man in the painting.

She gestured towards a stack of cardboard boxes in the corner.

"I moved in here at the start of this month."

"When we last met, I thought you were Egil's latest conquest," I said.

She laughed, and again I heard the tenderness in her laughter. She took a step back from the painting, reached out her hand, and made a tiny white brushstroke at the woman's throat before withdrawing her paintbrush.

"There."

We stood for a moment, considering the woman in the painting, her face half turned away so that it was impossible to see what emotions she was hiding. Maybe the stormy clouds said something about what was going on inside her, but it was ambiguous.

"Now it's your turn," Anita said. "Do you want to get undressed?"

My cheeks burned.

"Oh, you meant naked?"

"If that's okay?"

I turned my back to her and began to take off my clothes. She had seen me naked before, but undressing deliberately was different. Now the whole point was for her to look at me. I set my clothes in a pile on the floor and sat down in the armchair in the corner.

"Is it okay like this?"

She nodded, and I now saw that her cheeks were red, too. She picked up a brush and turned the easel so that she could stand and look in my direction.

"Just let me know if you get cold."

The room fell silent, apart from the low sound of Anita's careful brushstrokes. I wondered what would happen to the painting, who would see it. I wasn't used to someone being able to observe my body like this, but as she painted, I became accustomed to the feeling.

"I have to admit—I'm curious," I said. "*Were* you one of Egil's conquests?"

She shrugged. "I end up doing a lot of things."

"Same here," I said, "but that doesn't answer my question."

"I know it must seem strange," she said.

Her smile disappeared. Several seconds passed in which she simply painted in silence. The light from the skylight gave her hair a white glow.

"It's all right," she said finally, gesturing towards the painting of Birk. "An arrangement that works. He's away for weeks at a time, and I can be here and do the work I want to do."

She glanced over at me, seeming to compare me to something on the canvas.

"By the time I found out I was pregnant, it was already too late to have an abortion. We decided to try to make a relationship work, for the baby's sake. So I moved in with Birk."

She inhaled, let out a long sigh. "I guess you wouldn't have done the same," she said. "You seem so free. For me, it didn't feel like a choice. But looking after a baby all alone—there wouldn't be much time for art."

Her voice cracked. Instinctively, I got up from the chair, went across to her and hugged her. Her hair flowed over my face like lukewarm water. It felt like hugging myself.

"Don't cry," I whispered. Stuck out the tip of my tongue and licked the salty tears from her cheek. She giggled. I stroked her slightly damp hair, touched her throat with my fingertips.

It felt more intimate than it usually did. Something entirely different to this cold, aimless pastime I'd been making attempts at previously—and usually while in an intoxicated state. This was more honest, in a way, filled with more blushing and giggling, as if with open faces. I trembled as I ran my hands over her body, felt the glow of her skin and found that she tasted like caramel.

I had my head under the duvet, my mouth buried in Anita's wet labia. She writhed, emitting tiny whimpers, and suddenly it seemed that there was someone there who answered. A similar sound from elsewhere in the room. The sound didn't seem to be abating, but rather to be increasing in volume and intensity. I wondered whether there was something wrong with my ears. It wasn't until afterwards, when I set my head beside hers on the pillow, that I saw where the sound was coming from. There, in a corner just behind a wardrobe, was a basket. In it was a miniature black poodle with a motley litter of puppies.

"Aren't they lovely?" Anita laughed as she got up, pulling a blanket around her and walking over to the basket. She picked up one of the tiny puppies and carried it across to me. It landed on my chest, and immediately began to toddle across the duvet. Its ears were small, curly flaps on its little head, flecked black and brown.

"This little darling got out and went on a date with the neighbour's King Charles spaniel. If you know anyone who'd like a little mongrel to take care of, just let me know."

I held my breath for a moment. Felt my pulse rise again when I looked down at the tiny, curly creature. I opened my mouth; a reflex. Didn't want to say anything, but it was as if my lips and vocal cords had a will of their own.

"Actually," I said, then swallowed, "my grandmother just lost her dog. I think she'd be really up for getting another."

I buried my face in the dog's fur, wanting to wipe away the idiotic words.

"Great, that's perfect!" Anita cried. "She can have my favourite."

Mariam

Ålesund
Tuesday, 22 August 2017

Nero hisses as I push him down into the large suitcase I've purchased from Carol, and which I've punched with holes using an awl so he can breathe. His open jaws are bigger than my face, a whitish-pink palate with two rows of small, transparent teeth. They're almost invisible, but they're there. Were it not for the teeth, his mouth might have given the impression of being a pink tunnel to paradise. A ridiculous thought.

I close the lid over him and zip the suitcase shut. He hasn't spoken to me since I came back. Maybe it can be different this time—a friendship, mutual.

I start the car's engine and drive towards the town centre. It's a bright day, and the roads are empty. I move up through the gears, watching all the small houses rush past. On the main road between some small rocky outcrops, the nostalgia truly hits home. How many times have I driven these roads, through this tunnel, past the Sunnmøre Museum where boats lie bobbing on the fjord, through the next tunnel, until I can soon see the first signs of Ålesund town centre before me. My body lightens, as if I'm approaching something exciting. It makes me want to listen to music, so I turn on the radio, but it's the news. They're talking about the disappearance and the police search in Kristiansund. I turn it off. Can't bear to remember that she's gone.

I drive through the town centre a few times to take a look around. The town hall has been given a facelift; McDonald's has become a Hennes & Mauritz. But the starting point is still the same—the buildings, the streets. It feels as if I've gone back in time. I half expect to take a look in the rearview mirror and see a girl twelve years my junior reflected back at me, to be able to turn and see my two friends sitting in the back seat. I drive on, past the old cinema and down Løvenvoldgata, taking a left at the lights I have a feeling never worked—that these lights must have been standing here flashing amber for twelve years. At the next junction I turn right and drive past the old bus station, where we spent so many evening hours sitting and smoking on one of the hard wooden benches with a view of the asphalt and fjord, asphalt and fjord, all that Ålesund is.

The nostalgia is slipping away, replaced by the old feeling of boredom I so often felt when I lived here. On the other side of Hellebroa, where the roundabouts have been turned into junctions controlled by traffic lights, I take a left in the direction of Steinvågen. I drive on across the bridge out to Skarbøvika, past the small boats and the old high school, farther out past the rows of terraced houses and detached properties, back to a familiar neighbourhood. I know exactly where to park the car.

I pull the shiny gold key from my jacket pocket—the one that was in Iben's jewellery box—rubbing it between my fingers. The key to my room. It means something. I don't understand how Iben could suddenly have it, but this key proves that the disappearance must have something to do with me. This isn't just a key—it's a message.

The first thing I have to do is see my old room. I never thought I would one day come back here—this place belongs only in the worst of my nightmares. Still, for whatever reason, I was drawn back here.

I open the car's back door, crawl in beside the suitcase and unzip it. The snake slithers out over the edge, its coil bulging out across my lap. He moves towards the window, seeking the house.

"Do you recognise it?" I whisper.

He says nothing, but there's no doubt that the answer is yes. He licks the air with a tongue that has also grown longer. Then the silence is broken by a whisper, like a light breeze in my ear. It's enough for me to know that nothing has changed. He's dissatisfied in my company, at having been held captive all these years, and now at having been shoved into this suitcase. He doesn't care whether or not he gets to see our old shared home again. I swallow.

"I have to put you back in there, just for a little longer," I whisper. "I'll make it up to you later, I promise."

With great effort I manage to force his body back into the suitcase and zip it closed.

A light drizzle lands in my hair as I get out of the car. I think of how rain on one's wedding veil is said to bring good luck, and how it didn't rain when I got married. There wasn't a cloud in the sky that day, it was one of the few truly hot days of summer, and I started to sweat at even the slightest movement. I remember what it was like pulling on my close-fitting dress, how it clung to my skin with perspiration. How I looked at myself in the mirror and thought it wasn't me, that I looked like some big white animal on its way to the slaughter. But with time, I got better at being Mariam. Now it's she who feels like a stranger.

I see from the name on the mailbox that the same landlady still lives on the ground floor; she hasn't ended up in an old people's home just yet. She's such an old biddy, that woman. I walk down the steps towards the basement entrance. The light is on, and I can hear heavy music coming from inside. I creep over to the kitchen window, which is ajar, and peer in. A man stands bent over the kitchen counter, wearing boxer shorts and a black T-shirt. His beard is shorter than before, but his hair is longer and paler; he almost looks like Jesus. It takes time for him to notice me, but when he does, he jumps and comes all the way over to the window. I can see how his features look older. I stand there, looking back at him and waiting. Then the recognition clicks into place.

"Fucking hell, Liv," he says.

As I laugh, I think my voice sounds as if it actually belongs to Liv. It dawns on me that this is how I used to be—playful. I've lost that part of myself completely. Over the past few years so much of my life has been about doing things right. Raising my child in a responsible way, ensuring she gets healthy meals and that the house has clean windows. Maintaining normality. For Liv, this serious normality was something that happened elsewhere—never where she was.

Ingvar disappears into the apartment, soon after appearing again at the front door. He holds it open for me, wearing a Slayer T-shirt and a pair of sweatpants. From the look he gives me, I think he finds my appearance terribly straitlaced, but he smiles and hugs me. I walk after him, through the long hallway and into the living room. The music is still on, but at a lower volume. Ingvar starts to roll a cigarette.

"I thought you must have died ages ago," he says.

He puts the cigarette between his lips and holds the packet of tobacco out to me. A rollie, I think—wasn't that what we always called them?

"I quit."

He shakes his head. Lights his rollie and gets up to open the terrace door, letting air and sunlight into the apartment. I look around the room. The carpet has been replaced with linoleum. A larger TV, speakers and new curtains; new shelves have been put up, but the red chest of drawers in the corner is the same. Ingvar's posters hang on every wall; his guitar stands beside the sofa.

"So how you doing, stranger?" Ingvar asks.

"I've changed."

"Yeah, I noticed."

"Got a husband and a kid."

He raises his eyebrows.

"Liv, that's great! At least one of us turned out okay."

"Egil?" I ask.

"In prison. Stabbed a guy while he was drunk."

Ingvar picks tobacco from his mouth, then rubs his fingers together above the ashtray. Egil used to be the straightest of all of us—at least to start with, when I first moved in. I look at my hands. Clean nails painted a pale pink, a wedding ring. How ridiculous it all seems in this room.

"You?" I say.

He shrugs. "Same old, same old."

"Are you still making music?"

"Of course. The band broke up, though. I've had a normal job for about ten years now, driving a delivery van."

"There's something I need to talk to you about, Ingvar."

He looks down at the table. Probably thinks I want to talk about that night. And I do—but not for the reasons he's imagining.

"You don't watch the news, do you?"

He shrugs again. "It's only ever total shit, whatever's going on."

"I have quite a bit to tell you. I'm not entirely sure where to start."

Ingvar leans back. Puts his feet on the table and starts to roll another rollie.

"So just start talking."

Liv

Ålesund
Wednesday, 6 October 2004

I sat in the library reading room, trying to read about unstable column fractures, a kind of spinal break that most often occurs in patients with osteoporosis. The illustration was a drawing of the spine, with the ligaments added in blue. I set my fingers on the drawing. Straightened up, considering just how essential the spinal column is to the body. The very centre of the body's movement and internal communication. It struck me that the snake skeleton was the essence of the human one. Apart from the head, the snake's bone structure consisted exclusively of a backbone and ribs, not so different from the way a human skeleton looked from the waist up. Without limbs, snakes had mastered the spine; it had developed to its full potential. I tried to imagine what it would be like to lose these limbs I carried around with me, to be nothing but a spine and reptilian brain and to slither lightly across the earth.

My telephone made a noise from where it sat on the table in front of me; several heads dotted around the reading room turned to look in my direction. The message was from Anita. *Thinking of you!* Anita was heavily pregnant now. Just a few days ago, on the last day before Birk returned home, we had slept naked in her bed, feeling Aurora kicking against our fingers. It was such an intense feeling, to see someone with a real live person inside their body. When I first met Anita in the bathroom of the flatshare, the baby in her belly was a snail-like creature, its skeleton just a spinal column. She hadn't even known that she was pregnant. Now the little girl inside her had ears and fingers, and would have a chance of surviving even if she was born premature. Every time Anita asked me to touch her stomach, I felt an aversion, as if the thing inside her might come out and eat me.

Thinking of you! I hadn't been thinking of her. When I couldn't see her, I entered a state of emptiness and snake-focused fascination. It was Nero who filled my days now, as if he were my lover now that my spouse was busy elsewhere. I wasn't sure why I thought of her this way—as my spouse. I knew only that I felt good when I was with her, when I didn't have to be alone, when I could set my head against her chest and hear her heart beating. But at the same time, there was something frightening about her growing belly, about all the stability with which she surrounded herself, and her worries on the baby's behalf; how she thought about what she ate all the time. She was simply becoming more and more grown up.

In a way, it made me feel assured to know that she had Birk. I didn't need to be afraid that she might want anything more than what we had. I didn't need to fear that she would find out what I had done, how I had watched her beloved curly-coated puppy sink down Nero's throat as if into quicksand. Anita regularly asked me how the puppy and my grandmother were getting along, and I had to lie, over and over again. I typed out a quick *Thinking of you too*, sent the message and switched the phone to silent.

I had just turned back to the unstable column fractures when I felt a hand touch my shoulder, making me jump. I looked up, and saw Egil's slightly sunburned face. He was wearing a white shirt, his hair neatly slicked back.

"Oh my God," I whispered, bending over in my chair.

Egil began to walk towards the door, gesturing for me to follow. I quickly gathered up my things and went after him.

"What are you doing here?" I said once we'd moved out into the hall.

Egil stuffed his hands into the pockets of his chinos and shrugged.

"It's not as if it's possible to get hold of you any other way. I bumped into Anita earlier—she's big as a house!" He gave a brief laugh. "So I thought it was about fucking time you stopped hiding from me."

We found a vacant seating area in the foyer. Egil sat down, one foot propped on the opposite knee.

"Anita says the two of you have got something going," he said.

"So?"

He glanced up at the ceiling.

"It doesn't make any difference to me. I just thought I'd let you know that's what she's saying."

"Is that why you came here?"

He sighed. Around us, student voices merged into a background hum.

"I just don't think you should cut us off completely because of what happened."

I leaned forward.

"By 'what happened,' I assume you mean stealing my key, letting yourself into my room and doing whatever the hell you wanted, just so you could frighten the life out of the entire party?"

"I'm sorry for that last thing," he said, "but the first isn't true. I told you the truth—the door was already open."

I fought the impulse to throw something, or to get up and leave. Dug my fingers into the edge of the sofa.

"Ingvar's been really down since you left."

"What does that have to do with me?"

Egil shook his head.

"He didn't mean to hurt you. He's just a big pussy."

"That's bad enough."

"Okay, but I hope you and I can still meet up sometimes."

"We'll see," I said, letting my head drop back onto the sofa. I realised that this was something I had missed. Everyday life in our shared flat, just hanging out together.

"How was your summer?" I said.

"So damn boring. Not to mention fucking awful. Next summer will be better. I'm going to take a road trip through the USA. Hollywood, Las Vegas, Memphis, Chicago, New York."

I laughed.

"I'd forgotten just how much of a cliché you are, Egil. Does that mean daddy has turned the money tap back on?"

He fixed his blue eyes on me.

"Sorry," I said. "Old habit."

"Well, anyway, the answer is no," he said, "but it doesn't matter. I have a much better idea. A real Al Capone kind of thing."

I laughed. "You mean to say you actually have a plan?"

He glanced around him. Got up and came over to the sofa where I was sitting.

"I'm going to rob my dad," he whispered. "I'm going to do it."

"Seriously?"

He put on a big white smile.

"I've never been more serious about anything in my entire life," he said. "I've been dreaming about this since I was a little kid. That fucker has no idea how much he's going to regret everything he's ever done. Are you in?"

I looked at him.

"Oh, come on! Come on—it'll earn you so much cash. It's gonna be totally crazy."

"It *is* totally crazy, Egil."

"How come you're not cool anymore?"

"So *that's* why you came here?"

He sighed.

"Ingvar is game, but I want to keep him out of it. The guy is stoned literally all the time now, I mean it. He started drinking, too—and that's what worries me most. I'm afraid to leave him alone if he's been drinking, you know, because of his epilepsy. David says it isn't wise to involve him in the plan, and I agree."

"So you've started hanging out with David Lorentzen?"

"Yeah—why shouldn't I?"

"That means you already have someone who can help you rob your dad—you just want to drag as many people as possible into the prison cell with you."

"Into the *fun*, you mean. Come on."

I shook my head. "Keep me out of it, too."

Reptile memoirs

Slipping across the woman's sleeping body reminded me of hurrying up my mother's spine, back when I was an unwitting child. I could cross it, and the world was mine. I crept from her feet, up over her belly. Her body was salty with tiny drops of sweat. Prey without fur are the best kind. The contact between tongue and body is more intense, the heat closer. Still, I couldn't make her my prey. She was too large, I was too small. No matter how hard I stretched my wretched body, I hardly came up to her thighs.

Sleep made her face stiff, as in death. Her breath and warmth were the only signs that she was alive. I crept up to her ear, lay close against her and touched her tender earlobe with my tongue. It tasted bitter, of earwax. I withdrew my tongue, lay completely still for a while before I opened my mouth. Then began to whisper, quietly.

The words I whispered were among the few I understood, words I had learned from the many humans with whom I had come into contact. I whispered *food* and *hunt*. Then a third word: *prey*. The words were good, but the sound was lower than my own ears could detect. Still, I knew I made sounds, because her ear quivered as she listened. Her face twitched in tiny contractions. She skipped a breath; her skin became covered in goose bumps.

During the day, I waited. First, she became more restless due to poor sleep. The next thing that happened was that she turned away from other humans, moving closer to me. She shut us away in the tiny room and did her lonely activities. She opened her mouth as if in a desperate hissing, unparalleled and free of enemies.

After a few days, the next phase began. She started to wake in the night and look at me. She whispered back. At that point I knew it wouldn't be long. Soon, I would be able to coil myself around a juicy, furry animal. Animals that were either too small to run away, or which had been tamed by humans. Not difficult prey to catch, but they pulsed in my coil and gave me the wonderful taste of fresh flesh and blood.

Instinct was a word I had learned from the humans. They used it about everything other animals do, as if it were only humans that have consciousness, or only animals other than them that act instinctively. But my actions towards her were conscious, deliberate, and her resulting actions—they were instinct.

Liv

Ålesund
Saturday, 5 February 2005

I buried my face in Anita's soft stomach. It was now almost completely flat again after the birth. She giggled and writhed. Her breasts bulged beneath the bra she hadn't wanted to take off even in bed—she said that they were heavy, and ached. If I came too close to them, she would pull away. She got up from the bed and put on her dressing gown. Walked over and peered down into the crib where Aurora was commencing her little run-up to tears.

She had screamed all through the night; the sound of her crying still vibrated at my eardrums. For her part, Anita seemed to have become immune to it. At least it seemed as if she had no problem tolerating it as she walked and pushed and comforted the tiny creature she held in her arms. Perhaps this was the way a mother should be, consumed by her child. I had ended up taking a walk around the block with the black toy poodle, thankful for a little silence. I walked through the snow, imagining that the dog was sniffing around for her puppies, even though I guessed she'd probably forgotten them long ago. I hadn't been able to bear the thought of giving Nero any live prey since that day last summer, when I had carried the puppy home. What I had done was unforgivable. Anita must never find out.

Now she came towards me, carrying the half-sleeping baby, its head full of dark hair. Right now, the little girl looked peaceful. During the night she had been red with agitation, an openmouthed and screeching little monster. It occurred to me that there was no guarantee you would love your child, no matter how wanted it was.

"Have you noticed any difference?" I asked.

Anita smiled, surprised.

"Difference in what?"

"In you. Since you became a mother."

She lay Aurora on her belly on the mattress.

"I don't know. I hadn't thought about it, but maybe I have noticed something. Not since I had her, necessarily, but I think something has happened, gradually."

"What?"

"I think I've switched out who's most important. It's always been about me, me, me. Now everything is about Aurora."

Aurora flailed her arms and legs, as if she were trying to figure out how to move forward.

"It sounds nice," I said.

"Yeah. I don't miss being so obsessed with Anita all the time," she laughed. "I feel sort of—wiser."

I thought of my own mother, or the woman who claimed to bear that title. I wondered what had gone wrong, why she had never gone through such a change.

"Now I just have to figure out what I'm going to do about Birk," Anita said. Her face darkened. "If I'm strong enough."

"But isn't it an arrangement that works, all the same?"

She shrugged.

"It *was* an arrangement that worked. Or rather, I convinced myself that it was. But now I understand what I've been doing. It's prostitution, and self-harm."

I looked around me, at the fancy bedroom with its dark lacquered wood, the windows in the sloping ceiling. Anita had said that the woodwork was old, that it was difficult to maintain, but beautiful. Those were the kinds of things that grown-up people said. Birk had inherited the house; he was the third generation to live there after his mother was diagnosed with early-onset Alzheimer's and ended up in a home. Was this a brothel? Was I one of its customers, an arrangement that worked—for now?

"There's something you don't know," she said, a paleness coming over her face. "I have to tell someone, otherwise I won't be able to—"

Aurora lifted her little head and let out a grunt. Anita automatically stretched out and moved her slightly, even though there probably wasn't anything wrong with the way she was lying there.

"Promise me you won't judge me?"

"Why would I do that?"

She moved her hands behind her back, unhooked her bra and slipped it off. Put it down on the pillow. Her breasts bulged, swollen and heavy with milk, large nipples and fine veins beneath the pale skin. He had punched her left breast. A bluish-green bruise almost completely covered the outside of it.

"The other bruises disappeared after a few days," she said, "but right here, he really slammed into me. You should have seen what it looked like when it was fresh."

I reached out my hand and touched the bruise with my fingertips. Her breast vibrated with her heartbeat.

"He's so jealous," she said. "Accuses me of all kinds of terrible things. He says he can't be sure that Aurora is his, even though all you have to do is look at her to know she is. He's jealous of my paintings, too. Says that I'd be happier if I stopped painting, and that I'd be a better mother to Aurora. That I don't take good enough care of her because I'm buzzing around in my own head. He's threatened to burn all my palettes and brushes several times—he doesn't understand that without my paintings, I don't exist. There's more me in them than there is in this body. The easel is my heart, my palettes are my lungs—truly, that's how it is for me."

"So you're going to leave him?"

"Yes, I want to leave him."

She swallowed, bowed her head. Shook her blond hair several times.

"Fuck," she said. "Really, fuck. That's the first time I've said it out loud. What am I going to do?"

I looked at Anita's bent head. Thought of myself, how I had taken Nero and my most important clothes and simply moved out of the flatshare that day. How I found it so easy to close doors behind me. Maybe it wasn't like that for everyone, even after having lived with someone for only a few months.

"I'm so scared," she said. "Scared to stay, and scared to leave. I'm mostly afraid of what he might do. There's a voice inside me that says it was just this one time, that he's not going to do it again—but I don't want to listen to that voice. I have to get out. Get an apartment, somewhere I can hide."

Anita put her head in her hands and began to sob loudly.

"There, there," I said, feeling awkward. "You must have family you can stay with for now?"

"I have a room at my mum's place, but I don't know how long I'll be able to stay there. I don't know whether I've told you, but Birk is the son of one of Mamma's best friends, and we've broken up and got back together several times. Mamma was overjoyed when she found out we were moving in together. She's convinced he's the perfect guy for me."

"I'm sure she'd soon change her opinion if you told her what he's done," I said, feeling weird and cold. I'd spoken like someone who knows something about mothers and daughters.

Anita wiped away her tears, shook her head.

"I'm so scared," she said again. "I don't know if I can do it."

Just then, Aurora began to cry, a piercing howl. Anita lifted her to her battered breast, guiding her nipple into the baby's mouth. Aurora soon began to make contented noises, like some kind of murmuring machine. I wondered whether I had ever drunk milk from a breast. It was hard to imagine.

Mariam

Ålesund
Tuesday, 22 August 2017

I insert the old gold key into the lock. Try to turn it, but it's not like in the fairy tales where a long-locked door is finally opened. The door has been open the whole time. I was the only one who ever locked it.

"Egil took over your room after you left," Ingvar says. "I mean, he's been in prison, moved in with someone for a few years and then ended up in prison again, so it's mainly only been me here, but I haven't needed this room. He won't be needing it for a while, either, so you may as well use it." He pauses for a moment. "While you're looking for your daughter."

The air in the room is stuffy, and a new, unfamiliar smell has entered it, but it's still my old room, even though the carpet is gone, the walls have been painted a pale grey, and the bed has been exchanged for a new one. The plant that stood in the corner is no more; an old Nintendo and a cardboard box stand in its place. The room's main feature is still there—the window facing the garden and the plum tree. On the floor are a towel, some boxer shorts and a pair of Nike trainers. I think there's something missing, the thing that would really make this Egil's room, until I turn and see the poster on the wall beside the door. Glossy, silicone, with long brown legs. I turn to face Ingvar, holding up the gold key.

"Have you seen this since it disappeared?"

Ingvar stares at the key, wrinkles his brow.

"No. I haven't seen that since you lived here."

"This key—to this room—was in Iben's jewellery box."

"You're kidding."

"Do you remember the night it disappeared?"

He looks down at the floor, kicks at the door sill with his foot. He's never been good at conflict. It was his cowardice that enabled him to invite my brother here that night, as if they were good friends.

"Somebody who was here that night took my key, and kept it for all these years. Whoever that person is somehow made sure that it ended up in my daughter's jewellery box. They were sending me a message. It's serious."

"Who do you think it might be?"

"The way I see it, there are two people who could have taken my key that night: Egil or Patrick. They both had reason to want to go into my room. Egil because he wanted to get the snake, Patrick because he's Patrick. He probably wanted to snoop around in my stuff or something like that." I imagine Patrick picking up an item of my clothing and sniffing it. "I can't imagine anyone other than the two of them wanting to get in here. Can you?"

Ingvar shakes his head, seems embarrassed.

"If it was Egil, he might know who sent me this message. So I have to speak to him. If it was Patrick . . ." I swallow. "Well, yeah, then it was Patrick."

"It can't have been Patrick. Did he even know what the key was or what it was for?"

I think of the day I met Patrick in town. When he leaned forward to touch the key with the tip of his finger. *Have you become a latchkey kid, Sara?*

"At the very least, he knew it was mine. He saw me wearing it. It wouldn't have been much of a leap to guess that it belonged to a door that was mine."

"You're afraid, aren't you?" says Ingvar. "That it's Patrick. Just remember that there were loads of people here that night. It could have been just about anyone."

I shake my head.

"Just about anyone hasn't made sure that my key ended up in my daughter's jewellery box around the same time that she's disappeared. It has to be someone who knows me. Somebody who wants something from me."

Ingvar shakes his head, his long hair dancing.

"I just can't see it," he says. "Patrick has always been so . . . pitiful. Do you really think he made his way to Kristiansund to kidnap a child?"

I stare at him. Feel a strong need to finally sock him with the punch that has lain dormant within me since that night. I end up hitting the wall behind me instead.

"You're defending him," I say. "You're still friends."

"No, no, we're really not. I see him around all the time at Smutten, but I never talk to him."

"That's what you said back then, too."

He looks down, like a little boy. "This time it's true," he mumbles.

We stand there for a while without saying anything. Ingvar scratches his beard and glances behind him, as if looking for an escape route.

"Have you kept any of my old things?" I ask.

He clears his throat.

"Check the storage closet—there might be something in there."

He nods towards the small door in the wall. I open it, turn on a light inside. In the box room are many of the landlady's old belongings. A large trunk, a cast-iron bottle rack, a box full of all kinds of junk. A black bin bag has been set atop a cardboard box labelled BOOKS. I open the bag, stick my hand into it and pull out a sweater that seems familiar. I drag the bag onto the floor and turn it upside down, so books, CDs and various toiletries pour out. A dress I used to wear all the time, a perfume I can't even remember. I don't usually tend to travel back in time—I only ever move forward. There's something wrong about looking back. You don't recognise yourself.

I walk over to the window and peer out at the garden and the plum tree. Feel for a moment that I'm still Liv looking out—but only for a moment. Next I see Iben hanging there, dangling from a rope attached to the tree, swinging back and forth. I squeeze my eyes shut. Sit down on the bed and take a deep breath.

"Are you okay?" Ingvar's voice is gentle.

"Leave me alone."

He closes the door behind him; I hear his footsteps disappearing down the hall. I lie down on the bed, looking up at the white ceiling tiles. When Iben was six years old, she once drew an animal on the wallpaper of her room, something halfway between a dinosaur and a cat. When I first saw the drawing, I thought the animal's long, slim neck was a snake, and my heart skipped a beat. I was unreasonably furious at her for drawing it. I sent her to her room, threatening that she wouldn't be allowed out until she had washed away every last trace of it. She couldn't manage it, no matter how hard she scrubbed, and that had in fact been my aim—to make her understand what she'd done. I've been so hard on her.

On the nightstand are porn mags, condoms and a green slice of bread. I now understand where the smell is coming from. I sit up again. Almost retch as I shove the bread onto one of the magazines and carry it out into the hall. Ingvar's music is back in full swing, stinging my ear canals. My ears have become sensitive. I have no idea what band it is either; haven't kept up with that kind of thing.

In the kitchen, the bin is so full that I have to take the bag out in order to make space for the mouldy bread. I throw the porno mag in at the same time—it looks like an antique. Maybe it's something Egil feels nostalgic about, but I couldn't care less. I tie the bag's handles and carry it out, feeling like a goddamn mother, a mother who might never have the chance to come and clean up her daughter's flatshare. Could Patrick have killed her? Should I have gone straight to his place? I step into my shoes and go out to the dustbin. Shove the bag down into it and only just manage to close the lid.

Only when I'm outside do I go to the car and get my suit-cases. Think I can hear just how much Nero hates being moved around while inside that dark space. I drag the suitcases after me. Stop on the steps, pick up the suitcase with Nero inside it and walk down. The suitcase is so heavy I almost collapse under its weight. It won't do to move him around so much. I drag the suitcase into my room and park it neatly beside the window before I go and get the other.

Nero tries to attack my arm when I open the suitcase—I leap back. Whisper that I'm sorry. Offended, he disappears under the bed. I let him lie there and calm down for a few minutes while I look for clean bedding in the wardrobe, where everything is crumpled up into a ball: clothes and towels. There are boxes of painkillers and more magazines, and an unopened bottle of beer. In the end I manage to find a sheet, duvet cover and pillowcase, and begin to make the bed. I left this life—I've become someone else. Every cell of my body has been replaced since I was last here. Part of me misses that earlier version. Another knows that she never wants to go back.

When I'm done, I lie down on the floor and look under the bed. Nero is curled up, his head behind the nightstand. I try to draw him out, but he just lies there, threateningly opening his mouth. There's something behind his coil. It looks like a photograph. I reach for it, but he darts at me in attack. I manage to grab it and pull my hand away just in time.

When I enter the living room, Ingvar is sitting there with his eyes closed, listening to music. He's playing air guitar with his fingers. I sit down on the sofa beside him, nudge him in the shoulder and hand him the picture I've found. It was taken here in the living room. Ingvar, Egil and me sitting on the rug in the apartment. In the background is the lower half of the TV, and the bench illuminated by the red of the lava lamp.

"That's from a long time ago," he says. "The good old days."

"I found it on the floor under the bed, but I couldn't see any others. Do you know where the rest of my pictures are?"

Ingvar shrugs. "Maybe Egil took them to prison with him, or something like that."

That sounds unlikely.

"So you don't have any?"

A strange expression crosses Ingvar's features, as if his mouth has been sewn shut. He closes his eyes and leans his head back against the wall.

"No," he says. "None."

He's lying to me. I don't understand why.

"Can I borrow your phone?" I say.

Liv

Ålesund
Wednesday, 13 April 2005

I stuck my fingers in my ears. Shoved them in to block out Nero's insistent hissing. Closed my eyes so that I wouldn't have to see him coiled up there on the bed in front of me. All night I had struggled to sleep because of his furious noise. I had to find some food for him, something he wanted to eat. Rats no longer satisfied him, and he regarded all dead animals with contempt. He tried to bite me on several occasions this week—one time I sprayed Listerine on him to make him keep his distance. Every single day I felt that I was failing him. I just couldn't bear the thought of another kitten or a puppy like Anita's. He knew what this meant. That I had started to put others before him.

My phone vibrated somewhere nearby; I found it lying under a pile of clothes on my chair. It was so cramped and messy in this apartment—that's what I told Anita every time she begged to come and see where I lived. It was she who was calling me now.

"Where are you?" she asked. "Can I come over?"

I glanced down at Nero, who opened his jaws, showing me his pale-pink palate. It reminded me of something—something I couldn't quite grasp.

"I'm kind of busy."

"It's bad," she sniffed, her voice high-pitched and thick. "A total emergency. I've done it. I've left Birk."

I inhaled. Stared at the pink tinge of Nero's open mouth.

"Mamma won't help me," she sobbed. "I'm sitting in the car. Mamma thinks Birk and I have something valuable that I shouldn't throw away. She doesn't want to listen to me. Accused me of lying about him, of only thinking about myself. She said that Aurora needs her father."

She let out a husky wail, and in the background Aurora also piped up. It sounded as if Anita took the baby in her arms, began to rock her to sleep.

"I don't know what I'm going to do," Anita squeaked. "Can we come and stay with you for a few days, just until I find something else?"

I opened my mouth to say that it was so cramped here, that it was a mess—the usual arguments. I imagined what it would be like to have Anita and Aurora here, with the snake hidden somewhere in these paltry few square metres. It was impossible. But then I started to imagine Anita sitting in the car with the baby in her arms, her cheeks stained with mascara. If she couldn't find somewhere to stay, she would have no other choice than to go back to Birk. And what would he do to her then?

"Give me an hour," I said.

* * *

I carried the bag in which I had put Nero carefully down the stairs and back into the flatshare—I could hear him hissing furious commands from inside it. I had failed him. Of course he wanted to get out, he wanted to be free and hunt and live in harmony with nature. In his mind, there should be nothing to prevent him from slithering straight out onto the grass and making his way off into the forest, even if he might freeze to death in just a day or two. There was still only the mildness of spring in the air—but he could still freeze to death at night.

The door was open; I went into the hall and kicked off my shoes. It was quiet in the apartment, no music, which probably meant that Ingvar wasn't home. On the other hand, I could hear Egil's voice coming from the living room. It sounded as if he was speaking on the phone.

"I should have done it ages ago," he said. "I've never been so sure of anything."

His voice sounded fervent. I stuck my head around the door, knocking lightly on the doorframe.

"I have to go," Egil said. "I'll call you later. We're doing this!"

"What are we doing?" I said after he had hung up.

"The robbery. This Saturday. In three days!" He clapped his hand against his mobile. "Pappa has an important dinner with a client in town that day. He gave me access to his calendar years ago when I lived with him, so we could schedule when we would see each other." He laughed. "That says a lot about my father. Anyway. I know where he usually parks the car, so all we have to do is wait and attack him."

Egil pretended to punch his phone with his fist.

"Bam! Hit him from behind. When he's flat out, we'll steal the keys to the house. I know where the safe is, and I've given the code to David. Easy. You can still get in on it if you want."

I shook my head. "I still don't intend to go to prison."

His eyes met mine, and he gave me a roguish grin.

"But I haven't told you the best part. On Saturday it'll be the first-ever football match at the new stadium. The city will be crawling with people wearing football shirts, so all we need to do to make ourselves invisible is dress as if we're going to the game. It'll be the perfect crime."

"Who's going to hit him in the head?"

He grinned.

"I'm going to do it—with pleasure."

"If he sees you, he's going to know who mugged him."

"Obviously we're going to hide our faces, and it'll happen fast—he'll never have a chance to recognise me."

He smacks his own palm again. He seems overeager, almost manic.

"And you think you'll be able to do that? Hit your own father in the head? I mean, you're really going to need to hold your nerve."

"What is it you want, anyway?" he said, frowning.

I set the bag on the floor and opened the zip. Nero lay still, licking the air with the two tips of his tongue.

"You can have him," I said.

Egil stared down at the snake, the irritation from a moment ago seemingly erased.

"Do you mean it?"

"On one condition. You can't ever tell anyone that I had him. You have to say that you only just got him, just now."

He laughed.

"But I've told everyone—"

"Make something up. And talk to Ingvar, too. I've never had a snake. Do you understand?"

He nodded. "If it's that important to you."

"And especially don't tell Anita."

"Anita? But she used to hang out with us when you lived here—I talked about the snake all the time back then."

"Well, I told Anita that you've been lying this whole time. And she believed me. But now you've finally been able to get yourself a python to play with."

Egil took a seat on the leather sofa; I bent down and stroked Nero's scaly head. Silently, I told him that this was for the best. Our relationship was a black hole that was eating me up. It was time to put some distance between us before it swallowed me completely.

"Now do what you want," I said to Egil.

Then I got up and started to walk towards the hall. Wanted to get out of this house as fast as possible, to put this phase of my life behind me. Every minute of my life up until this point had been parenthetical. Maybe my life would really start this time.

"Have a good road trip!" I shouted on the way out.

Mariam

Ålesund
Tuesday, 22 August 2017

I sit on the bed, my legs pulled up under me. Listen restlessly to the ringing on the other end of the line. Egil is the reason I came here. He has to know something. Either he took the key himself, and is responsible for where it ended up afterwards, or he knows who might have taken it. He knew everybody back then, darlings and criminals alike.

"Ålesund Prison," a cold male voice says.

"I'd like to speak with one of your inmates, Egil Brynseth. He's an old childhood friend of mine."

"Telephone conversations and visits have to be arranged in advance."

"How far in advance? I'll only be in Ålesund for a few days—I'm just visiting."

"It varies. Let me take a look—call us back in an hour."

I give the man my details and hang up. My fingers are trembling as I punch in Tor's number. If everything were business as usual, he would be busy at work, but I don't expect things to be business as usual. Tor answers in a thick voice; it sounds as if he's just woken up. He never usually naps in the middle of the day.

"Is something wrong?" I blurt out.

A few long seconds pass before he answers.

"You're asking me if something is wrong?" His voice cracks.

I swallow. "I don't know what to say."

"Say that you'll come home."

I imagine him lying there in bed, fully dressed and red-eyed. There's something wrong with this picture. Tor isn't like this. Tor is strong. For as long as I've known him, he's used his sensitivity as a force to be reckoned with. He builds safe environments—creates, strengthens and transforms.

"I can't."

He hangs up. I sit there, watching Nero trying to find space for his large body under the chest of drawers. I count to one hundred in my head, then dial Tor's number again. It rings for a long time.

"Yes?" he finally answers.

"I think Iben is in Ålesund."

"If you have information, you have to give it to the police. You're not a detective. You're playing with my child's life."

"She's not your child, Tor," I say, regretting it straightaway.

"Of course she's my child. I can't sleep at night. I've been put on sick leave. Today I was offered some pills to calm me down, but the only thing that will help is to find Iben."

"That's the only thing that will help me, too," I say, immediately realising that this isn't entirely true. It's helped to come here. It helps that Nero has climbed up onto the bed and is now resting here, across my stomach. This attempt to flee, back to another time, where the tragedy hasn't yet happened.

"I so wish I could come home right now—I will come home, when I'm ready. But there are people I need to speak to, people who might not want to talk to the police. I know I'm doing the right thing."

"You know nothing!"

I study Nero's unmoving figure. He's so much bigger than he used to be, but he's the same. I try to understand how I might explain this to Tor. His world is so different from the one I'm currently in. For him, it's easier. Laws and rules have to be obeyed, customs must be followed—there's no alternative for him. Everywhere, eyes are turned in his direction, assessing everything he does. That's how it is to be a politician—everything he does is in the public interest. If he keeps information from the police for my sake, it might be enough to derail his career. Still, this is something I have to ask of him, without him even being able to know why. If I told him why, our marriage would be over.

"I'm calling the police today," Tor says. "I'm going to tell them that you've left, and that you have information you believe might lead them to Iben. They'll find you."

"Can't you just wait one more day? Trust me. I would never have asked you if this wasn't really important."

He's quiet. That means he's either shocked by my behaviour, or that he's thinking.

"If they ask, just say that I went to visit family," I say. "Burn the note I left. Tell them you never intended to mislead them, you just didn't think it was important to tell them I was gone. Blame the situation we're both in. And if they don't ask, don't say anything. Just give it one more day."

"If Iben is alive," Tor says, "one day might be the difference between life and death."

"That's exactly why I need you to wait," I say. "This isn't something the police can do. I have to do this myself." The words make a knot form in my stomach, right below the warm area where Nero is resting.

"Is there something you haven't told me, Mariam? Is it him—Iben's biological father? Do you know who he is after all?"

"I'm sorry," I say. "There are some things you simply don't want to know about me. Will you give me one day?"

He sighs.

"I have to think about it."

Once he's hung up, I lay flat on the bed and stare up at the ceiling tiles I studied so often during the years in which I lived here. I understand that Tor is desperate, and I'll understand if he calls the police right away. It bothers me that he has to go through this alone. Still, I can't turn back now. I have to find Iben.

Liv

Ålesund
Thursday, 14 April 2005

Anita passed a hand over one of the biggest bruises on her thigh. She kept her T-shirt on, said that she didn't want to show me how bad it actually was. Aurora lay on a baby duvet on the floor, a pink blanket pulled over her. She had slept through the night, perhaps worn out after everything she'd witnessed yesterday.

"Mamma didn't even want to see Aurora," Anita said. She wiped away a tear that had landed on her leg. "She's been hard to get on side before, but now . . . I can never forgive her."

I put my arms around her. Gently stroked her back.

"You're tough," I said. "I'm proud of you."

A sound pierced the room, and Anita jumped, so I let go of her, pulling back. It was her phone, vibrating on the bedside table. She picked it up, read the message.

"It's Birk. Again."

She threw the phone so that it flew across the room and landed in the pile of clothes I had gathered in the corner.

"I have to tell you something," she said. "I don't have the money for my own apartment. And I've no idea how I'm going to get it. Mamma isn't going to give me anything."

"What about your dad?"

She shook her head.

"He'll just say that I never should have given up my studies at the Norwegian Business School in order to become an artist. I'm going to have to get myself a job. Something that can earn me some money, fast."

"So live here for now," I said. "Until you find a better solution."

Just then we heard a loud crack—it came from the window. Another crack, and then another. Now we could see that someone was throwing stones. Anita got up, went over to look.

"No, Anita!" I cried, but it was too late. She withdrew.

"He saw me," she said. "How did he find me?"

"It must be the car."

"I didn't think he would come looking," she said. "He's crazier than I thought."

"He's probably gone around throwing stones at every window where there's a light on inside."

"What do we do now?"

The doorbell rang. Anita shrieked and curled up in the bed, pulling the duvet over her.

"Let's just hope nobody lets him in downstairs," I said, cursing my own words. Of course somebody was going to let him in.

We sat there, unmoving, and waited for several seconds. Finally we heard the echo of footsteps running up the stairs. Somebody grabbed the door handle, tried to turn it. Then there was the sound of a voice swearing, followed by a hard hammering on the door.

"Should we call the police?" I whispered.

"No! No, please."

"Why not? If I don't, the neighbours will."

Anita leaped over to the pile of clothes and rummaged around in it until she found her phone.

"I'm calling Egil."

Now Aurora woke up, too. The baby's anguished cry rose and fell, out of rhythm with the hammering on the door. Anita picked her up and rocked her as she held the phone between her cheek and shoulder. Then someone answered, and she began to talk over the sound of the crying, over the shouting from the man in the hall. I held my breath.

"I'm not leaving until you talk to me, Anita," Birk shouted through the door. "I'm sitting down on the steps now, and I'm going to sit here until you come out."

Anita hung up. I looked at her, standing there in nothing but her T-shirt, her baby in her arms. How calm she suddenly seemed despite the situation she was in—almost as if ready to fight.

"He said someone called David can probably help," she said. "Egil's calling him."

Hardly five minutes could have passed before I heard David's voice out in the hall. He must have run straight out of his apartment and over here. There were a couple of hard knocks at the door.

"Open up," David said.

I went over and twisted the lock, and David entered the room backwards, pulling Birk, twisting his arm behind his back. He crushed him against the door, twisting his arm even further until Birk gave out a howl of pain. David forced Birk's head against the door and leaned all the way forward.

"You've touched Anita for the last time, right?"

Birk nodded as well as he could with his head held fast.

"Now you're going to go home, and you are going to behave yourself so that we never have to see each other again. I'm going to be watching at the window to make sure you've gone."

He opened the door, shoved Birk out into the hall and slammed the door behind him.

I'd managed to throw on some clothes, but Anita had been busy with Aurora and was still only wearing her underwear and a T-shirt. She sat on the bed, rocking the baby, who had finally stopped crying. She didn't even seem to notice David's gaze, which flitted between me and her. Then David went over to the window. I went with him and saw Birk walk out of the building and across to a car. He seemed to be in great pain, nursing his arm.

When we turned back around, Anita had pulled the duvet over her.

"Thank you," she said. "That was quick."

David nodded. "I'm guessing that's his kid?" Then he shifted his gaze in my direction. Set his dark eyes on me.

"Anyway," he said, smiling. "I do this kind of thing for money, not for thanks. You know that, right?"

Anita turned pale.

"Because I'm guessing you must be able to afford it. Otherwise you wouldn't have ordered the torpedo."

He looked at me again, a hint of laughter in his eyes, and I realised that he'd probably just made all this up on the spot. Was it a way of getting one over on me? His eyes drilled into me, challenging my ability to win staring contests. I was still good, but he was a pro.

"How much?" Anita said. Her voice was shaking.

David looked up at the ceiling. Stuck the tip of his tongue out from between his narrow lips.

"I have an idea," he said. "On Saturday, I have a little job that needs doing. If one of you helps me with it, we can call it quits. Oh—and I'll even throw a few thousand kroner into the bargain."

David smiled at me, defiant. Now it was *his* turn to humiliate *me*, that smile seemed to say. Now he wanted to see me work for him. I bit my lip. Tried to think of another solution, but my mind was a complete blank.

"I'll do it."

Anita's voice was firm this time. She had already shown that she knew how to handle herself, and now she seemed eager to prove it.

"Anita—" I started.

"I'll do it," she interrupted. "Egil has already mentioned it to me, anyway—don't try to change my mind."

Aurora started to scream again. Her powerful cry cut through the room.

David laughed a brief, high-pitched laugh.

"I like you already, Anita."

Ronja

Kristiansund
Tuesday, 22 August 2017

I have foam earplugs in my ears, blocking out the humming of the machine. Instead I hear my own heartbeat, feel the vibrations when my feet hit the treadmill, the sweat that runs down my face to drip from my chin. I have to run without stopping, to push myself harder. My muscles can do it, my muscles can do it.

I want to focus on running—to refuse to let my head think about work right now. Want to shut out the divers who sink far too slowly into the water, who should instead be hurtling down into the depths. The helicopters that take too long—they should be whizzing through the air as if in an action film. The ground is on fire beneath our feet, we have to search, but I also have to run—if I don't, I'll go insane. I have to run and give my mind some rest, so it will be ready to do what it can to help.

This is what the investigation is like—a treadmill we're running on, without getting anywhere. No matter how fast we run, we remain in the same place—and maybe we'll never find her alive, the little blond girl who's laughing with her mother in the photograph, two happy girls in matching sweaters. If she's still alive, she must be held captive somewhere, gagged and bound, even starving perhaps. I mustn't think about it. I have to think of the sound of my own heart, the buzzing of the treadmill, the smell of my sweat, and focus on keeping up the intensity.

I keep an eye on how many kilometres I've run, the incline and speed. The equipment registers my pulse, too, and I know how much my body can take, that I can push myself even further. Past glimpses of memories of the hours spent in the car with Birte on our way from place to place, the people we've met; last Friday's drunken memories of me and August in a close embrace on the dance floor. How I later staggered home to sober up because a little girl was missing.

I pick up my towel and wipe my face without stopping. When I run, I always take out my contact lenses so I don't have to see the other people in the room. I can't take any more input, can't bear colours, light, voices—all I want is to feel my heart beating. It usually helps to run, but today not even running keeps the thoughts at bay. In my head is an image of a little girl lying battered and bruised on a stone floor, crying because we haven't found her yet. Tomorrow we're going to make even more inquiries, and I, the rookie, am going to conduct even more interviews—what if I ruin the entire investigation? Me—who couldn't work on the case on Friday night because I was drunk and messing around with my colleague.

I slam the button to shut off the treadmill and wipe my face again. It's no good. Today not even running helps. I have to do something, anything.

Mariam

Ålesund
Tuesday, 22 August 2017

"Mariam Lind," I say. "I was told to call back. It's about Egil Brynseth, who I need to see as soon as possible."

"He says he knows you," says the officer. "You're old friends?"

I clear my throat.

"That's right. From when we were kids."

"You have a clean record," he says. "Usually it takes time to be able to visit an inmate, but if you're only in Ålesund this week, we can make an exception. You can come this Thursday, at ten thirty."

"I can't come earlier than that? Or speak to him?"

"That's the best I can do," he says.

Ingvar looks up as I walk into the living room. He's sitting on the sofa with his electric guitar in his lap and a plectrum in his mouth. He's been passionate about music as long as I've known him. Not in an ambitious way, not because he dreams of becoming a rock star—or at least I don't think so. It's more something he can't live without, as important to him as sleep and food. I've never had anything like that. True, I've built up a company from nothing, have invested God knows how much time in it. It was something I wanted to do, and which I succeeded in, but there's no passion in it. I could have abandoned it and never looked back. I've hardly thought to check whether my deputy is managing to keep control of the new project—I simply slammed that mental door shut when Iben disappeared. How many other doors can I close?

"I can't visit Egil until Thursday," I say, slumping down on the sofa beside him.

"That's fast. I haven't been allowed to visit him at all," Ingvar says. "They've got it into their heads that I have friends 'in the scene.'" He makes air quotes with his fingers.

"Well don't you?"

"It's years since I hung out with any of those people."

I nod.

"So when you're not working or hanging around here, what do you do? Who do you hang out with?"

Ingvar reaches for his pouch of tobacco.

"I'm at Smutten quite a bit, have a few friends who hang out there."

"None of the people you used to hang around with?"

He shakes his head and takes out a fresh cigarette paper.

"Or—well. Yes. Maybe."

I sigh.

"So what are you going to do now?" he says, lighting his rollie and brushing away an ember that falls onto his jeans.

"Like I said, there are two people who could have taken the key—Egil or Patrick. It's too long to wait until I can speak to

Egil. So I have to get hold of Patrick. If it's him . . ." I stop myself.

"I don't think so," Ingvar says. "I just can't see it."

I look down at my phone. My hands are shaking just at the thought of opening a website, starting to look. Something stops me. I hand the phone to Ingvar.

"Do you have his number? Or do you have him on social media or something? Can you try to get hold of him?"

"But I told you that I don't—"

"Can you find him?"

He starts to tap the screen. Sits there like that as I watch him. He's older, with wrinkles at his forehead and new depressions in certain areas of his face—he's hollowed out. There's always been something slightly apathetic about him, and this seems to have become more pronounced as the years have passed. Then he makes a noise. Lets out a kind of whimper with his breath. It seems unconscious.

"What is it?" I say, and he straightens up.

"Nothing. He's on a few music sites I use. I'll send him a message there."

"What about a phone number?"

"I can't find one. He might be ex-directory, or have a secret number."

I nod. "Send a message to every profile you find—tell him you have to talk to him. Don't tell him what it's about, just that it's important."

If Patrick has done something to Iben, then he'll know that the messages are coming from me. Maybe that's what he wants—to make me come back. Why else would he send me a strategically placed message in Iben's room? Something only I would understand.

I take out the key, letting it dangle from its chain in front
of me. Follow it with my gaze as it rotates in the air, around
and around. I spread my fingers inside the chain so that it
opens into a kind of heart. When this key first disappeared,
I also disappeared from this apartment. I no longer felt safe
here. Now I'm back, going around in circles, becoming a snake
that bites its own tail. I have to relive everything I've spent my
entire life trying to run away from.

"If he doesn't answer," I say, "I'll have to go visit her
tomorrow."

For a moment it seems as if he's wondering who I'm talking
about, but then he gets it. I never say *Mamma*.

Ronja

Kristiansund
Tuesday, 22 August 2017

August looks at me in surprise as I come walking down the corridor at the station.

"Are you working now?"

I shake my head. "Not really. I just have something I need to sort out in the office."

He nods. Looks around him in the otherwise abandoned corridor, following me as I take the few steps over to my office. He stands in the doorway as I go in. I sit down on the desk chair and look towards him, hoping he isn't planning on having a chat right now. He smiles, and nods towards the enormous jigsaw puzzle of the Rakotzbrücke in Germany that hangs on the wall above my desk.

"That's a lot of pieces," he says.

Mamma and I spent a total of six months completing the puzzle. We would roll it up on a tablecloth each time we did a bit, so we could continue later. It became our joint project. Other colleagues who have seen the jigsaw have laughed at it.

They think it's nerdy to hang a jigsaw puzzle on the wall at work. None of them understands what it means to me.

"It's a *Teufelsbrücke*," I say. "A devil's bridge. It's constructed as an optical illusion. Do you see—it looks like a perfect circle of stone."

He laughs. "Yeah, very cool. Is it like the entrance to hell?"

"Or the exit," I say. "Depending on which side you're standing on."

"Perspective," he says. "Interesting." He nods towards the picture. "It reminds me of the Infinite Bridge in Aarhus. Although that bridge isn't an illusion, but a true circle—you can walk around and around it for all eternity." He laughs. "That's also a kind of hell, in a way."

"Why did you leave Denmark?" I ask.

"Because I was walking around in circles." He laughs. "No opportunities for development, either at work or in the relationship I was in. I wanted to try something new. And I have family up here."

He stands there rocking on the soles of his feet.

"Listen . . ." he starts, his Adam's apple bobbing up and down his skinny, poorly shaved neck.

I shake my head. "You don't need to say anything. Just leave it be."

He shoves his hands in his pockets, perhaps wondering whether he should say something regardless, but he stops. When he holds his head like that, he's sort of handsome, in the way that boys were in high school. It's about perspective—like the jigsaw puzzle.

After he's gone, I fire up my computer and open the program in which all criminal cases are stored. Search for the right case and find the first interviews. Click on Roe Olsvik's

interview with Mariam Lind just hours after Iben had disappeared. There's the sound of somebody clearing their throat
and the rustling of papers as the sound file begins to play.

"Let's see," Roe says before pausing. "I've been provided
with a reasonable summary of the statement you've already
given, but I have some additional questions."

Liv

Ålesund
Saturday, 16 April 2005

Anita had pulled on a pair of black jeans, a black T-shirt and an orange and blue hoodie with a football logo and zip at the front. She tugged her hair into a bun at the nape of her neck, lifted the hood over her head and hung a matching scarf around her neck.

"How do I look?"

I laughed. "Like a football supporter."

She looked at herself in the hall mirror.

"I could use some lipstick," she said. "Maybe some earrings."

"Only if you want to attract attention to yourself."

She pulled out her nose ring and set it on the kitchen counter.

"I won't be long," Anita said. "The bottles of milk are in the fridge—heat them to body temperature in the microwave. Nappies and wet wipes are in the changing bag. If for some reason you have to go anywhere, just use my car."

"I'm not going anywhere."

"Just in case . . . you know."

It hadn't occurred to her until last night that she might get caught—she had lain there crying in the dark for several hours. I tried as hard as I could to convince her not to go through with it, but it was no use. She imagined all kinds of awful things that might happen if she pulled out now.

The doorbell rang, and from the window I could see that it was Egil down there—he waved his scarf above his head. From one of his hands hung a supermarket carrier bag. Anita pulled on her shoes. Stopped for a brief moment, as if she wanted to tell me something, then shook her head.

"I'll see you soon," she said. And then she was gone.

Aurora lay on the floor, sleeping and still. With any luck, she would sleep until Anita got back. I'd never had anything to do with babies before—had no idea if I would manage to get her clean if she filled her nappy, or if I'd be able to put a new one on her. I glanced down at the tiny human; she was snoring lightly. Her nose was so small, her lips puckering as she slept. She looked like her mother. An absurd copy in miniature, almost frightening, but not only that. She sort of looked like me, too. She could just as easily have been my child. I'd never imagined it before—had never considered that possibility. But right then I thought that one day I might be someone's mother. Why not?

Outside, I heard a group of male voices singing a football song, probably on their way from the pub to the match. The thought of Anita out there risking everything right now made me dizzy. I just hoped it would all go as smoothly as Egil seemed sure it would.

Just then I heard a piercing howl. Aurora screamed, becoming almost blood-red in the face. I held her close against my chest, as I had seen Anita hold her, and tried to lull the tiny creature to sleep. She was hot and heavy in my arms, yowling out a possessed yearning for her mother. I rocked her as well as I could, taking care not to drop what Anita had entrusted to me.

I opened the fridge and took out one of the small bottles of Anita's breast milk. I put it in the microwave to heat as I tried to soothe the baby—she seemed to have the world's strongest vocal cords. I took the bottle of milk from the microwave, but it was far too hot—the bottle burned my fingers—and I ended up dropping it into the sink. Aurora screamed. I'd have to try another bottle.

This time it went better. I bounced Aurora on my hip and dripped lukewarm milk onto my wrist as I had seen Anita do. Sat on the bed and tried to put the bottle's teat to the baby's mouth. Aurora howled and twisted and started to cry more loudly.

"What is it, little one?" I said, rocking her. Maybe it was the lack of her mother's scent, or the bottle that was a poor replacement for Anita's warm nipples. I tried again, but Aurora bristled, resisting with everything she had. Her howling exploded against my eardrums, hard and painful. I tried to push the bottle into her mouth, tried to soothe her, but nothing worked. In the end I sat there, half-heartedly rocking the little creature, hushing and shushing her. Then the telephone rang.

It was Ingvar's number on the screen. At first I just wanted to let the phone ring until it gave up. But then I changed my mind. Aurora's crying filled me with an aggression that I wanted to take out on somebody—anyone at all. I threw myself forward and grabbed the phone, ready to fight.

"What do you want?" I shouted above the baby's shrieking.

On the other end of the line I could hear music from *Dope-throne*, Ingvar's favourite album.

"Hello?" I said. "Are you there?"

Aurora continued her long, grief-stricken wailing. The music was still playing, but Ingvar was silent.

Ronja

Kristiansund
Tuesday, 22 August 2017

"August! August!"

I stand in the corridor, shouting in the direction of August's office. I haven't heard whether he's left—I've been far too busy listening to the interviews. But now my body is vibrating with anxiety, and if August isn't here, I don't know what I'll do. "August!" I'm just starting to take long strides down the corridor when he appears in the doorway. He's smiling in surprise, puts a hand to his hip.

"What's up?"

He's flirting, and it's my fault. If only I could take back that kiss, undo the whole thing.

"Can I show you something?"

He accompanies me to the office. Sits on a chair right next to me in front of the computer screen. He's wearing a nice aftershave, the same as on Friday. These are the kinds of things that tempt me. Scents—even the completely ordinary kind that anyone might see fit to spray on themselves.

"Birte advised me to watch and listen to some of Roe's interviews, for tips. Good questions, tells from body language or voice—that sort of thing. So I've been watching a few from different cases." I click on an interview in which Roe is talking to a man who was taken into custody in connection with a series of rapes.

"This case was just awful—do you remember it? Four girls aged between twelve and fourteen. I was so filled with rage when we brought him in that I didn't know what to do with myself. Look at Roe's body language. He's sitting in a forward leaning position, his arms uncrossed; his voice and attitude are calm, right?"

August leans forward. Puts on the headphones and listens to what is said for a few minutes. Then he leans back and takes the headphones off again.

"What's your point?"

I fast-forward to where the interview is nearing its end.

"Here's the critical part of the interview, where Roe—after having let the suspect speak freely for a long time and asking good, open questions—starts to present counterarguments. Everything he does is completely by the book. Listen to this part. Does it sound as if he's pushing the suspect, or does it sound as if he's staying neutral and letting the suspect make his own statements?"

August puts the headphones back on, his expression focused as he listens, then takes the headphones off again.

"The latter. He did a good job."

I close the interview and find the next case I want to show August in the system.

"This is the interview Roe conducted with Mariam Lind on Friday. There's only a sound recording. Could you listen to this?"

"I've already heard it. It was terrible. He got agitated; she got defensive."

I nod. "Would you listen to it again, now?"

August does as I ask. He listens patiently as I sit there almost bouncing on my chair next to him. I curse my body for being so full of all kinds of conflicting emotions. He's perfectly fine, but not exactly my dream guy. Still, my body is trembling. If he were suddenly to make a move, I don't know whether I'd reject him. It's all so complicated.

August takes off the headphones. Looks at me expectantly, doesn't want to speak until I've explained why I asked him to listen to the recording. The manner of a true investigator— someone who waits and scrutinises, who always listens and takes note of the details before starting to draw conclusions. The recipe for avoiding the trap of confirmation bias. I take a breath.

"In all the interviews conducted by Roe that I've watched, he's done everything strictly by the book. He lets the interviewees speak freely, asks just a few open questions, and several times asks the people he's interviewing to think carefully and provide a detailed description of the incident. He uses the same phrasing as the interviewees, tells them 'you just said' and so on, uses memory-stimulating techniques with questions linked to senses and emotions, listens actively to what is said and waits until the interviewee has finished giving their description before providing contradictory information. All this is correct procedure. But in that last interview with Mariam Lind, he's completely different. He asks too many questions at once, so she's unable to explain herself. He interrupts her and pressures her. Don't you think it strange that he asks her straight out whether Iben was in the boot of her car? Or that he—in not so many words—basically calls her a bad mother?"

August lowers his head and nods weakly. "Do you think this means something more than that he simply got agitated because the case is so serious?"

I nod. "He's worked serious cases before—spoken to the worst kinds of offenders. All without raising his voice or acting unprofessionally in any way."

August puts on the headphones again and plays the interview from the beginning. Listens to the voice on the recording, his face creased in concentration. When he's finished listening, he sets a hand on his knee, as if to support himself.

"Even if he thought the first interview covered the most important details," August says, "that's no reason to do a bad job himself."

"He thinks Mariam has done something to Iben. That must be why. He's convinced that she's guilty, so he's unable to stay neutral. But that's still strange—for someone with so many years of experience. So many terrible cases he must have been involved in, so much suffering. This can't be the first time he's been convinced that someone is guilty of something gruesome. He knows that no matter what we might think someone has done, they have the right to be heard."

August shakes his head. "I don't understand why he would be so convinced, either. There's currently no compelling evidence against Mariam Lind."

I look at the computer screen, trying to recall Roe's friendly attitude in the first of the two interviews, the serial rapist right in front of him. Try to make that correspond to the last

interview with Iben Lind's mother, in which his voice seems
to be indignant with rage.

"And there's something else," I say, picking up my phone.
"On Friday, in the bar, I wrote a message to Roe on this and
showed it to him. I still have his answer saved here." I show
August the message.

*It's always okay to be angry. Not at the bad guys, not when
making arrests or during questioning, but otherwise always.*

"How could he write this and then go off and conduct such
a terrible, furious interview that same evening?"

August frowns. "You have a point."

"It's strange," I say. "It almost seems as if this case affects
him personally in some way."

Roe

Ålesund
Saturday, 16 April 2005

"Roe, do you have a minute?"

Sverre stuck his bearded face around the door to my office. This was obviously not a day on which the people of Ålesund were taking it easy. After several rounds of inquiries after a break-in at Kipervika, I thought I'd have time to do some paperwork with a cup of coffee and the football on in the background. The first match ever to be played at the new stadium, but from the look on Sverre's face I knew I could kiss goodbye any hopes of watching the game. Something else had happened.

"Can't you see I'm sitting here enjoying the view?" I said, waving at the grey concrete block that housed the Rema 1000 supermarket opposite. If you bothered to look up and tried to ignore all the asphalt, you could actually see that there was quite a nice view from here—some mountains in the distance at least—but I rarely tried.

"There's been an assault," said Sverre. "We need you."

I jumped out of my chair and hurried through the corridors after Sverre. He held his access card to the door and ushered me out into the connecting passage, closing the door behind us as I held my access card to the next door.

"A man was found on the ground in the pedestrian zone. He had head injuries. He got up when a passerby went over to him, but he seemed disoriented and couldn't remember what had happened. He's being taken to the hospital by ambulance now. The man hasn't been identified—his wallet is missing. Witnesses said two individuals ran from the scene wearing Ålesund FC shirts, blue hoodies and orange scarves, and jeans."

We got into the lift.

"That sounds like half the city today," I said, pushing the button. "I just hope they're not actually going to the match."

Sverre nodded. "One of them had a Rema 1000 carrier bag in his hand. Let's hope he keeps a good hold of it."

We came out into the underground car park; I went around to the driver's side of the car. The radio crackled as I started the engine. Someone cleared their throat on the other end.

"Parkgata. We've apprehended a suspect in the assault. Seized a weapon and stolen property in a Rema 1000 bag. We don't know where the other suspect is. According to witnesses it might be a woman."

I grabbed the radio. "Wait for me—I want to talk to him before you take him in."

The radio crackled.

"Good luck."

I started the blue lights as we entered the flow of traffic making its way towards the stadium. Cars crept up onto curbs and down side roads in order to let us pass. Most pedestrians were wearing hoodies or fleece jackets with the Ålesund FC logo, and many had matching scarves. Looking for the right person among these crowds would be hopeless.

On the way up Løvenvoldgata I turned off the blue lights, but there was little point in doing so. The first car had its lights on even though it was parked, flashing its blue lights as if there had been a major accident, and not just an incident in which a couple of youths had beaten a guy up. A small group of bystanders were watching from the other side of the street. I couldn't see what they were seeing until I got close—one of the police officers had restrained and was openly arguing with a young boy. He seemed distressed, shouting and cursing and trying to break free—he fell over and was yanked rather than helped up again. This must have been going on for quite a while. I took a deep breath and got out of the car.

"Hi," I said in as friendly a voice as I could muster. The police officer turned to face me, but I wasn't looking at him. I looked at the boy, finding his eyes with mine and giving him a smile. "I don't think we've met." I reached behind his back and took hold of one of his restrained hands. Gave him a solid handshake. "Chief Inspector Roe Olsvik. I'd like to have a word with you once we're in the car."

"Go to hell," spat the boy.

The police officer tightened his grip on the boy's arms, but I lifted a hand to signal that he shouldn't bother.

"I may very well be going to hell, but I hope that's a few years off yet. How about you?"

The boy looked down, kicking childishly at the ground with his white trainers. They looked as if they might be fashionable, but I'd stopped knowing what was trendy long ago.

"I just have to do one little thing before we go over to the car," I said. "I have to check your pockets and pat you down to check that you don't have any more weapons on you. Just to be sure that our driver doesn't get a bullet in the back of his head."

The boy shook his head. "I don't have anything on me."

I lifted my hands.

"And I believe you—but I have to do it anyway. Because if it turns out I'm wrong and you have a weapon, it won't help a damn that I believed you, will it? So. This won't take a minute."

I patted down the chest and stomach of his football sweater, felt his trouser pockets and legs. Then I moved to stand beside him and gently took his arm, as if we were an elderly couple. He twisted and writhed.

"I know, I know. But let me tell you something: if you cooperate with me, you'll end up in exactly the same position as if you cause a ruckus. The only difference is that if you cooperate, this will be much easier on all of us."

The rookie grabbed the boy on his other side, and we led him over to the car. I asked him to mind his head as he got in. He calmly slumped down as we fastened the handcuffs in front of his body and put on his seat belt. Then I went around to the opposite door and got into the car beside him.

"Well done," I said. "Now we're going to take you to the police station, where they'll examine you and ask you a few questions. I suggest you cooperate. Maybe you'll find out that this was the best thing that could have happened to you—the fact that you got arrested today. I hope so."

The boy stared straight ahead at the windshield.

"I'll leave it to my colleagues to ask you all about the details. The only thing I need your help with is finding your coconspirator. Can you help me with that?"

The boy seemed to consider this, weighing the pros and cons. He didn't know that he didn't have to say anything. The only thing I could hope for was that some of my words might reach him, and that he would want to change his life—do something right. He took a deep breath. Slowly let it out again.

"I don't know her," he said. "Today was the first time I'd ever met her. She didn't want to tell me her name."

I nodded. "That's okay. That's the kind of thing I want you to tell my colleagues. What I need to know now is where this woman might have gone. Can you tell me that?"

The boy couldn't be much older than twenty-two. I wondered where his parents were, whether they knew what he was up to. Some parents gave their children far too long a leash. Not that I could talk—I'd been no better myself. It was just a good thing my daughter had never ended up part of the scene to which this boy likely belonged.

"She has the keys." The words fell out of him.

"What keys?"

He clenched his hands into fists.

"The plan was that I was supposed to bear the brunt of it if things went wrong. I was supposed to steal his wallet and phone; she would take the keys, deliver them to a car. They're driving to the house to empty the safe."

I grabbed his hand as he said this. Gave it another firm shake.

"Do you have the address?"

He nodded; wrote down the address on the notepad I handed to him.

"You've done the right thing," I said. "Thank you for the nice chat."

His eyes were suddenly uneasy.

"Don't be afraid," I said. "It's not as scary as it seems."

"I'm an idiot," he said. "I thought I was a totally different person, like, I could be a gangster or something. How is he?"

"He's at the hospital."

I turned to leave, but the boy cleared his throat.

"Thank you," he mumbled.

I turned, and gave him a small smile.

As soon as I'd closed the door behind me, I ran across to the nearest officer.

"It's a covert burglary. We have to go to the guy's house."

The officer shouted the message to the others and hurried towards a car; Sverre was ready and waiting in ours.

"Everything indicates that the man at the hospital is Halvor Brynseth, principal shareholder in Brynseth Shipping," he said.

"I know—the kid told me. We have to get moving."

I gave Sverre the address and he entered it in the GPS.

"Klokkersundet," he said, showing me an aerial photograph of a house the size of three regular detached properties.

I grabbed the police radio.

"Car two, follow me. Car three, drive home with the accused and follow after."

The two cars confirmed from their relative positions. I asked Sverre to read the address over the radio, and stepped on the gas as we moved down Rådstugata towards the highway. Again, we had to weave our way past excited football supporters on their way to the game. The match was sold out, and the sun could even be seen peeking through the layer of cloud. I sent good thoughts to the players before once again banishing the match from my mind and speeding past the cars that pulled over onto the hard shoulder to let us pass. If we were lucky, they wouldn't have much of a lead—but it was impossible to know.

The drive wasn't long. I soon turned off at Borgund, drove past the road to the Sunnmøre Museum and continued towards Klokkersundet. Turned off the sirens when we started to get close. Finally we turned into a huge, empty driveway surrounded by an enormous property. The windows looked dark. Sverre was out of the car before I'd even managed to turn off the ignition and before the next car managed to pull up beside us. We ran up the steps to the front door, where Sverre already stood with his finger on the doorbell.

"We're going in," I said. "Come on."

Sverre pulled on a pair of gloves and grabbed the door handle—the door opened immediately. We followed him inside, splitting up to clear the house. I went right with Sverre, where we found a kitchen the size of a small apartment, a living room, two bathrooms and four enormous bedrooms. As we checked the first floor, a message came over the radio that the third car was on its way. Which was good—the house was far too big for us to manage on our own. As we were on our way back down the stairs, the radio crackled again.

"Office on the first floor, west wing," said one of the officers. "There's an open safe here. It's empty."

Liv

Ålesund
Saturday, 16 April 2005

I had dressed Aurora in too many clothes, or she was hungry, or she was mad at having to be fastened into her car seat. Her bawling drilled into my head, sharp and excruciating. I didn't stop to give way at the roundabout, turning abruptly and almost hitting a drunken football supporter who was taking far too long making his way over the pedestrian crossing. Aurora screamed—it seemed she never took a breath. How on earth was she able to howl like this without stopping to breathe?

"Shut up!" I shouted. "Shut up, I'm trying to think!"

But Aurora's voice only seemed to increase in volume as I drove on towards Skarbøvika, where the cars were fewer and I could put my foot down, feeling the resistance in the turns. I continued on past all the houses, keeping going, keeping going. What lay behind me didn't exist; nor did that which lay ahead. All that existed was the incessant screaming from the back seat, the baby that didn't have to breathe, and the thought that Ingvar had probably just had a seizure while all alone.

I stopped in the parking space in front of the house. Aurora was strapped in with all kinds of belts and buckles that were just as hard to get open as they had been to fasten. I put the crying baby over my shoulder and ran as fast as I could. Hurried down all the stone steps—it had to be possible to get her to calm down, but there was no time now. I had to find out what was going on.

The front door was open. Inside, the air was stuffy. Music rumbled through the apartment, mixing with the noise Aurora was making. The same CD was still playing.

"Ingvar? Ingvar?"

The music was too loud, as was Aurora's screaming—I couldn't think. I bounced her in my arms and hushed her. Hurried into the living room where the music was pouring out of the stereo system and turned it off. Aurora hiccupped in fright for a moment before she started up another round of violent cries. I put her down on the armchair and ran towards Ingvar's room, where the door was ajar.

He lay on the bed with his eyes closed, his phone in his hand. On the nightstand beside him was a glass of what looked like whisky, and an ashtray with a pungent lit joint in it. I couldn't see whether he was breathing, only that he was unmoving, stiff. I ran across to him, grabbed his arm and shook him, but he didn't move until I was close enough to put my hand over his nose and mouth to see whether he was breathing. Then his eyes flicked open, and a smile spread across his thin face.

"What the hell?" I said.

Ingvar sat up, laughing briefly, holding up his palms. "Listen, before you completely lose it—"

"What do you mean, before I lose it?"

I got up from the edge of the bed, where I'd been sitting like a worried nurse.

"It was Egil's idea. I've tried to call you so many times, but you never pick up the phone. Egil thought there was a much greater chance of you answering if you knew that he was busy with the robbery. That you'd be afraid I'd had an epileptic fit. He suggested that I call you, and not say anything, to get you to come over. So we could talk."

"And that's supposed to be funny?" I said. "That I drove over here at top speed because I thought you were dying?"

"I'm sorry, I—"

"No," I said. "'I'm sorry' isn't going to cut it. I don't have time for this bullshit."

"I just wanted to—"

I slammed the door over the sound of his voice.

"Yeah, great fucking job!" I shouted through the door. "Great job showing that you're someone who can be trusted!"

I listened through the door, even though I knew I wouldn't receive an answer. He was too much of a coward for that. He'd stay in his room now, right until after I'd gone.

I kicked the laundry rack so that it tipped over, jangling as it hit the ground. Then I stopped.

It was far too quiet. I could hear my own thoughts, my heart beating in my chest. I could hear the sound of my feet as they took their first tentative steps towards the living room door. Had she finally decided to go to sleep? A mixture of relief and unease washed over me. I slowly walked the last few steps over to the door. Stopped for a moment before I stepped over the threshold. Stood there, trying to understand what I was seeing.

Reptile memoirs

I lay hidden under the large piece of furniture that the humans tended to sit on. Resting my head on my belly, I slept. I was weak after having been starved for weeks, and starved of all hope, too, because it seemed that my power over the warm woman was lost. The male humans gave me nothing, either. They wanted to lift me and carry me around, but they did not feed me properly. The only thing that helped was hiding.

What woke me was not the usual vibrations with which these male humans liked to fill the rooms. I had, in a way, got used to those—or I was tired enough that sleep won out. What woke me this time was a smell. I tasted the air from where I lay, my taste organ seeming to light up from the inside. A sweet smell that reminded me of the warm woman's scent, but purer, even more refined. A smell that seemed to carry all my dreams within it.

I crept forward, licking the air, and was struck yet again by how wonderful the smell was. It was coming from the smaller piece of furniture. I couldn't see anything from my position down below; had to steal around and climb up into it in order to see. It was a tiny person, entirely new. Never before had I seen such a creature, so defenceless and yet so human. It glowed with heat, seemed agitated by something. A violent, invisible force was coming from its tiny mouth, a sound that made the chair vibrate around us.

I felt my teeth contract. Kept control of myself for a split second in order to truly savour the pleasure at having found such fantastic prey, before I darted forth. Sank my teeth into the little neck and felt the sweet, bloody juices run down my throat.

Ronja

Kristiansund
Wednesday, 23 August 2017

It's six o'clock in the morning, and I'm already at the office. None of the other investigators have made it in yet. I'm so tired I could faint, but feeling determined nonetheless. On the desk beside the computer, along with a double latte and a bag of baked goods from the kiosk, is a spiral-bound notepad. On it I've noted the way Robert Kirkeby described the man he saw Iben talking to outside Storkaia on Friday. A big man. Wide jaw, grey shirt. His nose like a large hook, a witch. A carrier bag from the Cubus clothing store in his hand. This last note I've underlined several times.

I hadn't thought of it before—not until early this morning, when I lay awake thinking of Robert Kirkeby and what a shame it was that he couldn't explain what he'd seen in any coherent way. How I wished we had another witness in addition to him, or some other sort of evidence. Something to strengthen his testimony, give him the credibility he deserves. I so wanted this for Robert, who maybe never in his entire life felt valued, important. That was when I remembered something he'd said. The carrier bag from Cubus. There are no Cubus stores in the area where the man was seen, apart from the one at the Storkaia shopping centre.

Roe Olsvik has already been through these recordings, but he's been focused on Mariam's and Iben's movements. He hasn't been looking for this—a big man with a wide jaw, hooked nose and grey shirt. If I look through all the surveillance footage from outside Cubus, it should be possible to identify some candidates.

I drink the coffee and eat a bun, feeling a certain joy at the combination of working out hard five times a week and eating delicious, unhealthy baked goods. I'm not such a damned "good girl" as everyone thinks.

The footage shows many customers going in and out of Cubus. I've seen nobody who fits the description so far. They're too young, or they're women, or they're wearing a sweater, jacket or shirt that's the wrong colour, or they don't have a bag in their hand upon leaving the store.

Shivers of tiredness run down my spine. There's something numbing about watching this stream of people moving past the camera. Maybe it would have been good to sleep for a while after all. I'm not actually supposed to be at work just yet—I could take a nap on the sofa in the break room, as Roe did when he spent the night here. Roe. There's something about the guy. Always so gloomy—when you talk to him, it almost seems as if he's taking umbrage. He can't have been like that when he first started as a police officer. He's probably still affected by the . . . tragedy. The rumours had spread quickly, of course, when he started here. Apparently he was ill for a long time afterwards. That's not so strange. Can you ever be well again after something like that?

The tiredness overwhelms me, and my head starts to nod. The flow of people becomes a blur of colours on the screen. It would be good to close my eyes, to disappear for a moment. Dream about the time Mamma and I sat together doing the jigsaw puzzle, how immersed in it we were, her fingers moving so lightly as she searched the sea of pieces before us. No, I mustn't sleep now. I have to pay attention. Just think if I miss the perpetrator. I force my head out of its thick doze. Lean forward, and press pause.

The image freezes as a single man is making his way past the camera. He's broad shouldered, middle-aged, his hair flecked with grey. He has a wide jaw, a hooked nose, and a bag from Cubus in his right hand. The remainder of my coffee has gone cold, but I empty it down my throat all the same. As I set the cup back on the desk, my hand is trembling.

Liv

Ålesund
Saturday, 16 April 2005

I stood bent over the flower bed behind one of the landlady's rosebushes, a small trowel in my hand. If she looked out of the window now, she'd hopefully just think I had finally decided to do some gardening. Using the trowel, I dug down deep. Helped the process along with my hands, the soil getting under my nails and making my skin slick and brown.

Beside me in the grass lay Aurora, the baby with the damp skin and big eyes, neatly wrapped in her pink baby blanket. Nero was furious when I pounced on him to prise her out of his coil. He threw himself at me and bit me on the arm, leaving a deep wound. Wouldn't let go until I took the lava lamp from the TV bench and hit him over the back with it.

I set the trowel aside, sticking my arms down into the hole and pulling up more earth with my fingers, the soil burrowing deep beneath my nails. Every now and then I stared at the bundle that lay beside me. I pictured the scene again and again—how I had entered the room and seen that it was already too late, that he had killed and suffocated tiny Aurora, and that it was all my fault. I did my best to push the awful images away as I pulled up fistfuls of earth, creating a huge mound of soil, and it occurred to me that by the time I was done, more earth would remain aboveground than below. I realised that burying the little body would not make her disappear, but that earth would be replaced by body, that I was exchanging a body in return for earth. The thought churned within me, making me anxious and afraid. Earth was no replacement— earth could not be put in a pram or sleep on your chest. The soil was cold, the edges of the grave visible. Might they come here with cadaver dogs and find her? *Cadaver*—such a grue- some word. It sounded as cold as stone.

I'd managed to get her away before Ingvar could come out and see what had happened. If I could only hide my tracks—in the soil, the grass—nobody would ever know where to find her. I could get away. I lifted a hand to my face, tried to wipe away the tears with a dirty hand. The soil was hostile and caring at one and the same time—a despised friend. If only I could bury myself in this garden, too, so no one could ever find me.

Burying a tiny baby's body in broad daylight. But I had no choice. I had to get away from here. I had to bury the body, the corpse, the death, and then I had to get away. Start over. I'd become someone else before—I could do it again now. Someone entirely new. Fresh and clean; someone who cared only about good things. Could I be like that again? I dug my fingers into the sides of the hole, dragging them upwards and scraping two piles of earth over the edge. It felt as if the dig- ging would never end. The hole was still so small, and every time I dug down, more soil seemed to run back into it. This must be my punishment—to dig in the soil for all eternity.

Farther down, the earth was harder, clumped and full of stones. I used the trowel to scrape down the walls and loosen the packed earth. My fingers were cold and wet. My shoulders ached, my hands were tired, but I had to keep going, had to dig through the pain.

In the end I could stick my entire forearm down into the hole, bathing it in the dirt. Now I just had to stomach the thought of putting a little baby down there in that hole. Of covering it over, letting the earth close around it, blocking out everything that had been turned upside down, flames and cockroaches in my soul. My tears mixed with the dirt. I couldn't take any more, but I had no choice. I grabbed the pink bundle, which had now turned so stiff and cold that it no longer felt like a baby. The pink blanket was quickly dirtied by the soil on my hands. I leaned forward, slowly started to lower her down.

"Liv?"

I looked up. A couple of metres away stood a figure wearing an orange and blue football sweater. She had its hood pulled over her head. She looked at the trowel, the piles of earth and the hole and the dirty baby blanket in my hands.

"Liv . . ."

The baby landed in the hole with a dull thud. I threw myself forward, pushing the largest mound of earth with my hands and torso so that it fell over her.

"No!" Anita screamed.

She ran towards me. Grabbed hold of my arm and dragged me away, starting to scrabble through the dirt with her fingers.

"Don't do it, Anita," I said. "You don't want to see her like this."

"Get away from me!"

She suddenly had a strength I'd never seen in her before. She shoved me backwards, so that I landed on my back on the ground. All the air was knocked out of me. Beside me, I heard Anita commence a high-pitched, agonising wailing. She rocked Aurora in her arms, back and forth, as if in a trance.

"You can't be here!" I shouted. "You have to go home, to your house. You've never been here—you don't know me. You have to leave Aurora here. Aurora is dead, you have to leave her here, and you have to bury that sweater."

Anita continued to rock the baby. I went over to her, tried to touch her hair, but she didn't seem to react. I tried to open her arms, but they seemed glued to the baby's body.

"You have to let her go, Anita."

Anita turned towards me. Her face was distorted with rage.

"Stay away from my baby," she hissed.

Then she got up and left, her arms embracing the dead body. That was the last time I saw her.

Roe

Ålesund
Saturday, 16 April 2005

We gathered in the meeting room for a quick update on the robbery case. I should have finished my shift ages ago, but with a case like this I could keep going into the night if necessary. The small meeting room was soon crowded with officers, so I would keep it brief.

"Why don't you start, Sverre," I said. "I observed parts of your interview with the kid. Can you give us a report?"

Sverre nodded. "He's probably withholding information from us—he's stubborn. He's determined that he didn't know the name of the girl he carried out the mugging with, but he's given us a description. He's also given us the name of the person he's working for, which doesn't seem to check out, so either the guy has given him a false name, or the boy is lying. Nor does he want to give the names of any of the others who were involved—he's afraid of the consequences. We're going to interview him again this evening."

I nodded. This was what I had been afraid of.

"What are his contacts like?" I said.

"He claims not to keep company with anyone dodgy, and says that this was a one-off incident. He was under the influence of alcohol when we apprehended him, and he's tested positive for hash and marijuana. He has a link to David Lorentzen and his scene—we've been trying to get Lorentzen for dealing for a while now."

I had long been responsible for keeping an eye on Lorentzen. His network was extensive and complicated—there were many criminals who moved in those circles—but he had proved difficult to catch.

"Lorentzen has a solid alibi. He was at the football match, confirmed by security camera."

"That doesn't mean he's not involved," I said. "I'm sure Lorentzen doesn't do his own dirty work."

Neighbours of the burgled house reported a large group of people hanging around close by just before the robbery—several of them in football shirts and all wearing hoodies. The gang left the scene shortly before the police arrived. A neighbour claims to have seen them driving a grey car, but couldn't say anything about the make or model. Looking for a grey car containing people wearing football shirts would be like looking for a needle in a haystack. It seemed hopeless. I ended the meeting by saying that we'd be in touch in a few days.

"Trace evidence might be important," I said. "We'll also have to get a forensic sketch done of the woman who participated in the mugging. If we can find her, we might get some information as to who's behind all this."

After the meeting I went back to my office. It was already late in the afternoon, but I had to note down a few key words for the report before leaving for the day.

I opened a drawer and took out my mobile phone. More than twenty missed calls. The first at three o'clock this afternoon, the last more than an hour ago. The name on the screen: Kiddo. I looked up at the photograph on the wall above my desk. She'd left a message. I called my voicemail.

"You have one new message."

Her voice was faint and choked with tears.

"Pappa, you have to call me straightaway. Please."

That was the entire message. I hung up and scrolled down to her number.

"This is the voicemail for . . ."

I hung up and tried again.

"This is the voicemail for . . ."

I got up. Tapped her number again as I walked out of the office and down the corridor, towards the stairs.

"This is the voicemail for . . ."

I took the stairs two at a time, making my way towards the exit as fast as I could, running out to my car.

"This is the voice—"

"This is—"

Reptile memoirs

When the lid was lifted, I saw her face. Something was dripping from it—salty drops from her eyes. It happened when humans were sad. Their feelings apparently emptied their bodies of salt and water. I had never understood why. We were in a foreign room. Dark, except for a few strips of light. I licked the air, searching for threats, but sensed none. The room smelled like every other human home I had known. On the floor where I was released was a soft rug. The room was about the same size as the warm woman's, with a bed and a small table.

The next moment, a new smell arose. I recognised it.

"This was my son's room," the cold woman said. "But now it belongs to Nero."

"Thank you so much for taking him," the warm woman said. The scent and heat of her left the room.

The cold woman brought a bowl of water, and a cold carcass that she set on the rug like an insult. I refused to eat it—let it lie there, rotting. Nor did I eat the next carcass she put in front of me. I was famished, but waited for something better. The warm woman had taken the fantastic prey from me—even hit me in order to take it—so I was still starving. I had never felt so close to death.

In the end, I had no other choice. As the sun rose and fell, rose and fell, and this country's season changed from cold to hot and back again in an eternal circle, I learned to hate myself enough to swallow the cold carcasses I was given. As I ate, I fantasised about the day I would be big enough to kill these malicious human animals. The cold woman and the hot woman would go first. I would be sure to make them suffer.

Roe

Ålesund
Saturday, 16 April 2005

I accelerated as I came out into Skarbøvika, on the way to Kiddo's house on Hessa. I was probably overreacting. Maybe it wasn't as bad as I'd imagined when I heard her voice on the answering machine. Maybe that spineless guy of hers had left her. Still, I couldn't rid myself of the thought that she would have called Ingrid if that were the case—not me. Kiddo and I had so little contact. We probably hadn't spoken since I last visited her, two weeks after she gave birth. That's already a long time ago.

I took a chance and called again, increased my speed when all I got was her voicemail. She would either laugh or be angry when I turned up at her door after a single telephone call—when she realised that I'd shifted into catastrophe mode for her sake. *So now you're here*, she would say, *just because you think I need a policeman*. But at the same time, I couldn't help but think of her voice on the phone. She'd seemed upset and afraid, like a small child. It sounded as if something inside

her had broken when I hadn't picked up the phone. Why had
she called me? Maybe she was in trouble—maybe this really
was something she needed her policeman pappa to sort out.
We have many fine memories from out here on Hessa, back
when Ingrid and I were still together and Kiddo was small.
Hikes to Sukkertoppen on Sunday mornings, swimming off
the rocks below, celebrations on Constitution Day when our
daughter played the flute in the school band. The annual lighting of the Sankthans bonfire. I had a photograph of Kiddo
standing in front of the fire when she was eight years old. She
had a stick in her hand, with a sausage on the end of it. In the
background the enormous Slinningsbålet fire towered above
her, surrounded by water and boats on all sides. The little girl
smiled, satisfied, pointing at the flames that licked at the tower
of wooden pallets. It was a powerful photograph.

Over the roundabout I took a sudden turn and ended up
behind another car. I missed being able to put on the blue
lights and sirens and overtake all the traffic, but soon I could
see the turnoff up towards Sukkertoppveien, where she lived.
I took the turn and slowed down, my pulse hammering in my
ears. Had I not just told myself that this was probably nothing?
That she was going to be mad at me when she saw me turning
up like this? That she would stand there with the baby on her
hip and say, *Oh, what do you want?* And I would answer, *You
called, and then you didn't pick up when I called you back.* At
which she would raise an eyebrow and say, *Relax, Papps, I got
hold of Mamma.* But then why was I so afraid?

Just when I'd managed to calm myself down, I saw Kiddo's
house. It was an idyllic old wooden house, painted red, with a
large garden outside, but today the image was spoiled by a grey
cloud of smoke rising from just behind it. At first I wondered

whether they were having a barbecue in the garden—but wasn't it too big, this cloud of smoke, to be coming from a barbecue? And anyway, it didn't seem to be coming from the garden. As I approached, I saw that the smoke was coming from the house itself, surrounding the roof from the rear side.

My pulse quadrupled—shaking, I managed to force the car down the verge and struggle out of my seat belt. I called Kiddo again as I got out of the car, prepared to calm myself down again, relax, relax, it's just a coincidence.

"This is the voicemail for . . ."

There was no reason to worry—this was probably just a small garden fire that looked as if it were coming from the house.

"This is the voicemail for . . ."

I started to take long strides in the direction of the smoke. Ran the final stretch towards the front door and opened it. A thick, hot cloud poured out. It filled my nostrils, eyes and mouth, blanketing me like a darkness. I heard the crackling of the flames inside. Wanted to run in and look for her, but it was too hot, too close. I shouted for Kiddo as loud as I could, but other than the crackling, the house was silent.

I called the fire department as I ran around the house and tried to open the terrace door. It was locked. Flames licked up the wall from the kitchen window. I gave the address in a shaking voice as I tried to fix a clear image in my mind of the flames, to memorize what the smoke looked like. It was important to take photographs early during the fire if you could, for the sake of the investigation. I didn't have a camera, so I would have to trust my memory. I wasn't even certain she was at home. Maybe she had left the message while she took the baby out for a walk, to try to get her to sleep. I heard the sirens approaching, so ran around the house trying to view the fire from all angles—it might be important. Kiddo would say that this was typical of me, to think like a policeman even when I didn't know whether she was trapped in a fire, whether they were . . . I called her again.

"This is the voicemail for . . ."

The sirens were closer now; I saw the huge fire engines, which hardly had enough space to squeeze themselves down the street behind the house. The flames had already spread to the roof and were coming up from the chimney. The whole house was on the verge of being ablaze. The taste of smoke was heavy in my mouth and nose.

"This is the voicemail for . . ."

The firefighters stormed towards the house, preparing their hoses and ladders. The flames licked up over the roof and walls, like a tongue tasting the sky. The heat. My face was burning, even though I had moved back from the house and now stood several metres away.

The police cars arrived just moments later. There wasn't enough space for more vehicles in the street, so they had to park farther down the road. Curious neighbours had begun to emerge. Police officers came running. Sverre was the first to reach me.

"You're here, Roe? I thought you'd gone home."

I dialled Kiddo's number again. Looked up at the flames as the voicemail sounded once more.

"This is the voicemail for . . ."

"I just hope there's nobody in there," Sverre said. "It looks too hot for the smoke divers."

The house glowed against the sky, a burning heat radiating from it, as if from Kiddo herself. It glowed just like the beautiful energy in her, everything that made her so good. So many times I had thought that this flame, this thing that existed in her—that it could never be extinguished. I'd been afraid that the flame was too strong, that it would eventually consume its bearer. Never had I thought that a flame from the outside, that a heat like this . . .

My mind melted, all thoughts evaporating. It was the flame that did it. The flame, rising like a snake towards the sky, a glowing, hot-tempered dragon. Nothing was darker than that flame which had just broken into me, burning its way deep into my brain.

"Anita," I said. "My daughter. This is her house."

Mariam

Ålesund
Wednesday, 23 August 2017

I wake from the weight of something pressing against my chest. Nero is resting his head against my ear, lying completely still. I study the scales of his face, the hollows of his cheeks where he takes in heat from the surroundings, the ever-open stone eyes that never reveal whether he's asleep or awake. His camouflage was probably practical for free tiger pythons that hunt on the ground, between stones and leaves atop the soil. Against the faded blue bedding it only made him more visible.

The next time I wake, he's lying beside me. He stretches his long body, awake now in the light from the window. I stretch out an arm and stroke him carefully over his back, feeling the tiny scales against my fingers. He's so huge now, much longer than I am tall. I carefully touch his face, and he turns towards the movement, licking the air.

"I know where I have to go," I whisper. "I have to go to the only person I can imagine wanting to do something like this. I'm so scared."

I try to take a deep breath; don't want to feel the nausea that wells up at the thought of what I have to do. The only thing I've ever been sure that I would never do again. But I no longer have any choice.

In the kitchen, Ingvar is doing the washing up. Music booms from the stereo system. I knock lightly on the doorframe with a knuckle, and he looks up.

"There's coffee in the pot." He gestures with his head towards a blue pot on the counter. I take a mug from the cupboard.

"Will you be home today?"

"I have to deliver a few things, but I'll be home this afternoon. I'll leave the door open so you can come and go as you please." He pauses. "If you need any help with . . . anything, I'd be happy to help you when I get back. Just say the word."

I get goose bumps. Think of the night that Patrick was here, how Ingvar had spoken to him as if it were nothing at all. Not to mention the day of the robbery, when he called me and pretended he'd had a seizure. Ingvar can't be trusted. My only reason for being here is that this house, this apartment—it means something.

"I don't need help," I say.

I get into the car, close my eyes and imagine ash falling from the sky like snow. Maybe today will be the end of the world, so that none of this needs to happen, so that I don't have to make this trip. A lump forms in my stomach, deep inside me, but I start the engine regardless. Begin to drive the long road inland, back towards the city. Today might be the end of the world, blood might run in the streets, a meteor might crash into the earth. According to Norse mythology, when everything expires the Midgard Serpent will come ashore, slithering across fields and meadows. I imagine how it will tear up houses, farms and public buildings with its mighty coil. At the end of all things, it won't matter whether or not I've managed to find Iben, or what happened to her. We will all be made to suffer.

I accelerate down the slip road onto the highway. The middle of the day is the best time for driving these roads. I pass the football stadium, which was new back when I left this place. I drive on beyond Moa, where I take the turning for Sula. I haven't seen him since that night. Can still feel how the anxiety tore through my body at the thought of meeting his ice-blue eyes.

I pull over onto the hard shoulder, take a deep breath. My heart is hammering against my rib cage. I close my eyes and imagine the Midgard Serpent slithering across the road, sweeping all the cars aside. There's still time for it to turn up. I cast this wish out into the universe, but when I open my eyes the road is still intact, the cars still driving along, undisturbed.

The house is at the top of a hill, not far from the quay where the tiny passenger ferry from Ålesund docks. I feel queasy as I park, regret not eating any breakfast. I get out of the car and look up at the house. Walk up to the front door. The label bearing the name Scheie is gone from the doorbell—it looks like a completely new intercom system. I count the number of floors to find the right bell. Press and hold the button for a long time, in spite of the regret that already burns through my body.

Roe

Ålesund
Saturday, 16 April 2005

Outside the window, the evening was cast in a flashing blue—flash, flash, flash in the night. Voices hummed from somewhere far away; the crackling of radio static could be heard. I sat on a sofa in a strange living room that a neighbour had offered for the police to use. They brought me in here when they found out that I was a relative. Put a blanket around my shoulders like I was some patient in shock, but I didn't remove it. I actually felt cold. Cold in the body and hot in the face, as if the heat still remained in my head, my eyes, my brain.

The last time I went over to the window and looked out towards the house it was empty and black, like the burned corpse of a giant spider. The water that the firefighters continued to pour over it was transformed into a damp grey smoke. She had called me. An hour and a half before I arrived at the house, she had called me. I had heard such despair in her voice. Maybe it was a sign that she wasn't inside, because then she would have surely called the fire department, and not me? Perhaps she was feeling desperate somewhere else entirely—maybe what she was feeling so terrible about had already blown over, a mere trifle, something we could laugh about when I next saw her. She probably wasn't in the house. Maybe it was like those people you heard about, those who should have been at home when a horrible accident happened, but due to some chance occurrence were unexpectedly somewhere else. People who had taken the bus in the wrong direction, had got stuck in traffic or forgotten something and turned back just in time. Those kinds of things happen all the time; they're far from unusual.

Of course it was a tragedy regardless. The house burned to the ground, all their belongings gone. All the pictures Anita had painted over the years, which filled her now blackened and charred studio. The walls that were also full of drawings and paintings—she was so talented. Not enough to be able to live off her art, of course, but she really had a gift. Now it was burned away—all of it. A tragedy—but as long as she turned out to be alive, she could always paint more.

When Anita quit her marketing degree—which I had paid through the nose for—so that she could become an artist, I was furious. She still hadn't understood what a stupid idea it was to go through life without any form of fixed income. As artistic as she was, she could have given herself some security by working a day job. Ingrid, on the other hand, supported her from the start. The last time I saw her, she spoke so warmly about how talented our daughter was, how happy she was that Anita had found Birk, that she could live out her dream in his loft studio. I'd ended up the one who was labelled unfair—the father who wanted to dampen the flame in his daughter, who wanted to make it less of a towering Sankthans bonfire and more of a smouldering ember.

She couldn't be tamed, our daughter. Maybe I should have been more understanding, but I was so afraid that she was going to throw her life away.

The door opened. Sverre took a few slow steps towards me. His gaze was directed at the floor.

"How are you?" he asked.

He approached, seeming cautious, as if he was dreading speaking to me. He looked like a little kid, the way he walked across the room. It was so irritating—so bloody irritating. It wasn't as if I was made of glass.

"Don't ask me how I am," I heard myself bark, my voice unfamiliar. "Tell me what's going on."

Sverre cleared his throat and sat down on the edge of the sofa, hands in front of him. Looked as if he had wanted to come here and show compassion.

"Anita isn't answering her phone," I said. "All I get is her voicemail. She might have gone out somewhere, might have felt better and taken a walk. Right?"

Sverre met my gaze, suddenly calm. He leaned closer to me, seeking intimacy.

"Surely you haven't given up looking, because you think they were in there?"

"Roe."

"No," I said. "Don't sit here and say 'Roe' to me. Don't spend time talking to me at all—get out there and find my daughter and grandchild." I threw out an arm, wanting to show him what I thought of the fact that he didn't have the entire fucking force out searching. "I don't want to hear another word from you. Not another word, until you've found them."

"Roe, listen to me." Sverre gripped my arm, looked me in the eyes. "We've found remains."

"Remains?"

My face burned, as if scorching hot. I wanted to pull away—
didn't want to hear—but Sverre held me, his grasp firm.

"We've found charred adult human remains inside. It seems
to be a woman. She has her arms around a baby."

Remains. Fragments. A soot-black spider's house, legs
towards the sky. I had seen such remains before. Scorched
and blackened bodies with exposed teeth and eye sockets, or
nothing but the skeletons remaining in a charred room. I knew
all too well what burned human flesh smelled like. I felt sick
just at the thought of it.

"You're wrong."

Sverre shook his head.

"No, Roe. We're not wrong."

Mariam

Ålesund
Wednesday, 23 August 2017

She's standing in the doorway as I come up the stairs. She's wearing a dress with a pattern of blue flowers, and her long nails are painted red. The skin of her legs shows signs that she's starting to get old. An unnaturally brown complexion and short, bleached-blond hair—none of it helps. When she was younger she was a natural blonde, like me.

"Let me look at you," she says, grabbing my shoulders. "I saw you on the news. You really look like a grown woman now. And here I was, thinking you'd never even start wearing makeup."

I twist out of her grasp like a teenager.

"Are you not even going to give your mother a hug?"

I can smell her duty-free perfume from where I'm standing.

"I'm not staying long," I say.

She goes into the apartment, gestures to me to come inside. In the hallway, a piece of paper featuring the calligraphed words

HOME IS WHERE THE HEART IS has been stuck up on the wall. This is some new hobby she's started—when I lived here, most of the walls were bare, no more than a mirror and the odd poster. The words are a lie. There is no heart in this home.

"I have to speak to Patrick," I say.

I don't like the way she smiles.

"I haven't seen Patrick in a long time," she says. "He moved out . . . Two years ago now, was it? He doesn't even want to celebrate Christmas with his mother anymore."

"I can understand that. Where is he living now?"

She straightens a lock of hair with her long nails.

"I think I have his address."

She waves me further inside; I take off my shoes and go into the living room, which has been decorated and furnished in shades of cream. Only the angles of the room are recognisable, the sharp edges in my memory. I sit down on the sofa as she rummages through some papers in a drawer.

"You haven't visited him since he moved out?" I ask.

"I was there once, when he had just moved in. He doesn't want anything to do with me, says I've ruined his life."

"Is he keeping to himself? Or does he have friends?"

She comes over with a little address book, sets it on the glass table in front of me.

"What do I know? You've disowned your mother, the both of you. I can only assume that you're managing fine without me."

I sigh.

"We've managed without you for a long time."

I look up Patrick's name in the address book and rip out the entire page. She makes as if to protest, but then thinks better of it. Picks up the phone.

"I'll call him," she says. "That's probably easiest."

I wait as she holds the receiver to her ear. It strikes me that she has probably shown her fingernails more care throughout her life than she has her own children. She shakes her head.

"He's not picking up. Do you want the number?"

I note down the digits next to the address and get up. Move across to open the door to the room Patrick and I shared. I'm expecting to find it in the same state as when I left, but it has been turned into an office with a desktop computer, a white wardrobe and a sofa bed. In the corner where my bed once stood, where I would lay stiff with fear that Patrick would wake up and want something from me, there's now a laundry rack hung with white sheets.

A poster used to hang on the wall above the bed. A green snake coiled around a branch. The snake had its head turned towards me, almost making eye contact. The poster was company for me during those evenings. I could lie in bed and study it, pretend we were talking. When Patrick wanted something from me at night, it was the snake who helped me. I could glance up at it and see the creature smiling. As if it wanted to say that the pain would pass, just like my awful dreams. That it was watching over me. If I wanted, the snake and I could run away together. The snake from the poster, and I from my body.

On the wall where the snake poster used to hang is now a picture of a lily. She has erased every trace of us.

Was it solely his fault? He was a lonely, hormonal teenage boy, and the woman who was supposed to help us become people was elsewhere. But on the other hand, if he's taken Iben, I don't know what I'll do. Because then Iben will be destroyed, too.

I close the door, walk out into the hallway.

"Where were you last Friday?" I ask as I put my shoes back on.

"When she disappeared? Do you think that I—"

"Just answer the question."

She lifts her gaze to the ceiling.

"I've got a job on the Sulesund ferry, in the café. I was there all day. I was so sad when I saw you'd lost your daughter. I hope they find her, Sara."

"My name is Mariam," I mumble as I move towards the door.

"Apparently so."

She takes a tentative step towards me, but stops. Realises that I don't want her near me. I don't believe in the slightest that she didn't know what went on here in this house. She just chose to turn a blind eye.

"There was a man here," she says as I squeeze my way past her. "Before the summer. I told the police about it, too. An older guy, who I'd never seen before. He asked after you, showed me a photograph. Seemed angry when I didn't want to answer his questions. I was scared, so I slammed the door in his face."

I stand there beside the front door.

"An older guy?"

"Broad shouldered, grey-flecked hair, maybe in his fifties."

I thank her for the information, feeling that I can't stand to be in this apartment for a second longer.

Roe

Ålesund
Saturday, 16 April 2005

I hugged Ingrid for the first time in almost ten years. It was a long hug, which reminded me how there were actually times during our marriage when we managed to be a safe harbour for each other. Her tears made the front of my shirt damp; I hadn't been able to cry just yet. It was as if the fire had dried out my tear ducts. A glowing behind my eyes, dry as a desert.

The next moment, Ingrid was beating her fists against my chest.

"She called you," she sobbed. "She called you, and you didn't answer."

My knees suddenly stopped working. They buckled under me as if I were a ragdoll, seeming to pull me down after them. Birk, who was standing just behind Ingrid, came and grabbed my arm, wanting to pull me up again.

"Let go of me, for fuck's sake," I said.

I grabbed the arm of the sofa and hitched myself up; managed to sit down. Had to lift my knees with my hands in order to move my legs into position.

Ingrid's face had the same white expression as on that day when Anita was five and in the hospital with a broken arm, but her features were drawn tighter. Right then, her new husband was sitting in the car—of course, the coward always kept his distance whenever something serious happened. He was the same back then, too, when the moving company had carried all of Ingrid's furniture out of what had been our shared home. Not to mention every time I had to meet Ingrid because of something pertaining to Anita. He would stay in the car, or he'd be in another room or somewhere else entirely. Any opinions he might have about Anita I heard only through my daughter or my ex-wife. He never seemed to support Ingrid, to hold her. He was just a shadow. This was the guy she had left me for. Things really must have been bad between Ingrid and me back then, worse than I was able to appreciate at the time.

"I have to go out there," said Birk, pointing towards the hall. "They want to talk to me."

He left. Ingrid covered her face with her hands and cried in long sobs.

"I just don't understand," she sobbed. "I really just don't understand."

If there was one sentence I heard often when meeting next of kin in connection with everything from suicides to violent crimes, it was this: *I don't understand*. It was a common reaction. People couldn't make the tragedy fit with the image they had of their family member alive and well. Until now I had understood what it meant only in theory. I had partly felt it when my mother and father died, but not like this. I truly did not understand. I had a vivid image of what a female body lying dead in a burned-down house looked like, but I just couldn't place my daughter in the scenario. Not to mention Aurora. The baby had burned in the house, along with her mother. I just didn't understand how it could happen.

"She sounded so desperate on the phone," I said. "As soon as I heard her voice, I knew something was wrong. It doesn't make sense. If it had been the fire, she would have called the fire department, got out."

"Why did she call you?" Ingrid said. "Why not me? I don't understand."

I took a breath, trying not to imagine what it was like to inhale thick, toxic smoke.

"Was there anyone who wanted to harm her?" I asked. "Anyone you know of, who might have done this?"

Ingrid stared at me, openmouthed.

"You're saying you think someone did this on purpose? That it was murder?"

She started to cry again, a new, desperate sobbing. "No, Roe. I just can't talk to you. You're so fucking . . ."

I was immediately reliving one of the last arguments we had when we were married. *You have a bigger heart for drug addicts and car thieves than you do for me and your daughter*, she'd said. *You would have given us far more attention if we were both dead and you were the first to arrive on the scene.* After which she made a sweeping motion with her hand, swiping a vase from the table. It rolled across the parquet flooring to stop by the door. There was water everywhere, and we had to interrupt the argument in order to wipe it up.

"I'm sure it isn't you who's going to be investigating this," Ingrid said now. "And your colleagues haven't asked me any questions yet."

"They will," I said. "That doesn't mean it's murder, only that questions have to be asked. Do you understand?"

"But you think it was murder?"

I shook my head. "I don't think anything," I said. "I'm just asking you. Is there anything I should know?"

Ingrid wiped her face with the sleeve of her sweater.

"Anita came to me a few days ago, with the baby in her arms. She wanted to leave Birk. Said she was in love, that there was a new man she'd started seeing. She made all kinds of awful accusations against Birk—I told her that she really ought to think things through. She and Birk had such a good relationship, she was everything to him."

It hurts me to hear that Kiddo had received such an answer from her mother. I would have told our daughter to leave him right there and then. Birk wasn't worth the socks on her feet. I didn't believe for one second that he had supported her by letting her go around as a stay-at-home mother with an art studio in his house. What he wanted was for her to be financially dependent on him.

"Did she tell you his name?" I said. "The new guy?"

Ingrid shook her head. I looked out of the window, down at the shoreline where we used to go swimming when Anita was little.

"Did Birk know about this new boyfriend?" I said.

Ingrid looked at me for a moment. It took a few seconds before she realised what I was asking. Her mouth fell open, her expression moving from sad and confused to furious.

"No, Roe—you know what? Now you're going too far."

Mariam

Ålesund
Wednesday, 23 August 2017

I drive into the car park in front of a white apartment building with green balconies, reminiscent of something out of the Eastern Bloc. Clasp the steering wheel with both hands as I try to summon the courage to get out of the car. I'd hoped he would still be living at home, but of course I'd also feared that I would have to jump out into the unknown once again. I set my forehead against the steering wheel and take a deep breath, forcing away the memories that rush over me. This was why I wanted to get away from everything, so I'd never have to see him again.

It should be in the first stairwell. My legs feel heavy as I tramp up the steps to the first floor. There's no name on the doorbell; it feels as if people are trying to hide wherever I go. A shudder runs through me. I swallow and push the button, and it responds with a deep buzz. I pull back my hand again. Want to turn and run down the stairs, but force my feet to stay glued to the floor. Is this enough of a sign of the love I have for my daughter, the fact that I stay standing here?

I hear the sound of footsteps from inside, which means he's home, even though it's the middle of the day and he should be at work—if he even has a job, that is. I try to prepare myself mentally, but every single memory I have of his face makes me feel sick. I stand up straight and lift my head, want to make myself tall so he'll understand I'm no longer his little sister. Then the door opens. A woman looks at me. She must be over fifty. She smiles expectantly—she's probably the kind of person who likes to talk to door-to-door salesmen or anyone else who comes knocking.

"I'm looking for Patrick Scheie?"

From inside the apartment I hear sounds coming from several other people, or from a TV. The woman looks at me, surprised.

"I'm afraid I don't know who that is. Perhaps you have the wrong address?"

"I was told that he lives here."

She looks up at the ceiling, thinking.

"I've only lived here for five months," she says. "Maybe he was the man who lived here before me. I didn't know his name."

She's talking to me as if I'm a lost little girl. Strangely, it feels good. "What was his name again?"

She has a smile that makes me want to move in with her. But I've been fooled by that feeling before. I shake my head. "It doesn't matter—I'm sure I'll find him."

Roe

Ålesund
Friday, 22 April 2005

Sverre kept his jacket on. He followed me into the living room and sat down on the chaise longue. I hadn't made coffee. Since the fire, I'd been living on crispbreads and cold drinks. Anything hot, even coffeemakers, made me uneasy. Take your time, my doctor said, prescribing a sedative that I had no intention of taking. The only thing I wanted was two weeks of sick leave to get back on my feet—literally. I needed to get my legs to stop feeling like jelly beneath me, to get my brain to stop melting and then get back to work. The only thing that helped was that Birk had been charged and taken into custody to be thoroughly investigated. Ingrid was furious, believing I had incriminated him, but he hadn't needed me to look guilty—he'd managed that all on his own.

"Are you sure you're ready for this, Roe?" Sverre sat leaning forward, his hands clasped between his knees. He looked anxious. "The boss has said that it's fine, as long as you understand what it means. Do you understand what it means, Roe?"

I had insisted on this, just as I had insisted on seeing her. Everyone had advised me not to see Kiddo, but I'd insisted. I regretted it now. The image of her death was layered over the living memory of her like a black film. Still, I had to do it, had to know. Couldn't go around pretending she wasn't dead, with all the concrete details that involved.

"I'll tell you everything, including what we haven't made public, if you believe you really want to know. But of course you have to understand that the usual duty of confidentiality applies, and that you won't be able to work on the case."

I nodded.

Sverre took a deep breath.

"The fire started in a frying pan containing olive oil. At first glance, this could just look like carelessness, of the kind we often see when young people who are drunk or elderly individuals fall asleep in the middle of preparing food. The hot plate that the pan was on was turned to the highest heat. Whether this was done by Anita herself or by someone else is hard to say."

"What about the cause of death?"

"Anita was found on the floor just outside the kitchen door. The autopsy found traces of soot in her throat, trachea and lungs, and elevated levels of carbon monoxide in the blood, as well as some cyanide. This indicates that she died of smoke inhalation from the fire. However, upon examining her body, it was also found that she had received a blow to the back of the head with a heavy, blunt object."

I looked down at my hands. They had suddenly started to shake. I placed them on my knees and hoped that Sverre wouldn't notice.

"She was hit in the head with a heavy object," I managed to say. "So we can say with some certainty that it wasn't her who started the fire, either."

"It looks like a typical attempt to hide a crime, but we have very few leads to go on."

"And Aurora?"

He sighed.

"Aurora is difficult. But we're fairly certain she was already dead when the fire started. She had no soot in her lower airways, nor any carbon monoxide in her blood. Her cause of death is unclear, but her body appears to have sustained injuries consistent with being crushed. The clearest sign of this is several broken ribs. Her skin is too damaged for us to conclude what caused the injuries, but her torso was squeezed extremely hard by some external force. Suffocation seems most probable; there are no signs to indicate any other cause of death. She appears to have sustained no head injuries of the kind observed on Anita's body."

"I don't understand." The words tumbled out of me.

"There's something else we also need to talk about," said Sverre. "We have to release Birk. We don't have enough to hold him."

I got up. Began to pace back and forth across the floor.

"So what you're saying is that Anita and Aurora are dead, and he's going to walk free and receive the insurance payout on the house?"

"You know how it is, Roe. The door was unlocked—in theory anyone could have been in there. Whether the fire was started deliberately is unclear; the two deceased have different causes of death and very different injuries. One of our main hypotheses is that we may need to look for two killers."

"Have you corroborated Birk's story? That he was out taking the dog for a walk and just happened to have left his mobile phone at home? It stinks."

Sverre nodded. "I completely agree with you, Roe, but that alone proves nothing. And you mustn't forget that even if someone had seen him leaving the house right before the fire, that still wouldn't prove he was guilty of murder. It's all circumstantial evidence. Half the house is completely burned—we have very little to go on. Of course, we're going to continue the investigation, but we have no compelling evidence."

"Then you haven't looked hard enough!"

Dark spots danced in front of my eyes, and I felt my legs turn soft beneath me again. I slumped to the floor. Sverre came over and grabbed my arm; I waved him away. Dragged myself over to the sofa and hitched myself back up.

"Anyway, we couldn't put you or Ingrid through a court case that ended with Birk being acquitted—I know you know that," Sverre said. "And I think you also know that he doesn't have the strongest motives. Something against Anita, perhaps—but why would he want to harm his own daughter? I don't think it's good for you to be involved any further now, though. Do you have someone you can speak to?"

Mariam

Ålesund
Wednesday, 23 August 2017

I borrow the telephone in a shoe store in Moa. Walk away slightly, so that the girl at the cash register won't hear me, and call Patrick's phone number—the one I was given by the woman who calls herself my mother. She hasn't spoken to her son in several months, hasn't tried to contact him other than the occasional call to this number, which he clearly never answers. She's just as indifferent as she's always been, in other words. As far as she's concerned, he could have been swallowed up by the ground, drowned or murdered. She'd never know. I let the number ring until it goes to voicemail, then dial again. Let it ring again. I don't want to leave a message—it feels too difficult to free my voice. I'll have to ask Ingvar to do it.

I get the sense that someone is watching me, but I push the feeling away. Walk between the racks of trainers and high-heeled shoes as I think. What if it wasn't Patrick or Egil who took the key, but someone else who was at the party? I have no idea how many people were there that night—in

principle, it could have been any one of them. A hidden
enemy, or somebody I thought was a friend. But then I
remember, and a thought strikes me—something that hasn't
occurred to me before: earlier that day, when I was in the
shower, Anita came into the bathroom. I didn't even know
her at that point, but how do I know that she didn't take
the key? Could Egil have told her about it—asked her to go
get it for him, so he could open the door? If so, she hid it
for a long time afterwards. A shiver runs through me at the
thought of being tricked by her, but something doesn't add
up. Anita is dead. She can't have been the one to put the key
in Iben's jewellery box.

Out of the corner of my eye I think I catch sight of someone standing outside the store, peering in. I turn towards the
figure, for a moment convinced that I'm being followed, but
the man is already moving away. It takes so little to unsettle
me. I have to get back to the apartment. Get Ingvar to call
the number, see if Patrick answers then.

I return the telephone to the woman at the cash register.
Have just begun to walk through the shopping centre towards
the exit when another shudder runs through me. I really am
being followed—there's a man, with black hair and a black
beard, the sleeves of his grey shirt rolled up to reveal his hairy
arms. He's portly, and the forearms sticking out from his shirt
are large and bulging. It's now many years since I last saw this
man, twice just in passing, but I know who he is. I've seen
him in the vibrant acrylic colours of a painting, in the same
way he probably remembers me from one. I consider turning
away, leaving and hoping that he doesn't follow after me, but
he can't do me any harm here among all these people. And I'd
really like to speak to him.

I stop and nod my head faintly, just once. See that he starts to walk towards me, hands clenched into fists. He stops just as I think he's about to try to walk straight through me. He's tall and broad-shouldered, flecks of grey in his dark beard. He could easily be the man who visited the woman who called herself my mother. Looking for me.

"You're Birk," I say. "Anita Krogsveen's partner."

Birk is breathing heavily.

"I'm Mariam," I say. "And I usually win staring contests."

Roe

Ålesund
Tuesday, 26 April 2005

I stood at the graveside, shaking. Aurora and Anita, the two most incandescent people I'd ever known, side by side. Already half consumed by flames, and now the earth would take the rest. Sverre stood and held my arm so I wouldn't collapse. There was no strength left in my body. On the other side of the grave was Ingrid. Her husband stood beside her—a useless shadow as usual. It was her so-called son-in-law she leaned on. The guy who had been charged, who had been remanded in custody for the crime that had led us all here. Ingrid had given him her full support all the way.

I hadn't shed a single tear. The sockets of my eyes were like burned paper; there were deep wounds behind my eyeballs. I tried to see something good in the sea of flowers before us, to find comfort in the fact that so many people wished to show how they missed the mother and baby who had died, that they cared about us, but it was no use. All I saw was Anita's naked, charred eye sockets, her teeth exposed because her lips had been burned away. In her speech in the church, Ingrid had said that we had to remember Anita as she was in life. That we must make sure her life won out over her death—it was just the kind of empty thing people said. When it was my turn to speak my legs refused to move, so I remained seated. Simply shook my head and clamped my fingers around the piece of paper and its words deep in my suit pocket—words I couldn't bear to say. Luckily Birk stayed silent, too.

As soon as the priest had cast earth onto the two white coffins and the gathering had sobbed its way through "Gje meg handa di, ven," two little girls from Ingrid's side of the family stepped forward. They each set a single rose alongside the other flowers. It struck me that there was nobody left now, nobody who would come after me. The bloodline was broken, and the person who had done this to Anita—whether it was Birk or somebody else—had also put an end to me. Was that a selfish thought?

The mourners began to move, lining up to embrace Ingrid and Birk, to take their hands and look deep into their eyes. I wanted to slip away, but soon the same people were swarming around me, squeezing my hand and talking about Anita. I hadn't seen many of them for a decade or more, friends and family of Ingrid's, goading me, acting as if they cared. Question after question was thrown at me—has it been tough? Are you holding up? I nodded to everything and backed away, wanting to flee. My heart pounding, I saw dots before my eyes and felt dizzy. My chest tightened; the air felt like thick clay, and I had to lean on the first person who would be able to hold me up. It was Birk. He opened his mouth to say something but I twisted away, took several steps across the grass and dropped to the ground like a drunk.

The next thing I knew, Sverre and Ingrid were standing over me. They each grabbed an arm and pulled me up, conducting me safely away from the crowd.

"What happened?" said Sverre.

I opened my mouth to say something. I wanted to say that I didn't know how I was going to get through this, that I was alone, but I couldn't make a single word pass my lips.

"I think you should take yourself home," Ingrid said.

There was concern in her voice, but a hint of something accusatory, too. She had wanted a better father for her daughter. She had thought that for many, many years—I knew that well enough—and now it was my fault that she no longer had a daughter.

"Why don't you say that to Birk?"

"Because Birk hasn't just fallen over, Roe."

"Come on now," said Sverre, and led me off towards the car.

Ronja

Kristiansund
Wednesday, 23 August 2017

Yet again, I sit and smell August's aftershave as he watches the video clips of the surveillance footage from the Storkaia shopping centre. Not only what was recorded outside Cubus, where Roe Olsvik walks past looking exactly as Robert Kirkeby described him—grey shirt, wide jaw, broad shoulders, with a carrier bag in his hand—but also what was captured outside the supermarket, which shows Roe peering through the window, as if he's watching something inside. Not long afterwards he strolls out through the same exit through which Iben will soon come running.

I get up and walk over to the jigsaw puzzle that hangs on my wall. Every time I look at the strange image of the bridge reflected in the water, I feel a kind of craving. Perhaps it's the mouth of the devil tempting me, pulling me towards it, or perhaps we're on the inside, looking out. Or maybe both sides are just the same. The bridge says so much about us humans. How we let ourselves be tricked, see reflections in the water and think we're looking at the thing itself. How we can stare at a tiny piece of the world and believe we can see the whole picture.

"Fuck," August says in Danish. "That's why he's been so acting so strangely throughout this entire case. He's involved."

What does the Rakotzbrücke look like from the other side? Perhaps there's a shadow there, so the reflection in the water can't be seen in the same way. Maybe the water is muddy, or full of fish swimming around.

"We have to talk to Roe," I say. "There must be an explanation, don't you think?"

"Explanation? He's been hiding this from us this entire time! I think we have to investigate him as a suspect and consider taking him into custody. If we ask him about what we've found out he'll be on his guard, he'll have an opportunity to prepare. We should continue with the investigation until we have enough to catch him by surprise."

It occurs to me that it isn't the fact that Roe Olsvik has hidden something from us that's interesting—what's important is why. This *why* might be so big, and so strange even to Roe, that this is the reason he hasn't said anything. Regardless, it isn't those of us among the lower ranks who get to decide any of this. We have bosses for that kind of thing.

"We have to speak to Shahid," I say.

Roe

Ålesund
Monday, 2 May 2005

The nerve fibres of my brain were on fire. A flame licking its way along my neural pathways and down my spinal column, spreading until I was glowing on the inside. It was the sun outside the window that made me burn like this. I felt as if I was going to spontaneously combust. On the desk in front of me were cases from as far back as two weeks ago. Cases that had simply remained there and which I had to clear up, pick up the thread again, but I couldn't do it. It was hopeless trying to concentrate while my body was alight with Kiddo's flame. The fire, shooting across walls and roof tiles into my brain. Kiddo's body like a lump of coal. There was so much that didn't add up—her voice on the phone, this fire in a frying pan in the middle of the day, the baby who seemed to have been crushed to death. What did it mean?

I had to get up. Go somewhere, fill my head with something. I walked over to the door. Took a deep breath. The air didn't seem so thick today. I opened the door and walked down the hallway.

"Roe! I heard you were back." Sverre walked towards me, a half smile under his beard. "How are you?"

I cleared my throat. "Oh, you know, better. Time to get back to work before the whole place falls apart."

Sverre gave me a half hug, which I didn't return. He seemed to have become a hugger too, now. The relationship between us had changed forever.

"I've been thinking of you," he said.

I looked down, suddenly embarrassed.

"I was just on my way to get a cup of coffee."

Why hadn't I been there when she needed me? Me, the old grouch, who had left my phone in my office and not had it on me like every other grown person would. I had just wanted to concentrate on work, putting everything else aside. Now I would never know why she called. For the rest of my life, I'd have to hear her tear-choked voice as it sounded that last time on the telephone and know that she might be alive today if only I had picked up when she called.

Ingrid rang me often these days, reminding me of precisely this. *How could you have left your phone behind, Roe? To think that you didn't answer the last time she called you!* And then the more worrying: *How are you coping with this all alone? Do you have anyone to talk to?*

The easy conversation abated as I entered the break room. They treated me with such a strange reverence, for some reason or other. I walked over to the coffee machine, feeling their eyes on my back. I could almost hear their thoughts: *Roe isn't exactly easy to talk to anymore, so it's hard to know what to say.*

It feels sort of disrespectful to laugh in front of him—they were full of these kinds of notions. As if I'd turned into a fucking porcelain figurine. Hadn't I handled far more crises than any of them? Talk all you want! They looked at me—looked and looked. Suddenly I missed being shut in a room by myself, staring at the wall as if waiting for it to go up in flames. *Spend time with those closest to you,* the doctor had said, *time with those you love. Time heals.* He prescribed medications, but I didn't intend to take any of that shit. *Take time with those closest to you.* For the past two weeks my closest friend had been a white brick wall in my apartment—I'd had time to study every scratch and every crack in the paint.

I gulped down coffee until it made me cough. I wanted to leave, but didn't know why. Anita, the baby—there had to be some lead they hadn't checked, there had to be an answer. Had they looked for this new boyfriend? I had to ask. They would answer if I asked. But at the same time, I didn't know whether I'd be able to. I might just explode.

"Boys." Sverre was standing in the doorway, his face a blazing shade of red. "Something's happened. We need you right away."

I dropped my cup into the sink. Followed Sverre, taking quick steps, squeezing my way past a couple of the others.

"Tell me what's going on."

"Are you ready for more death, Roe?"

"Just tell me what's happened."

"We're going to Løvenvoldgata. David Lorentzen's apartment. His mother called. Her son had said he was going to visit her, but he didn't show up. So she went to his apartment and let herself in with the spare key. There was a body inside, a man."

The group behind us was abuzz. A body. They wanted to know who it was. It was a possible murder. I took the driver's seat, adjusted the rearview mirror and stepped on the gas. Quickly reversed out, a pounding in my veins.

"Are you sure about this, Roe?" Sverre asked.

Everything was pounding. The blood behind my eyes, in my throat. "Haven't you had David under surveillance these past weeks? What happened?"

"It was de-prioritised."

My knowledge of the circles David Lorentzen moved in might be useful in this case. It was an opportunity to transfer my thoughts to something else, to contribute to something. I turned the car into Løvenvoldgata, braking abruptly in front of the patrol vehicle that was already there. I threw myself out of the car, towards the house. I jogged up the steps to the first floor—in my mind I was somehow on my way to save Kiddo, running to her. I stopped outside the door, where an officer was standing guard. Pulled the plastic covers over my feet, tugged on the suit and hood. Still breathing heavily. The officer stepped aside so I could go in. A tripod had been set up in order to photograph a footprint in the hall. The smell reminded me of the time several years ago when Ingrid and I had come home to a broken freezer after a holiday, before we had Anita. Water on the floor—water on the floor and blood, the stench of rotting flesh. I grabbed the arm of the man who was standing there taking photographs.

"The body," I said.

He jumped, and I saw myself in the hallway mirror behind him, towering there like a bear. I let go of him, took a step back. I'd got myself worked up, shifted into crisis mode, but this wasn't Anita or Aurora—this was someone else entirely.

"He's in there."

I was almost panting. Zigzagged my way between stains and other possible evidence on the floor and tried to breathe—in through the nose and out through the mouth, the doctor had said—or breathe into a paper bag, breathe. Inside, behind the door, I followed the stench and saw the body of an adult male lying there, swimming in its own juices from decomposition. The skin of the face and body was swollen, and had a greenish tinge to it. The mouth was open and appeared to be full of larvae. I took a breath. Took another, but the air was foul-smelling clay, filling my mouth. I gasped. Hot, stinking clay that burned in my chest. I tried to inhale again, but all I could feel was a hard lump in my chest that burned. Couldn't get enough air. I opened my mouth as wide as I could, but there was no air, only heavy, hard clay. Then everything turned dark.

Ronja

Kristiansund
Wednesday, 23 August 2017

Shahid gestures to two straight-backed chairs in his cramped office. There isn't much luxury to go around even for managers in this line of work. Above the desk hangs a photograph of his wife and his teenage daughter. This case must be difficult for him. He always appears so professional, maintaining a distance from his work, but I can imagine how he must have hugged his family extra hard over the past few days—when he's had the chance to go home, that is.

The boss doesn't say anything, just waits for one of us to start speaking. The authority in his bearing seems so natural, so easy. In the end, I'm the one to break the awkward silence. I start to speak in a disjointed torrent of words—start going on about the witness who saw a man with a Cubus carrier bag and the surveillance footage from Storkaia. Shahid looks at me with obvious scepticism—I see it straightaway—but it's too late to stop, to take it all back now.

I look at August, feeling like a child when he nods encouragingly at me. I speak constantly, don't even stop to take a breath, feel my cheeks grow hot and my hands clammy. The boss's authority makes me feel like a kid trying to explain something to her teacher. And the words do not sound convincing—they sound clumsy and confusing, incoherent. I start to analyse everything as I speak, lose the thread of my argument, but I've already started to tell him what I found out. I half-heartedly force out the rest of the explanation and exhale.

Only now do I hear a fly buzzing on the windowsill, butting the glass. Shahid leans back in his chair and puts his hands behind his head. He takes a moment to think through what I've said, weighing every word. This is something I don't recognise in myself just yet—the seriousness that seems to kick in around the age of thirty, that makes someone seem like a true grown-up.

"I think you'll find it's just a misunderstanding," he says. "Of course the fact that Roe was at the shopping centre should have been mentioned in the report, but it's probably just an oversight. He probably didn't think it was important."

That's a relief. The boss agrees with what I first thought, before I let August convince me otherwise. It could be as simple as Shahid says—just an oversight. We don't know anything yet.

"He hasn't simply neglected to report that he's on the footage," says August. "He was observed talking to Iben before she disappeared."

Shahid frowns.

"But we agree that this eyewitness isn't one-hundred-percent reliable?"

He stares at each of us. I nod.

"Have you asked Roe about this? I'm sure there must be an explanation."

"We came to you first," says August. "Because there's something that doesn't add up. There are several things that are confusing—it seems that Roe is involved in this case in some way. That he knows more than we do, and is deceiving us."

"That's a serious accusation."

"We're not asking for anything other than permission to look into this in more detail," August says.

"Well, I'm afraid that's not something I'm going to grant you. Iben Lind's disappearance is far too serious for us to be spending time on trivialities. As I said, I'm sure there's an explanation. If you like, I can give Roe a call right now and ask him. He's off sick today, but I'm sure he won't have anything against a quick phone call."

"But then he'll know!" The words slip out of me.

Shahid looks at me, surprised.

"Roe is not a criminal, he's a colleague. I'll give him a call, and we can put an end to all this."

My face grows hot. I glance at August, feeling stupid. I'm not sure why I need to look like I agree with him, when in fact I don't.

August looks at Shahid and nods.

"Don't give it another thought," August says. "I can call him."

The boss looks from August to me. I hold back a sigh, give an eager nod.

"Great. So now we can put this behind us, right?"

We nod again, both of us, like a pair of naughty schoolchildren.

"By the way," Shahid says as we're about to leave. "When Roe called in to say that he's ill, he also said something else. He has a suspicion that Mariam Lind isn't at home, as her husband has said. Could you check that out—as discreetly as possible?"

Once we're safely back behind the closed door of my office, I look at August. I feel relieved, in a way. It seems like the right thing to do, to contact Roe and get him to explain. Of course the whole thing must be a misunderstanding.

"Maybe we should go see him instead of calling," I say. "I'm happy to come with you."

August plants a hand on his hip and smiles.

"I don't intend to do either of those things—I just wanted to stop the boss from calling him. We have to make a plan."

Mariam

Ålesund
Wednesday, 23 August 2017

It's still early in the day, the café sparsely populated by mothers with prams and the odd solitary figure. Birk goes and sits down at one of the tables towards the back of the premises while I walk up to the counter. He doesn't want anything—at least, nothing but an answer. When I set my cup on the table and take a seat across from him, the questions are hissed from between gritted teeth.

"What happened that day, Liv?" he says. "What did you do to them?"

Something tightens at the base of my throat. Even though I'm used to lying—even though I've done nothing else for the past twelve years—this is tough. Some lies are more difficult than others.

"Anita and I were together," I say. "She wanted to leave you for me. Other than that, I did nothing. I didn't see them that day, and I don't know what happened." I swallow and grip my cup. "I'd already left. I knew that the relationship between her and me wasn't going to work, and I had enough problems already."

"What happened to Aurora?" His dark beard makes him look like an angry caveman.

I hide my hands under the table to conceal the fact that I'm shaking. I've spent twelve years practising in case someone should ask me these questions. I take the time to slowly shake my head.

"I'm so sorry. I wish I knew. I didn't even know that either of them was dead until I saw a photograph of the house in the newspaper." I stutter a little, clear my throat. "To be completely honest, I thought it was maybe you who did it. You were taken into custody, after all. I followed the case."

The police thought it was him. It was so obvious that someone had attempted to hide their crime, and it's always the boyfriend or husband, isn't it? As far as I'd read, they had released him due to lack of evidence. Had he somehow looked me up, figured out who I was? Had he become convinced that I was behind what happened back then, and so sought revenge by taking my child from me, the way I took Aurora from him? It sounded crazy, but people have done crazier things. I've done crazier things.

"When did you find out about me, Birk?"

He lifts his gaze again.

"I've seen the photograph of you everywhere. In the newspapers, on TV, alongside your daughter. I saw that photograph and thought you looked so damned familiar. It took a long time before I realised that I recognised you from some of Anita's paintings. From late in our relationship. That was when I realised that it must've been you who killed Aurora, and now you'd killed your daughter, too. I've already told the police all this. I know someone on the force in Kristiansund, so I called him right away. I've been surprised that they haven't brought you in. Instead, you turn up here."

I shake my head.

"I haven't done anything to my daughter. I'm convinced that Iben is alive. I'm going to find her."

Convinced. That's what I need to be.

He sighs. "After the fire, I was so angry that they were wasting time arresting me instead of finding out what really happened. That they weren't spending their time trying to find the fucking *lover* I knew she'd had, and who was to blame for everything. The lover who turned out to be a *woman*."

"So you had a motive for kidnapping my child. If you believed I killed yours." My voice cracks.

He looks at me, a deep darkness in his eyes.

"I know what you did to Anita," I say. "I saw the bruises."

He blinks for a split second too long, enough for me to see that he's now suddenly on his guard. I'm not the only one with something to hide.

"I was at sea when your daughter disappeared," he says. "I came home Friday evening."

I take a big gulp from my cup of coffee. Think of Iben when she was the same age that Aurora was when she died. How I carried her all the time, rocking her to sleep and holding her close to me. I used to think that if she could just live to be a single day older than Aurora, everything would be okay. A ridiculous thought. The tragedy was already in my blood, in my DNA, and Iben's, too.

"It's strange," says Birk, "that they haven't followed up on my tip. Have they really not even asked you about it?"

Roe

Ålesund
Tuesday, 1 December 2009

White flakes outside the window, the first snow of the winter. I sat up on the sofa and fumbled for the bottle of pills and mug of water, swallowed two Effexor. I shouldn't have been taking them. They took away my ability to think, made me sluggish. Made me forget things, think less clearly. But if I didn't take the pills I wouldn't manage to eat anything that day, would drink no water, breathe no air. *Just temporary*, the doctor said, *take your time, spend time with those closest to you.* My closest friend, the white brick wall. I knew every nail hole, every undulation in the texture of the paint. Around me, the dust bunnies grew in the nooks and crannies; once bright green plants had long since turned to corpses, the leaves draped over the edges of their pots. Take your time—I took four years.

The first snow. Soon it would be Christmas, and this year, as last, I would sit here alone and try to think that in just a few more hours it would be possible to turn the TV back on. Kiddo was dead. Aurora was dead. It felt wrong that the pills stopped me from feeling it more intensely. I could sit like this and say it to myself: Kiddo is dead, Aurora is dead, I am dead. I felt nothing. I shouldn't take those pills. Should be clear of mind, prepared, ready to find out what had happened. There had to be evidence that proved somebody was to blame for all this. If it was Birk, there must be conclusive evidence. They hadn't looked hard enough, and as time went on, it would become harder to find. Perhaps it would disappear completely. *Take your time.*

I went over to the fridge. There was nothing in there except for a mouldy piece of cheese, a packet of butter and a Munkholm beer. I sighed and threw the cheese into the bin. *One day at a time*, the doctor said, *write lists of what you're going to do each day.* Today I should go to the store, buy something to eat. Make a proper dinner. I often made dinner when Ingrid and I lived together. That's what I was supposed to do. Use the oven, and see that it was okay to do so.

My winter coat was at the back of the closet between my suit and a blazer I had never worn. I stuck my hand into the pocket of the suit jacket and pulled out the programme from Anita and Aurora's funeral. Ingrid had stood there, clasping a note in her hand, and said, *We have lost a child and grandchild, but we'll try to think of all the times we shared.* Always so fucking positive, Ingrid. I jammed my hand into the other inside pocket, but the piece of paper featuring the speech I never gave was gone.

I pulled on my coat, hat and gloves and went out into the snow. Lately I'd often thought that it might actually be possible to get over it. Start living again with the knowledge that there was a big black hole in the world, one in the shape of a burned-down house. After all, I had managed to live without

Kiddo before—I hadn't had much contact with her after she had grown up. Only once had I visited her after she gave birth; I didn't know Aurora at all. It was the pills talking when I thought like this—that it was possible to lose a daughter and a grandchild and still live—but I couldn't be a police officer and constantly pop pills. Three afternoons a week in the archive, sorting old cases so as not to lose my job. *Take your time*. Hoping that nobody would see me on the way in or out and—God forbid—want to chat. Hoping that nobody looked me in the eyes. For the most part they avoided me anyway. *Take all the time you need*, the boss had said. A zombie former police officer wandering through the snow.

Nobody recognises me at the local grocery store, even though I've always shopped here. There's a constant stream of new, young faces—it probably isn't a place you want to stay working at for very long. I stood by the shelves, trying to remember how I used to make gravy—was it just flour, butter and salt, or was there something else? It was as if my memories of cooking had been packed at the bottom of a cardboard box that lay in a storeroom at the back of my brain. I remembered that it needed bouillon. Went to the checkout, picking up two bars of chocolate along the way, and then looked down at the conveyor belt as the products were scanned. Looked down at my wallet, took out my card and paid. The boy behind the till put my items into a bag for me; I thanked him without looking up.

"Hi," a voice said, a figure by the door. I guessed it was a greeting intended for somebody else. Began to walk away, taking my bag with me. Then I felt a hand on my shoulder. It was a young boy. Semi-long hair and leather jacket, in his twenties.

"Hi," I said, wanting to leave.

"Don't you recognise me?"

I shook my head and impatiently walked past him, out onto the street.

"You're a policeman, right?"

I turned and looked at the boy.

"You arrested me once, a few years ago. I'll never forget your face."

A narrow face, low forehead, eyebrows that almost joined in the middle, but not quite. He'd had short blond hair when I arrested him.

"I got you for a mugging," I said. "It was your father, wasn't it—the man you robbed?"

"I'd hoped I might run into you one day. You know, it meant a lot that you were decent to me back then. I wasn't used to anyone of your age being decent to me in that way."

"Thanks," I said, pausing for a moment. "Was David Lorentzen the guy you did the job with?"

Outside he lit a cigarette, didn't answer the question.

"I heard that somebody killed him. I was brought in for questioning, but I couldn't give them anything. Did they ever get anyone for it?"

"I don't know anything about it," I said. "I've been on sick leave."

He came closer. "I hope you won't mind me saying this, but your pupils are huge."

I turned my gaze to the floor.

"It's a side effect of some pills I'm taking."

"Anxiety?"

I nodded.

"Just temporary, right?"

"Temporary for four years."

He took a long drag on his cigarette. Blew smoke from the side of his mouth.

"Seriously?" he said. "That's long enough. It only gets harder to quit the longer you're on them. My mother was on that stuff for years." He held out his hand. "You wanted to introduce yourself to me last time we met, but I wasn't exactly obliging. Will you give me a second chance?"

I took his hand, gave him a real handshake.

"Hi. I'm Roe."

"Egil Brynseth," he said. "Nice to meet you."

Ronja

Kristiansund
Wednesday, 23 August 2017

The door opens, and the nurse comes in along with Robert Kirkeby. Just like last time, he doesn't look at our faces but instead casts wary glances from side to side, his gaze flitting about the room in a way that makes me think he doesn't quite believe what he's seeing. He sits in exactly the same place as before, whispering a few words to himself under his breath.

"Hi, Robert," I say. Robert looks up at me and August in fright before turning his face back to the tabletop. "You were a big help to us the last time we were here, but now we need your help again. I have some photographs to show you and wonder if you could tell me whether you recognise any of the people in them. Do you think you can do that, Robert?"

A few seconds pass. Robert looks down at the tabletop, whispering to himself.

"Iben Lind, Iben Lind, Iben Lind," he says.

I nod.

"Yes, this is about Iben Lind. I'm wondering whether any of these men are the man you saw her with on Friday?"

I set the photographs on the table. Six different faces—I push them forward so that they're right in front of him. It feels wrong to be going behind the backs of Roe and the boss in this way. For all we know, Roe might have a good explanation as to why he never told us he was on the surveillance footage from Storkaia, but August wanted to talk to the witness first. So that's why we're here, and all we can do is hope that something useful comes of it.

"Iben Lind, Iben Lind, Iben Lind," Robert Kirkeby mumbles. "Everyone believes them, everyone believes them, but they lie straight to your face. Standing and talking to little children—the police are in on it, the police have been infiltrated, just look at Tom Cruise. Where does he get his money from? I see it, right enough."

The nurse leans forward. "The police are only here because they need your help, Robert. Do you recognise any of the men in these pictures?"

Robert leans forward so far that he almost headbutts the photographs on the table.

"Talking to Iben Lind," he says. "Talking to Iben Lind, arguing and talking to her, then she disappears."

I hold my breath.

"Yes, Robert," the nurse says calmly. "Are any of these men the man you saw talking to Iben Lind?"

Robert's torso begins to sway back and forth. A loud hacking sound comes from the back of his throat. He hacks several times more. Then he stops, looks down and spits a long, thick gob of spit that lands precisely on the table in front of him. He leans back; August and I simultaneously lean forward, across the table. There, in the only photograph bathed in Robert Kirkeby's enormous gob of spit, is Roe Olsvik's face.

"It'll never hold up in court," August says when we're back outside.

The slightest glimpse of sun can be seen between the grey clouds. I feel my stomach contract. In court?

"Maybe we should go and speak to Roe now?" I say meekly.

August looks at me, astonished.

"You want to go and talk to him now, when the witness has just identified him?"

Some expression crosses his face, the authority of someone with years of experience talking to a pitiful rookie. What do I know about the right course of action? Maybe I'm just influenced by the boss. A typical *good girl*. Still, that's what you're supposed to do—listen to the boss.

"We have to make a few phone calls," August says once we get into the car. "To people in Ålesund, people who know Roe. We have to find out what his connection to this case is."

His connection to this case. That's precisely what we could have asked Roe about.

"You're sure we shouldn't just go to him directly, talk to him?"

August looks affronted. Then he smiles.

"Call Birte," he says. "See what she thinks."

Roe

Ålesund
Tuesday, 5 June 2012

All around me, time didn't pass—it flew by with jet propulsion. Rushing past at a speed that broke the sound barrier, while I sat frozen. Staring at the brick wall and watching the plaster flake off, tiny white specks that landed on the laminate flooring. This was how I let time go by—hours, days, weeks, months, years. I was like a figure in a snow globe, with plaster instead of snow. I wondered whether some ill-tempered God was sitting up there shaking the cursed thing while laughing his head off.

The inside of my head was far too crowded. Every time I tried to sleep, my mind was full of memories. The pills that had kept them at bay had been flushed down the toilet two weeks earlier. I'd be turning fifty-five soon, and I intended to celebrate my birthday quietly and privately, free from all that shit. I knew I should try to get some sleep before Egil arrived, but I just couldn't manage it. Behind my eyelids were Anita's charred remains. I knew I had to clear away the dishes that stood on the kitchen counter, but I simply sat there, staring. Soon Egil would come. He would come and grab hold of me and say, *Do this and this, Roe—it will do you good.* That was the kind of thing I wanted. A parent. Me, a parent myself, who had been the best . . . I put my head in my hands.

It had been nice, lately, with Egil. We'd met a few times at a café, talked about our lives, and it all seemed so simple, suddenly, in the light of the life of this young boy who had managed to get a grip on himself. Last time, he'd started to talk about his father. He said that during his childhood, anytime his father was home, he was drunk—as was his mother. On the outside, everything was about status and money, but within the house's four walls there was only loneliness. He remembered the feeling of being forgotten, how both his mother and father were always busy with their own lives. He could remember hiding to see how long it would take before somebody found him. As a young man, he ended up caught in the same trap, his drinking getting heavier and heavier until he abandoned his studies. He had blamed his father for every drop he drank, he said. Right until his father wanted to take away his allowance, too. That was when he had started to plan his revenge.

When the doorbell finally rang, it hit me that I didn't have anything to offer him. Not so much as a cup of instant coffee. I sat there for a while, considering whether I should just not bother opening the door, whether I should postpone the visit. Then the doorbell rang again, and I remembered what Egil had said, that he hadn't been used to somebody of my age being decent to him and how that had meant a lot. I got up and went over to the door.

Egil gave me a firm handshake and entered the tiny hallway.

"It's so cool to be able to come here," he said.

At that moment I felt afraid. He had expectations that would be crushed as soon as he saw my apartment, as soon as he realised that there really wasn't anything left of me other than a wretched police officer on long-term sick leave who couldn't get back on his feet. But when Egil walked into the living room, he didn't seem to react negatively at all. He found himself a space on the sofa next to the crumpled wool blanket I had left there, looking past the chaos of glasses, cups, and plates on the table as if it was all beyond his field of view. I sank down onto the sofa, feeling old when I said I didn't have anything to offer him. No pretzels or Danish pastries, the kind of baked goods Ingrid would set out when we had visitors, back when we were together.

"I'm so happy to hear that you've finally stopped taking those pills," he said. "That's good. You can't process anything if you're high."

"I'll admit it's cost me a lot. But still, I feel better without them. I think I'd rather feel the pain than not feel it, if you know what I mean."

"Met any ladies recently?" he said, looking up at the ceiling and suddenly making me remember how young he was.

"I gave all that up years ago, when my wife met a weak motherfucker she liked better than me."

I thought this would make him laugh, but he only shook his head slightly.

"I don't understand what *that* has to do with anything. What your wife did, I mean. If you met someone, I bet it would help your mood."

"Women cause nothing but trouble."

He nodded. "True. If you take away 'nothing but.' They cause a lot of other things, too. You should try online dating."

It's so typical of young people to say "must" and "should" to mature adults. Anita used to do it, too, when we were in touch. She also used to say that I "should" try to find someone new. Just as her mother had done.

"What about you?" I said. "Is love still blooming?"

Egil laughed in a feigned sort of way, as if he had prepared for this question.

"We're moving in together."

He beamed when I congratulated him, seemed shy and in love, looking up at the ceiling again. I immediately began to think about how I had been at his age. How I'd thought that there was something outside of me, another person, who could make me whole. I'd abandoned such fairy tales long ago, but I remembered how good it had felt.

"So you're doing well," I said.

"Yeah, I am actually. Really well."

He got up and went over to the window. Outside there was nothing but trees and grey streets; the snow never settled here for more than a couple of days.

"Good place to live," he said. "Central. I hope we can find a place like this, too."

Then he turned to face the only decorated wall in the room, where two paintings hung in the light from the window. I'd wanted the sun to fall on her face every once in a while. He stopped, moved closer to the images.

"That's you," he said, pointing at the painting titled *The Policeman*. She had captured me in the typical position, with my gaze lowered and deep in concentration, brow furrowed. The light fell on my head and the grey skin of my face. It must have been hard to be the daughter of a man who never looked up from his paperwork.

Egil studied the other painting more closely. The fine lines along her throat, the blond hair half falling into her eyes. Anita was so good at self-portraits. It was as if she came alive again for a moment every time I looked at the painting. Ingrid had given me the two paintings after the funeral. So we could remember Anita as she was, she said. As if it were possible to replace my memory of Anita's blackened skin with a memory in which she was breathing and had rosy cheeks. That wasn't how it worked. Both memories existed—all the memories existed—and still the memory of her death was the strongest.

"That girl, there," Egil said, pointing at the painting.

"That's my daughter."

Since Anita died, I had carried a small, sharp folding knife in my pocket every time I left the house. For protection. At night, I dreamed that I held the knife to the throat of the person who killed her. Generally, the murderer's face flickered with Birk's dark beard. I dreamed that Anita lay dead, charred on a stretcher, but then she took a breath and the colour returned to her cheeks. I dreamed that the ash fell from her body, and that she became a smiling, warm child again, at twelve years old, six, four.

He looked at me, pale.

"That's your daughter? The girl who died?"

His words burned in my ears; it became hard to breathe. I started to wonder about this idea of taking my time, which the doctors were continually nagging me about. How much time? How much time would help?

Egil studied the painting, frowning.

"Was there something you wanted to say?" I said.

"No," he said quickly, shaking his head. "She was just so pretty."

Ronja

Kristiansund
Wednesday, 23 August 2017

We're sitting in Birte's car, all three of us, outside the local psychiatric outpatient clinic. Birte drove straight over here when I told her what we'd discovered. She's been doing voice exercises and has shifted into acting mode, and now she taps "call" on the phone that is connected to the car's speakers. August and I sit in the back seat as the phone starts to ring. Birte is enjoying herself now that she has the full attention of an audience. She purses her lips in a special way, posing, as if she's already in character.

"Yes, hello, Sverre Nakken here."

"Hello," chirps Birte. "This is Birte Lie from Kristiansund police station."

Birte had been in complete agreement with August, saying that we had to go against Shahid and investigate further. She even gave us a quick lesson in acting techniques for the occasion.

"Kristiansund, right. Awful, the case of the missing girl. Is there something I can help you with?"

It was Birte who thought we should start by calling Sverre Nakken, but that we shouldn't reveal our real reason for calling. She thought we should try to avoid creating a situation in which he might start to defend his former colleague or call Roe as soon as he hung up. For the time being, both she and August agreed that it was wise not to reveal what we knew, or what we were trying to find out.

"Thank you, Sverre, I appreciate that. But this isn't about that case. I'm calling because my new colleague, Roe Olsvik, has just turned sixty, and we were thinking that we should arrange a bit of a party for him, since it certainly doesn't look as if he's going to do it himself." She chuckles, as does the man on the other end of the line.

"Are you sure he'd want you to do that, though?"

Birte giggles.

"He doesn't have a choice. He *has* to be able to celebrate his birthday—that's the way I see it. The reason I'm calling is that we wanted to invite some family and old friends of his, but we don't have the details for anyone he knows, apart from his colleagues."

Silence falls for a moment. The man clears his throat.

"You know what—if I were you, I don't think I would invite anyone else. Colleagues are enough."

Birte looks as if she's holding back a sigh. Presses her lips together and forces a smile.

"Can't you think of anyone he would appreciate having there?"

"I'm sure you're all aware of his past. What happened to his daughter and grandchild, and that he was on sick leave for years. I honestly don't think he has anyone left—"

"His ex-wife," Birte interrupts. "Do you think you'd be able to give me her number? Just so I can see what she thinks?"

Silence again.

"Well . . . I think he's actually trying to get away from every-thing these days, but . . . you could always call Ingrid and ask."

"Ingrid, right."

Birte notes the telephone number on the back of a receipt and thanks Sverre for his time. She hangs up and waves the receipt over her shoulder.

"Now it's your turn, August."

August gets into the driver's seat and picks up the phone, calling the number Birte was given. His slim hand is trembling slightly. The phone rings just a couple of times before a woman answers. Her voice sounds delicate, almost feeble.

"Hi," says August, adopting a mild tone. "Is this Ingrid Krogsveen? I'm calling because I have a colleague, Roe Olsvik. Is he your ex-husband?"

"Yes?"

"As I said, I'm his colleague, and a friend. I'd very much like to invite his family and friends to a party to celebrate his sixtieth birthday, but I'm not quite sure who to invite."

"Oh, I see. Is he really that old?"

Her voice is flat, almost indifferent. "There's nobody to invite," she says. "His parents are both dead. His father died . . . was it fourteen years ago? Drank himself to death, or so they say. He lost his mother even further back than that. Of his immediate family, there's only me left." Her voice increases in pitch as she says this last sentence. "And I'm not sure I'm up to it."

"I understand, though I'm sad to hear that. But perhaps you can help me with what I might say in my speech. How would you describe Roe as a person?"

"Oh, I don't know if he'd be that interested in any descrip-tion I'd give. He was a kind man when we were together. Not around much, but kind and good when he was. Of course in recent years he's turned hard and dark, after what happened to Anita. But, well, you can't say that."

August takes his time.

"What do you mean? How was he different before?"

"Oh, he was more open, enjoyed life. Not as angry as he sometimes seems now. I haven't seen him since before the summer, but still. It scares me actually, the way his personality changed."

"He doesn't say very much to me, either," August says. "He bottles it all up. I wish I could be of more help."

August's voice is calm and composed. He's doing an excellent job. Nobody would have any doubt that he must be a good friend of Roe's.

"That's so typical of Roe," Ingrid says. "He wants to be strong, but I think he has bigger problems than the people around him realise . . . No, now I'm speaking out of turn. Of course this isn't material for a speech. If you want to give a greeting from me, say that I've always regarded him as a good man."

Silence descends. August drums his fingers lightly on the steering wheel.

"There's something I've been wondering about," he says. "His daughter had a partner she lived with, didn't she?"

"Birk?"

"That's him. What was his surname again?"

"Fladmark, but I wouldn't invite him. Roe never liked him, and for a long time he was convinced that it was Birk who killed Anita."

I enter the name into directory enquiries as Ingrid speaks. Her voice begins to crack.

"Oh, I'm sorry—well then of course we won't contact him. Thank you very much for your help, Ingrid."

"Thank you for calling," she says. "As I said, I would have liked to be there, but I just don't think I can manage it. I'm sorry."

"Don't worry about it," August says.

When he hangs up, Birte and I sit there, stunned, for a moment.

"Jesus," Birte says. "That was really good, August. You have a talent."

August tries to act as if the praise he receives from us is no big deal, but the redness at his throat gives him away.

It's my turn. My hands are clammy as I get into the driver's seat. I look down at the phone, then up into the rearview mirror.

"I don't think I want to do this," I mumble.

"What was that, Ronja?" says Birte.

My hand is shaking. "I don't think we should do this," I say. "We were given an order."

Birte laughs her piercing laugh. "Give me the phone," she says.

I pass it to her, and she enters the number. I set my hands on my thighs, still trembling as Birte sets the phone against my ear. She giggles almost inaudibly.

"Hello?" says the man on the other end of the line. "Hello, is there somebody there?"

"Hi," I manage to say. "Is this Birk Fladmark? This is Ronja Solskinn calling from Kristiansund police station."

"Finally," he grunts. "I thought you'd never call."

Roe

Ålesund
Monday, 2 March 2015

"Well, hello there stranger!"

Sverre beamed when he caught sight of me walking down the corridor of Ålesund police station, and I immediately felt a warmth spread through my chest, as if I had returned to my old life, ten years ago now. I took his hand and gave it a good squeeze.

"Are you back, or . . ."

A simple question—as if I'd been gone for a week, not a decade. Still, there was a new uncertainty in his tone, a crease to his brow that was probably due to my tendency to pop up on the premises only to disappear again before the day was out. This time, however, it was different. This time I wanted to stay.

"Yes," I said. "I'm back."

The offices were the same old cubicles that seemed to have stood there since the dawn of time. I'd been given a new office, but it was only new in the sense that it was different from the one I had before. This time, I'd have an office job in criminal investigation. My days in the field were over. The boss had said I could spend the first day getting settled in, and I intended to do so. I set a few books on the empty shelf and ripped away a few comic strips the previous occupant had left on the corkboard. A temp had worked in here before me, long enough to be transferred to a permanent position. That was all I knew. I didn't know who had quit, whether anyone had gone on leave or left town. Before what happened to Kiddo, I knew everything about everyone in this building. Now I'd have to start all over again.

I pushed up the sleeves of my sweater and started the irritating job of connecting all the cables to their relevant sockets. Whoever invented the computer could have made the whole thing a little more intuitive. Still, I was happy that nobody was standing over me trying to help, that I didn't have to talk to anyone. There would be more than enough time for people to say *We thought we'd never see you again*, or for Sverre to finally ask *How come you never returned my calls?* Because now, things would be good again. I was back.

When I had finally connected all the cables to the PC and started it up, I sat back in the chair with a sigh. I was sweaty from the sunlight that beat against the windowpane, and so opened the window a crack. I'd only recently started going for walks. Before Kiddo, I used to go jogging and lift weights. Now I suddenly needed simple walks, where I could listen to the screeching of the seagulls and smell the sea. Make my way down to the water's edge and feel the wind in my face. There probably weren't many people here who could understand that, but Egil did. That was what was so great about him. He seemed to understand everything.

I opened the program for archiving old ongoing cases—it was many years since I had last used it. I'd have to refresh my old knowledge, bring all the dead paperwork back to life. I searched for the last major case I was involved in, and which had also contributed to my breakdown. David Lorentzen. The case was still unsolved. There was too little evidence. Or rather, there was too much evidence. I began to open the many files containing reports from the forensic examination of the body, biological findings from the crime scene, interviews with witnesses. Pretty much the entire drug scene seemed to have been brought in at some point or other. Still, nobody knew what happened that night. Most of them used each other as alibis. It seemed hopeless. These people were used to lying. You sat across from them, fully aware that they were lying to you. Hardly any of them would agree to give so much as a fingerprint for fear of becoming a suspect. It wasn't much use having piles of DNA at a crime scene if nobody was willing to cooperate and be tested, and there was no way to charge one person rather than another.

The autopsy report concluded that David Lorentzen had been dead "between five and fifteen days." The body had advanced livor mortis and was leaking decomposition fluid. The estimated time of death was also based on the life-cycle stage of the larvae present when the body was found.

I clicked through the documents and discovered that the last confirmed sighting of the deceased was on Saturday, 16 April 2005, the day of the first football match at the stadium. He had been brought in for questioning at Ålesund police station in connection with the mugging and the break-in at Halvor Brynseth's home. Whether he died on this or one of the subsequent days was, however, unknown. He may have died as late as the following weekend. Witnesses gave substantially different statements—very few wanted to admit to having ever been at Lorentzen's residence, while others claimed to have seen him around that time. I went back to the autopsy report, in which the medical examiner had concluded that the deceased had consumed alcohol in the hours before he died. Not surprisingly, his blood also tested positive for several narcotic substances.

I clicked through to other documents, scanning the huge volume of material. Interviews with the deceased's mother, Karoline Lorentzen, who had let herself in and found her son dead in the bed. Clicked further and found an image of his living room, in which bottles and cans were scattered around along with full ashtrays. It looked as if he'd just had a party. Back in the autopsy report I found that traces of female DNA had been discovered on the deceased's penis, which indicated that he had engaged in sexual intercourse soon before he died. There were also traces of adhesive from gaffer tape on his hands and feet, but the tape had been removed. The cause of death was suffocation caused by an object pressed against the deceased's throat. The murder weapon was presumed to be the lamp on the nightstand, which seemed to have been thoroughly cleaned.

Several of Lorentzen's friends were suspects in the murder, but no one was ever charged. One of them submitted their fingerprints and DNA, which matched those found on a large pile of gaffer tape discovered in the bin in the kitchen. The fact that he wasn't charged was understandable—the gaffer tape featured DNA from at least six individuals, male and female, in addition to Lorentzen himself. The same was true of the bottles and cans, as well as cigarette butts found around the apartment.

I closed all the documents. Clicked to open the one named
"Forensic Sketch, Scene of Mugging." Since such a brief time
had passed between the two incidents, and they happened
such a short distance from each other, a connection had not
been ruled out. The image appeared, a woman in her twenties
wearing a hoodie and football scarf. My heart turned over in
my chest.

"I thought you didn't have to work today."

Sverre stood leaning against the doorframe, watching me.
I minimised the forensic sketch and opened another random
document, which happened to be an image of the crime scene,
Lorentzen's rotting body on the bed.

"I was just interested in a case."

He came closer.

"Is that David Lorentzen? Wasn't that the case where you—"

He stopped himself, or I stopped him with a look.

"I always thought it was a woman who killed him," he said.

"Why do you think that?"

"I can't prove it, but he slept with a woman before he died.
And his hands and feet had been bound with tape, and he'd
been strangled. It seems like the work of somebody who knew
she wasn't strong enough to do it with her own hands. Don't
you think?"

I shrugged. "Or a man who wanted to be certain he'd be able
to get the job done, and not end up being beaten up himself?
Or some kind of blackmail?"

"That was what the boy—Egil Brynseth—thought."

"And there's something else," I said, but stopped myself.
"No, forget it."

Sverre nodded. "Are you getting out and about, Roe? Have
you met anyone lately?"

I turned to face Sverre, who gave me the look everybody else seemed to be giving me these days. "You too? I'm constantly getting that stuff shoved down my throat right now."

"You should try online dating."

"Excuse me," I said. "I think I'll set this aside for now and go home. Short first day."

"Lucky you."

Sverre backed out of the doorway and disappeared. I waited a few seconds before I opened the forensic sketch again. She would have done a much better job of drawing it herself, but the eyes were unmistakable. It was Kiddo.

Ronja

Kristiansund
Wednesday, 23 August 2017

It falls silent in the car after I've hung up with Birk. I first meet Birte's gaze, then August's, then look down. I clear my throat.

"Mariam Lind knew Roe's daughter," I say.

"Roe's daughter's partner gave Roe a tip, which he hasn't checked out," August says.

Birte presses her lips together. Shakes her head slightly.

"Why wouldn't he tell us about Birk's suspicions regarding Mariam Lind?"

"Maybe that's why Roe has been so obsessed with her," August says. "Because of this tip."

"But why lie?" says Birte. "Why not tell us about it?"

I think for a moment. Why would somebody lie about something like this—that was the real question. Had he told us about the tip, it would have strengthened his reasons for wanting to investigate Mariam Lind. And that's what he wants—he's been talking about it from the beginning.

"I think only Roe can answer that," I say.

"Yeah—the questions he needs to answer are starting to pile up," Birte says. "I think we have to bring him in."

"Bring him in?"

"If Roe had told us about this connection," Birte says, "then not only would it have linked Mariam Lind to both cases, but it would have linked him to both cases, too. Maybe he wanted to direct attention onto Mariam, without coming under scrutiny himself."

I look at Birte.

"Do you think that Roe—"

"At the very least, I think we have to dig a little deeper. He's lied to us, he has a connection to both cases, and if he thinks Mariam Lind killed his daughter and grandchild, doesn't that give him a motive for committing the same crime against her?"

August clears his throat. "Let's not go jumping to conclusions," he says. "How about we first do what Shahid said—visit Tor Lind for an explanation as to why he hasn't told us that Mariam has disappeared?"

I nod.

"Let's go."

Birte takes over the driver's seat and I get into the passenger side as usual, while August drives his own car. He follows right behind us as Birte drives confidently, chin raised and eyes glued to the road.

"There's nothing going on, by the way," I say. "Between August and me."

Birte laughs. "That's for you to manage exactly as you please, Ronja."

"I'm not managing anything."

We drive inland, towards Nordlandet. I think about Roe and how friendly he can be towards me, almost as if he's happy to see me. Perhaps I remind him of his daughter. It's hard to imagine him as the potential murderer Birte has hinted he could be. Other police officers have said that he's sometimes aggressive and sharp-tongued, but he's never been like that with me. I know full well that anyone can turn out to be a murderer, but when it comes to Roe I really just can't see it.

I learned two important things at the Police University College: The first is that you always have to ready yourself for the worst imaginable outcome—the worst-case scenario—in order to be prepared. The other is that you must never draw conclusions too early; you must keep an open mind. We mustn't be biased, mustn't assume that something that might look right is in fact correct.

"Can you drop me off at the footpath?" I ask. "Instead of driving all the way up to the house?"

"How come?"

"I just want to follow the route Iben supposedly took. It might also be a good idea to surprise Tor—people sometimes speak more freely when the visit is unexpected."

Birte brakes and pulls up neatly beside the pavement. She calls August on her mobile.

"August, stay where you are for ten minutes."

Birte looks at me and laughs. "Well, off you go then."

I jump out of the car and start to take the shortcut, past the place where the comic book was found, and up the gradual slope. This is likely where she was running, until somebody stopped her. There's an area of the path that is hidden, where a car would be able to pick up a little girl without anyone seeing.

In my head, I try to go through what I need to ask Tor Lind about. *Where's your wife, Tor? Why haven't you told us about this? I seem to remember you said she was asleep upstairs the last time we were here, and that you didn't want to wake her.* I imagine his face, how his gaze will wander as he searches for an explanation, but then I stop. I take long, careful steps backwards before I turn and jog back to the car. Birte winds the window down.

"What is it, sweetie?"

"Shhh," I whisper. "It's Roe. He's standing behind a car in the car park. He's spying on the Lind family's house with binoculars."

"Shahid said he was off sick today," Birte says automatically. Then she falls silent.

"What should I do?" I ask.

Birte thinks for a moment, then jumps out of the car. She walks back to August and says something I can't hear. August pulls out onto the road as Birte starts to run up the path towards the house. I run after her, suddenly confused. It feels like we're back in primary school and I'm the girl at the top of the class who wants to go find the teacher because he hasn't turned up, while all the other kids just want to skip the lesson. I always hated being that girl, and right now it's taking all my strength to suppress the instinct.

We're soon well within Roe's field of view; he would see us if he turned his head. But he continues to look through the binoculars, studying the house.

"Hi, Roe," says Birte. "What are you doing here?"

Roe lowers the binoculars. He stares alternately at the house, at Birte and at me.

"I thought you were off sick," she continues.

"Mariam Lind isn't home," Roe says. "She hasn't been here for two days."

"What are you doing here? Why are you so interested in the family? Why didn't you tell us you already knew Mariam Lind?"

Roe immediately looks afraid.

"We know everything, Roe. We know you were at the Storkaia shopping centre, that you hid the fact you were there and that you spoke to Iben Lind before she disappeared."

He seems to weigh several options. Turn and run through the Lind family garden or jostle us aside, beat two police-women unconscious and flee. I try to imagine his bulky body hobbling through gardens and over fences, but he just stands there. Then August pulls up beside me.

"I think you need to come down to the station, Roe," Birte says.

Roe

Ålesund
Monday, 2 March 2015

Egil beamed when he opened the door and saw that it was me. He was wearing a small apron dusted with flour.

"It's Roe!" Egil shouted into the apartment. "How nice to see you, Roe. I wish people younger than you would turn up unannounced. It pretty much never happens." He extended his arm, gesturing into the bright hallway. I took two steps inside and stopped.

"I have to speak to you," I said.

"What's going on?"

Right then, I started to shake. The strength went out of my legs, and they became weak; cowardly muscles, cowardly skeleton. I squeezed my eyes shut—not now, please, no more of this now—but it was so intense. Egil grabbed my arm, led me into the living room and managed to get me to sit down on the sofa. I kept my eyes closed, heard him go off to speak to his wife. Behind my eyelids I saw the cloud of smoke that had poured out when I tried to open the door to Kiddo's house. If only I'd arrived earlier. If only I had answered the phone when she called. The least I could do was find out what happened to her, solve her case. The least I could do—and even that I couldn't manage. There'd been a living piece of the puzzle right in front of me for years—I had spoken to him, enjoyed hearing about the good times in his life, had treated him like a son and not just some scumbag. He had visited me, stood in front of the painting of my daughter. He knew, and he never said a word.

Somebody came closer, bending down just next to me and setting something on the table. I opened my eyes and saw that Egil had put a glass of water in front of me. He took a seat on the corner sofa, folded his hands.

"What did you want to talk about?"

A coward—that's what I was. I couldn't even confront a criminal without my legs turning to jelly. I drank greedily from the glass, wanting to put out the fire with the water—to extinguish Anita. As if I longed for stillness, for an inner life that wasn't boiling under high pressure. I yanked out my new mobile phone—which even had a camera that could take good photographs—and held it out to Egil so that he could see the forensic sketch.

"That's Anita," I hissed. "That's fucking Anita, Egil!"

Behind me I heard the kitchen door close. Egil scooted forward to sit on the edge of the sofa, looking down at the floor.

"I'm trying to understand," I said, "but my mind is seeing nothing but red, I'm so damn pissed. You have to explain this to me."

I threw the phone onto the table. Egil grabbed it, looked at the sketch. The girl in the orange and blue hoodie, the scarf around her neck. The blond fringe, the eyes that had looked at me in expectation when she was a child, lit up by the idea

that Pappa was magic—with Pappa, anything was possible.
The same eyes that in her teenage years had started to view
me with scepticism, irritation. She had learned—not only was
Pappa not capable of magic, he wasn't even an especially good,
ordinary Pappa. He would forget to pick her up from school
because some thrilling crime had been committed. He would
come home late and fall asleep like a log on the sofa while she
ate whatever she could find in the fridge. *We were too young
to become parents*, Ingrid had said so many times, but for me
it didn't feel that way. It was more as if I became a worse and
worse father with the passing years. I had spent hardly any
time with her. And now everybody kept insisting that time
heals all wounds, but every hour of the rest of my life would
be time I could never choose to spend with her.

"Don't you have anything to say?"

Egil fiddled with my phone.

"I didn't want to ruin your memories of her," he said. "That's
why I didn't say anything. Something like that wasn't in her
nature, she was just desperate."

"She was the girl who did the robbery with you? Back then,
you said you didn't know her. Which is true?"

"I sort of knew her. I met her at the Norwegian Business
School when she was studying there."

"You didn't give her name in order to protect her."

Egil nodded. "I didn't want to drag anyone else into it. It
was *my* plan, a stupid act of revenge against my father."

"You have to tell me everything now, Egil. Who was it who
put you up to this?"

He shrugged.

"Well, 'put me up to it' isn't entirely accurate. I suggested
the plan to David Lorentzen."

"How did Anita end up involved?"

"She called me, said she was desperate—she wanted to leave Birk and needed to borrow some money. She was crying and distraught. I didn't have anything to lend her, but I suggested she could help with the robbery."

"So it was because of you. It's your fault she got dragged into it."

Egil nodded, put his head in his hands.

"I really fucked up. Really."

"Egil," I said. "What happened to Anita and Aurora? Why are they dead?"

He shook his head, which he propped in his hands.

"I don't know what happened after the robbery. I got arrested, didn't I?"

"Do you know who this new boyfriend of hers was—the one she wanted to leave Birk for?"

He shook his head again.

"I need one hundred percent honesty from you now. You won't lie to me ever again?"

Egil shook his head.

"I won't lie to you again."

Mariam

Ålesund
Wednesday, 23 August 2017

Ingvar is sitting in the living room watching TV when I get back. It's the news; the photograph of Iben and me appears on the screen, even though there are no new developments to report. I close my eyes, try to pretend the photograph doesn't exist. It was Tor who gave it to the *Tidens Krav*, and obviously to other media outlets, too. When I found out he had shared the photograph, I worried somebody would recognise Mariam as Liv. Still, I let it happen, didn't stop it. I'd imagined that Iben would see herself and her mother in the newspaper and on television, and feel guilty. What a mother I've been.

"I thought you didn't watch the news," I say.

"But you're on," Ingvar says, lowering the volume. "How did it go?"

I sigh and cast the key onto the table, slump down onto the sofa beside him. Want to lean my head against his shoulder, to be Liv hanging out with her old friend, but I resist the impulse.

"Have you heard from him?" I ask, but Ingvar only shakes his head. I hand him the note with the phone number written on it.

"Could you call him for me? Leave a message if he doesn't answer?"

Ingvar is wearing a T-shirt that says ACID KING on the front, with a picture of a wizard on a motorcycle. He picks up the phone and enters the number. Gets up as it starts to ring, pacing back and forth across the floor.

"It's Ingvar," he says into the phone. "Can you call me when you get this?"

He hangs up and sits back down. Again I start to think about the day I bumped into Patrick in town. *Have you become a latchkey kid, Sara?* My brother couldn't have been clearer in his message to me. I had to find him.

"You said you tend to see him at Smutten," I say. "How often?"

Ingvar looks up at the ceiling.

"It's a while since I've been there. I don't remember."

"Would there be somebody there who knows him?"

Ingvar's gaze begins to wander. Is something making him nervous?

"Yeah. Probably."

"So we'll go down there, talk to everybody. Somebody there must know where he is, or who we can talk to."

He gently lifts his shoulders. "Fine by me. Do you want to eat something first?"

Ingvar turns, grabs the remote control, and is about to turn off the TV when he stops and instead turns up the volume.

On the screen is a press conference from Kristiansund police station—I recognise the building. I've never met the man who is speaking—a man who appears to have a Pakistani background, with a solemn air about him. *Shahid Sethi*, it says at the bottom of the screen. He's heading up the investigation.

"We have requested that this individual be taken into custody based on the overall evidence in the case," says Sethi.

"Shit," Ingvar says. "They've brought somebody in?" The policeman on the screen points to a journalist who asks whether there is still hope of finding Iben alive, but the police don't wish to speculate at this time.

"Look at this," Ingvar says. He's opened an online newspaper on his phone. "They say it's a police officer who's been taken into custody."

I shake my head. It isn't possible.

"Can I borrow your phone?" I ask. Ingvar hands it to me without hesitating, and I dial Tor's number. "I'm watching the news," I say when he answers. "Do you know anything?"

"Not much. A man, a police officer. They won't give me his name or describe him to me at this point. They're interviewing him now and have promised to provide more information as it becomes available."

"It just doesn't add up," I say. "It can't be some stranger—it has to be somebody who knows us. Who knows me." As I speak, I squeeze the key in my fist. Hold it up, as if to show it to Tor, even though he can't see me.

"I know," Tor says, but it doesn't sound as if he knows anything. "There's probably more to this case than they're telling us. We just have to wait and see. I'm just glad that something is finally happening."

On the screen, the head of the investigation refrains from answering several insistent questions from the journalists.

"Just so you know," Tor says. "The police know you left. They'll probably be busy with this for a while, but you should probably get yourself home sharpish. I just hope to God that something in all this brings Iben back."

Roe

Ålesund
Sunday, 12 March 2017

"Do we really have to go through all this again now?" Ingrid said, pouring more coffee into my cup. We were sitting in her living room, on a glossy new white leather sofa—Ingrid bought new furniture all the time; she was constantly shopping for something that might bring her a sense of peace. As usual, the airhead of a guy she left me for had withdrawn into his office.

"This is the last time I'll ask," I said. "I've been to see Birk today, too."

"You've spoken to Birk?"

"I asked all the usual questions. Whether it was him who killed them, whether he knew who did, all of it."

"You mean you terrorised him again by subjecting him to a load of accusations." She shook her head. "Birk is innocent. My heart is absolutely sure of that."

"So who does your heart say killed them?"

"You never stop, do you, Roe? Do you understand what you're doing? You're reducing our daughter to a criminal investigation that isn't even yours to solve. Not to mention that it's *unsolv-able*. The case has been closed. It was a fire. There's no further evidence. Can't you just let our daughter rest in peace?"

"That's what I'm trying to do. I want peace, and I want to give her peace—that's why I'm leaving town. This is just an attempt to leave behind all the questions before I go."

She crosses her arms. "Fine. Ask away—come on."

"There must be something we've overlooked," I said. "Something we've forgotten from the period just before Anita died, something we should have known about her. Can you remember her talking about people she knew other than Birk?"

"As I've said a thousand times, I don't know anything, no more than that she was seeing somebody else. I don't even know how long it had been going on."

"When she told you about this other guy," I said. "Can you repeat what she said?"

"She was distressed. She said she wanted to leave Birk. Said she was in love. I asked who it was, and she said it was some-body her age. Someone who understood her, she said, and who was kind. I didn't want to hear any more about it."

"You didn't ask his name?"

Ingrid shook her head. "I've answered these questions so many times before, Roe. I'm actually glad you're moving. For your own sake. You need to get away. Kristiansund is nice, you can start over. I hope you can leave all this behind you and start living again."

I knew she was right. This town was a big black hole in my heart that never healed. I couldn't walk through the streets without staring at all these fucking people who were alive instead of her. Including myself—my own reflection in the store windows haunted me. I needed to get away.

"I have to go through her things again one last time before I leave."

Ingrid waved me away, irritated. "They're where they always are."

Anita's childhood bedroom was full of paintings. Most of them were hanging close together on the walls; others leaned against them on the floor. So many copies of Anita's naked face staring straight ahead, looking up or down. Other people, many from Ingrid's family. Babies and elderly relatives. I trailed my fingers over a painting of a baby with an open mouth and blood on its teeth—a funny picture. Straightened a framed sketch of Ingrid and her husband. It was good that some of the paintings had been saved, even though so many must have been destroyed in the fire.

When Aurora was a newborn and Birk was away at sea, Anita came here often. Ingrid helped her with the baby, and Anita could draw or paint when she needed a break. According to Ingrid, she had often sat on the bed, sketching with charcoal while Aurora slept.

Three sketchbooks were neatly stacked atop a chest of drawers. I took them over to the bed, sat down and began to turn the pages. As usual there were many self-portraits, and a few portraits of Ingrid and the baby. Quick sketches of bodies without faces, somebody standing beside an easel or holding a child in their arms. She often drew the things that caught her attention, so there were a few drawings of odd subjects, perhaps an attempt at a new style. It looked as if she was trying to do something a little more symbolic. There was a sketch of a room with a bed and a nightstand, a chest of drawers, not so unlike the room she had here, but with a strange difference—a snake. It lay curled up on the bed, its head resting on its coil.

She had drawn it several times, once hanging over the shoulder of a woman. I wondered what had interested her about this snake, the symbol of evil itself. Might it mean something?

One of the drawings in particular captured my attention. She had used yellow pastels and drawn a chain with a key on its end. The chain was curled up like a snake. I turned more pages and found that Anita had drawn the same chain around the neck of a young girl with dark hair and dark eyes. I thought I'd seen that chain and key before somewhere.

I got up and went over to the dressing table that stood at the opposite end of the room. This was where she had kept her jewellery box. I opened the box, rummaged around among pieces of silver and gold jewellery, and finally found what I was looking for. A shiny gold chain with a key on its end. This was what she had drawn. So simple and fine.

I carefully put the sketchbooks back in their place. Glanced around at all the art supplies Anita had left at Ingrid's house. Various types of paper, chalks and ink. I lifted the shiny glass paint muller that was being used as a paperweight. Anita had explained its use to me, how it could crush pigments into fine powder in order to create paints.

"I'd really like to take something of Anita's with me," I said to Ingrid as I came out of the room. "Is it okay if I take this?" I showed her the chain with the key on it.

"I don't remember having seen that before," she said. "Of course, just take it."

She gave me a long hug and wished me well in Kristiansund.

"But don't take the past with you," she said. "Leave it here. You'll see it does you good."

Mariam

Ålesund
Wednesday, 23 August 2017

A Led Zeppelin guitar solo fills the dim premises as we walk inside. Not many people have arrived yet. A tired-looking woman in her fifties, wearing a miniskirt that shows her big white thighs, is chatting to a man of around the same age at the bar. They both look drunk, the man hanging over the counter and pointing at the bottles of spirits that line the wall. A gang of bikers, ranging in age from eighteen to almost seventy, sit around some large tables made of beer barrels. One of them is wearing a studded leather waistcoat; another has a tattoo of a Viking on his arm. On the wall above them hangs a deer head. Ingvar leads the way. We walk past the bar and into the back room, where two girls are playing billiards. They lean over the table, laughing loudly, obviously drunk, even though it's still early in the evening. Off the billiard room is a separate room containing tables and chairs, but no people.

"It's still early yet," Ingvar says, looking at his phone.

We go to the bar. I feel overdressed in the dress and jacket that suits my new life. Nobody else in here looks like this—so proper. When I lived with Ingvar and Egil, this was one of our favourite haunts, one of the few places in town where Ingvar would agree to go. The old me stood on these tables singing along to rock classics, bet money on who would beat whom at billiards, argued with random drunks and scrounged beer when I didn't have money. I once felt as if I owned this place. Smutthullet, or Smutten—this was where it was at. The man behind the bar is in his late thirties; his hairline has started to recede. He wasn't here back when I laid waste to this place as a young girl. I still remember the names of the people who worked here back then.

"Do you know Patrick Scheie?" I ask the man behind the bar, but he only shakes his head. I turn to the pair sitting on stools at the counter. "How about you two? Patrick Scheie—do you know him?"

They look at me as if I'm asking whether they believe the moon landing was real. I grab Ingvar by the arm, pull him a little closer.

"Let's split up," I say. "I'll ask the girls in the back, you ask this lot in here." I jerk my head towards the motorcycle gang.

I cast a glance at the entrance. Even though the chance of Patrick just wandering in here today isn't especially great, my pulse has quickened.

As Ingvar moves off in the direction of the bikers, I walk to the back of the premises. The two girls at the billiard table seem too young to be here, and they're too busy with their game to notice somebody looking at them. One of them, with blond hair, tries to take a shot with the cue behind her back. The other, who has dark, reddish hair, laughs at her technique.

"Who's winning?" I ask.

"No idea," says the redhead, and both of them laugh. "You want a go?"

I take the cue. "Solids or stripes?" I ask.

Both girls shrug.

"We just play for fun," the blonde says.

I lean over the table and take aim at the red. Shoot so that the ball lands in the top pocket with a loud thunk. The girls cheer, easily excited. They seem so easy and happy—carefree. I hand the cue back to the redhead.

"I'm looking for Patrick," I say. "Patrick Scheie. Do you know him?"

The blond girl looks up.

"I know who he is. Haven't seen him for a long time, actually. He tends to pop up now and again. Usually a real pest when he does." She looks at me. "I hope you're not offended I said that."

"Don't worry, I know what he's like. You don't know whether he's moved, made new friends?"

She shakes her head. I thank them for the brief game and go back out into the main room, which has started to fill up. Wonder whether I can bear to be Mariam for the rest of my life. The person I was here, that girl, she's still inside me somewhere—every now and then I feel a pang of longing for her. But what I forget is that she had it difficult, too. The good memories are distortions of reality. It wasn't fun, standing on the tables and howling to the music. It was exhausting. Just passing attempts to fill the emptiness.

Ingvar is sitting alone at a table, his face turned towards the entrance, a glass in front of him. He seems so apathetic just sitting there, dispirited.

"Is that alcoholic?" I ask, pointing at the glass.

"No. Don't be stupid."

"Did you get anything out of them?" I ask, nodding at the bikers sitting behind him. He shakes his head. Looks down into his glass.

"I didn't get anything from the girls in the back, either."

I sit down on one of the barstools at the beer barrel table. The door opens, and more people come in. I'm sure I'll find him. There aren't many places you can hide in this city, where everybody knows everyone.

Ingvar nods to a couple of tough-looking guys who appear in front of him. They both have beards, and one of them is wearing a leather jacket with a biker logo. When Ingvar introduces me, they look me up and down, apparently confused by my presence here. I look at the two men. Wonder for a moment whether one of them was actually sitting with the group in the corner when we came in—the group Ingvar was supposed to go talk to. The one with a tattoo of a Viking on his arm. He looks at me, puts a hand in front of his mouth.

"It's you," he says. "Iben Lind's mother."

That photograph of Iben and me in front of the clothing store mirror. It seems so long ago.

"That policeman, the guy they arrested. Do you think he's the one who took her?"

I shake my head. "I think it has to be somebody else. Somebody who lives here in town."

The two men sit down at the table. They look at me, expectantly.

"Patrick Scheie," I say. "Do you know him?"

"Haven't seen him for months," says the guy with the leather jacket. "Do you think it was him? I mean, yeah, he doesn't seem quite right in the head, but . . . Do you really think he could have done it?"

"Patrick is missing," the first guy interrupts. "He didn't turn up at work, is what I heard. They found his apartment empty."

"Missing?"

He nods.

"I have a theory that he's moved to a secret address. There were people who were after him—rumours had been going around about that guy." He shakes his head. "He might have fled abroad, too, for all anyone knows."

I look at Ingvar, who seems surprisingly unaffected by this news. I turn back to the two men.

"So he's vanished?"

"Without a trace. Don't you think it must be that policeman they've arrested, though? Or do you have another theory?"

I reach out my hand and pick up Ingvar's glass and take a big swig. It feels very rude. Like the kind of thing Liv would do.

"Excuse me," I say.

I get up, my legs unsteady, and walk towards the toilet. I just want to be alone, to think. I try the door, but it's locked. If Patrick has done a runner, it will be difficult to find him. If he's really the one behind all this, that is. It's about time I spoke to Egil. He might have the answer.

The door to the toilet opens, and a familiar figure walks out. Her grey hair hangs loose, falling down around her shoulders. Her dress is dark purple, and baggy around her body. She puts her arms around me in a hug.

"My darling!" Carol smells of wet dog and perfume.

I accompany her outside so she can smoke a cigarette out on the deserted street. I'd completely forgotten how I would sometimes bump into Carol here, and how well we got along

as the evenings progressed. At one point, Carol was more of
a mother to me than my real mother.

"I'd hoped you'd come see me today," she says, blowing
smoke towards the sky. "I saw on the news that they've arrested
a policeman."

I shake my head. "I don't think it's him," I say. "It has to
be somebody who knows me. Someone who wanted to do
me harm. You remember how I told you about the key in the
jewellery box? It has to be someone from here."

"You're wrong, dear. It's him. A policeman from Ålesund.
He turned up at my door, just before the summer. I swear. He
was from the police, and he was trying to get into my house."

She laughs, loud and heartily.

"At your door? Why didn't you tell me?"

Carol cuts off the laughter.

"I didn't want to scare you. At the time, I didn't know that
he was bad news—I thought he was just an ordinary cop.
Anyway. He was angry, and wanted to come in. Asked whether
I knew you. At first he didn't want to admit that he was a cop,
but when he did—well, you know. I asked him whether he
was in the mood for a fight with my dogs."

She laughs loudly again. I remember the policeman who
talked to me the day Iben disappeared. He had spoken with
an Ålesund dialect. Could this be the same policeman that
Birk said he knew in Kristiansund?

"I don't get it," I say. "I don't know any policeman. Can I
borrow your phone?"

Carol hands her phone to me. I open the web browser
and search for Roe Olsvik, Kristiansund police station. A
photograph of a police officer appears. Broad shouldered,
hair flecked with grey. The description also fits the man who

visited the woman who calls herself my mother. I show the photo to Carol.

"Is that him?"

Carol squints at the phone.

"Oh yeah, that's him. I remember him well—a stern man, he was."

I feel a tear run from the corner of my eye—I'm not sure which part of my cold heart it comes from. Carol's smile fades; she comes towards me. Puts her motherly arms around me.

"Don't cry, darling. Chin up—they've got him. And next they'll find your daughter."

Ronja

Kristiansund
Wednesday, 23 August 2017

On the screen, I can see Roe in the custody cell, his head bent. He's sitting on the mattress on the bench, a blanket over his lap. On the wall above his head is a mural of an excessively happy clown, its yellow hair sticking out in all directions. Roe doesn't seem like the type to be encouraged by the colourful paintings in the custody cell—one of what we call the "happy cells"—but he doesn't protest. In fact, he hasn't said a word since he was brought in. August, Shahid and Birte have peppered him with questions, but so far he's just sat there, pale and exhausted. Now he's been locked up, he's put his head in his hands. Even Shahid seems to be convinced that Roe is the offender now, after they searched his apartment and found the walls of the bedroom covered from floor to ceiling with images of Mariam Lind. There were also some documents from cases he's no longer working on, fingerprint kits and other investigative materials. It's starting to look bad for him, I have to admit, and the longer he stays silent, the more suspicious he seems. Why isn't he saying anything? Doesn't he intend to defend himself? We have to figure out what all the photographs and documents mean. And if Roe continues to refuse to speak, it could take us months to find out.

"It's so damn hard to get him to talk," August says.

I jump—I hadn't realised he was standing beside me. A pale stubble has begun to appear on his chin.

"This is to your credit, all this," he says.

"What's to my credit?" I sigh. I feel powerless.

"The case is pretty much solved, thanks to you."

"You really think it's solved?"

"All we need is for him to start talking."

"Confirmation bias," I say. "This is an example of confirmation bias—we're only looking for what confirms our hypothesis. You said it yourself to Birte when we were in the car: don't jump to conclusions. We don't actually know what happened."

I find the key to the cell in which Roe is sitting. Leave August, jogging down the steps to the basement and the cells.

A surprised expression crosses Roe's face when he sees me enter. I leave the door ajar and sit down on the bench beside him. Then he smiles. I wonder again whether I remind him of his daughter—the girl who died. That must have been so hard for him.

"I don't think you've done anything to Iben," I say. "But they do."

I point at the camera.

"Is it hard to talk about her?" I ask. "About Anita?"

He looks down at the floor.

"I really think you have to," I say. "You have to explain to us what everything means; otherwise nobody will ever find out what happened to your daughter."

He continues to stare at the floor. His eyes are sort of empty and blank, as if he's withdrawn somewhere deep inside himself. Then he turns to me and nods.

Roe

Kristiansund
Tuesday, 6 June 2017

I cursed the alarm clock that woke me yet again in this hovel of an apartment in this completely ordinary town—so fucking similar to Ålesund, only smaller. I gritted my teeth and sat on the edge of the bed, straightening my spine and trying to figure out whether everything was in place. On the floor, copies of documents from the David Lorentzen file were strewn around me. Moving had changed nothing. I was still bound to the town I had left. I'd just have to go farther, dammit, next time I moved. Or make sure to leave everything behind when I did. Anita. Aurora. David. Egil. Pieces of lives that were no longer related, since there was always something, somewhere, that was too painful.

I bent down, swept up the papers and put them in the plastic folder on the nightstand. Nobody knew I'd made copies of the documents and taken them with me. If I solved this case, then I would also solve the rest, I was sure of it. I went out into the kitchen, started up the coffee machine and took out bread,

butter and cheese, setting it on a plate with a cracked rim.
Went over to the front door to collect today's copy of *Tidens
Krav* from the doormat. I'd ordered delivery of the newspaper
as soon as I moved. Had decided that I would live this life at
full force, that this town would become mine. It was unbe-
lievable how naive I had been. It's now several months since
I moved here, and this is still a foreign place. I was trying to
accept the advice that people seemed to keep throwing at me
from all directions every time something difficult happened.
Take your time. But time was inconceivably long, and at the
end only death awaited me.

I poured myself a cup of coffee and opened the newspaper. It
was June. The main story was about how new documentation
had been submitted in the appeal regarding the hospital. The
case seemed without end—the people of Kristiansund talked
of nothing else. I could understand it; I, too, was frustrated at
all the merging of local hospitals and police stations around
the country. But I was tired of reading about it. I buttered
a slice of bread as I turned the pages, reading the headlines.
Stopped at OptiHealth Wins Tender Round. A small group
of people standing around a marzipan cake, most of them
women. OptiHealth was a company that hired out personal
assistants. Now they had won a significant contract with local
government, but it wasn't the article that interested me, it was
the photograph. More specifically, the woman standing on the
far right and smiling, short blond hair and long fringe, a cake
server in one hand. Her hair was shorter and lighter, and she
was older and thinner, but it really looked like her.

I flicked back through the photographs on my phone to find
the images I had taken of Anita's sketches from the sketchbooks
she'd left behind. It was strange. Could it really be the same

woman? According to the article her name was Mariam Lind, and she was the owner of the company. I did a search for her name online and found that she was married to city council member Tor Lind. She didn't have her own Facebook account, but her husband had posted a photograph of himself and his wife along with a smiling little girl called Iben. The girl wasn't looking into the camera, but towards something behind it and off to the right. A shudder went through me when I saw her. There was something so strangely familiar about that face, but I couldn't put my finger on exactly what. I searched her name, but the only thing I found was a post from the middle of January about her eleventh birthday.

I searched for Egil's phone number in my list of contacts. The number rang for a long time, and I shuddered when I reached the voicemail message that transported me straight back to that day. I quickly hung up, but decided to try one more time.

"Hello?" It was a man's voice on the other end of the line, but it wasn't Egil's.

"Is Egil there?"

Silence on the line for several seconds.

"Egil is in prison," the man said.

Mariam

Ålesund
Thursday, 24 August 2017

I wake gasping for breath. Panting in the half-dark room, light penetrating the gap between the curtains. No air. I try to move, but my arms are held fast. I'm enclosed in a muscular coil, flecked brown, black and yellow. I open my mouth and stretch my neck, writhing in the snake's thick embrace. I turn my head to one side and look straight into Nero's gaping mouth. He's now big enough to set his jaws over my entire head. Black dots dance before my eyes. I shake my head. Shake and shake, tears spattering in all directions.

Then he lets go. The air hits my lungs like gravel. I curl up, coughing hard; my chest is burning. He gathers his body near me, his tiny tongue peeking out of his closed mouth. Then he turns his head and slithers slowly down from the bed. Exhibiting his coil in slow motion, letting each patch of colour dance past me until his tail disappears over the edge. My heart pounds hard in my chest. This is the first time he's properly attacked me.

I'm still shaking when I find Ingvar sitting in the kitchen, smoking. The smell has long since lost all appeal for me. Still, there's something pleasurable about the idea of sitting at the kitchen table with the window open, just smoking.

"Latest news." He points at the radio. "They've released the policeman."

"Can I bum one?" I say.

He throws me the pack of tobacco. I take it between my hands, pull out a delicate paper and start to fill it. Realise that I've forgotten how to roll a cigarette. The tobacco isn't behaving as expected; it remains thick in the middle, thin at the sides. They've released the police officer, but I'm not done with him. I have to find out why he's been looking for me. Why did he want to talk to Carol? Perhaps he was also the one who wanted to talk to my mother, and the others too. I set the terribly rolled rollie between my lips and light it. The burning paper and tobacco sting my lungs. I cough, and Ingvar laughs.

"Do you remember, Liv, that first evening after we'd moved in together? We sat up all night, just the three of us, smoking and talking shit. I remember thinking you were the coolest girl I'd ever met."

"I remember it really well. It was so nice, the two of you letting me live here without knowing anything about me. I didn't even pay rent that first month."

"Well, you didn't have anything to pay it with."

"But what meant the most to me, what made it possible for me to stay here, was that you let me feel safe. I could talk about my past, or not, if I didn't want to. You seemed to understand that it would be like prodding at a viper's nest."

Ingvar takes a last drag of his rollie and stubs it out in the ashtray.

"A viper's nest, right. And apropos that—what happened to Nero in the end?"

"I released him into the forest," I say. "I had no other choice."

I didn't need to hide the truth—Ingvar would probably have been happy to see Nero again, but the lie spilled out automatically. I didn't want to share him. The fact that Carol knows he still exists is one thing; Ingvar, on the other hand, doesn't need to know. Who knows what he would use that knowledge for?

"But that would have been like killing him," Ingvar says. "I thought he was really important to you."

I'm about to answer, but stop. Above our heads, the creaking of the old landlady crossing the floorboards can be heard. To think I never thought of this before. I stub out my half-smoked cigarette.

"I'm going upstairs," I say. "I have to speak to her."

In the hall, I have the strange sense that I'll find the grey trainers I wore all the time when I lived here, and am disappointed when they aren't there. It's Mariam's shoes that I find in the hallway instead, even if they aren't as freshly polished and shiny as they were two days ago.

I walk up the stairs to the ground floor and ring the doorbell. I've actually only ever seen her a handful of times, and when I did she hardly showed any interest in me. She takes her time coming to the door. I can hear her moving inside. A slight clinking sound as she looks through the peephole before turning the lock, opening the door with the chain on. Her spine is curved; she has white hair that lies flat against her head, and which isn't sufficient to cover a mole on her scalp. She squints at me through the thick lenses of her glasses.

"Who is it?"

"It's Liv," I say. "Liv, who lived in your basement some years ago."

"You'll have to excuse me. My eyesight is so bad, I'm afraid."

"It's also a long time ago."

"Was there something you wanted? I think you've paid for this month already."

An extra wrinkle appears in her brow, as if to say she doesn't have time to waste on her tenants—as long as they're paying.

"It's about something else. I wondered whether someone knocked at your door a few months ago—a middle-aged man? Broad shoulders? Might have been a policeman?"

She seems to light up.

"There was a man here, before the summer. He was from the police—very pleasant. He asked me quite a few questions, but I couldn't answer all of them. That's right, he asked about you, too, but of course I didn't have anything to tell him. Have you spoken to him?"

I nod.

"Has he been to the apartment downstairs?" I ask.

"Oh, but of course. I don't make a habit of letting myself in down there, but when it's the police—well. He just wanted to see one of the rooms—even had the key to it himself. It was a good thing he did, because I didn't have any other keys. He spoke to that boy who's now in prison."

"Egil?"

"Oh, I don't remember any of their names. But he's in prison at any rate, and likely deserves it, too. The policeman had the key for the room inside, so I let him into the apartment."

"Was this the man?"

I show her the photograph of Roe Olsvik on Ingvar's phone. She leans all the way forward, so far that her glasses almost touch the screen. Then she nods.

"Yes, that's him. Such a nice young man."

Roe

Ålesund
Tuesday, 20 June 2017

I parked at the side of the road in front of the framing store. This would only be a brief visit. Ålesund was a town I had already left. Hopefully nobody would see me before I was gone again.

I took a few steps across the street and up towards the looming yellow prison building. I had been here many times over the years, but always in connection with work—never with a visitor's pass in my pocket. I rang the bell and was let in with a buzz. The prison officer smiled from door number two.

"I didn't know you had friends in here, Roe."

I couldn't remember the guy's name. He couldn't be more than twenty-five, and he had an irritatingly sharp voice, like steel wire. I locked my phone and wallet in one of the small lockers, stuck the oversized key chain in my pocket so that it bulged out—it was obviously something one of the inmates had made in their woodwork class. I handed my visitor's card to the officer and walked quickly through the metal detector before he managed to make a big deal out of it.

The prison was more than 150 years old, and well past its use-by date. A wonderful building and a great location, too—for a museum. Right in the town centre, where people lived just across the street and could look in on the inmates. But there were far too few places suitable for a high-security prison for all of Western Norway. There were more people from Bergen here than there were people from Ålesund—although the sentencing queue for locals was long enough.

The officer left me alone in the tiny visitor's room. On the cold brick walls slender trees had been painted, growing from floor to ceiling. Little birds sat on the branches or fluttered about the tiny forest. It seemed as if the artist had attempted to depict jailbirds as something beautiful and melancholic. Maybe this was what the dreams of the people incarcerated here looked like. I took a seat on the black leather sofa and closed my eyes, imagining the birds flapping around and screeching in distress.

Egil grinned as he came through the door. He pushed up the arms of his sweater and gave me a handshake that ended in a semi-hug.

"Well, this is unexpected."

He sat down on the chair in front of me. I put my hand in my back pocket and plucked out the photograph I had printed from my phone.

"What's that?" he said.

"Do you know who the person in this photograph is, Egil?"

He stared at the photo, obviously surprised. He ran his fingers through his hair, an involuntary gesture.

"No. No, I don't. Is it a drawing?"

"Anita drew it. If you know the model, I want you to be completely honest with me."

Egil shook his head. "I have no idea. I've never seen her before."

"Are you lying to me, Egil? Are you protecting this girl?"

"No. I know nothing. Nothing."

"Do you know what it means if you're lying to me? I've lost my daughter and my grandchild. You're refusing me the right to know what happened to them."

"I know nothing about what happened. Honestly."

Holding the photograph, I lowered my hand. So I'd been right. He'd been lying this entire time.

"You don't know what happened, but you know who she is."

I held up the gold chain with the key. His grey-blue eyes widened; his face became tense.

"Where did you get that?"

I thought of the young boy I once thought I'd managed to reach, a boy I'd helped, who wasn't used to anyone my age being decent to him. It had given me hope—made me want to get back on my feet and do more things right. Now it struck me that I hadn't done anything of value at all. He had built his life around an entirely different view of right and wrong—the morals of the street.

"I found it in one of Anita's jewellery boxes. I know it belongs to this woman she sketched."

"Fuck," he said. Clenched his fists in his lap. "I can't protect her forever. She's just not right in the head, that girl."

He seemed to think for a while. Then he leaned forward.

"That key belongs to a room in my flatshare. Or rather, it's my room now. Before, it belonged to Liv. There's a few of her things in there we haven't gotten rid of; they're in a black garbage bag. Tell Ingvar that you're there to pick something up for me. If he won't let you in, just threaten him with all you've got."

I clasped the key between my fingers in my jacket pocket as I walked back to the car. It couldn't wait. I would only be here for a few days. Had moved, started a new job and a new life. Shouldn't be here in the past, shouldn't be carrying the burden around with me like a bag of worn-out clothes or an old TV. But I had to be sure that I left no stone unturned when I abandoned this town for good.

There was nobody home in the basement apartment. The windows were dark, and nobody opened the door when I rang the doorbell. I tramped my way back up the steps until I was standing outside the back door on the ground floor. Then I saw a woman in the window, white-haired and with her neck bent, behind the short kitchen curtains. I went over to the front door, thinking I may as well try. Rang the doorbell. She came and opened the door a crack, wearing thick glasses and a suspicious expression.

"What's it about?"

"My name is Roe Olsvik—I'm a police officer at Kristiansund police station. I've been in touch with Egil Brynseth. I've been given permission to search his room, but I'm afraid I don't have a key to the front door."

The woman didn't need to be asked twice. She found a spare key and pulled on a thin coat, then walked ahead of me down the stairs.

"I'm not allowed to snoop on my tenants," she said, "and nor do I. But I won't say no to the police. They're a certain type of people, my tenants—I dread to think what it might look like in there. I haven't been inside in . . . oh, I don't know how many years! But, well, they pay their rent on time. Here—please." She gestured towards the door, standing there as I entered a hallway filled with shoes and clothes. "I'll wait here—I don't want to snoop."

Egil had said that his room was just to the left of the bathroom. I tried the door—it was locked. I took out the gold-plated key, stroking it with my fingers for a moment. Behind this door might be answers to more questions than I would care to ask. Or it might be yet another dead end. I stuck the key into the lock and turned it.

The room was small, containing nothing but a bed, a wardrobe and a chest of drawers; the floor was littered with a few stray belongings, presumably Egil's. A pot containing the remains of what had once been a plant stood beside the window. The curtains were half drawn. The air had the close, stuffy smell of a boy's bedroom—it took me back to my youth. I opened the door to the storage closet and found what Egil had told me about. Two large black garbage bags. I opened one of them and stuck my arm down into it. Pulled out a black sweater and a photograph album. The album was full of photos—most of them taken at parties. I sat on the bed and began to turn the pages. This woman was in many of the images, drinking, red-eyed, sticking out her tongue. In one of them she sat with a group of young people in front of a TV screen, an unfocused picture from a wildlife program in the background. In another, she was walking on her hands while somebody held her feet. She seemed like the life of the party. Between the party photographs, there were others—everyday scenes from the kitchen and living room. In one photograph she sat cross-legged on a bed. In her arms she held a python. There were several photographs of this snake—of Egil and Ingvar holding it, too, but in most of the pictures it was in her arms or over her shoulder.

I put down the album and searched through the bag. Found cheap jewellery and clothes, along with shoes and various other bits of girls' stuff. I rummaged around and grabbed something hard, which turned out to be a baby bottle. Then I pulled out several pieces of baby clothing and a little teddy bear. My chest burned. I imagined tiny Aurora's charred body, with its broken ribs, suffocated. Then my fingers closed around something that felt like a telephone, large and lumpy, with an antenna. I pulled it out. It was pale purple in colour, and it had just one button that could be used to turn it on and off. It was a baby monitor. I recognised it. I had given it to Anita as a gift when Aurora was born.

Mariam

Ålesund
Thursday, 24 August 2017

I had once been on a guided tour of Ålesund Prison when I was in primary school, but I have only a distant memory of a prison yard and concrete. I recognise the faint but familiar smell of old art nouveau buildings as I inquire at the window and am directed to a metal detector, which I walk through. Then I'm led into a small room where the walls are decorated with a large painting of trees and fluttering birds. There isn't much to do in this room other than sit and stare at the artwork. I take a seat, and wait for the door to open again. When it does, Egil smiles his typical, charming smile. As soon as the prison officer leaves us, he comes over to me and gives me a long hug.

"Jeez," he says, sitting down beside me on the sofa. "*Here's* somebody I didn't think I'd ever see again. And looking so elegant, too."

He looks at my shoes, my pressed trousers, and again I have the feeling of being overdressed.

"So how's it going, jailbird? Are they giving you enough food and fresh air?"

"It's so boring! I'm practically climbing the walls, but hey, it's my own fault. How are things with you, Liv?"

"It's Mariam now."

"Mariam, right. Mariam Lind. You've really created a new life for yourself, haven't you?"

He looks at my hand.

"Married to a politician, with a lovely family and an important job that probably rakes in the dough. You've left the past behind like an old jacket. Before all this happened, I mean. How are you?"

I consider telling him how I am, but he doesn't deserve to hear a damn thing about me.

"I'm not here to make small talk, Egil. I'm actually pretty busy. I've lost my daughter." I glance over my shoulder at something that looks like a camera.

Egil shakes his head. "They're not watching us. They only do that if someone they don't trust comes to visit."

"Good. Then you can tell me how you could do something like this to me."

He looks at his hands. The lines on his face have deepened since we lived together. He has a few grey hairs.

"I suppose you mean this thing with Roe Olsvik." Egil waits. When he doesn't receive a reply, he continues. "I know it was stupid, but I didn't have much choice. He already knew too much, and we were friends. I couldn't stand keeping all these secrets from him any longer. Anyway, he's kept everything I've said to himself. Otherwise you'd be in here, like me."

He speaks quickly, obviously afraid of my anger.

"I have to admit, Liv—I didn't want to lie. I'd already lied so fucking much, and he thought of me as a friend even though I was a total fuckup—and that meant a lot. Anita had sketched you—he had photographs of her drawings. He even had the key to your room, Liv."

"Wait—I'm not entirely following, Egil."

"Anita Krogsveen. He's her father. I told him I didn't think you could have anything to do with it. Her death, I mean. Even though—to be completely honest—I wasn't really sure. You kept so many secrets from us."

I take a deep breath, close my eyes. Imagine Iben's blond hair, which I combed with my fingers when she was little because she didn't like to have it brushed. As blond and thin as the hair on Anita's head, and as fine as Aurora's baby hair. I so often think of Iben in the past tense. Is she now part of the past?

"You said he had the key?" I say.

He nods. "It must have been Anita who stole it from you. Roe found it in her childhood bedroom, at her mother's house."

Anita. I close my eyes again and think of how she had come into the bathroom, rummaged around in my makeup bag and said that I had interesting eyes. And then she had gone to check whether the rumours were true—that I had a python in my room. She knew I was lying the whole time. Tears begin to run down my face, dripping onto my neatly pressed trousers.

"So stupid," I say.

I had thought I needed to hide Nero from her. I'd hidden him the whole time, and she let me believe that she didn't know a thing.

"So you told him what the key opened," I said. "You let him go into my room."

"Well, technically, it's my room. Your things had been there for twelve years—I figured you weren't going to come back and claim them."

"What if he's killed her, Egil? Did you think of that?"

He shakes his head. "He hasn't."

I hold up the gold key in front of his face. Let it dangle there before him.

"Do you know where I found this? In a jewellery box in my daughter's room."

Egil stares at the key.

"What? But how did it end up there? Do you really believe that—"

"I'm absolutely sure, Egil."

"So then why are you here? Shouldn't you be out there trying to find your daughter?"

I stare at the floor.

"Yes. Yes, I should, I just . . . I was so sure it was Patrick."

"Patrick?" Egil glances towards the door, then turns to face me again and moves closer.

"Patrick is dead," Egil whispers. "We did him in."

"Did him in?"

He moves even closer.

"Me and Ingvar—we did him in. Nobody's ever going to find him, either. It's as if he's vanished into thin air. Or into the belly, more like." He puts a hand to his chest, blinks. "I'd have ended up in prison regardless, but that's just because I'm such a lousy criminal. I never could keep my mouth shut."

Egil laughs briefly. Then he gets up and bangs on the door; calls the guard.

"Go—now," he says as the door opens and the officer walks in. "Find her."

Reptile memoirs

Time passed. My body became long and heavy, and I didn't leave the bed unless I felt the need to stretch out in the narrow rays of sunlight from the window.

Twice I was visited by strange humans. Customers. The first were a group of males with hair on their faces and clothes that were dark and smooth and decorated with sharp objects. They were boisterous, passing me around, and they smelled strange. The men mumbled among themselves. Used words I had heard before, *skin* and *lovely* and *valuable*. One of the men stroked me with his fingers as he held my coil. I had just woken, was full of anger and longing for prey, so I attacked the first hand I saw. Got a good grip on it, too. The hand was dirty and hairy. Its owner used more words I recognised. *Shit. Monster.* He dropped the part of my body he was holding, and I fell to the floor with a smack. The pain lasted for a long time afterwards. I thought they would come back, but they never did, despite my lovely, valuable skin. Perhaps the cold woman's price was too high.

The second time I was visited by only one human. I thought it must be a male, covered by a large white outfit that concealed his head and body. Over his mouth was also something white, and his hands were covered by a transparent membrane. He reminded me of someone, a distant scent behind the plastic of the flatshare, but it was hard to distinguish one human from another. The man had a large black bag between his hands, so shiny that it reflected the light from the window. I licked the air and tried to identify a bitter, acidic smell, but it was too weak.

The man unfolded a large piece of shiny material and laid it on the floor. Then he opened the black bag. The smell tasted of death, congealed blood and hardened skin. First, the man pulled out a dismembered arm. Set it neatly on the floor and pulled out a leg, which he set beside it. He put another arm beside the first, then did the same with the other leg. The upper and lower body had been parted from each other at the navel. Finally, he held out the head. He held it dangling by the hair. The lips were swollen, several teeth were missing. The skin around the pale eyes was also bloated. The man put the head beside the other body parts. Scrunched up the black bag into a ball. Then he turned and left.

I didn't want to eat the deceased human. The body wasn't fresh, it was already food for insects and carrion birds, but the cold woman had starved me for such a long time. I knew this food would be all I'd be given for a long time. And so I ate, even though there was something sour about the taste, even though it made me nauseous to feel the stiff arm glide down my throat and gullet. I swallowed all of it. In the months that followed, I couldn't bear the thought of food, and nor was I given any more until I was again close to dying of hunger. When I was finally served the usual cold carcass, which at least smelled fresh, I accepted it immediately.

After the last visit, the cold woman cleaned the room. She shut me in a cage while she did this, and the air smelled of strong cleaning products. I watched her from behind the bars, fantasising about the day I would take her by surprise, how I would make her death throes long and agonising. She would feel her breath leave her slowly, she would panic and stink of fear. Her long grey hair would stick in my teeth.

By the time the warm woman came back, I had long since given up on her. That day no longer had any meaning for me. It could just as easily be a sign that I was dead, but there she was. I licked the air and sensed new scents along with the old. She couldn't hide herself from me—I could not be fooled by the reek of perfumes. She lay down as she used to and let me embrace her, as if submitting herself as prey. She was fresh and glowing—and I was hungry.

Roe

Kristiansund
Friday, 7 July 2017

I dropped my speed to below thirty, letting the car glide almost soundlessly into Siktepunktet. I drove to the end of the street, saw through the windows that the lights in the house were off. It was a small, terraced house with a fenced-in garden at the front, along with a terrace, neither ugly nor idyllic. It looked like any regular house in any Norwegian neighbourhood, but it was the devil's house. I pulled into the parking area. Turned off the engine and sat there, pretending I was checking something on my phone as I watched what was happening through the window. I heard children playing nearby, but couldn't see them, nor the car I assumed belonged to Mariam Lind.

I had driven up here once a day since early in the summer, just to take a look. Sometimes the windows were illuminated; other times they were dark. Sometimes the car was in the driveway; sometimes it wasn't. I generally stayed for a few minutes before driving away. Why I did this, I wasn't sure. Perhaps I hoped for an opportunity to speak to one of them—to interrupt their family idyll. If anyone began asking questions, I could quite simply say I had taken a wrong turn. But if I bumped into her, or anyone else from her family, that would be another matter.

I put my phone away. Looked out over the empty streets and thought of all Egil had told me about this woman, Liv, now Mariam. What he thought had gone on in that room—I didn't want to think about it. Couldn't bear to think about it. I closed my eyes and tried to push the thought away, but it clung on. Aurora's delicate ribs, broken as if she had been squeezed by something. On one point I agreed with Ingrid—Birk didn't have motive to kill his own child. A snake, on the other hand, needed no motive. It needed only a devil of a person who brought the hunter to its prey.

I opened my eyes again. Decided it was time to drive away, but then I noticed a child coming up the hill. A young girl with long, blond hair, thin and wispy. Hair that was electric, seeming to float around her head. She was wearing a red jacket that was slightly too big for her. When she came closer, I saw how much she looked like her mother. I rolled down the window. Whispered a little "psst." She stopped and looked at me. I whistled and waved her closer, and she took a few short, slow steps in my direction. She looked sceptical. Had probably learned all about the kind of people you should watch out for. I pointed to the house.

"Is this the house where Mariam Lind lives?"

She looked up at the house. Nodded.

"Are you her daughter?"

She nodded again.

"You're just as pretty as she is," I said, and winked.

She twisted her body, looking shyly at the ground.

"I have something of hers," I say. "From when she was young." I leaned out of the car window, holding out the gold chain with the key on its end. "You can have it, if you like."

PART THREE

Roe

Kristiansund
Thursday, 24 August 2017

The knife is sharp against my thumb. I've lost count of how many times I've stood here like this and felt the blade against the fine ridges of my skin. Always knowing exactly how to touch it without cutting myself. In the mirror on the wardrobe door I look crazy, standing here with the knife. Lifting my hand and brandishing it in the air as if to fight off some invisible enemy. Who knows—had I been there for Kiddo that day, maybe I could have done something to prevent it. I would have done anything—even if it involved slitting someone's throat.

I point the knife at Iben. Her throat is exposed, delicate tendons and veins under the pale skin. I poke her gently with the tip of the blade. Pick at the surface of her pale-pink skin, at her throat and her cheek. She accepts this without looking away, smiling her stiffened smile. A shy, reserved smile, a face like her mother's, with a reticent sort of charm. Mariam's gaze is penetrating—she stares until you feel like ice. Her daughter isn't like that. She's soft, and far too kind for her own good. I don't know why I'm standing here destroying the photograph. Perhaps to make myself realise that she's dead. The entire town now understands that she's dead. Just like my Anita and my Aurora.

If only I had managed to figure it all out earlier. If only I had kept my head above water and not collapsed like a hopeless idiot, wasting precious time staring into my own darkness. Maybe Iben could have been saved.

I start to rehang the rest of the photographs that my colleagues confiscated when they arrested me. Photographs of Liv, of this python. All these images make me feel sick. I've carried this nausea constantly in recent months, along with the dream of doing real damage to her. Of not only seeing her behind bars, but really trying to hurt her. As she hurt me. That's why I spoke to Iben. I was willing to use her daughter against her, to do harm. Outside the shopping centre, I wanted to tell her all about the person she called her mother. It was a desperate act, an attempt to make her understand. I said that she had to know you can't trust anyone—least of all grown-ups, not even your own mamma and pappa. Then I told her that her mother was a murderer. She wanted to leave, and it's possible that I raised my voice and grabbed her arm, that she shook it in order to break free. Then she ran—fast, faster, up the road—and disappeared.

The folder of documents from David Lorentzen's case lies on the nightstand. I open it, flick through the sheets containing photographs and reports. The case is apparently irrelevant, but I can't quite let go of it. For a while I thought that maybe somebody linked to the mugging had killed Anita, for some reason unknown to me. How would I know—me, the person who would never have believed that my own daughter was

capable of committing a crime? At one point I was so distressed
that I even visited David Lorentzen's mother, spreading all the
photographs and documents across her dining table—reports
she shouldn't have seen, newspaper clippings and photographs
of Mariam and Iben. I've long since lost the ability to think
rationally. I still have so much anger in me, even though I
know I can't use it for anything but cooking my own brain.

The doorbell rings, a long and hard noise penetrating my
body. I put the knife in my pocket, take a deep breath. Pull
myself together and go out into the hall, set my eye to the peephole. She's standing there, staring straight at me, her narrow
lips forming a smile. She seems to be making fun of me. *I know
you're in there*, her eyes say. She's wearing lipstick, is smartly
dressed in a blouse and neat trousers. A small handbag hangs
over her narrow shoulder. She looks like the businesswoman
she's managed to become. She probably has a weapon hidden
in the handbag, but she's smaller and weaker than I am. The
self-confidence she's shown by coming here—she'll regret it.

She grips the strap of her bag as I open the door.

"Mariam Lind," I say. "Welcome." I bow lightly and let her
into the hall.

She tramps inside, keeping her shoes on, and takes a seat
on the edge of the sofa. Stares at the apartment around her.

"You don't have much here."

"I have what I need."

She gives me a look that says she's seen right through me.

"I visited Egil in prison," she says. "I was there today."

I wait for her to say something more. Of course it had to
turn out like this; at some point she would find out what I
knew about her. So she's been in Ålesund while she's been gone.
Maybe that's where she's hidden her daughter—her daughter's

body. She's done something stupid now, by coming here. She thinks she can catch me unawares, hit me in the back of the head—just like she did with Anita.

"I see," I say finally. "Did you say hello from me?"

"He told me to come here straightaway. When I told him about the key."

She holds up the chain with the gold key, lets it dangle from her hand like a pendulum.

"It was in Iben's jewellery box."

I nod. "So what do you want from me?"

The hard, cold look in her eyes disappears, and now they shine. She looks at me, her gaze suddenly pleading.

"Where is Iben?" she asks. "Can I see her? Please?"

Ronja

Kristiansund
Thursday, 24 August 2017

Birte munches on potato chips as she pages through the documents in the file from the David Lorentzen case. She has her feet up on the table and reads, the bag of potato chips in her lap beneath the sheets of paper. Just looking at the pile of paperwork on the desk makes me feel exhausted. Copies of all the case documents, newspaper clippings and photographs Roe has gathered over the past few months. With the flat of my hand I fan out a pile of photographs. Mariam Lind as a young girl with dark hair. Of course, people change. They try out a new identity, or change their name. On the other hand, it's pretty unusual to change your name, place of residence, appearance and personality all at the same time. That kind of thing must come from a strong sense of desperation, or the need to get away from something. Could it be as Roe suspects—that Mariam had something to do with the deaths of his daughter and grandchild? Is she now also guilty of having done something to her own daughter? I pick up a photograph in which she has a python hanging over her shoulder. I wasn't sure whether such a snake would attack a little baby, but a few Google searches left no doubt. This type of snake is a known pest in Florida, where owners release them into the wild when they become too big to handle—they go on to attack everything from possums and raccoons to alligators. A little baby surely wouldn't be a problem. Roe finally got what he wanted. We searched the area through which Mariam Lind had driven after visiting the shopping centre with Iben on Friday. The police in Ålesund have been made aware of the circumstances and have given us access to the case involving the deaths of Anita Krogsveen and Aurora Krogsveen Fladmark—and they're looking for Mariam. It shouldn't be hard to find her—after all, she's been moving around the town for two days already. Everyone who knows her will be interviewed; there will be witnesses who have seen her. The only question is how much time we have; if this also turns out to be a dead end, we'll be back at square one. Roe is convinced that if we find Mariam, we'll find Iben—but what if he's wrong? Even he has the feeling that there's a piece of the puzzle missing. Something in all this material that might give us answers as to where Iben is.

In my dreams, she's still alive. She glances up from a white box where she's been hiding this whole time, and laughs because she's managed to trick us. In the photograph from her eleventh birthday, she looks as if she's been captured while laughing this way, as if she's without a care in the world. A child's laughter, because life is a game. I wonder whether she'll ever be able to laugh like that again.

Birte continues to munch her potato chips. She's obviously grumpy because I was the one who managed to get Roe to talk. She's worked here longer than I have, and she wants to be the best. Even though we're not actually in competition with each other, it probably still smarts for her. Probably best that I leave her alone for a while, until she's got over it.

Roe has carried these secrets for a long time. He's been afraid of casting a dark shadow over his daughter's memory. For it to become known that she participated in a robbery. Might there be something there, in that robbery? Roe believes that if we could just find a connection to David Lorentzen's death, everything would fall into place. That's why Birte is reading the file so tenaciously. She wants to be the next person to make a breakthrough.

I've just stood up to go get a glass of water when the door opens and Shahid walks in.

"There you are," he says.

"Is there something I can do?" I say.

"August is about to conduct another interview with Tor Lind—can you observe it, as you did before?"

I cast a glance at Birte, but she's already disappeared into the documents again. Shahid opens the door so I can walk ahead of him.

Mariam

Kristiansund
Thursday, 24 August 2017

"What are you talking about?" Roe Olsvik sighs. "I have no idea where she is."

He sounds truly irritated, but I'm convinced that he's just a good actor. You have to be, if you're going to keep an entire life secret from everyone around you. If there's anyone who understands that, it's me. You can't pretend that you're someone else—you have to become the other person absolutely, completely—split yourself in two and think as the second as much as you thought as the first. In my case, the first person is damaged; that's why the second person exists. It must be the same for him.

I'm about to reply, but instead I break down. Desperately try to wipe away the tears as they come, but still end up a mess. I don't know how I could think I'd manage to maintain a tough tone, challenging him and demanding his respect before I put him on the spot. I should have known that I'd unravel after hardly any time at all. As I'm sitting here like a lost child on his sofa, I'm Mariam. Not Liv—who might have punched him

in the gut—but a desperate mother who just wants to know
that her daughter is alive. He looks back at me, searching my
face. His brows are low, frowning.

"What do you want?" he says.

"Can't you just tell me whether she's dead or alive?"

Then it hits me that he seems different from the last time
I saw him. He seems more aloof, in a way—more calculated.
There's something nonchalant about his manner.

"I think that's for you to tell me."

"I'm not going to play this game, Roe."

"No. *I'm* the one who's not going to play any game," he says.
"You picked her up on your way home from the shopping
centre and took her somewhere. I don't know whether you've
killed her or not—she might be at the bottom of the sea, or
you might have her locked up somewhere. What do I know?"

"You haven't even looked for me."

He looks down, his fingers digging through the grey roots
of his hair.

"All this is my fault," he says. "You killed her because you
knew I'd spoken to her. You couldn't risk her giving everything
away."

I vigorously shake my head. Something is terribly wrong.

"You killed her to save your own skin," he says. "Just as you
ruthlessly murdered a tiny infant."

"You're someone other than who you claim to be," I say.

"I wouldn't be—if it wasn't for you."

This last statement gives him away. He grabs my arm and
pulls me up. Grips me hard, his fingers digging into my skin.
My handbag sails across the floor, and at this moment I realise
what I've done. I've made the same mistake, the one I said
I would never make again. I've believed myself invincible. A

glinting knife appears in front of my face. The blade has several notches in it; the shaft is military green. It looks like the type of knife used for hunting.

Roe presses himself against me.

"If one more lie passes your lips, it will cost me nothing to use this."

It becomes hard to breathe. The blade of the knife flashes before my eyes. His body is so close; he smells sharply of sweat. My stomach, chest and head hurt. I have to think clearly. Am I wrong—has Roe not taken Iben? After all, the police have released him, and he seems convinced that *I'm* the child murderer. Maybe he'll cooperate if I don't resist. Together, we can find out where Iben is.

"Let me go," I whimper. "I'll tell you everything, I'll behave myself, if you just let me go."

He doesn't listen; simply holds me even tighter. Starts to jostle me ahead of him, so that I almost fall to the floor. I plant my feet in front of me for stability and permit myself to be led out. He wants to get me out into the hall. Keeps hold of my upper body with one arm while he brandishes the knife with the other. Pushes me ahead of him, through the hall and into another room.

And here we are. Liv and Mariam, step by step from playful young woman to adult and mother. I'm neither of them, and both. On the inside of the wardrobe door is a photograph of Iben, smiling. The image has been damaged, its surface ripped. It takes a moment until I understand which photograph it is. It's from the local newspaper—Iben's birthday in January. A beautiful picture of her—of course it was Tor who took it. He's always been best at taking photos of her, while I move through my life like a sleepwalker. This is my punishment.

Liv

Ålesund
Saturday, 16 April 2005

I held down the button for the doorbell for a long time, feeling how it buzzed beneath my finger in rhythm with its ringing. In the apartment, the lights were on. I hoped he was alone. At least it was his shadow that moved behind the door's textured glass window, lifted the curtain to see who was outside. I didn't have anywhere else I could go.

"Liv!"

He was obviously happy to see me. Happier than I wanted him to be, perhaps happier than he wanted to let on. His boyish smile didn't fit his tough-guy persona. David opened the door wide, revealing the illuminated hall with its yellow and brown striped wallpaper and the old telephone table with the swirling pattern on its seat. I'd said it looked like an old man's apartment. He hadn't responded, so I still didn't know whether he had inherited the place or acquired it through some other dealings.

Perplexed, he glanced at my bag as I set it down in the hall, stuck through with holes as it was in several places. I stepped out of my shoes and hung my jacket on one of the coat stand's hooks. Even the carpets looked old.

"I need a favour," I said. "A place to stay the night, without too many questions."

"So it's over, between you and your girlfriend?"

I cleared my throat.

"Without too many questions, as I said. I'll find somewhere else tomorrow."

I sat down and opened the bag in which Nero lay sleeping, his eyes staring as usual.

"Can we warm up your bathroom so Nero can stay in there?"

"Feel free."

I turned up the bathroom's underfloor heating and lifted Nero into the shower cubicle. He seemed to settle down fairly quickly.

David stretched out a hand, showing me farther down the hall. It struck me too late that this was the last place I wanted to be. Even more so because I was wearing a skirt he might think I had put on for his sake. It was both his and my Achilles heel, the fact that he liked me. Still, I had no other choice but to come here. I walked ahead of him, feeling his eyes burning into my back. Then we rounded the corner and entered the living room. The table was overflowing with bottles and full ashtrays. There were empty bottles and cans on the floor, and on the window ledges, too. On the TV screen was a frozen image of a woman standing with her legs apart and her ass towards the camera, so you could see straight into her cunt and anus.

"I don't have a guest room," he said. "We'll make up my room for you, and I'll take the sofa."

"That won't be necessary—the sofa is fine."

The sofa was far from fine, dusty and full of stains as it was, but I didn't want to owe him anything. And I especially didn't want to sleep in his bed.

Without further comment, David settled down in the armchair and pressed Play. Moaning filled the room. High-pitched, fake sounds from women who would never have been given a role in a Hollywood film. I stood there in the middle of the room, not sure what to do with myself.

"There's plenty of beer in the fridge, just help yourself. I don't have any food."

"It doesn't matter. I'm not hungry." I left the room. The moaning from the TV continued to reach me as I made my way into the bathroom.

Nero was lying completely still on the floor, resting his head on himself as he usually did. As I approached him, he opened his mouth and hissed at me. I backed away. His anger was enough to make my head explode. He was drilling into me, a nagging voice from an animal denied its prey. I had failed him, and he knew that I didn't intend to take him with me when I left. I couldn't keep him, couldn't keep anything from this life. He would drive me insane if I took him with me.

I stood before the mirror for a long time, studying myself. My eyes were reddish, my hair hanging heavily around my face, and I looked tired, pale. Still, I felt no need for sleep. The exhaustion I felt couldn't be relieved in any simple way. It was eating me up from the inside, gnawing at my muscles and tendons. I felt as if my blood had been diluted. Every time I closed my eyes, even if just for a split second, the image of Aurora's dead body appeared behind my eyelids. It was as if she remained in my pores, that there was an imprint of her on my retinas. I wished I could cry, scream, smash something. But I only stood there, looking at myself.

Tomorrow I would go and speak to Carol. She'd help me make the necessary arrangements to start over somewhere else, but she wouldn't let me stay overnight, not with the situation the way it was now. She wouldn't risk so much for my sake. So I'd had no other option but to come here. Just one night. Then I would disappear. I would vanish into thin air, become invisible. Tomorrow, it would be as if I had never existed.

Roe

Kristiansund
Thursday, 24 August 2017

I am another. The fingers that tighten the rope around the narrow female wrists are not my own. They belong to a man I don't know. Someone who feels certain that he can do harm, should he wish to. The Roe I know never tries to dominate women, but the Roe who is acting now, he's fastening the ropes that bit tighter, just because he can. He's the same person who spied on a family, who drove up to their house and rolled down the window and spoke to an innocent little girl. And who later tried to speak to her again, which must have frightened her. It's like overstepping an undefined yet dangerous boundary. He knows all this because he's worked with offenders for years. He knows that these apparently insignificant boundaries are more dangerous than they seem. Criminals often begin with the small stuff. Criminals justify every transgressive act, step by step. I've acted like a criminal for a long time. With good intentions, but I've been a criminal all the same. I've long since lost sight of right and wrong.

She tries to make herself more comfortable on the floor, but with her hands bound to the bedpost, she's unable to. The rope digs into her, holding her tightly. She whimpers.

"I'll confess to everything," she says. "I'll take my punishment. Anything. Just please let me go look for Iben."

I sit down on a stool above her legs. So full of rage that the Dictaphone trembles in my hand. I set it recording, and lean forward so she can speak right into it. The knife quivers in my other hand.

"Tell me your full name."

"Mariam Steinersen Lind."

"What about your birth name?"

"Sara Scheie."

"Why did you leave your hometown, adopting a new name, a new identity?"

She smiles. For a moment I glimpse something within her that is far more dangerous than this miserable mother.

"Where should I start?"

I move the Dictaphone to be sure that it adequately picks up the sound.

"Start where you think the story begins."

She twists her body. Looks up at the ceiling, thinking for a moment. An expression crosses her face as if she's looking for a poetic line.

"That first time," she begins, "his body was a paradox. Like living granite, or silken sandpaper."

I realise that she's going to take her time with this story— perhaps she's dreamed of being able to tell it, for all these years. Now she finally has the opportunity. She takes a deep breath. Searches for the next sentence.

"He was hard and soft at the same time. Coarse and smooth. Heavy and light."

Liv

Ålesund
Saturday, 16 April 2005

David was at least just about enough of a gentleman to make up the sofa for me. The sheet was yellowed, but it would do. The table was full of more beer bottles—he had drunk most of them. I'd had a bit to drink in order to stay on good terms with him, but not enough to get drunk. Now he leaned back in the armchair and lit a cigarette, slinging his sweatpants-clad legs over the armrest and looking at me.

"So why did you come here, exactly?" His expression was playful. He blew a cloud of smoke up towards the ceiling. I helped myself to the pack, lit up. "I mean, I'm sure there are plenty of other places you could spend the night."

"I wanted to stay with someone who was enough of a criminal for me to know I could trust them."

He grinned. Pointed with the hand that was holding the cigarette towards the duvet across my knees.

"Do you need a T-shirt? Or do you sleep naked?"

"A T-shirt would be nice."

He got up, the cigarette between his lips. Came back and threw a black T-shirt into my lap.

"I'm in there," he said, pointing into the dark of the bedroom. "If you need anything."

He stubbed out the cigarette in the ashtray. Downed the rest of his beer before he left.

I lay on my back atop the duvet. Looked up at the ceiling, where fine, straight lines divided the white surface into rectangular pieces. It was a long way up, higher than the ceiling of the apartment I'd just come from. I suddenly remembered the time I'd got high, when I'd lain in our living room watching the ceiling undulate as if it were breathing. What had been calming about it had also been frightening—it was visible on the outside, but it came from the inside. What I had seen was my own breath—my own interior—rising and falling. It was deeper than I was aware of, this interior, and so often beyond my control. Nero had helped me for a while. He had swallowed some of the burden, taken over some of what seemed most difficult. But at the same time, I realised now, he had also made the burden grow larger—and not just today. It was so hard to understand such things.

He was shut in the bathroom, but I could hear him all the way from here. He had long since found a way into me, into my head and my body. The scaly snake's body slithered through my veins, rasping against cell walls and reminding me of what I had done. Now it was time to get rid of him, too. I would have to make it on my own. The only way to destroy him was to become someone else, but I still didn't know how.

Roe

Kristiansund
Thursday, 24 August 2017

I get up to change the cassette in the Dictaphone. Evening has fallen; the apartment building is deserted. A scream would probably make a few souls stop what they were doing, perhaps go to the window, but they would just as quickly tell themselves it was probably nothing. I've toyed with the thought while I've listened to her; watched her face as she's described what she did to those innocent pets. She blames the snake. Says that he asked her to do it—like some kind of strange voice in her head—but she's given herself away. She *enjoyed* it. So it's hard to believe that it was actually an accident that led to a little child being subjected to exactly the same suffering. Part of me says that it can't be true. That I mustn't let myself be manipulated by her fake emotional outbursts, her crocodile tears and the small glimpses of something that looks like empathy.

"I'm thirsty," she says. "Could I have something to drink?"

The question quivers there in the room. I don't want to answer. As if I'm not thirsty, as if I wouldn't like to take a break. But it's not possible, everything has to be on tape before I dare stop.

"Okay," I say, starting the Dictaphone again and sitting down on the stool. "So we've got to the day you were supposed to look after Aurora. How did that day begin?"

"Can I have a glass of water?"

I smile at her. Catch myself and turn serious.

"When you've told the whole story, you can drink as much water as you want. So—Saturday, sixteenth of April 2005."

She sighs. Almost looks as if the tears are about to start running again.

"What happened that day, Liv? Where was Anita going?"

She shrugs.

"She'd got a job. It was only supposed to take a couple of hours."

"Anita was involved in the robbery, along with Egil," I say, and she nods.

"I was watching Aurora, in my apartment. I'd never looked after a baby before and was really nervous. Especially when she woke up and wouldn't stop crying. And in the middle of all that, Ingvar called me. We had an agreement that if he called me or Egil without saying anything, we should assume he'd had a seizure and go help him. I got there as fast as I could. But it turned out he was pretending—a really bad attempt at becoming friends again."

"Then what happened?"

"I didn't leave her lying there like that, unprotected, for very long. I didn't even know that Nero was in the living room, but when I came back . . . It was awful."

Tears run down her cheeks, dripping from her chin. She actually seems truly sorry for what happened. Not that I haven't seen offenders cry before, but they tend to give themselves away. There's something about the time at which they start to cry—the way it seems premeditated.

"Was that when Anita came back?" I whisper.

She nods and hiccups.

"The last thing I wanted was for her to see it." She shakes her head. "When she got back, I was burying Aurora in the garden."

I swallow.

"What about Anita? How did she die?"

She shakes her head.

"I don't know. She took Aurora with her and left. That was the last time I saw her." She bows her head.

The story makes far more sense than I, in my dark cloud, could have imagined. I never thought that what came out of this woman's mouth might make all the pieces fall into place. How Anita was at home and alive prior to the fire, and how Aurora was smothered, but not devoured. It makes sense in its absurd way. The only thing I don't feel sure of is whether she's telling the truth about that last part. Was this really the last time she saw Anita? It's impossible to know. She's a liar by nature.

"Who do you think killed Anita?" I hear myself ask.

"Birk," she says straight away. "That's the only thing that makes sense. Do you know that he hit her? She had huge blue bruises all over her body. That was why she wanted to leave him."

I start to shake. Squeeze my fingers into my palms in order to stop it.

"If I'm to believe that you haven't done anything to Iben," I say, "then who did?"

She shakes her head.

"I have no idea."

I cast a glance at all the photographs on the wall. If it isn't her, then we're back to square one. I can't trust her, but at least I have a confession for one crime, and now I'm going to get hold of my colleagues. They have to help me do everything we can for Iben. As I bend forward to turn off the Dictaphone, she whispers something.

"What did you say?"

"I'm sorry."

Then something happens. A pain rips through my side, spreading across my chest. I collapse, falling forward onto the floor. Mariam has worked her hand free and has found the knife and thrust it into me—I can feel it with my fingers. Blood covers the floor, pumping out of me. Blood everywhere, on my hand and shirt—my own. Then the air gets heavier, like thick clay. I gasp and gape, gulping for breath. Now I'm dying. This is where I was always supposed to end up.

Mariam

Kristiansund
Thursday, 24 August 2017

My hand is red with Roe's blood. He collapses onto the floor, a dark stain spreading across the carpet. I break myself free, get up and wipe off the blood on my blouse, which is now ruined forever. It doesn't matter. The only thing that matters is Iben. I go across to the wall that Roe has decorated with photographs from my past. The answer will be here somewhere. I just have to find it. I take down the pictures with a bloodstained hand. Most of them I'd forgotten. They're distant memories from an intoxicated life, when I had no control over my own impulses. I have red eyes and a distant smile, am doing all kinds of ridiculous tricks for the camera. Playing a game. I've always been that way. Is there anything about me that is truly real? I stop at a photograph that reminds me of something. It's me, Ingvar, Egil and David, whose arm is outstretched, holding the camera. In the background is a TV screen with a snake coil on it, which he's only just managed to get in the frame. I can't remember David being there that night.

I take the photograph down and compare it with the one I have in my handbag, which I found when Nero slithered under the bed in my old room. In this one, David must be behind the camera. He was the one who was there that night when I lay on the sofa, high and watching the ceiling breathe—the guy I could remember only as a face without features. The guy who said he knew where we could buy a snake.

I put the photographs in my bag, simultaneously grabbing the Dictaphone from the nightstand. I have to find somewhere to get rid of it, somewhere they won't look. From the floor, Roe emits a few desperate wails, which I do my best to ignore. It isn't too late, not yet. I can still find Iben alive and get out of this without ending up in prison.

Just then, I catch sight of a folder of papers on the nightstand. I open it. It's the documents from David's case. Photographs of his body after it had been lying there for several weeks. I sit down on the bed and flick through forensic reports, crime scene photographs and DNA profiles for which they never found a match, memos from interviews with witnesses. I won't know what I'm looking for until I find it. But then all at once, the pieces fall into place. I should have realised it long ago.

Roe groans as I leave the room. I slip out into the hallway, taking quick steps towards the front door. Should anyone look out of the window now, they'll see a woman in pressed suit trousers, a blouse and high-heeled shoes, her clothes covered in dark stains. I have to get going. It's a long drive.

On the ferry, I change into a dark pair of trousers and a black, high-necked sweater. Get back into the car and drive ashore, letting the road lead me all the way up to the house that lies there peacefully in the light of the setting sun. I've never been so full of emotion, and I've never been so calm.

"This time, you're coming with me," I whisper. "It's time for your reward."

I open the boot and the suitcase containing Nero. He immediately darts forward—I only just manage to stop him from sinking his teeth into me. With great effort I manage to force him back down into the suitcase and zip it shut. It must be the blood. It makes him hungry, gets his instincts going.

I lift out the suitcase, carrying it with long steps to the back of the house, where a window is open. It gets so hot in this house in the summer. I push the suitcase up towards the window, opening the zip so that the only natural way out for him is into the cellar. He disappears behind the glass, and I close the window behind him so he can't get out again. The snake seems to be smelling his way around his new surroundings— perhaps he's caught the scent of the zoo that is this house. I send a thought his way, silently asking him to help me.

I knock my usual hard, long knock using the door knocker. As before, I hear the barking and running of the dogs inside, and as always Carol's patient steps and calming voice come after them. Her radiant smile when she sees me is just as convincing as always—the actress turned criminal. Her dream had been to become a movie star—she had lived and worked in Hollywood for years, but pregnancy had made her fat; the long nights awake gave her tired skin and stole her concentration, and she needed money to keep the kid alive. Nothing ever came of her acting dreams. She stopped colouring her hair, stopped wearing makeup, let her body deteriorate. Moved to Norway, got married. I know her as Caroline Holloway, a beautiful name for an actress. The police report, though, gives her Norwegian name. Karoline Lorentzen.

"You came back," she says.

Her smile quickly fades. I don't need to say anything—she's seen the words in my eyes. All these years that we've known each other, and we didn't really know each other in the slightest. I follow her down the hall. The dogs shuffle along in front of me, hungry for attention and perhaps also for meat.

Carol turns right, moving into the kitchen. She goes towards the stove in the corner, takes the coffeepot down from the wall like the ageing woman she is—she wants to make coffee for me, the old-fashioned way. Wants to act as if nothing has happened, as always.

"Carol," I say. "You know I don't want coffee. I want my daughter."

Carol looks at me, her dark eyes flashing.

Reptile memoirs

After all these hard years, the warm woman and I were once again back in the house from the past. I was now an old snake, and she was older, too. Her temperament had calmed, she seemed less short-tempered, more sober-minded. This time, when she lay beside me in the same bed where we had once slept, her eyes dripped with the same salty tears as back then. Over years of contact with humans, I had learned that this was sorrow. A specific kind of feeling that they distinguished from all the other types of negative emotions they produced—anger, anxiety, fear. They used all these feelings for something. For communication, and to exchange gifts and actions; for self-defence. It was incredible that they needed so many.

I stretched out my body beside hers, measuring myself against it. Was thrilled to see that I now reached far beyond her pale head and naked feet. Finally she could become my prey. During the night, as she slept, I burrowed beneath her back, finding my way around her soft belly and encapsulating her in my coil. If she woke now, it would already be too late. I had her. My muscles were far stronger than hers. I tasted her in the air, then began to enfold her, preparing myself for this huge meal.

But as soon as I had begun to tighten my body, she woke up. She gasped for air, looking at me with terrified eyes. She fought me as any animal would, thrashing and struggling to get free, to breathe. Puzzled, I watched this indignant resistance from the being who for so long had held me captive, held control over my life.

I opened my mouth in order to finally consume this meal I had dreamed of for so long, but stopped. I came no further, was stuck. Something held me back. She squirmed within my coil as I tried to understand. I finally had to let go of her, twisting myself to break free.

I hissed in fury when I discovered what this curious enemy was. A single thread from the pillow had become hitched on one of my teeth. I turned and licked the air, seeking the warm woman who was now on her way out of the room. The next chance I had, I would manage it. Next time.

Ronja

Kristiansund
Thursday, 24 August 2017

I lay my head on the papers in front of me as August leads Tor Lind ahead of him, out of the interview room. It's as feared—Lind can't help us with anything. Of course he never told us that Mariam had left town, but beyond that he knows nothing. We have the telephone numbers she's called him from, but nothing that tells us where she is right now. Not to mention the fact that Lind obstinately defends his wife, despite all the evidence with which he's been presented. He doesn't recognise the woman being described to him, has problems believing she exists. He's angry and sick of being presented with things that happened before he got to know her. He knows Mariam—not Liv, not Sara.

I'm tired. I've had little sleep over the past few nights—my body has wanted nothing but to be awake and working to find Iben. I've been in this state for a while now, and it's wearing me down. We've come a long way in just the past twenty-four hours, but it feels as if we're moving slowly, as if we're caught in something viscous. Am I ready to give up? I sigh and lift my head to see August leaning against the doorframe.

"Were you asleep?"

I shake my head. "I'm just starting to lose hope."

There's something reassuring about the smile he gives me. He's a good guy. Stable, calm. It's just all ended up so ridiculous, the whole thing.

"You know, August," I say. "On Friday. I shouldn't have . . ."

His gaze doesn't falter; he smiles at me expectantly.

"I'm afraid you might think . . . Well, it wasn't exactly the wisest . . . I mean, it wasn't exactly planned . . ."

"We were drunk," he says. "These things happen."

I'm not sure whether that's what I meant to say. It's so hard to know what you want—there's more than one right way of looking at things. There's so much to consider—you don't know whether to listen to the voice that says we work together, that we should keep our work and private lives separate. Or whether it's okay to bend the rules, if another voice suggests that. For me, the Rakotzbrücke has never been the entrance to hell, and nor has it ever been the exit; it's just a bridge, and on the other side is more water, more nature. Maybe you'll never know whether it was wise to stand there looking at the tempting other side of the stone circle, or whether it was a good idea to get into a boat and row through. You can always turn around and row back, but by then you might have already become someone else.

"I found something." Birte's voice interrupts us. She comes and stands beside August, waving a newspaper clipping in her hand. I take the clipping, holding it up while August moves so close to me that I can feel the heat from his body. The clipping is from *Tidens Krav*, from January of this year, congratulating Iben on her eleventh birthday.

"I've already seen this," I say.

"She was born in January."

I look at the photograph of the apparently carefree young girl.

"So what?"

"She was born in the middle of January 2006! Almost nine months to the day after Anita Krogsveen died. And we still don't know who her father is."

"It was a rape," says August.

"But where did it happen? In Kristiansund?"

I look down at the clipping.

"That's what she said when she was interviewed—that it happened in Kristiansund."

"What if that was a lie?"

Just then, Shahid hurries through the door. He seems worked up.

"We need you, right away," he says.

"What's going on?" I say.

"The police in Ålesund have interviewed Egil Brynseth, who is currently an inmate at Ålesund Prison. Mariam Lind visited him today. He says she seemed convinced that Roe had done something to Iben. She left there earlier today, to find Roe."

I leap to my feet. "We have to get to his place. Now."

Liv

Ålesund
Saturday, 16 April 2005

I woke with a cold shudder. At first I thought the cold was coming from inside me. A flaming icicle in my nipple drilling its way out. Still dreaming, I thought I had a tiny baby in my arms. It was trying to drink my milk, but was instead pierced through by an ice-cold stake. I thought I could see the child's brain matter flowing down my chest, but then I woke up and opened my eyes to the dark.

David was sitting on the edge of the sofa next to me. He stared at me, looking straight into my eyes with a stiff grin as he pinched my nipple between his fingers. When I pulled away, he laughed. Another man would have shown signs of embarrassment, but not David. Instead, he set his hand on my thigh, squeezing it right at the top next to the edge of my underwear. Something tense came over him, as if he had turned angry without stopping smiling.

His hands were strong. A pulsating thud from his thumb, which dug into my thigh. The smell of him was a mixture of alcohol and sour tobacco. I kept trying to get up, but was pushed down each time by a hard hand against my shoulder. Any movement only led to more resistance. I felt something damp against my hip. Looked down, and saw his dick sticking out over the edge of his boxers like the root of a tree. I closed my eyes and immediately received a blow to the face, so that the back of my head smashed into the hard edge of the sofa behind me.

"Don't close your eyes."

A panting voice, stinking of beer. He couldn't have brushed his teeth tonight, nor yesterday, either. He pressed his forehead against mine, so that I was forced down against the edge of the sofa. Its wooden frame dug into the back of my head, my neck. His dick moved against my skin, and I felt something viscous pooling in my diaphragm, a black tar in my veins that made everything slow. My heart was giving its all to get my blood flowing. He tugged up my half-closed eyelid, staring into me with a big, shining dark eye. Dank breath over my mouth and chin, saliva in my mouth. He clawed around with his hand down there, ripping at my underwear to remove it. I should have done something else. I should have slept in the car, or just driven all night to get away from everything, but back then I still believed myself indestructible.

The piercing sound of fabric being ripped, the elastic of my underwear being stretched and broken. He forced my legs apart and penetrated me with a rough thumb that scraped against my skin. Pain in my lower abdomen. Another failed attempt to get away. I received another smack to the face, which cracked through my teeth and tasted of metal.

"I said, do not close your eyes."

I closed them anyway when he thrust his way into me with the swaying tree root, pushing a hairy thigh into my hip so hard that I felt as if the muscle was about to be ripped clean off. Something ran into the corners of my mouth, collected around my tongue and grew. I took aim and spat, but only hit myself—my chin and my throat and the oversized T-shirt. Another blow came, and this time I spat blood into the centre of his face; with the next crack, I finally lost a tooth. It scraped against my tongue as the dry tree root pushed forward, again and again, a rough branch burning against flesh.

I despised my breath, which moved slowly in and out of me, keeping me alive. I had to get out of my body if I was going to survive. I had to give myself some brightness, something white. Rays of sunshine from the sky, grass and trees, all white in my head. But when I closed my eyes and tried to disappear, I received a blow that sent me back to reality, hurtling me back to the scraping pain and stinking breath. A tree root stinging and grating against all the soreness, continuing to chafe for what seemed like hours. In the end I just lay there and took it, staring glassy-eyed into his shameless face.

When he was done, he sat on the edge of the sofa and pulled on his boxer shorts. He turned his back to me. I lay there, looking up at the ceiling as I heard him flick a lighter; smelled the scent of marijuana. He smoked the joint in silence as I lay behind him and waited, a burning pain between my legs.

Mariam

Ålesund
Thursday, 24 August 2017

Carol lightly pats the Weimaraner on its skinny head.

"I think you've lost your mind, darling. I'd do anything to help you find your daughter."

She's using her cosy voice, as if she's talking to the dog. She bends down and scratches it behind the ear. The dog whines and wags its tail, blissfully unaware that it's in the middle of a tense situation.

"It's too late to put on an act, Carol."

She looks up. "You're accusing me of acting?"

"Is she alive or is she dead? Your grandchild?"

She shakes her head.

"You're David Lorentzen's mother. You lied to me when you said that you didn't let Roe Olsvik in here. He was here, told you everything he knew, and you realised that Iben must be David's child. Am I right?"

She looks up. Reaches out an arm and opens the oven. Just then it occurs to me that this isn't the oven she usually uses—it's the old one, the one on the opposite side of the room. She sticks her hand inside it and pulls out a revolver with a shining grip, like something out of an old Western. Carol straightens up and points the gun at me.

"Do you know that's the first time anyone has told me I have a grandchild?" She lifts her chin and chest, as if offended. "You want your daughter. I want my son. Is my son alive, Liv?"

It feels as if ice and crushed glass are running through my veins. The smile on her lips is so reminiscent of her son's that I can't believe how I could have missed it.

"Tell me how you knew, Carol—that David is Iben's father."

"That cop was here—he spread all his documents out over there," she says, gesturing towards the kitchen table. "Photographs and newspaper clippings. That was the first time I saw a photograph of your daughter, from her eleventh birthday. I've never seen anyone so like my son. She was born nine months after you came to me to drop off the snake—around the same time my son was murdered. I remembered how quickly you wanted to get out of town, and that same day was the last time anyone saw my David. Nobody else he knew would have done something like that. It was hateful what he was subjected to, and they knew he had slept with a woman. That must have been you."

"Can I see her?"

She gestures towards the cellar door with the revolver.

"Please. Be my guest."

She wants me to go first. Gestures with the revolver again, and I open the cellar door, start to walk down the steep, narrow stairs, step by step, down into the lair. I don't know exactly where Nero is, but I can sense his presence. It's as if he's creeping through my veins, as if he is here through me.

"And for all these years I've been the guardian of your madness," Carol grumbles behind me with her American lilt. "Without knowing what kind of an excuse for a human being you are."

I've never been down these stairs before. All the times I've been here, I've stayed on the ground floor or I've been up in the loft. At the bottom of the stairs is a small sitting room with a fireplace, a bed and a fat old TV.

"I let him come here as much as he wanted, when he needed to get away from that awful scene."

I have to laugh.

"David *was* the awful scene, Carol."

In a split second Carol's nails are gripping my neck.

"Well, you certainly beat him at being the bad guy, didn't you?" she spits.

She touches my temple with the muzzle of the gun, and for a moment there's something about her smell that overwhelms me, something about the taste in my mouth that reminds me of that night on David's sofa when he thrust that tree root into me, when he wouldn't stop hitting me. I thought about the tooth I'd had to spend several thousand kroner to replace.

"You don't know what you're talking about, Carol."

Carol holds me tightly. Unlocks the door to the next room, a small storage space with no window. There, on a chair in the dark, sits a blond-haired girl. Her head hangs heavily against her chest; her eyes are closed, and the floor beneath the chair is coloured by a dark stain.

I no longer care about my own life. I shove Carol aside and run towards the little feet, the blond hair, the young skin. My baby, who I had learned to love—even though it seemed impossible after everything that happened. It was for her that

I changed everything. My name, my body, how I spoke and behaved—she was the reason I could truly make that change. I shake the skinny little girl's body until she lifts her head. Looks at me with half-open eyes beneath heavy lids.

"Iben. Iben."

Iben opens her eyes. They're shining below their pale lashes.

"Mamma."

I hug her close. Stroke my hand over her thin, fine hair, now sticky with dirt. Iben, who is always so good at keeping everything clean—we never have to nag her. Now she smells of shit and urine. She must have been here by herself for a long time, unable to go to the toilet when she needed to. On the table is a plate and a glass that indicate she's at least been given something to eat.

"Sweetie. Mamma's here. I'm so sorry."

I hug her again, even harder this time. Then there's a bang at the wall. Plaster sprinkles down onto my head.

"Let her go," says Carol, pointing the revolver at Iben's head. "Or I'll put a bullet straight between her eyes."

Reluctantly I let Iben go and take a step away from her. Then it's Carol who is holding her in her arms, who's hugging her tightly but still sticking the revolver into her face. Iben seems to be holding her breath. She looks at me, beseeching.

"Please, Carol," I say. "She's innocent. I'm the one who deserves to die."

"Am I hearing this right? Are you saying I should kill you instead? Is that it?"

Iben whimpers.

"If you'd asked me, all those years ago, whether you should kill me or my son, I would have said *kill me*. Did I get to choose?"

"I can explain."

"You're going to tell me everything, and my grandchild is going to listen to everything you say."

Carol presses the revolver to Iben's temple; Iben squeezes her eyes shut, whining. I look around me for a solution—a knife, a hammer, anything—but the room is almost empty. I look towards the door, but I can't go—can't leave Iben here alone.

"Your mother is a murderer. Did you know that? She killed a man. Come on, Liv. Tell us what you did."

Liv

Ålesund
Saturday, 16 April 2005

When he finally left me, I got up to go to the bathroom. Nero hissed angrily as I moved him out of the shower. A sticky clump of David-slop ran down the inside of my thigh, dripping in large pink drops on the floor. I grabbed the showerhead, turned it on full blast and set it between my legs, letting the hard jets of water take what could be cleaned away. Nero hissed at me from over by the door where he was lying. I heard furious words, commands to win back control.

On my way back to the living room to pick up my things and get out, I saw that the door to the bedroom was ajar and heard the regular rhythm of his snoring. Carefully, I pushed the door further open. The room was dark. The stuffy smell of sweat made a wave of nausea spread through me. All I wanted was to get out, away. But still, I stood there. From where I was standing, I could see the chest of drawers in the living room, on which the TV stood. I went over to it. Began to open the drawers, which were full of everything from broken CDs to trimmed Zippo lighters and old batteries and cables. In one of the drawers I found a bundle of banknotes. In another I found the gaffer tape they'd been using on each other that night I had been at the party here.

I went back to the doorway, where I could still hear David's snoring. I could leave and never look back. But at the same time, I knew that if I left now, I would always feel small. I would forever go around with this sneaking feeling of having let my body be destroyed yet again. Nero was right, I couldn't let him win this. So I went back into the room.

I began by winding the tape around his feet—three complete revolutions. I fastened his hands to each other, binding and binding them together with long strips of tape, until they became a single long arm at the front of his body. Then I attached this long arm to his body and the bed, using several long strips. I took my time. The last piece of tape I set over his hairy lips.

Carefully, I got onto the bed, one leg either side of his taped body, a greyish half mummy. I leaned over and pulled out the plug of the lamp on the nightstand. The lamp was steel, with a long, narrow neck. I set the lamp against his throat, just above his windpipe. Still the low snoring came from his nose. I started gently. Not with a clear plan of going through with it, just driven by an immediate intense need to do something. I pressed harder, and it wasn't until he couldn't draw breath that he woke. His eyes grew large. He looked down at himself, at his body bound with tape.

"Look at me," I said.

He did as I asked. Stared at me with those dark eyes—trying to say something, trying to scream, but all sound was dampened. The pain between my legs guided my hands—a stream of blood that seemed to be flowing more easily already, from down below and upwards, out into my slender woman's hands. He moved his lower body in a writhing fight to break free, but in vain.

Roe

Kristiansund
Thursday, 24 August 2017

Someone is shaking me. There are flashing lights—someone is holding up my eyelids and shining a light into my eyes. There are several people in the car, wearing red suits with yellow reflective patches. On a stand beside me hangs a bag of blood, with a tube that snakes its way down into my arm. Reflections of the blue lights on the ceiling and in their faces. I feel dizzy. I must have been given something for the pain, something strong. Still, the pain in my side is so great that I can't bear to be awake. I feel sleep tempting me. Anita is waiting for me at the edge of the forest—I can return to her whenever I choose.

"Roe."

The voice is familiar. To my right sits a young woman, her face ablaze with stress. Ronja. She touches my free arm.

"Roe, you have to stay awake."

I cough. Somewhere nearby I hear the crackling of the radio. Somebody is speaking on the other end of it, but I can't catch the words.

"Give me a moment," Ronja replies into the radio. It crackles. "Just prepare the units to respond as soon as we have an address. Roe? Roe, are you there?"

Anita is waiting for me at the forest's edge. She smiles at me, says everything will be okay. I close my eyes, try to conjure her up again, but there is only darkness.

"Roe!"

Ronja continues to call me back to the pain. I moan, see that there's a woman standing behind Ronja, wearing a paramedic's uniform. Is she the one who will take me to Anita?

"Why didn't you use the alarm, Roe? You were supposed to press the button if she came, or call us. Not let her in—not speak to her, let her stick a knife in your gut. That was the only thing you had to do. What on earth were you thinking?"

I groan. "I had to be sure she'd be convicted."

"So getting stabbed—that was the solution?"

"The Dictaphone," I say. "Did she take it with her?"

"Of course she took it with her."

"Excuse me," says the paramedic. "It's urgent—the operation."

"I just need to get a few answers out of him first," Ronja says. "You have to tell me, Roe. Where will we find Mariam Lind?"

I can't bear to speak—it hurts so much. And what do I have to say, anyway?

"We have police officers ready to respond in both Kristiansund and in Ålesund," she says. "They just need to know where to go. Please—can you tell us?"

Mariam

Ålesund
Thursday, 24 August 2017

I am another. My daughter sees her mother's real face for the first time. I've sat down on the floor; Iben is sitting opposite me with Carol's arms around her skinny shoulders. Iben listens, disbelieving and frightened, to the words that come out of my mouth, hearing my idiotic and defensive attempts to soften the facts, make it not sound so bad. But I didn't kill David in self-defence—it was revenge. Carol's face is dark. When I stop speaking, she squeezes her eyes shut, presses her lips together. She slowly shakes her head.

"You can't lie about my son."

"I'm not lying, Carol."

"In that room there was only you and him. He no longer exists. You taped his body to the bed and killed him. I think maybe he didn't want you, something like that. You like to kill. You kill animals and people—I heard it all from the policeman. Oh, if you knew how I cried. For so many years I've asked myself what happened to my son. I've even thought that maybe he did something, that he deserved it—but according to what the policeman said when he came snooping around, you're a killer. You don't need a reason."

I know that she's right. I enjoyed killing David. I've had to make what little heart I have myself, but I love with that little heart all the same.

"Then I found out what had happened, that I had a grandchild. I wanted to get your daughter away from the monster you are, to give her a new life. You wanted to keep her for yourself, to destroy her. There's no love in you—you're destroying her. It's better she stay here with her grandmother, I thought—but you deserve to watch me kill her."

"Do you hear what you're saying, Carol?"

Carol sticks the revolver into Iben's mouth. Her eyes widen, look red.

"Your mother wants to blame my son for the fact that she killed him. As if he killed himself—but that isn't what happened. *She* killed him. So many people had nasty things to say about him, but they were wrong. He was a wonderful son."

"I'm sure you knew him just as I knew him, Carol. Don't lie to yourself. Do you remember how I looked when I came to you back then, after staying with David? You asked me what had happened—do you remember?"

Carol forces the revolver farther down Iben's throat. Iben gurgles and retches, tears streaming down her soft cheeks. I want to rush to her, but I don't dare. Carol is directing all her anger at Iben now—it won't be long before the pistol goes off.

Just then, a large, undulating body slides across the floor. I blink. Nero licks the air with his split tongue and turns his head in my direction.

Roe

Kristiansund
Thursday, 24 August 2017

"We've overlooked something," I say. I take a breath, my entire side splitting with the effort.

"I need to know *what* we've overlooked," says Ronja. "Help me to think."

"I've been thinking for twelve years."

She moved from Ålesund to Kristiansund twelve years ago, just after the incident involving Anita and Aurora. What had she done with the snake? She might have killed it, or set it free in the forest, but something tells me that it was too dear to her for her to be able to let it go completely.

"Iben was born in January," Ronja says.

I cough, and the pain sweeps through my side.

"I don't know what the significance is," she says, "but we've forgotten to think about Iben's father. The rapist. Do we really know that Mariam doesn't know who he is?"

"Excuse me," says a paramedic urgently. "But he really has to go into surgery now."

Two men in paramedic uniforms begin to lift my stretcher between them. They start to walk towards the exit. Lights flashing outside, ambulances and police cars. I'm set on another stretcher with wheels.

"Birte noticed Iben's date of birth," Ronja says. "It's almost nine months to the day that Anita died. She must have been conceived right around that time."

My head is heavy. The pain in my side makes trying to stay awake hopeless. I just want to sleep. Just want to go to Anita, she's waiting for me at the edge of the forest, but I make a last-ditch effort to think as the lift doors open and I'm wheeled down yet another corridor. As it dawns on me, I gasp too hard and almost pass out.

"David Lorentzen," I manage to force out. "He slept with a woman before he died. Check the DNA against Iben's—it'll match."

"First we have to find Iben."

David Lorentzen's mother had said she only wished she could be of more help when I went to see her in the hope of discovering the link between the deaths of my daughter and her son. She listened to everything I said, watching as I spread the documents out on the table before her. She'd been particularly interested in the newspaper clipping from Iben's eleventh birthday—so interested that I'd found it odd. That was before the summer, before Iben went missing. I should have realised the connection then.

"I think she's with her grandmother." I cough. "Karoline Lorentzen."

I cough so much that it feels as if my heart is about to explode. Ronja is told to leave me be. She protests, but is quickly led away. I have nothing more to give her, anyway.

"Karoline Lorentzen! Karoline Lorentzen!" I hear her shouting into the radio as she starts to run.

Reptile memoirs

Ever since I was small enough to fit in a jacket pocket, I had looked forward to the day when I would be big enough to swallow the cold woman. When that day finally came, I couldn't believe I was lucky enough to find her sitting downstairs, unaware.

She fought with every limb, but she didn't stand a chance against my far stronger muscles. I had long since become superior to humans' dancing skeletons, was no longer impressed by their vertical bodies. I squeezed the air out of her as I once would have done to a rat, until she stopped thrashing around. Her body was soon brought into my mouth. Her skin had an exquisite flavour, pure and refined. I squeezed extra hard in order to savour how I forced the life out of her. And now she surrendered, letting me crush her, without the slightest resistance. This was the largest, the most difficult and yet the simplest prey I had ever devoured.

Never before had I taken so long to swallow. With great effort I let her go down, little by little, until I could close my lips around her large feet. As I squeezed her down those last few centimetres, all kinds of flashing lights could be seen outside. The floors vibrated beneath human feet. Carrying such a heavy burden cost me much, but I finally managed to creep beneath a low table in a corner where I could hide, where I could lie still and let my body digest its prey. After such a nutritious meal I wouldn't need to eat again until white rain began to fall outside the windows.

As the stomping feet approached, I lay in the shadow, believing I was well hidden. They were more concerned with the tiny human than with me, which suited me well. But then, out of nowhere, a head appeared in front of me—one that belonged to a male. The male called out loud noises and waved with his arms. I hissed as loud as I could, opening my jaws and revealing myself, but the male did not back away; he was insolent and wanted to touch me, wanted to pull me from my hiding place. Arms held me firm, pulling me up into the air, floating above all safe havens.

With the prey in my belly, I resisted fighting, but I had no choice. Lashed out for limbs as best I could. Other men came, shouting and holding my head.

I hissed out all the human sounds I had learned, but if they heard me, they pretended not to understand.

Ronja

Molde—Vestnes
Thursday, 24 August 2017

We drive past the queue and straight onto the ferry. We're on our way to Ålesund in case they need help. If Iben is alive, we have to bring her home. The glow has returned to Birte's freckled cheeks—driving purposefully, she stops right at the ship's front barrier. I've never travelled the drive from Kristiansund to Molde at such speed before. August pulls up beside us.

The police in Ålesund have promised to keep us updated on the ongoing operation at Karoline Lorentzen's house. They've acted quickly to get the relevant arrest and search warrants in place and are on their way. The operation is happening right now. They're going in, and if we're right—if we really are right—then the girl might be alive. Every time the radio crackles, I jump in my seat, thinking that this will be the time they say they're ready to storm the house.

I hold my breath, waiting as the ferry moves away from the quay. I turn and watch the rear mouth of the ship as it closes. When I was little and took the ferry, I was always fascinated by that mouth. How it closed behind us, and then the other opened up in front. As if we were swallowed by a monster we had to trust would spit us out on the other side.

The radio crackles again. I look at Birte, and she meets my gaze. I can see that over in the other car, August is listening to the radio, too.

"We're in," the radio crackles. "One dead, two alive and out of harm's way."

"Who's dead and who's alive?" I say into the radio.

"Suspect Karoline Lorentzen is confirmed dead, killed by a python. One of the sickest things I've ever seen, to be honest. Mariam Lind and Iben Lind are alive. Neither is seriously injured."

Birte and I cheer in unison. We howl and hug each other. August looks like he's cheering over in his car, too. He gets out and throws his arms in the air, and Birte and I each get out too. Birte hugs him first—she throws her arms around his neck. Then it's my turn. I take a running jump and wrap my legs around his waist, hear him groan in surprise, but I just laugh. The mouth of the ferry has slowly begun to open. I look down into August's face, which is so close.

He smells good, and surely one little kiss won't hurt.

Roe

Kristiansund
Monday, 4 September 2017

There's a crackling sound somewhere nearby. The sound of long-extinguished flames, the embers of which have never stopped glowing. Kiddo's glowing essence has long since faded—it's only her flaming death that I will always hear and feel. And yet there's something from the outside that manages to break in. I open my eyes, and see the nurse approaching. She straightens the bedsheets that lie over me.

"I don't think there's anybody as kind as you," I say.

She smiles as she checks my cannula and changes the bag on my drip.

"You're not so bad yourself," she says. "With everything they're writing about you in the newspaper. You're famous."

She points to the newspaper she's set on the nightstand, which I haven't bothered to open.

"You have a visitor," she says. "Are you up to it?"

"As long as it isn't a journalist."

She gives me a little pat on the cheek. Turns and leaves. When she reaches the door, she looks back, checks whether I'm watching her. I close my eyes and rest for a few minutes. All the medication makes me so tired. It's as if the days are one single, long dream. Sometimes, when I wake, I'm not sure whether I've dreamed it all—everything that happened with Anita and Aurora, with David, Iben, Mariam. I exhale. In the dream, Iben sits at a desk, drawing. Her blond hair is pulled back into a ponytail at her neck. As I approach, she turns. Look what I've drawn, she says, lifting her picture so I can see it. It's me, standing beside a big house with a red cross on the roof, holding a balloon. She's drawn a big heart on my chest. But the face of the girl who has drawn this is not Iben's. It's Anita's, and she drew that picture when she was seven. The building with the cross on it doesn't belong to that drawing, but everything else is real.

When I open my eyes again, I'm still dreaming. It must be a dream. Beside the bed stands a girl with long, blond hair. Her gaze is serious, her head tilted slightly to one side. She looks at the cannula in my arm. On the other side of the bed stands Ronja, smiling with her lips pressed together.

"Are you awake, Roe?"

I take a deep breath.

"It's so good to see you."

I turn towards the pale-haired girl. Her eyes are on my face now. She seems a little shy.

"Roe," Ronja says. "Don't you recognise Iben?"

Of course I recognise her. Still, there was a delay—and her name, as Ronja speaks it, makes tears run down my face. Such a hopeless crybaby I've become. Iben looks much older than she did the last time I saw her. She's lost something, the innocence in her eyes. I take her hands in mine. It hurts my side, but I do it anyway.

"Iben wanted to meet you," Ronja says.

"It's so good to see you, Iben."

Iben looks at Ronja. She's unsure how to reply.

"You don't have to say anything," I say quickly. "It's just nice that you wanted to come see me."

"Roe is the one who saved you," Ronja says to her. "We would never have found you, if it wasn't for him."

It's also my fault you had to go through all this, I think. *If it wasn't for Roe, you would still have a mother, and the innocent view of the world a child should have.*

"Oh, don't embarrass me, Ronja—not in front of such a nice young lady."

Iben giggles.

"Now tell me, Iben. Are you back at school again?"

The girl shakes her head. "I'm going for two days next week."

I nod. "It's okay to need time. Remember that. Even though things might be difficult for a while. The more you accept that it's okay to need time, the better you'll feel. I used to hate it when people told me that, but it's really true."

Ronja, standing at my side, nods. I take a deep breath and continue.

"The worst thing you can do is start to think that you should be doing this or that. That's when you start to hate yourself. Listen to the doctors—accept help and take it easy."

I hear how wise this sounds. It's been twelve years, and I've finally learned this myself. All the energy I wasted before I was ready for it.

"Mamma's in prison," Iben says.

"Yes, I know. I'm sure that's hard to think about."

She nods, holds something out to me.

I have to laugh when I see what it is. It's a drawing, of a man with a key in his hand. The man has a big smile on his lips.

"Thank you very much," I say. "And I hope you know that it was wrong of me to speak to you in the way that I did. You did exactly the right thing, running off—I was a stranger."

She nods.

"I'm going to hang this on the wall," I say. "It's really great."

She nods again.

"I wish I could spend all day with you, but unfortunately, I don't have much strength at the moment."

"We have to go anyway," Ronja says, guiding Iben ahead of her. "Thanks for letting us come visit—I'll see you soon."

She waits until Iben has gone out into the corridor, then remains by the open door and turns back to me.

"We've reopened the case regarding Aurora and Anita's deaths," she says. "Birk has been charged with Anita's death, and for starting the fire. He was the one who did it, Roe."

At hearing this, I try to get up; pain sears through my side. I drop back on the bed—Ronja comes to my aid, but there's nothing she can do. Let it hurt as much as it wants. Physical pain is manageable. It makes sense.

"We found the weapon that was used to strike Anita," she says. "It was in Anita's childhood bedroom at Ingrid's house—a glass muller. Birk had hidden it after the fire and then took the first opportunity to put it back there. After several interviews with everyone involved, we got Birk to confess."

I've now discovered that the other type of pain—the unmanageable pain—doesn't have to grow. Instead, it can subside, diminish, and at certain times it's even possible to forget to feel it at all. It hasn't been that way so far, but it might be, someday.

"Thank you, Ronja," I say, gripping her hand. "I'm so glad you told me."

She leaves, and as soon as she does, the nurse is back. She's carrying a tray of food—juice, a bread roll and a small bowl of meat stew.

"You look like you might be ready for food," she says, knowing me all too well already. "I'll just put it here, so you can eat it whenever you like."

"Thank you, that's kind of you."

I set my hand over hers as she straightens the sheets.

"When I get out of here," I say, "how about we go out to a nice restaurant? Your choice."

She nods, a slight blush spreading in her cheeks.

Epilogue

I parked the car I had purchased from Carol in the street just a few metres from Kristiansund police station. David was dead, and if there was one place in the world I thought they wouldn't look—if they were ever to look for a crazy, murderous woman—it was here. Right under their noses. I hadn't dared to turn on the radio, thought I might hear the voices of all the people looking for me. I couldn't even bear to get into the back; I just lowered the driver's seat and tried to get comfortable. Within a few minutes, I was asleep.

When I woke, the sun was shining through a layer of rain on the windshield. I was freezing cold, so started the engine to get the heating going, along with the windshield wipers. The street was almost deserted, apart from a single figure far up ahead, a woman pushing a pram. I watched her in her thick coat, the way she walked hunched over, a hat pulled over her head, looking only at her child. It struck me that it might be possible to replace the destructive love I felt for Nero with something better.

I went around to the boot and opened my suitcase. Found a woollen sweater and a raincoat that I pulled on, plus a shawl to hide parts of my ruined face. I took my phone from my pocket and threw it into a puddle, getting my trainers wet when I stamped on it. I already knew it was possible to start again. That first time, I had been a child, still searching. This time I would do it properly, as an adult.

I walked towards Kristiansund town centre, looking around until I found an open pharmacy. The girl behind the counter stared at me—my scarf over my face, my hat pulled over my head and my bulging, leaking black eye. She opened her mouth to say something, but stopped as I came over and heaved disinfectants, bandages and gauzes, painkillers and a few makeup products onto the counter. I paid using notes from David Lorentzen's stash.

Back in the car, I sat in front of the rearview mirror and tried to tend to my facial injuries. It was the black eye and my mouth that ached the most. My jaw hurt, too, but I'd be okay. I smiled to myself in the mirror, revealing the gap left by the missing tooth. It would take time before I would be able to walk around anywhere unnoticed. In the meantime, I'd just have to patch myself up as best I could, concealing with makeup what could be hidden and covering the rest.

It took a few days before I found a place to rent. Until then, I wandered the streets, getting to know the town, learning all the street names and visiting the library to read the local newspapers. I didn't just want to move to this town—I wanted to become it, as if I had been here for years. I went into clothing stores, and after trying on countless outfits found a dress that suited me in a cute sort of way. Its skirt was longer than I was used to, the colour paler and the waist looser than I would usually wear—it made me look older. I bought a pair of earrings, too, and more makeup. Went to a hairdresser and asked if she could lighten my dark hair, bleach it as pale as possible and cut it short. She didn't want to cut so much of it off, but I insisted. The strands of hair fell to the floor like stones. I was on my way back to joining the world of the living. I found a room I could rent cheaply, but the money wouldn't last long. I had to get myself a job.

When I met Tor, I was working as a waitress in a restaurant. My teeth had been fixed, and the swelling on my face was gone. I'd become used to my new style, started to feel good in it, as if beneath a soft blanket. The day Tor and I met, he was eating dinner alone in the restaurant around five o'clock. I don't remember what he said, only that he had such a nice smile. I remember that he noticed my already protruding belly, but it didn't seem to frighten him. I felt adventurous, a tiny glimmer of the girl I used to be—the part of her I liked. So I wrote my phone number on the back of his bill.

Just a few months later, Iben came into the world. Tor was with me in the birthing room—he squeezed my hand and tried to be encouraging. I think he viewed it as a joint project, pushing Iben out of me. I told him as much as I dared reveal about who the father was. Tor was a man of justice—he hated the perpetrator intensely. Still, he was ready to accept and love the child. I thought I was ready for it, too, but giving birth to Iben took twenty hours. Even Tor eventually lost heart. But when I finally pushed all my remaining strength out of me like air from a balloon and the bloody child began to scream, I couldn't seem to take it all in.

The first thing I felt for Iben was nothing. It was a completely different type of love than I had expected—not the self-sacrificing love Anita had felt for her child. It was a love I had to learn over hours and days of sore nipples and long nights without sleep, without feeling anything but exhaustion and sorrow. I had to learn to love through years of potty training, language learning and countless arguments. I thought I'd never manage it, but I did. It took me eleven years, but I learned to love her.